More praise for *Bluebird, or*

"Written in elegant, spare sentences... *Bluebird* forms that rare, exquisite hybrid: a historical novel where the history lesson works to illuminate the life of the hero instead of the other way around... [The] character could have easily been whipped into a feminist cliché—a kind of late-eighteenth century Rosie the Riveter—but Kohler is far too subtle and sophisticated a writer to hard-sell the obvious angle."
—*Time Out New York*

"Enchanting... Kohler's elegant, clearly written prose conjures a heroine whose enthusiasm for life and learning is infectious, and whose disarming manner is immensely appealing."
—*Booklist*

"Sheila Kohler hitches her sensory-rich prose to a really good story: that of Lucy Dillon, an aristocrat (based on a real person) in Marie Antoinette's court."
—*More*

"I wondered when someone would adapt the intriguing worldly life, the rich inner life, and the marvelous prose of Mme. de la Tour du Pin as a novel. Sheila Kohler has netted this elusive subject like the rare butterfly she was—but alive."
—Judith Thurman, author of
*Isak Dinesen, The Life of a Storyteller*

"With her portrait of noblewoman Lucy Dillon, Kohler offers a wonderful story of a 'new genus' of womanhood at that time and demonstrates what a different, pacific, humane world a woman of her caliber could create."
—Lyndall Gordon, author of
*Vindication: A Life of Mary Wollstonecraft*

*continued ...*

## Praise for *The Perfect Place*

"Wholly entrancing...Kohler has a fine ear for truth and untruth and for the musical possibilities of their interplay."　　　—J. M. Coetzee

"Elegantly disturbing...the language of *The Perfect Place* yields beautifully to the constraints and expansions of its theme, becoming progressively more lyrical—and more gripping—as the truth emerges."
　　　　　—*The Times Literary Supplement*

"Chilling and poetic."　　　　　—*Cosmopolitan*

"Structured in a way that conjures up images of a very elegant striptease, this novel reveals itself in tantalizing, overlapping glimpses....Kohler's writing has a hypnotic, abstract allure."　　　—*People*

"Intense, beautifully written."　　　　　—*Vogue*

## Praise for *Crossways*

"There is a territory—fictional and psychological—that Sheila Kohler has now marked as her own. I am full of admiration."　—J. M. Coetzee

"Hypnotic...unsettling...a combination of domestic drama and psychological thriller."　　　　　—*San Francisco Chronicle*

"Sheila Kohler's novel *Crossways* is the gripping, often terrifying story of a man who can't suppress his violent impulses."
　　　　　—*O, The Oprah Magazine*

"Shelia Kohler's best yet...Exquisitely written and devastating in its depiction of a 'superior' family in a profound state of crisis."
　　　　　—Patrick McGrath, author of
　　　　　*Port Mungo and Spider*

"Compelling and beautifully nuanced...There is a fascinating interplay here of the lovely and the brutal—a story gloriously imagined."
—Elizabeth Strout, author of
*Abide with Me* and *Amy and Isabelle*

## Praise for *Cracks*

"Written with real atmospheric nostalgia that conjures up the wildness of the veld, and the passion and drama of adolescence...a sustained piece of storytelling, and a peculiarly satisfying novel."
—*The Times Literary Supplement*

"A disturbing note-perfect novel."  —*San Francisco Chronicle*

"In this vivid and haunting story...Sheila Kohler's writing—always elegant, often erotic—takes on the patina of myth."  —Amy Hempel

"Erotic and disturbing."  —*Vanity Fair*

"Delicious and dark...with sensuous, shimmering imagery, [Kohler] tells a story of teenage tribalism, awash with dreamy eroticism. Kohler's language is poetic and elegant and brilliantly visual....Hauntingly good."  —*Elle*

"An eerie, elliptical masterpiece."  —*Kirkus Reviews*

## Praise for *The Children of Pithiviers*

"Kohler's slim volume holds in its easy grasp the liveliness and the corruption, the yearning and the evil that run just below our civilized skins."  —*Time Out New York*

*continued...*

"Kohler weaves an intricate and endlessly surprising tale of betrayal. Her vivid, sensual writing and her heartbreaking account of the fate of two of the many children imprisoned in the camps of Vichy France make this a beautiful and important book."

—Margot Livesey, author of
*Banishing Vernona* and *Eva Moves the Furniture*

"*Children of Pithiviers* is amazing: stunning, rich, and multilayered."

—A. M. Homes, author of *Things You Should Know*

"Artful…sensual and psychological…it stays with you."

—*The Philadelphia Inquirer*

"Spellbinding…Kohler's elegant prose propels the sinister, almost dreamlike narrative."                                            —*Publishers Weekly*

## Praise for *The House on R Street*

"Sheila Kohler has achieved in this short novel a remarkable atmosphere, a fine, delicate fusion of period, society, and climate."

—Patrick McGrath in *The New York Times Book Review*

## Praise for *Miracles in America*

"[Kohler's] language is disquietingly vague, tantalizingly suggestive—like a painting done in pastels except for surprising streaks of dark, angry color. Her stories reflect a kind of genteel camouflage, with tenuous polite behavior masking frustration and desire."          —*People*

# Bluebird,

## or

## the INVENTION of HAPPINESS

*A Novel*

### SHEILA KOHLER

BERKLEY BOOKS, NEW YORK

THE BERKLEY PUBLISHING GROUP
Published by the Penguin Group
Penguin Group (USA) Inc.
375 Hudson Street, New York, New York 10014, USA
Penguin Group (Canada), 90 Eglinton Avenue East, Suite 700, Toronto, Ontario M4P 2Y3, Canada
(a division of Pearson Penguin Canada Inc.)
Penguin Books Ltd., 80 Strand, London WC2R 0RL, England
Penguin Group Ireland, 25 St. Stephen's Green, Dublin 2, Ireland (a division of Penguin Books Ltd.)
Penguin Group (Australia), 250 Camberwell Road, Camberwell, Victoria 3124, Australia
(a division of Pearson Australia Group Pty. Ltd.)
Penguin Books India Pvt. Ltd., 11 Community Centre, Panchsheel Park, New Delhi—110 017, India
Penguin Group (NZ), 67 Apollo Drive, Rosedale, North Shore 0632, New Zealand
(a division of Pearson New Zealand Ltd.)
Penguin Books (South Africa) (Pty.) Ltd., 24 Sturdee Avenue, Rosebank, Johannesburg 2196,
South Africa

Penguin Books Ltd., Registered Offices: 80 Strand, London WC2R 0RL, England

This is a work of fiction. Names, characters, places, and incidents either are the product of the author's imagination or are used fictitiously, and any resemblance to actual persons, living or dead, business establishments, events, or locales is entirely coincidental.

PRINTING HISTORY
Other Press hardcover edition / April 2007
Berkley trade paperback edition / March 2008

Library of Congress Cataloging-in-Publication Data

Kohler, Sheila.
    Bluebird, or The invention of happiness / Sheila Kohler.—Berkley trade paperback ed.
      p. cm.
    ISBN 978-0-425-21961-4
1. La Tour du Pin Gouvernet, Henriette Lucie Dillon, marquise de, 1770–1853—Fiction.
2. Aristocracy (Social class)—France—Fiction.   3. France—History—Revolution, 1789–1799—
Fiction.   4. France—Social life and customs—18th century—Fiction.   5. Hudson River Valley
(NY and NJ)—Fiction.   6. United States—Social life and customs—1783–1865—Fiction.
I. Title.   II. Title: Bluebird.   III. Title: Invention of happiness.

    PR9369.3.K64B68 2008
    823'.914—dc22

                                                                                    2007043412

PRINTED IN THE UNITED STATES OF AMERICA

10  9  8  7  6  5  4  3  2  1

This book is for Jeanette and Bernard Perrette
with gratitude for many years of true friendship.

*Il faut tacher de ne pas passer un jour sans acquérir une idée nouvelle; il ne faut dire de rien: "A quoi bon?" car tout est bon et utile à savoir dans le monde.*

One should attempt never to let a day pass without the acquisition of a new idea. One should never say, "What is the use?" for it is useful to know everything in the world.

—La Marquise de la Tour du Pin

# PART ONE
## The Diana

*W*HILE HIS FRENCH passengers huddle in their cabin, the captain of the *Diana* is approached by the *Atalante*, a French man-o'-war, at the height of the Terror. France is ruled by patriots in red caps and tricolored cockades, armed with national muskets and sabers, who have commenced a siege of retribution against their enemies. The instrument of vengeance is the guillotine. Every day, the tumbrils jolt heavily through the streets to the scaffold filled with the condemned. Eventually 14,000 will be executed.

## MARCH, 1794

The captain has been at sea for twenty days, going north instead of west, in wild winds, flying light in sleet and snow and a terrific sea, to avoid the Algerian pirates. Two leagues out from the lighthouse called the Tour de Courdouan, he has been obliged to change course. More than the terrible equinoctial gales, more than the French men-o'-war, more than starvation, he fears the Algerian pirates. He has heard of what they do to their captives: tongues cut off, other parts removed. He knows they prey particularly on American ships, as the American government, unlike the French and the British, has no treaty with them.

This is his first command, this sloop, the *Diana*, a wretched 150-tonner, one mast, wooden latches to the doors, not a bit of brass about it, and the only cargo the twenty-five cases his French passengers have brought with them. It rolls horribly even in light seas. He can barely stand upright.

It is mid-afternoon, but the seas are so high and the swirl of fog so thick, it is impossible to see the bowsprit. The deadlights have been put up.

The captain is used to high seas and fog. He and his first mate come from Newfoundland, that watery and fog-weary place, but he has always feared the sea, has never learned to swim, and has had only a short apprenticeship under Captain Loxley on the *Pigow*.

He has had to order the mainsail furled in this strong wind. Boyd, one of the sailors, has been up the mast to grapple with it. His crew consists only of the first mate, a cabin boy, and three common sailors, since his fourth caught his loose clothing in the rigging and took a terrible fall on leaving Bordeaux, and was lost at sea. The captain doesn't like to think about that, though he dreams of it. He sees the man falling through the twilit air, arms flailing, hands reaching for the rigging. In his dreams the man is somehow keeping himself afloat in the sea. He shouts after the ship that has been his home, fixing his gaze on the lantern at the stern, a speck of light that comes and goes with the waves.

Nights, the captain wakes with the screams from the French passengers in his ears. They had cried out for him to save the sailor, as he disappeared in the waves. He goes up for a turn on the deck, even if it is not his watch. He searches the waves as if he still could save the man. Could it have been done? Could he have thrown a barrel over for him and taken out a small boat? Should he, after all, have heeded old Harper who had told him to think of his ship first?

Thank God for old Harper, the mate, who, though new to this ship and bossy, and though the captain suspects he doesn't think much of him, has proven invaluable. Now he hears the hoarse voice of this mate on the watch, shouting, "French man-o'-war ahead."

The boat pitches so hard the captain is thrown against the chest that serves him as bed, bench, and storage, and bruises his hip. All the scuttles are closed, the air thick with the stench of vomit.

He lunges along the bulkhead and knocks on his passengers' door, lets down its top half, and glances in, as he tells them not to be alarmed but to stay out of sight, as there is a French warship ahead.

No need for the warning where the Frenchman is concerned. His pale face glimmers briefly at the captain above his high collar, before he shuts his eyes with resignation and turns away, lying flat on his back in his cot. He is still in his blond knee-breeches, his powdered hair, his silk stockings, the same clothes, almost the same position, as far as the captain can tell, he has been in since they set sail from the Bec d'Ambez three weeks earlier. He seems barely alive—more a marmoreal statue, so white, so cold, stricken with seasickness since he set foot on board, apparently surviving on weak tea and stale biscuits soaked in white wine, which his wife brings him. Still, his sufferings never seem to get the better of his good humor, and he laughs at himself and his extreme weakness and manages to comfort his children.

The Frenchwoman sits very upright on the sea chest with the faint light behind her. He likes her direct gray gaze, which is not soft at all. She holds her baby to her breast, covers herself with her shawl without haste but with a deft, decisive movement, not before the captain has seen a thin trickle of milk escape from her nipple.

A memory comes to him with an acute stab of desire: a woman turning her back on him, struggling with the fastenings of her bodice to cover her heavy breasts in the candlelight of some small room. But what room? What woman? Not his Sally, with the freckles on the bridge of her snub nose, the one who is waiting for him and hoping. Absurdly, at such a moment, the captain longs to lap at this woman's breast. He can almost taste her milk in his mouth.

For she, too, like the sailor falling repeatedly from the mast, has invaded the captain's restless sea dreams. She comes to him with the rocking of the ship in the night, bringing other women he has known in her wake. In his dreams the Frenchwoman comes to him without her long, dark dress, the one she has worn since she arrived on board, a shabby one, which hangs on her increasingly, stained on the shoulders with her baby's spittle, under the armpits with rings of sweat, and around the hem with brine.

In his strange dreams—strange surely for a man who does not know how to swim—he is swimming naked underwater, looking for her. He catches glimpses of her and then loses her again, repeatedly. He reaches out his arms, grasping. She swims fast, going through seaweed, coral, and flickering light, bubbles floating from her mouth. She swims easily, gracefully, in the full flowering of her youthful motherhood, her long ashy hair waving around her white breasts, her mouth open in a sort of cry or call. "Lucy," he calls out to her in his dreams, "come to me!" He calls again and again, as he has heard her husband do—a strange name surely for a Frenchwoman? Is she really French? She doesn't look French. Who is she?

Or sometimes she stands fully clothed before him, bends down to lift up her skirt at the hem, remove her woolen stockings from her slender legs, and then, barefooted, loosens the Madras kerchief that holds back her hair.

In reality she has not changed her clothes in twenty days or, the captain suspects, even brushed her mass of ash-blond hair, which in his dreams falls gently into his hands like sea anemones. The captain has never seen hair so thick or skin with such a blush in it or such a fine waist or such delicate feet. He has never seen as smooth and white a breast.

The woman has pleaded with the captain with much eloquence

and with tears in her eyes, begging him to set a direct course to Boston. Though she has not told him who they are, she has admitted what he has suspected from the first sight of them, that they are not who they have pretended to be, who their papers say they are: common citizens, the Latours.

Though she has not given him their real names, she has appealed to what she called his native gallantry, his generosity, his kindness, and her words or perhaps rather the captain's sea dreams have come near to persuading him. She is a persuasive young woman, speaking English like a native, better than a native. Will he ever hear English spoken more beautifully? Her tongue seems a bright, fluttering bird, landing gently here and there, illuminating the leaves.

What she apparently fears above all are her own countrymen, the French, who, she maintains, have gone mad with bloodlust, dragging their guillotines behind them into town after town. She tells him people are being paid twenty pounds for a pair of ears removed from an aristocrat. She has described the butchery in Bordeaux, replete with the sound of drums rolling before the fall of heads on the Place Dauphine. She has put her bone-white hands to her ears at the memory. She maintains no one is safe. She has begged him to save them.

But he has had to explain the greater danger of falling into the hands of the Algerian pirates and being sold into slavery. The Algerians keep their slaves shackled, chained to pillars, or thrown into rat-infested dungeons for years. The husband, albeit from his bed and in the voice of a dying man, has agreed with him, so that his wife, despite a flicker of impatience in her gray eyes, has had to submit, naturally. The captain has held to his northerly course despite the wind, the flooded decks, and the smashed bulwarks.

Now the Frenchwoman stares directly at him, her blue-gray eyes glazed with exhaustion and fear. When he first saw the couple arrive, walking along the dock toward the ship in the pale March afternoon light, he was filled with misgivings. *Trouble*, was what he had thought, and he had not been entirely wrong, though not for the reasons he had conceived. The young woman could not be more than twenty-five years old. She wore a battered leghorn hat aslant her head, the same dark-violet dress—or perhaps it is black, the woolen stockings, navy jacket, and grayish scarf, which muffled her face. The slight man had half-concealed his physiognomy in the hood of his dark, voluminous cloak. Despite their shabby clothes and half-hidden faces, something about the way they held their heads, the proud arch of the back, the elegance of the walk, immediately revealed their true status, and he wondered how they had escaped this long. Above all, it was the Frenchwoman's distant, unflinching gaze that gave her away.

When she proffered her hand in greeting in the English fashion, he saw skin so white and felt a touch so soft and yet firm, he could easily imagine her holding her skirt to curtsy before the French Queen. Now, after twenty days together on this small ship in such close proximity, he has dreamed of her hands otherwise engaged.

At the time he had even wondered in a mad moment if she might not *be* the French Queen herself, leaning on the arm of the French King, and that the news of the beheadings of these royal personages was not true. Indeed, such things are difficult to believe.

Yet her papers said she was a Citoyenne Latour.

But all mad musings aside—the woman must be half the age of the Queen, even if she were alive, surely—what he had worried most about was how to manage such a charge on his hands. He was a little reassured to find that, at least, she spoke perfect English, though her husband did not, only seeming to understand something of what was being said. Indeed, the woman looks more English than French.

He wondered how she would ever survive the hardships of such a voyage, the crossing of the Atlantic in midwinter in such a small ship, or even cope with the little brown-haired boy, who held tightly onto the father's hand, and the baby, who appeared to be—though the captain is not much of a judge of babies, never having married and being the youngest of seven children—not more than six months old. He was afraid this woman with her supple waist, her translucent skin, her fine hands, and her distant gaze would be delicate, difficult, and demanding, a spoiled beauty who would expect his cabin boy to wait on her like a maid, to attend to her, as she must have expected at Court surely, never having had even to dress her own hair, he would have wagered.

And the hardships since they set out were even more than he bargained for. There were days when the young captain has become confused in his calculations: in the thick fog and high seas he was frequently unsure of where he was. He had moments of deep discouragement, when he believed he might lose his ship, driven by wild winds too close to lee shores, or consumed in a conflagration, when once a lamp overturned. On this, his first voyage as captain, he feared that he would never reach his home port, Boston.

Supplies of food and water have become dangerously low, the voyage much longer and rougher than planned. The only biscuits he could procure for his passengers are hard enough to make the gums bleed and full of weevils and have already crossed the ocean more than once. The baby girl, he can see, is not thriving, not thriving at all, and growing thinner, paler, and quieter by the day. He fears that her name, Séraphine, may be all too apt.

Oddly enough, the Frenchwoman does not seem to have become afraid, even in the worst of high seas. On the contrary she seems to revel in her good health, energy, and competence. Rather than a hindrance, she has been a considerable help, rousing the flagging spirits of the men, supervising the cooking of the beans, and even finding time to do mending for the crew in quiet moments. Seeing him sewing on a button one afternoon, she simply took the jacket from his hands without a word and fixed the button firmly in a second, her deft fingers flying magically. Whatever her life may have been before this voyage, she now appears to excel in adversity.

At times when the wind was high, driving them toward the shore, lightning splitting open the sky, the mast about to crack, the deck flooded, and all hands obliged to go below for cover, falling down at each tumble of the ship, he has seen her face glow strangely in the flickering light of the tallows. Unlike her husband and even himself at times, she does not suffer from seasickness.

Nor does she seem to need much sleep. She is often awake and dressed in the morning before he is. Their cabins are adjacent, and the partition thin, and he often wakes, his dreams mingling with reality, so that he is not quite sure if he really hears her sweet voice, singing to her baby or to herself in her language, or if she is really moving about, perhaps down on her knees, scrubbing the floor, from the sound of it, with the vinegar she has been given.

He watches her escape the malodorous cabin whenever she has the opportunity. When she can get the cabin boy to stay with her older child, to whom he has taken a great liking, and while the baby sleeps, strapped in her bunk beside her seasick father, she spends much of her time sitting in the galley, apparently taking the opportunity to question Boyd, who serves as their cook, who seems to have fallen in love with her, as, indeed, they all probably have.

In reality, Boyd is no cook at all, but a broad-shouldered farm boy from the Boston area with a fresh complexion. The captain has felt a sharp twinge of jealousy—along with the husband, he suspects, who has told him laughingly, in his broken English, that the beans have turned to mush again, as his wife has forgotten herself with the young cook. The captain cannot imagine her forgetting herself with anyone. He has overheard her questioning the boy skillfully and in great detail about life in the new country, about the land, the customs, the prices of commodities, the taxes, the availability of property, as she warmed her pretty toes—he has never seen such narrow, delicate feet—by the fire, while getting soaked from time to time by an errant wave.

She goes back and forth all day long to the cabin to take her husband a little sustenance, reserving the best bottles of wine and more than his share of the fresh water for his tea. The baby girl, who appears to sleep all day, is fretful in the night, perhaps pushing teeth. The captain has been woken from his dreams by her piercing cries. He wonders when the Frenchwoman sleeps.

Now for the first time he can see fear in her gray-blue glassy gaze, her stiffly held head. She holds her baby to her breast with one arm, and with the other she clasps her little boy to her side. The boy strokes the captain's dog's head, between his knees. Black, a terrier bitch, who like everyone else has taken an inordinate liking to this French family, deserting her master to follow the woman around constantly, has her mouth open, panting, as though she, too, feels her distress. She stares up at the woman with practiced stillness, an attempt at invisibility.

Not for the first time, the captain regrets taking on these passengers, though the decision, of course, was not his to make. And what would have happened if he had not done so?

At the port of La Pauillac, where they had stopped briefly for supplies, he watched the woman's reaction to the story they had all been told, how this very French frigate that is now approaching, the *Atalante*, had met an American boat carrying French aristocrats fleeing their country near the entrance to the port of La Rochelle, had seized it, and taken the passengers to Brest, where they had been guillotined.

Now, with one bound, the captain is up the steps. There is a round of cannon, and the frigate declares her intentions. He heaves to and orders the American flag unfurled, watching the stripes flutter bravely.

The seas are high, the bowsprit dipping and rising. His small crew struggles to stand into the wind. The sloop is tossed about like a candle box. The captain stands on the bridge with his mate next to him, the spray in his face. His hip aches. His head swims. He is exhausted. After the customary questions about his origin and destination, he finds himself having to improvise. He says in as firm a voice as he can muster, "No passengers. No cargo."

To this the French captain replies, "Come aboard."

"Seas too rough," the captain cries above the sound of the wind.

"Then follow us."

He orders his mate to fall off and to follow as ordered.

He runs below and raps on the door. His passengers are huddled there in the half-light, in much the same position he left them. With as much optimism as he can muster, he tries to reassure them: "The fog is thickening, and besides, in an hour it will be dark."

When he leaves, the Frenchwoman turns to her husband and says it will, indeed, be dark soon. Surely, in this fog the captain will shake off the French ship.

Her husband mumbles something mournfully about the captain's inability to shake off anything. He has little confidence in him or his ship. He complains of the dreadful odor from the wretched hole that is used for their intimate needs, an odor that adds to his seasickness. He maintains the captain must be making errors in longitude as he has neither a sand clock nor a bell.

Lucy replies only that it would be wise to sleep while they can. She wipes her boy's face with a rag. She tells him to climb into his berth. He protests, saying it is too early. He is not sleepy. He is too hungry and scared to sleep. "Will the men with red bonnets be on the other ship? Will they make us go back to Bordeaux?" he asks. Lucy shakes her head. He begs for a potato. Surely at least one remains? She shakes her head again. She promises him a biscuit and some beans in the morning. He doesn't want any more beans, he whimpers, nor the biscuits with the horrid worms in them that give him a stomachache. He would like a potato, please. She puts her hand in his hair, pushes it back from his face, and shakes her head.

She offers her husband a glass of wine and water. She holds his head up, while he sips from the glass and then lies back, looking not so much green now as gray. He says he is beginning to believe he would rather take his chances with the guillotine than have to pass another night on this damned ship. "My dear, my dearest dear," he murmurs, miserably, "I fear we may have taken a misguided course."

She says nothing. *What other course could we have taken, after all?* She lies down and straps herself into her bunk, so that she will not fall onto and suffocate her baby with the rolling of the ship. At first she could not sleep in this halter, but she has grown used to it. At twenty-four she craves sleep like an animal, but has not been able to for more than half an hour at a time on this voyage. She lets her baby suck hard on her breast, her small face red with the effort. She can feel her little girl is not drawing down any milk. The child already has a tooth, and Lucy's nipples are sore and bleeding. How could her breasts not be dry? She has had to give up much of her share of water to her seasick husband, for his tea. She has hardly had time to swallow down a mouthful of beans. Her mouth is dry from the wine she drinks in lieu of water. Her head aches. The small pot of butter has long since been used up. Above all she regrets not bringing the goat along to provide milk for her children.

She slips her finger into the baby's mouth and lets her suck on that instead. "In America we will find you milk," she murmurs into her baby's fine, soft hair. "America, America," she sings softly in English while her husband groans, and the baby falls into restless sleep.

Lucy is overcome with weariness that strikes her like a fever. She wants only to sleep but she cannot; she is thinking of food. Constantly she thinks of food. She remembers the dinners at Versailles: the joints of scarlet beef, the fattened pullet, the wild fowl, the mutton sausages, the chicken *blondin*, the fritters of cauliflower and of leek, and the desserts, quivering mounds of jellies and *blancmange*. She would give anything for a thick piece of fresh white bread and butter. It is fresh bread she misses most.

She understands her husband's fears. After twenty days they are no closer to their destination than they were at the start and a great deal hungrier and wearier. She, too, has little confidence in this young captain. He seems hardly able to write and read, though he is a nice enough fellow. The only one who seems to know what he is doing on this ship is the first mate, Harper, who has a face like a nutcracker.

But the warm body of her little girl beside her and the rocking of the boat lulls her. She hears the voices of the sailors and the stamping of the bare feet on the deck above her head. She blinks. She says goodnight to Frédéric, who gives a soft moan in response, and, though he is not a religious man, is moved to murmur that they are in God's hands.

*God! What has God had to do with this voyage?* It is she who has obtained their passages on this small ship; she who has procured their permits from Tallien, the revolutionary, to leave France.

She would prefer a watery grave to the ignominy of the tumbril and the guillotine. She is not afraid of water. She remembers once, at fifteen, being caught in a flood on her way to Montpellier in her great-great-uncle's traveling carriage.

*The water was so high the doors had to be opened to let it pass through. We had to stand up on the cushions. Grandmother screamed at me to lift up my skirts. The thrill of the danger! The thrill of a voyage! The thrill of that trip!*

Now she is obliged to lie still, haltered in this narrow space like a beast. She is unable even to turn, while the ship blunders on toward the hoped-for dark, lurching back and forth, rising and falling, following the French warship. Is this to be the end of her short life? *Will the White Lady of my dreams come for me? Alive! I must stay alive!*

How can anyone even imagine the many splendid places where she has lived? The names run through her mind like a prayer: *Hautefontaine*, where she hunted in the summers as a child; *Spa* in Belgium, where she danced the gavotte for the man who is destined to become the Emperor of Russia; *The Hague*, where the Dutch women copied her clothes; *Le Bouilh*, Frédéric's castle, where they hid for many months. She remembers dinners with a liveried servant standing behind each chair. She thinks of all the things she left behind: her wedding gifts, clothes, materials, laces, harpsichord, her precious music, porcelain, books, portraits of her ancestors. She does not miss those things.

What she misses are the myriad sounds of the early morning in the forest at Hautefontaine, the tumult of the chase, the wild thudding of the horses' hooves, the white light of the Ile de France coming and going through the leaves, the French mud flying in her face.

What she thinks of are some of her earliest memories: the humiliations of her childhood, the penances and beatings, the loss of her first love, her maid, Marguerite, who was banished to the kitchens, and her grandmother's rages.

*I was never a child. I was never innocent.*

Now there is nothing but this small space, her husband and their young children, and the few things she has managed to bring with them. She lies, barely able to move, her back and limbs aching with fatigue, her mouth dry. She stares at the swaying blue curtain over the small porthole of their cabin.

She holds her baby closer, and her eyes grow heavy. Her vision blurs. She blinks but continues to see soft blue, the soft blue of the Queen's dress.

PART TWO

Childhood

## I

FTER ELEVEN YEARS of marriage to Louis XVI and after scurrilous attacks in the anonymous *libelles*, Marie Antoinette, Queen of France, finally gives birth to a boy, the Dauphin, Louis-Joseph-Xavier-Francois, and a ball is given by the Royal Bodyguards to celebrate this event.

### DECEMBER, 1781

*I saw the Radiant Queen, the Young Mother, in her blue dress with all her promise of happiness. I thought: I could be happy like that.*

Lucy almost said, *I could be the Queen.*

How many times in her life has she returned with yearning to that instant, at eleven years old. When she first saw the Queen, floating on the hand of a young guardsman, Lucy was standing by the side of a young page.

What comings and goings on the staircase and in the corridor! What whispers, muffled laughter, rapid footsteps, and wafting perfumes outside her room! How many footmen and maids, her governess, and even Marguerite, coming bustling into her room, having managed to escape from the kitchens and slip up the stairs, determined, "if it cost her her life," she had said, to see Lucy dressed for the Queen's ball. She stood before Lucy. She gazed, enraptured. She pressed her thin, reddened hands together against her heart as if in prayer, her artless eyes bright with tears of admiration and joy at the sight of her darling little girl in her white taffeta dress.

Lucy's mother had even sent up her own maid to help Lucy with her dress, her hair, and shoes. The recently acquired pert and pretty Miss B., Lucy's English governess, hovered impatiently behind her. She held her cape and tried to hold her hand. Sputtering a little in her excitement, white teeth protruding, she told Lucy her mother was ready to go, the coach was waiting, she was to hurry up and go immediately down the marble stairs.

Lucy had lived all her eleven years in this somber house, the Hotel Dillon on the Rue du Bac, the house of her grandmother and her great-great-uncle, Richard Dillon, Archbishop of Narbonne, without any protection other than that of her nurse, Marguerite, now banished to the kitchens and replaced by this plump, Protestant woman with her damp eyelashes, her sharp, glittering gaze, her urgent breath.

"She'll end up forgetting all her English if she spends another day with Marguerite," Lucy's grandmother had said. She had decided Lucy needed an English governess and chosen the pliable Miss B. Everything in this house belonged to Lucy's grandmother; she was in charge of everything, making sudden and unexpected appearances at awkward moments, keeping strict watch over her daughter, her granddaughter, the servants, the animals. "Trust is all very well, but control is essential," she had said.

*I will not let you control me.*

Lucy remembers shivering with excitement but also cold and fear, that damp December afternoon. A slight drizzle fell. Her mother had told her about the Queen's ball weeks before and had ordered her to say nothing to her grandmother, who would be unlikely to approve. *I will not tell you. I will not give you the pleasure of a response.* Lucy let them dress her and admire her, but she was wondering all the while what her grandmother would say. Her eyes watered from the smoky fireplace in the hall, as she stood in silence and listened to her grandmother's reaction to seeing her dressed, the flowers in her hair. *How could a mother and a child fight with such venom!*

Everything ached, as Lucy stood beside her mother: the arched insteps of her feet, shod in high-heeled shoes; the back of her long neck, carrying the weight of her hair, which had been scraped and piled high on her head and adorned with artificial flowers; the small buds of her breasts, which were squeezed together and pushed upward and forward. She hardly dared to move for fear the whole artificial edifice would crumble to the black-and-white marble floor.

Her grandmother was taking snuff. Her voice was punctuated with sniffs. Her cocker spaniel cringed at her feet. She leaned against the mantelpiece, lifted the back of her hand to her nose, gave Lucy one look, and said in her booming voice, "Absurd! You are not taking the child there! No children or corpses at Versailles."

Her grandmother seemed old to Lucy, though, despite her heavy build, not lacking in beauty, with her dark blue, shadowy eyes, her smooth olive skin, and her glistening plum-red mouth. Standing before her, Lucy felt as if she were facing a military commander of high rank. There was about her heaving chest, her tobacco-flecked, gray-black taffeta, a raw energy and violence she did nothing to conceal. Lucy had seen her turn in rage on an unsuspecting dog or servant as savagely as she did on Lucy and her mother.

At the sound of her grandmother's voice, Lucy's mother stood immobile. Already in her deep-blue velvet cloak, with the hood and elbow-length gloves, she hung her head, half-hypnotized by her mother's voice, despite the waiting carriage, the footmen hanging onto the back.

Her cheeks flushed with fever and rouge, she protested in a shaky, conciliatory tone, "But *Maman*! The Queen!" She explained that the Queen had expressly asked her to bring Lucy with her that night. The Queen was so happy after all these years at the birth of a boy and wanted everyone else to be happy, too. Marie Antoinette so loved children, Lucy's mother gushed. She loved, even at such a moment, to repeat the Queen's name. As though a spell had been cast upon her, she seemed transformed from a tall, brilliant, successful young woman into a pathetic child. Lucy turned away, embarrassed, aggravated, and afraid they would never go to the ball.

Above all, Lucy hated to see her grandmother turn this violence on her mother. Lucy preferred to be beaten or even shut up in the dark closet without food or water, where she could despise her grandmother and even show her contempt. She could think of what she knew, of what she had learned from her tutors, from her mother, recalling the Irish poems she knew by heart and that her grandmother ignored. "My little love, my calf, / This is the image, / That last night brought me / In Cork all lonely..." But when her grandmother turned on her mother and reduced her to fawning stupidity, she could only feel helpless and sad.

What was the point of explaining to her grandmother what she must already know, that there had been great joy at this birth. Lucy had been joyful. She had thought: *Now everything will be all right. Mother will be the Queen's favorite again.*

But her grandmother was not joyful. She had been enraged that Lucy and her mother had been invited to the ball and that she had not, and this on a night when Lucy's great-great-uncle, the Archbishop, was in Montpellier. Her mother would never be able to convince her grandmother to let Lucy go. She had never convinced her grandmother of anything, as far as Lucy could see. *Do what you want: walk out the door, head held high!* Was she not a grown woman, with an eleven-year-old child and a privileged place at court, one of only twelve ladies-in-waiting to the Queen of France?

"It's madness going out on a damp night like this yourself, in the condition you are in," her grandmother said, flicking the growing pile of tobacco garbage from her chest with thick, bejeweled fingers.

Lucy's mother looked down at her for a moment, hesitating, her gloved hand to her mouth, coughing her shallow cough. Lucy slipped her fingers into her mother's to augment her courage. More than wanting to go to the Queen's ball, more than wanting to go to Versailles for the very first time, she wanted to see her mother, for once, stand up for herself, and above all, stand up for her.

Lucy's grandmother sniffed and turned furiously on Lucy. Her voice thundered, "You know perfectly well your mother is ill. Neither of you is to go out tonight."

Lucy leaned as close to her mother as her wide paniers permitted. She was certain her grandmother was not concerned about her mother's health, but only about her own boredom without them. Lucy understood that her grandmother somehow needed these quarrels, as a fire needs wood. Lucy herself was just kindling.

Lucy stood stiffly in her white dress made expressly for this occasion and the flowers she had chosen for her hair. She stared down at the black-and-white marble floor. *I will not listen to your angry words.*

"If you disobey me, you'll be punished, you understand," her grandmother muttered menacingly, giving Lucy a look that made her feel as if she'd stabbed her.

She understood all too well. She recalled each of her grandmother's lashings with the riding crop, bending over the chair, a handkerchief stuffed in her mouth, and the times she had been sent to the dark, musty cupboard for refusing to spy on her mother. *I have a heart that scorns disguise and will not dissemble.*

"The Queen has asked me to be there tonight at her triumph," her mother went on in her painful, slightly hoarse, beseeching tone. She lifted her head and added with a little more resolution, "I cannot disappoint her." Lucy hoped this referred not only to the Queen.

"The Queen's only concern, as far as I can gather, is that the Countess Jules should be there. I doubt the Queen will miss your presence much, though Henri de Guéménée might, a bit," her grandmother replied cruelly, speaking pointedly of the Countess Jules de Polignac, who had displaced her mother from the Queen's heart, and of the Prince de Guéménée, who her grandmother maintained had displaced her father from her mother's.

At that, her mother made a strange motion. She lifted an arm to her flushed face, as if to protect herself, and swayed a little on her small, high-heeled shoes. But for once she did what she had wanted or, anyway, promised to do. They left in a confusing dash, so that Lucy had not even time to run downstairs to the kitchens to embrace Marguerite, as she had promised to do. She and her mother held hands and giggled like naughty schoolgirls. They panted as they tumbled into the carriage, their pink and white taffeta skirts all crushed together. They went so fast in her great-great-uncle's carriage, with its six swift horses, that her teeth chattered, arriving at Versailles just in time to see the lantern-men with their pikes light the torchères. *The sky suddenly cleared for a moment of blue, as it always did in the evenings in the Ile de France of my childhood.*

Despite all the din, the barking of dogs, the chiming of bells, the shouting of the changing guard, as they entered the gates Lucy had the impression of entering a fairy-tale palace of gold, silver, and precious gems.

Her mother counseled her not to be shy, as she so often, pain-fully, was. She told her, as they hurried up the stairs, "Hold your-self erect, my heart, be amiable to all, smile, and try to make a good impression. Who knows, perhaps the Queen will stop and look up at you. I've told her all about you and how clever you are, how many books you have read. If she considers you interesting enough, she might even wave her hand or make some other sign of her royal approbation."

These words made Lucy tremble with terror, confusion, and blind hope. If only she could help her mother regain the Queen's favor!

"It's a place where anything can happen to you," her mother went on, panting on the stairs, her cheeks a hectic red. "A word from the Queen, a minister, some high-placed person, as in a fairy tale, can change your life."

Lucy recalled how her mother's had been changed, first by her favor with the Queen, and now that she was ill, for the worse. Her place had been usurped by what she called the "Polignac gang." Despite her failing health and diminished status, she continued to assist whenever she could at some part of the royal ritual: prayers, petty levee, grand levee, mass, dinner, hunt, vespers.

Then Lucy saw a small kitten slither furtively along the wall of the gallery above the hall to retrieve an abandoned piece of cheese. Or could it have been a large rat with a long tail?

Her mother stared at her for a moment with a bewildered, almost surprised expression in her blue eyes. She leaned over her, kissed her on her forehead, nose, and cheeks. Then she was gone, leaving behind only a perfume in the air, a bittersweet smell of heliotrope, verbena, and jasmine. Lucy heard the click of her rapid footsteps retreating down the stairs and saw her shadow on the wall.

*Mother's existence was almost an illusion, my own invention, one that required continuous work to preserve. She was always leaving. She was a mysterious source of strange, seductive secrets. When she was there, I was often obliged to stand by, half-forgotten, and watch from afar.*

Lucy stood where her mother had left her, in the gallery, along with the other people who had not yet been presented to the Queen. All was gold and shadow in the *Salle des Spectacles*, an ephemeral, illusory place. Chandeliers dangled precariously from the ceiling. Garlands of real or artificial flowers hung from the pillars. Liqueurs of different colors filled large, make-believe shells. Lucy was certain the walls were of marble, but the young page at her side insisted they were only painted wood. He told her to touch them. "You see, just wood," he said, grinning at her surprise at hearing the hollow sound. Overhead in a sconce on the wall, a six-branched candelabra held candles. The flames danced in unison to the cold draft that wafted through the gallery.

Lucy might have considered she was dreaming, were it not for the young page, Alexandre. He had told her his name. She could see from his fresh, pink, girlish cheeks that despite an air of lassitude, he must not be much older than she. He boasted he had seen many of the Queen's balls, many of them much more amusing than this one. He waved his hand slowly through the air, as though he were already a hundred years old rather than fourteen or fifteen. He answered her questions distractedly, as if knowing much more than he probably did.

Lucy gazed down anxiously into the crush of courtiers in the great hall, staring at everyone and everything with extreme interest, but trying above all to keep her mother's fluttering fan in sight, as though her gaze could somehow hold her up, keep her well and safe. Her mother had not adopted the new, short *coiffure à l'enfant*, which the Queen had recently introduced because of her thinning hair.

Surrounded by a crush of people, Lucy lost sight of her mother. She hunted her with her gaze. Where had she gone? For one terrible moment she mistook another slender, blond lady in pink for her own mother. Had she been overtaken by a fit of coughing, as she so often was? Or, feeling weak, had she had to leave after just arriving? Might she have forgotten Lucy in her distress?

At that thought Lucy was afraid she would fall from the balcony where she stood. She leaned dangerously over the ledge, catching sight of her mother's fan with the roses painted on it that the Queen had given her. Her mother was chattering, smiling, and laughing. All her ardent admirers were clustered around her: the Duke de Lauzun, Liancourt, Axel Fersen. Lucy knew them all, because they came hunting at Hautefontaine. She saw the one her grandmother had mentioned with disdain, the Prince de Guéménée. How many times before had her grandmother admonished her, her ringed fingers clawing into Lucy's shoulder, "I'm counting on you to keep an eye on my daughter and tell me what she is up to." Lucy's grandmother had a passion for the possessive pronoun.

Despite the whispered insinuations, Lucy was certain none of these men could possibly be her mother's lovers. Lucy watched her and the faces around her for a hint of these secret liaisons, but could see nothing inappropriate in the way she turned this way and that, smiling and chattering equally with all of them.

Everyone Lucy knew wore the aura of another, half-secret life. She was accustomed to searching faces and listening closely to the silences between the words for what was omitted. She had always the feeling that people withheld what was most important. What did the young page, for example, know about the Prince de Guéménée? She turned to him and asked in a casual way if he knew the Prince. His black eyes wandered. He stood distractedly in the Queen's red velvet livery with the tight waist, the gold braid, and

the plumed hat, fidgeting and covering a yawn. Eager to be else-
where, Lucy supposed, he seemed bored by the conversation of an
eleven-year-old girl. But she was determined to take full advantage
of the opportunity. She wanted to know everything he could tell
her about the extraordinary scene before her, and above all, about
the many men who congregated around her mother.

"Oh, of course I know him. Everyone does. Henri de Rohan,
Prince de Guéménée, the grand Chamberlain, nephew of Cardinal Rohan and husband of the Royal Governess of the Household,
though she does not seem particularly interested in children or men
either, for that matter, but rather in dogs. She believes she can talk
to the spirits through them." He was showing off his knowledge
and, like her mother, liked to pronounce grand names. "They say
he has enormous debts." He spoke of the gambling that went on at
Court, of the extravagant fêtes the Prince gave, the huge sums lost
and won overnight. "Of course he's immensely rich, like all the
Rohans, but he's also the most extravagant."

Lucy wanted to say that almost everyone she knew had debts,
including her own Irish father and her great-great-uncle, an archbishop of the Church, but she said nothing further on the subject. She had already learned to ask people about themselves, so she
asked him about the school for pages at Versailles. He explained
that they learned Latin, German, fencing, and riding. According to
him, the Queen was excessively kind to her pages.

"My mother says she is very beautiful, that she has such beautiful skin, no?" Lucy asked, turning toward him again. Her mother's
eyes turned bright when she said the Queen's name. Her greatest
joy was to be alone in the Queen's company, when she had amused
her in some way, making her laugh at a witty comment.

The Queen was not actually so beautiful, the page told Lucy,
to her surprise. He let his brown gaze wander over her face, shoul-

ders, and hands. He drawled, "In my opinion the Queen's eyes are not beautiful at all, and her mouth is decidedly disagreeable. Also, she has something that might not be an advantage for a queen: her face shows exactly what she is thinking. You can read enthusiasm or disdain immediately." It was her carriage that was truly remarkable. "She walks like a goddess, as though she were surging hip-deep through water, head held high." Lucy tried to bring him back to the men who stood around her mother, but he seemed hardly to hear.

Her mother was fanning her face and talking with the Duke de Lauzun, who had recently come back from the war in America. Lucy wished it were her own father who had returned from the war instead, but he was far away in Tobago, in the West Indies, also fighting for American independence, with his Irish regiment. Lucy's mother had explained how important this area was to France as well as America, because of its economic value and France's rivalry with England.

Lucy returned to the attack. Had he had the privilege of seeing the Queen's new baby boy, the Dauphin? "Ah," the page said, snickering suggestively, "Yes, yes, I have seen the little Miracle, and he does not look very robust to me." She thought of her own baby brother's death, which had brought on her mother's malady.

Miss B. had told Lucy that the Queen had not had any children until her brother, Joseph, had come all the way from Austria to give his brother-in-law advice on how to engender an heir. She had hinted the baby might not even be the King's son. "What advice?" Lucy had asked her. Miss B. had muttered something Lucy did not entirely understand about the King being better at eating and hunting than at other duties he was called upon to perform.

Lucy saw her mother now talking to the handsome Swede, Axel Fersen, who, according to Lucy's governess, was the Queen's lover. She asked the page if he knew how the Queen had first met him. He told her about other balls, which he deemed more amusing, where everyone was masked and anonymous. Even the Queen was masked, he maintained, and taken for someone else. He raised his brown eyebrows suggestively. That was how she had met the Count.

"I know him quite well," Lucy said haughtily, for indeed she did. He, too, with the Prince de Guéménée and the Duke de Lauzun came to hunt almost daily when the family was in residence at Hautefontaine.

Lucy asked another question about Axel Fersen, but the page seemed not to hear or was anyway more interested in gazing down the low front of her dress, where all she had at eleven to pass for a bosom had been made as visible as possible. Lucy let him look.

The page giggled, shook the feather in his hat shamelessly at her, and confided in her *sotto voce* about the man who was in charge of the royal pages who had, heaven knows how, been awarded the cross of Saint Louis.

*All were there to advance their careers in some way. They looked through me, or beyond me, with an infinitely bored expression. Their gaze wandered from my face, to see if there was someone more important nearby, someone connected with the Queen or the King, someone who could advance their station.*

Lucy drew herself up and thrust out as much bosom as she was able. She caught sight of her mother, who glanced up at her and the page at her side. She fluttered her fingers and smiled vaguely up at them, with that surprised look on her face. The page commented politely on the sweetness of Madame Dillon's smile, her brilliant success at Court, and her friendship with the Queen that had caused Madame de Lamballe some chagrin.

Indeed, Lucy thought her mother beautiful: tall, slim, and graceful. Everyone, apart from Lucy's grandmother, loved her mother, she was certain. Why would the Queen not love her, too? And how could anyone have replaced her mother in the Queen's fancy? Lucy tried to smile back openly. She wanted to appear as lovely as she could for her mother, though she knew she would never be as beautiful. Her nose was too long, not fine enough, her eyes too small, not as bright as her mother's. She bit her lips to make them look red. Above all, what she wanted was to look grown up. Certainly she did not feel like a child. She had seen too much, heard too many bitter quarrels at such a young age.

And what about the page, young Alexandre? What was he thinking as he stood beside her? Was he really interested by this eleven-year-old girl? Actually, he was thinking about his disgrace with the Queen because of an escapade in Paris where he had been taken with one of the other pages by an older man. In Paris they had fallen for the same woman of ill repute, who is known to have given them both the same unmentionable disease. The page was suffering from a burning sensation in his most intimate part, and from the shame attached to the revelation of this malady that had been necessary in order to obtain some relief not only for himself but for his friend, who had been stricken even more seriously than he, Alexandre, had been.

At that moment Lucy turned away from him and peered down to watch the dark-haired Prince draw nearer to her mother and mutter something in her ear.

"They also say that he admires your lovely mother particularly," the page said, sidling up, following her gaze, and smiling suggestively.

Lucy attempted to reproduce one of her grandmother's most awful looks: a mixture of stern pride and passionate opprobrium.

"And you, too, I'm certain, will soon have many admirers," the page said, dipping his head a little and making his feather quiver.

For a moment Lucy wished she and her mother were both back in the dark, leafy forest that surrounded the house she loved. She wished she were at Hautefontaine following her mother's bay mare in the hunt as she had done since she was seven.

Above all, she prayed to find some way to protect her mother, who seemed to her an angel of light and shade. She wished she could be like Cleveland, in the book by the Abbé Prévost, who had hidden alone with his mother in a cave.

Then she noticed someone in the crowd who looked different from the rest, because she seemed to make no effort to be looked at, at all. Though Lucy had never seen her before, she was almost certain who this was: the Usurper, the one who had taken her mother's place in the Queen's heart, who made her mother mutter, "They flee from me who sometime did me seek." *Mother spoke to me sometimes in English and sometimes in French. And sometimes in both together.* Others courted her less, Lucy sensed, now that the Queen had lost interest in her.

"And who is the lady with the rose in her hair?" Lucy asked the page, looking at the woman in a simple dress who seemed to be wandering aimlessly through a field of flowers. "Don't you see: the one with the dark hair and the large, light eyes, in the white dress who looks as if she's playing a dairymaid?"

"Ah! They all like to playact, but, of course, that's the Countess Jules de Polignac," the page replied with a laugh.

"Oh!" Lucy said, her suspicions confirmed. Lucy watched her mother glance over her shoulder at the Countess Jules, who, all soft curves, walked on followed closely by a fine-looking man who seemed weighed down by many decorations. Lucy noticed a shadow pass over her mother's face as they approached. Lucy could feel her distress.

"She's the one the Queen likes best now?" Lucy asked though she knew all too well.

"Indeed, she's the current favorite—the Queen is besotted with her, she will have no one else near," the page whispered. "Though they say she's not very clever, the Queen will do anything for her. She adores her." Smiling languidly and moving forward with grace, the Countess approached the Prince and Lucy's mother. Lucy thought the Countess looked like the Madonna in an Italian painting she had seen in her great-great-uncle's house. She seemed to be the only woman in the room not wearing jewels of any kind.

"And who is the woman behind her, with all the jewels?" Lucy asked, watching someone who followed slightly behind the Countess Jules, like a squat shadow. She stared at the greedy, purple mouth, the shadow on her upper lip, the stubby hands that she waved in the air. She was talking to the Prince, who did not seem to be listening, but was staring instead at the Countess Jules.

"That's her sister-in-law, probably saying something clever," the page pointed out. The sister-in-law, the Countess Diane de Polignac, apparently thought only of acquiring an enormous fortune for her family. She used the Queen's infatuation with her sister-in-law to obtain it. "The Countess Jules is the bait. If you know what I mean," he said.

Lucy thought it better to nod her head. Then the page leaned closer to say, "It is said they receive 700,000 livres a year."

The Countess Jules leaned now on her lover's arm, the Comte de Vaudreuil, the man with all the decorations.

"The Comte de Vaudreuil is a very good actor. He does the Count Almaviva in Beaumarchais's play very well," the page told Lucy.

Lucy watched her mother put her handkerchief to her mouth to cover a cough. Her face was flushed and thin. Lucy wanted to reach for her hand, lead her to a chair, and tell her to sit down and rest.

Seeing them in all their splendor, she grasped the powerful influence of these Polignacs. She realized how they had gradually usurped not only her mother's place but that, too, of the Princess de Lamballe in the Queen's heart. Seeing her mother beside the fresh-faced Countess Jules, she was aware how exhausted she looked. They had been waiting too long for the Queen to open the ball. Perhaps her grandmother had been right, and they should never have come here.

Was there not some way she could guide her mother, so guiless, innocent, and unable to protect herself? Lucy, as though she were the older one, wanted to protect her. She wanted so much.

Then the doors swung open, and the usher called out: "The Queen!" Though Lucy had been waiting for this moment since she had first heard she was to come to the ball, she had difficulty believing what she saw.

*My head reeled. My face burned. My knees were unsteady. I was thrown into a state close to rapture as I watched the Queen advance on the hand of a young guardsman. The musicians struck up a minuet. It must have been Gluck.*

*For a moment I forgot the damp, the rat in the staircase, the impudent page at my side, even Mother, surrounded by all these admiring men. I saw only the Queen, who seemed hardly to be dancing. She floated through the room like an ethereal being, half-light, half-illusion, my illusion, my promise of happiness. I had brought her forth in her sparkling blue dress, strewn with rubies and diamonds, like the poppies in the wheat fields I had seen in the countryside in the summertime.*

The Queen's shining skin reflected the adoration of all the courtiers around her. They watched her at this triumphant moment.

She had finally produced a boy and succession was secure! Her sister-in-law's children would no longer inherit the throne.

Lucy's mother bowed her blond head and dipped low in a curtsy. She smiled with adoration as the Queen passed her, her face alight, her joy evident.

The Queen made a gracious salutation that somehow managed to encompass them all: her mother, and behind her, the Prince, Lucy's young and hopeful presence hovering above in the gallery, and even the young page, who had sprung to attention at the Queen's appearance with a brilliant smile. In the half dark, with all eyes fixed on the Queen, his hand, which had been lying quietly on the balustrade, slithered, like the rat she had seen on the staircase, inside Lucy's bodice and clamped itself around one very small bud of a breast.

## II

If she closed her eyes, she could shut out the outer darkness and hold her own light, some faint illumination, her own seeing and hearing, in her mind. She could pretend there *was* light out there, and sound, and above all, in the airless, narrow closet, that there was air and space. When she sat, breathless, immobile, cramped up in the dark, narrow linen closet for her penance, she could keep her eyes closed and imagine she was a lark, flying free through the trees. If she concentrated hard and thought of all those brave people who had gone before her, her ancestors, the ones called Wild Geese who were closed in crates for days to cross the sea, she might imagine herself lifted out of her body, just a vapor, the very air itself, slipping under the door, escaping into the long corridor and out into the street.

Then she might hear the sound of a key in the lock. She might catch a glimmer of lighter darkness and open her eyes to see Marguerite there, panting slightly, with her candle glimmering in her shaking hand and a piece of bread in her apron pocket and her pewter pitcher of water or, once, even a slice of apricot tart, sticky with syrup that she could suck from each of her fingers for solace. She could put her arms around her nurse's wide waist, lean her head against her soft breast, and listen to her whisper in the language she loved, *"Courage mon enfant, courage!"*

She might have fallen into a light sleep when the door would be thrown open and real light of day come in with the perfume she knew so well: heliotrope, jasmine, and verbena. Her mother would be there in the early morning, still in her rumpled ball gown. With her pomaded hair in disarray, she would laugh a little and tell her to come out quickly. She would whisper in appalled tones, as though this had never happened before, "But what have they done to my precious?" Her own mother would dare *her* mother's wrath to free her finally. After a night of revelry—she could smell the sour smell of wine and sex mixed with the perfumes—she would take her by the hand and help her to her feet, her legs all stiff with pins-and-needles, and bring her forth into light and air.

Sometimes, it might be her grandmother herself. She knew by the musty, tobacco odor of her that she was standing stolidly in the doorway. She imagined her face canted severely down, but kept her eyes closed. Her grandmother had finally come to free her from her penance and demand the satisfaction of an apology, which she gave with as much dignity she was able to muster. She opened her eyes and allowed her grandmother's navy blue taffeta dress, her violent red lips, her heavy breasts to enter the light of her consciousness.

# III

In that house the ceilings were high. The furnishings were heavy, pompous. My archbishop great-great-uncle, like the Prince de Guéménée, managed to live beyond his considerable means in great style. Everything was of the best quality. The candles, made of goat fat, came from Salzburg. The carriage was decorated with my uncle's coat of arms in silver. Yet, in my mind I often compared this elegant abode to Robinson Crusoe's island. I imagined that I, too, was stranded there, with an imaginary Friday to teach.

Not that I was often allowed to be alone. I was surrounded by an army of maids and footmen, coachmen and cooks, my own personal tutor, M. Combes, and so many costly things: my necessaire of rosewood that held perfumes and toilette instruments; my own secretaire, with its inlay of ivory, its lock, where I kept my secrets; my leather-bound diary; my harpsichord, which I practiced diligently daily, joyfully, leaving my conscious life and entering another realm; a sketch pad; my doll, made by Rose Bertin herself, the Queen's dressmaker, and given to me by Talleyrand, a friend of my mother's, on my seventh birthday; with a complete wardrobe: dresses, silk chemises, and stockings; and my precious books. I read them to find out about life.

I had to go up a small, twisting staircase and then slip silently past Grandmother's room to access my own, which lay at the end of a long corridor. Grandmother called out to me as I tried to slip by. "Lucy, come here," she bellowed. I had to assist at her toilette. One chambermaid powdered her hair, while her hands were manicured by another. Yet another massaged a *very visible and blue-veined leg, while her reader read to her from her favorite books. Oddly enough she loved* Manon Lescaut.

*She often received her guests almost naked, in her bed or during her toilette. Even my great-great-uncle might drop by at such a moment to report the latest event . . .*

*I escaped, whenever I could, to my canopied bed. I drew together its dark, dusty red hangings. I sat reading, playing with my doll, or even doing my petit point, behind its drapery.*

*It was here that I discovered the blood running down my leg one morning as I sprang from my bed. I thought I had injured myself in some terrible way. Mother had never told me what to expect, though she had dropped a few hints. My grandmother had enjoyed making veiled prophecies on the subject, I suspect. Still, I was quite unprepared until Miss B. laughingly informed me of my womanhood, which seemed hardly a laughing matter.*

Now Miss B. was at Lucy's side weeping profusely this cool, sodden autumn morning. She breathed heavily, snuffling through her small snub nose, her plump bosom rising and falling alarmingly.

*I was dreaming of the White Lady. I had seen her the first time when I had the smallpox as a little child. She was to come to me again and again in my long life, whenever death was near.*

She was walking across a field of soft snow, dragging Lucy by the hand. She wore a white gown with a long train that trailed behind and made a hushing sound. She kept telling her to hurry, they would be late. Lucy could not walk fast enough to keep up, her legs curiously heavy, her bare feet weighted down. Then she became aware someone was holding her hand and urging her to rise, to make haste.

Miss B. knelt by her bed, her warm breath on her cheek. She smelled of cheese. She must have been eating the Welsh rabbit she often had for breakfast. She murmured something dolefully about haste. From the distressed expression in her governess's globular eyes, Lucy could see that something was wrong.

"What is it?" she asked without wanting to know. Miss B. caressed her hand softly and wept. Her forehead was flushed and slightly mottled, her blond curls in disarray, her gown creased. Lucy regarded her suspiciously.

She did not trust any of the adults around her except for Marguerite. The plump English governess, Miss B., with the flushed forehead, the pink-and-white skin, the fat blond ringlets, the adorable protruding teeth and a taste for light literature, though one of the most attractive, was one of the least trustworthy in this household.

Her tears annoyed Lucy. She moved away from her. She turned her back, buried her face in her pillow, and hoped she would go away. She wanted to tell her to go and fetch her faithful Marguerite. Marguerite, though she could neither read nor write, had always whispered sage advice to her. She had taught Lucy about love. When Lucy had turned twelve, Miss B. had taught her about lust, reading her passages from light novels, the popular *livres du boudoir*, that make her flush and squirm.

Miss B., blowing her snub nose loudly, gave her the sad news in her high-pitched, slightly nasal English voice. "Darling girl, I'm afraid your mother is with us no more," she said. Lucy rose from her bed, ran to the door, and begged to go to her. She wanted to see her. She wanted to hold her in her arms. Please! Where was she?

"She's gone, my heart," was all Miss B. would say, restraining Lucy, leading her back to her bed.

Why had she not been called in the night? Had her mother not asked for her? Why had no one told her that her mother was dying and that she needed her? Why was she not with her mother at this last moment of her life?

Her mother had died alone, Miss B. informed Lucy tactlessly

and perhaps not even truthfully. *Surely it was not possible that she could have died without a priest at her side, in the house of an archbishop?* Lucy, half-blind with grief, guilt, and sleep, stumbled to the window in the faint dawn light. She stared out into the noisy street.

She asked if she might then be left, at least, for a moment alone, but Miss B. refused. There was no time to waste. Lucy must dress appropriately and go to her grandmother immediately. She must throw herself at her feet, beg for her protection. Already Miss B. was scurrying around looking for Lucy's black silk stockings.

But Lucy could not move. As in her dream, she felt in another atmosphere, as if the air were different, thinner in the head, as if she were on a mountaintop. Breathing was difficult.

How could her young mother, who had given Lucy her life, be dead? She had known she was ill, that she was suffering from her lungs. Perhaps she had even suspected she was dying, but she had not believed she would die *now*, not this night. How could this small shred of hope for any protection from her grandmother be gone? She clung to the last memory of her mother, lying half-asleep on her bed, one arm flung across her flushed face. She was murmuring about going to Naples with Henri de Guéménée. She had been planning a voyage to Italy, when Lucy had peeped in the door to say goodnight.

Lucy imagined her mother's lonely death in a maid's arms with a terrible and heavy melancholy. After all her success at Court, after the adulation from the many men around her, after visits from the Queen to her bedside, her mother had died with no one but a stranger to hold her in her arms as she slowly suffocated: no Queen, no husband, no lover, no son, no daughter, not even a priest was present. *You might die alone. You might lie like her in the arms of a servant, forgotten.*

"I will go to my father," Lucy objected. She lifted her head, trying to remember the last time she had seen him: three years before, when she was nine years old. He had left to fight beside three other Dillons, including Edward, the one they called the "Beau" Dillon, in the West Indies.

She remembered how he had lifted her high in the air and swung her around gaily, how her cheek had grazed his wig and knocked it askew, how he had laughed, taken it off, and put it on her head like a crown. He had promised to bring something special for his princess on his return from America. "America! America!" he had chanted in English. Her father always spoke to her in English. Surely he would want his princess to be with him, wherever he was, now that her mother was gone? She would go to America to be with him.

Her father was not on good terms with her grandmother, and he was in any case still fighting at Saint Christophe, Miss B. reminded Lucy. There were rumors that he would remain there to become governor of the island. It would take months to contact him, for him to even know his wife was dead, his daughter on her own.

"Cast yourself at your grandmother's feet and obtain her sympathy with your tears, your distress. She could simply abandon us, throw us out of the house, now that your mother is dead," Miss B. warned.

Indeed, she had been right to feel that this house was like a luxurious desert island, a dangerous one at that. What would happen to her now, she thought, looking at the rain falling against the window-panes. Was it possible she might be turned out of here, banished at any moment, abandoned as an orphan to some charitable institution? Surely her mother had left her possessions to her daughter and not her mother? She imagined what she would do if she had to make her own way and find her own food, out in the street like the child with the wooden bowl who called out for food. Who would help her?

*All my life I imagined dire situations in which I would be obliged to manage on my own to find food and clothing. I had made Marguerite teach me how to iron the clothes at Hautefontaine.*

"I won't go. I won't beg for favors from her. I won't be part of some play!" she said. "Not after what Grandmother did to Mother. She was the one who made her sick." Lucy sat back on the bed, arms crossed on her chest. She thought of all her grandmother had made her mother suffer, how she had refused to believe she was ill, even when she was spitting up blood. She was working herself up into a righteous rage.

"I'd prefer to run away alone. I'll go to Father in America. I'll get uncle to pay the passage."

Vaguely her father's youthful form and face came to her. It was his bright soldier's uniform she remembered most clearly, a tall man in the uniform of his own Irish brigade: a short red coat with daffodil-colored turnbacks on the cuffs and the lapels, white waist-coat and white breeches, the buttons shiny. She had put her fingers into the buttonholes that were trimmed with red twist.

"And how would you do that?" Miss B. asked her and cocked her head inquiringly and blew her nose.

Lucy thought about that. She said, "He likes me," thinking of her great-great-uncle saying to her, "You are a very clever girl, do you know that, Lucy? I'm going to make sure you have a tutor clever enough to teach you something."

Miss B. smiled. It was from the mouth that you could see she was smart, savvy, from the way she grinned, lifting up one corner of her plump, seductive lips. Now she lifted up Lucy's arms and pulled the nightgown over her head, catching a lock of her hair in a button.

"Of course he does, but you know the Archbishop only does what your grandmother wants him to do. He is entirely in her thrall."

Half-naked, shivering in the damp air, Lucy said she would work her way to the New World and to freedom. "I'll ask one of Mother's friends," Lucy said, blinking back tears, for how could she do something of the sort? Why would anyone want to help her? What could she do for them?

Miss B. shook her ringlets, her mouth half open, teeth protruding, panting. She always seemed slightly out of breath. She twitched her red nose, rabbit-like, and warned Lucy that her father would now certainly remarry.

"He will want a boy, an heir, after all—such a young man still, and so handsome, I hear. It's not at all certain your stepmother would want you to live with them," Miss B. warned and opened her arms and told Lucy to come and be comforted. Lucy went to her, trembling in the damp, chill air. She let her hold her, feeling her warmth, wanting desperately to allow herself to be held much longer, but knowing that this embrace was all the comfort she could receive. *I will not weep. I will not weep. I will not weep.*

Lucy shook her head, but allowed her governess to help her dress. She would go to her grandmother, if she had to. *I will not dissemble.*

"Do you want to be shut up in a convent, then?" Miss B. asked. She imagined it all too clearly: the monotonous, prayer-filled days, the long hours of solitude in a cramped space, the cloistered life. What she wanted to know about was the real world! She wanted to discover the truth that was so skillfully disguised from her.

"She would not do that to me, would she?" Lucy cried out, appalled, but as she said the words, and as Miss B. blew her little pink nose and raised her eyebrows, Lucy knew that, of course, her grandmother might very well do just that; and she would bruit the thing about so skillfully people would believe the idea came from Lucy herself.

But it was Miss B. who threw herself at Lucy's grandmother's feet. She fell to her plump, dimpled knees on the Aubusson carpet in the gray morning light and clutched at the hem of Lucy

Cary's black taffeta skirts. She opened her mouth wide, an obscene organ, showing all her small, glittering teeth. She wailed piteously and clasped her hands to her heaving breast. "Do not banish us, Madame! Have pity on this poor orphan child!" she cried out dramatically.

Lucy watched the scene, one she considered dreadful, tasteless, a scene of fraudulent grief played by the Englishwoman to retain her own position, no doubt.

She stood stiffly, miserably, in her dark dress, hovering in the shadows of the large room, frozen in her corner. She was unable to move, to speak, to weep, unable to show any sort of emotion at all. A sort of paralysis came over her. She thought only of her mother, saw her thin arched eyebrows, the staring pupils of her startled eyes, heard the sound of her skirts, her rapid steps on the stairs, and it seemed to her that her mother was running away from her once more.

Her grandmother sat at her dressing table, half-dressed, one maid beside her dressing her hair, another massaging a leg. She held her cocker spaniel fast under one arm. She lifted up her other hand to silence Miss B. She touched the cameo at her neck with one stubby finger. "Enough! Get up! Compose yourself!" she said. "As far as I know, you have not lost a relative. And you need not fear for your employ." Then her grandmother looked at Lucy and said, "*You* don't seem to be particularly affected by this sad event, Lucy. But then you never had much to do with your mother, did you?"

Lucy said nothing, only blinking back her tears: *I will not weep*, she muttered to herself as she had when she had broken her leg at seven years old at the hunt, and they had carried her on a stretcher made of bark and leaves through the forest, on the day of the feast of Saint Hubert. She would remember it all and find some way to leave this house, this woman. She would grow up fast!

IV

*Once—I must have been about twelve or perhaps thirteen, I saw my uncle in a strange position. I was bored and lonely, and left to my own devices in the gloomy rooms of the house on the Rue du Bac. I heard a strange strangled noise, coming from the linen closet. It was where Grandmother would shut me up if I had not behaved as she wished. I was afraid some small animal was trapped in there.*

*I opened the door of the closet and stood in the half-light. At first, I was not quite sure of what I was witnessing. Gradually, I made out my great-great-uncle in his violet robes. He was pressing against something that moved. At first I was not sure what it was. Then, gasping, my hand to my mouth, I recognized the under-chambermaid, not much older than I, beneath her white bonnet and her corn-colored hair that had tumbled around her shoulders in disarray. It was she who was making the strangled noise. She was trapped, half-propped up against a shelf of sheets, her skirts trussed up about her waist, her legs spread wide. Poor girl, puce in the face, she was sweating as she did when called upon to beat the big carpets in the spring.*

*I cried out. I was afraid my great-great-uncle would kill the girl with his awful weight. I could see he was pressing against her hard, with his big hands around her buttocks. He was struggling and straining against her. I wanted him to stop. Instead, he simply raised a beringed hand in the air elegantly, imperiously, as if in the middle of some very important sermon, which was not at any cost to be disturbed, and I felt obliged to flee.*

Now Lucy's great-great-uncle rose with a rustle of his robes from his dinner. He waved a scented handkerchief in the air with a beringed hand and said, "Ah Lucy, dear, did you know your father is back in France and would like to see you?"

She was fifteen.

Since her mother's death, she had been slow to give up hope for a miraculous reversal. Each morning she woke disbelieving, only to see the rain beating on the window. It seemed to rain constantly through those years of her young life: the weather associated with her mother's death. The rain echoed all the feelings of her heart.

Lucy knew her father had remarried against her grandmother's wishes, that her grandmother considered the woman, a rich Creole, entirely beneath them and refused to let Lucy meet her.

She rose from the table and followed her uncle as he went through the door, caught up with him in the corridor, and placed her hand in the crook of his arm. She leaned against him and whispered in his ear passionately, "I would so like to see my father."

Lucy's grandmother, following, shouted at her back, "I forbid you to go to your father's hotel!" her words hitting Lucy like a hatchet.

Lucy leaned a little more on her uncle's arm and cast a longing glance up at him.

"Ah, youth," he sighed, looking down at her.

"Make haste then, dear child. Only here for a short while. Leaving again for Tobago, where he has been made governor," her uncle bent down toward Lucy to inform her softly and to squeeze her arm against his ribs, not without kindness and a benevolent glimmer of complicity in his Irish eyes.

"He must be disappointed. I know he had hoped to have Martinique or Santo Domingo," Lucy said, for her father had served with great distinction, and had written to her of his hopes and expectations for the governship of these more prestigious places.

She saw a look pass between her grandmother and her great-great-uncle as they stood at the foot of the stairs. She was certain her uncle, following her grandmother's wishes, had not supported her father's candidacy.

Lucy was determined to see him before he left. She would go to him and ask him to take her along. She would leave this house and go to the New World. She slipped out of the house on the Rue du Bac, Miss B. at her side, one afternoon, going to her father's hotel.

She ran up the marble steps, her heart drumming, and Miss B. panting, rustling and crying out behind her in a yellow taffeta dress, "Wait! Wait for me, Lucy!"

Lucy, who had not seen her father for many years, was not sure she would recognize him in the street. He looked tall and slender, his skin somewhat darkened by the sun. The aquiline nose, the small mouth, the small black eyes, the chestnut-colored hair, which he wore drawn back from his face without a wig, made him resemble the bright parrot in the cage at his side eating a cherry. She embraced him shyly, not knowing now what to say. How could she ask him for anything? He stared at her, and there was a certain melancholy as well as surprise in his eyes.

"Oh, Lucy! You came to visit," he said, blinking, and holding onto both her hands. She noticed broken veins in his cheeks, a scar at the edge of his hairline. "What a joy to see you. I've called so many times at your grandmother's house."

"No one told me," she said, tears in her eyes.

"I was so hoping we could see one another again before I left," he replied. Lucy's stepmother murmured something from her couch. Her father turned and introduced them.

Stretched out by the fire, his new wife lay languidly on a day bed, covered in bright shawls, only the toes of her silver slippers visible, her stomach already swelling with her unborn child. Perched on a swing in a painted cage by her side was the brightly colored parrot, which kept crying out, "Hallo, good-bye, hallo."

Madame de la Touche, a woman several years older than Lucy's father, was sipping a cup of hot chocolate, her bee-stung lips stained at the edges. As she moved indolently, Lucy noticed her green taffeta gown and an elaborate silk turban and her heavy perfume that hid darker ones. She crooked a plump finger in a secret gesture to indicate Lucy was to approach and put her arms around her neck. Obeying, Lucy felt her soft bosom and smelled her odor of rut.

"I hope we'll be friends," she murmured into Lucy's ear. Her eyes were small, hard, and black.

Lucy drew back from her and turned to her father.

"I will write again to your grandmother and ask if she will receive us," he said.

She stared at him, thinking of her mother standing in the hallway that night before the Queen's ball. She could hear her begging tone of voice: "Maman, the Queen..." Why was her father, too, this brave man, begging from her grandmother? Why had he not run up the steps and carried her away? Lucy wanted to tell her father that he would have no answer to this letter.

Her father's new wife rose languidly from her couch, her hands on her swollen belly, smoothing the satin folds of her gown. She said they had, unfortunately, to go out. Lucy should have sent a note on ahead to warn them of her visit. A big-boned, indolent, rich woman with fine wrists and shrewd eyes. *Why did Father choose her? Why do people choose one another?*

"We must go, too," Miss B. said, "Your grandmother will be looking for you, and I'll be in trouble." Lucy picked up her father's three-cornered black hat that lay on a chair, and held it to her bosom. He took it from her gravely, put it on his head, and bowed slightly. Then there was nothing to be done but to stumble down the stairs half-blind.

Lucy was not to hear from her father again for several years, until he wrote to her to propose her marriage with Frédéric, Séraphin de Gouvernet, de la Tour du Pin.

# PART THREE
## At Sea

Frédéric Séraphin lies shivering, doubled up, the sweat breaking out along his back, leaning over the side of his cot in the dark. He retches as the *Diana* takes yet another terrible, shuddering lunge, but there's nothing left in his stomach, which is pinched and wrung out. He has not eaten for days. He lies back, head swimming, eyes misted over, throat aching, as the boat plunges and heaves through the fog, following the French man-o'-war. He tells himself to lie still, to think of other things, to close his eyes and forget this boat, which shakes as if about to split apart. Above all, he will not think about the dangers of following a French man-o'-war to a revolutionary tribunal and to the guillotine.

He tells himself to remember pleasant moments, to sleep, but he longs to stop this dreadful rocking, this prolonged and awful state of nausea. He tries to conjure up the stability of the rooms of the chateau of his childhood, Le Bouilh, to imagine strolling through the gardens, but all he can conjure up is riding through the night, the rain running down his back like ants crawling down his spine. For months he has been going from place to place, riding in carriers' carts, lying hidden under knapsacks and cloaks, not knowing half the time if his wife and children were safe.

Why do such terrible memories come back to besiege him, moments of terror and panic and not moments of joy? He has been hunted like a fox and hiding out alone, or worse still, buried like a mole, burrowing beneath the earth without sunlight or moonlight or even real lantern light, deprived of months of life, lying like this, on his back, watching spiders and other insects crawling in the thatched roofing of the locksmith's house. This has robbed him of his lively curiosity, his acquaintance with literature, with music, with action, the thrill of the chase. He has been slipping slowly back in the order of things to one of the lower species. All he has had to sustain him are memories, some of them memories he would rather forget.

Lying in the cover of dark, with Lucy beside him, their whimpering baby in her arms, his boy crying out from time to time in his disturbed sleep, he weeps at the thought that their young lives may end.

Who was it who had told him what the Irish Jacobites had been called, he wonders, as the boat leans dangerously, almost tipping him onto the floor? Was it Lucy's father, Arthur Dillon? Could it have been his old friend, Talleyrand? He does not recall, but he knows they had been named the "Wild Geese," because of the crates that were marked thus, in which they had stowed away when they left Ireland, after the battle of the Boyne in 1690.

He wonders just where his wild Irish goose is carrying him. Why has she chosen this endless, dangerous winter passage to America? He thinks about this brash new country she has chosen as their destination, a country whose freedom he has fought for but which has brought France nothing but heavy debt. Might it not have been safer to go to England, to her English family, or to their friends at Juniper Hall? Lucy has little love for the English, he suspects. Certainly she has little love for her grandmother, who is in England. But would they not have been better there?

He remembers the first time he saw Lucy's father, a tall, young Irishman, only eleven years older than he, riding through the smoke and noise of cannon, the shouts of men. That day had begun at six in the morning with an arduous ride across that wretched country, for so the island of Martinique had seemed to him. There were marshes and gray-green bush, the still sea shimmering endlessly in the distance. The British were entrenched on a hill, some thousand yards distant. He could see them on his approach, redressing their lines. He had reined in his horse and contemplated the scene, viewing them as if placed on parade for his inspection. The French and Irish battalions were still out of range of British guns. Then his commander, the Count D'Estaing, had given the order for the French infantry to charge. The British cannon battered large holes in the ranks, and in an instant this orderly world dissolved into smoke, noise, and confusion. He saw some French soldiers blown to pieces, others skewered and ripped open by pikes.

During the battle, Arthur Dillon was moving forward with his Irish brigade, using low brush and stunted trees for cover, and reassembling his troops for the next charge, this time from the flank. Frédéric followed at the head of his men. It was his role to encourage them, but when he opened his mouth to speak, his throat was dry and stiff and no word came forth. He saw Dillon waving his black hat, the gold braid flashing in the air, and shouting out above the noises of musket fire and screams.

Frédéric can still see him charging forward in his scarlet coat, white waistcoat and breeches, head tilted back slightly, riding with easy grace, one hand on his hip, going under the flowering acacia trees, the light and shade flickering on his freckled face. He remembers the man's recklessness, his ability to surge forward oblivious to the bullets flying about his head.

The battle was won that day more by the flight of the enemy, who had taken off in fright at this reckless assault, than by the Irish and French charge. The first men who scaled the hill found the British guns unmanned. As the British front line fled backward, they caused the next line to panic behind them. Yet the English had outnumbered the Irish and French troops. Arthur had not expected them to buckle so easily, he told Frédéric later.

Frédéric wonders now what mysterious elixir this man possesses. Dropped down on the alien and savage coast, commanding men fresh from Ireland, young peasants, with hands hardened by the plow rather than musket or pike, he moved among them and gave orders as though their success were casual and inevitable.

Frédéric has never had that kind of ease with the men in his command, never been followed with adoration. He is not sure where such authority comes from. Is it an accretion of the many battles an officer has fought, or some personal, almost magical power, or is it rather, because of his particular sense of humor, his Irish luck, his cunning and ability to devise imaginative change of tactics, to create surprise?

Frédéric had watched Arthur riding up and down the line that day talking to his men. Though his spoken English is rudimentary, he could see the effect Dillon had. The men, who an instant before had looked angry or terrified, grew quiet and thoughtful. Frédéric wonders what moves men into battle, why they would follow a commander with nothing in his hands but a piece of cloth with an Irish harp fluttering above him, a rousing anthem, an inspired word. Where does such power come from? And what is happening to Dillon now? Is a royalist general still able to fight alongside the French?

He sees Dillon's face in the flickering candlelight, rising after drinking a great deal of rum and still retaining his dignity, only the controlled movements of his shoulders, his stiff gait suggesting a certain formality.

It was after Frédéric had found him wounded and managed to help him to safety that day in Martinique, that Dillon had first mentioned Lucy and suggested an alliance between what he called their equally ancient and honorable families.

"I'm offering you what is most precious," he had said, grinning, as the sunlight played on his head. He had put his hand on Frédéric's shoulder, light as pollen, and looked directly into his eyes. He was one of those men who does not hesitate to put his hand on an arm, a shoulder, a back, to kiss a friend warmly on both cheeks. Frédéric was already half in love with the father, so why not the daughter?

Frédéric's father, when he had asked for his permission to marry Lucy Dillon, had talked at some length and with admiration about the military history of her Irish family, which could be traced back to 1185, when Henry Delion of Aquitaine was sent to Ireland. It was a family that had emigrated to France, following their Stuart King, James II. Thus Frédéric's father had favored this match. Frédéric considers his father might have been more ambitious, more engaged with the realities of the world around him. He spent too much of his time far from Paris and Versailles, building onto his own chateau in the Bordelais region in the hope of a visit from the King. And what did his father know about women?

Frédéric thinks about this family he was born into: men of great privilege, of high and rigid principles, military men, not used to having to find their way in life. His grandfather had brought him up to believe in diligence, discipline, and honor. He had been educated out of ancient books, brought up on the history of Roman heroes, instilled with an assurance in his own virtue, the value of his considerable French culture, his innate superiority as the eldest son of an ancient family, his good breeding—and above all a reverence for his military ancestors, for bravery in battle, for the rigor of the classics. His grandfather had made him learn long passages of Tacitus by heart.

His father had performed valiantly in battle and had advanced because of this. But he was hated by his mother-in-law, Mme. de

Monconseil, who had found him too severe toward the misconduct of her daughter, Frédéric's mother.

Frédéric never knew what his mother had done to shock his father so, in a society where the married aristocracy often lived separately and mistresses brazenly announced their commerce with married men. There must have been some knowledge in her circle, or at least speculation. Some would have known and some would have been able to guess, though no one has ever told him what they knew. All Frédéric remembers is his father's wrath that morning when he was six years old.

He remembers the scene so clearly, his father striding suddenly into his mother's bedroom, pulling apart the curtains with a sharp movement, the spear of light penetrating the room, his father's stiff white collar, the bright scarlet waistcoat, the lace ruffles at the wrists, the gold buttons flashing. He had stalked over to his wife's bed, his high, old-fashioned boots scraping savagely on the parquet floor. He swooped Frédéric up with one angry movement, disentangling his fingers roughly from his mother's dark hair. He had imagined the sensation of her thick hair between his finger and thumb for years afterward whenever he fell asleep.

She was gone, after that. By that evening, when he and his sister went to find her, her bedroom was empty, the portrait of her cold, lovely face no longer on the wall, all her things swept away, the floors scrubbed clean. It was as if she had never existed, as if some evil spell had been laid upon the whole house. A silence had replaced her murmuring, languorous presence. No one would say her name. He had not been allowed to see her again until he was quite grown, and she had become a white-faced stranger, with blank, shuttered eyes, though he had written her many letters: *Please come home. I promise to be good. I will be brave. I will be your Prince.*

His father never spoke of her, or allowed anyone else to mention her. He shut up the house in Paris and established the family at Le Bouilh, which he spent his days building and rebuilding. Every day there was a discussion over what might be expanded or adjusted. He was one of the few nobles who embarked upon such a grandiose project at that already uncertain time.

Frédéric kept a part of himself in reserve for his mother, should his prayers be answered and she be allowed to return to him. He remembered odd things about her: her fine ankles, the soft sound of her skirts, her many rings, which she would remove before she lay down, placing them in a little china bowl with a chink-chink that sounded like the sweetest of music. He remembered an air of Gluck's she played on the harpsichord, breaking off halfway through with a sigh, letting her long fingers linger on the keys, dreaming. Above all, he remembered her dark, thick, smooth hair. He could no longer go back into her closed-up room without a shudder. Much later he found what sounded like an echo in the words of an English poem, "Else a great Prince in a prison lies."

On his birthdays, she was allowed to send a small gift but no words. He treasured these and read secret meanings into them: a horse on wheels, sent for his seventh birthday, was to suggest that he ride daily, practice his skill at horsemanship, and become a brave cavalry officer, which he did become; an ebony crucifix sent him to mass every morning at dawn for years and made him pray for her return; the fables of la Fontaine, read and reread, until he knew all the words by heart, were the beginning of his love of books, which had all become letters from his vanished love.

Sometimes, with a pang of remembrance, he caught glimpses of his mother's face in his sister's finely etched features. She was a quicksilver girl with lighter streaks in her russet hair, slim and curious, with an ease and freshness about her. In the shadow of their mother's cloistered half-death, she developed a taste for life.

Frédéric's grandmother, Mme. de Monconseil, a great beauty in her youth, had been fond of him, and she had stressed the necessity of his marrying someone with a fortune, considering his own debts and his impracticality. "You will need someone to cover your expenses, young man, in case you lose more money on the gaming tables, or give it away to some charlatan. They say this Lucy is pretty enough and an accomplished, intelligent girl and not too spoiled. She'll be rich, too, as her grandmother's only heir. You'll be lucky if you get her."

Frédéric remembers Talleyrand, too, limping into the salon at the Palais Royal, with his cold, nonchalant air, leaning on the mantelpiece and saying, "Now, Lucy Dillon would make you a perfect wife. I've known her since she was a girl." But what had he meant by that? His wit was probably greater than his judgment, in this matter.

It was, however, principally his admiration for Lucy's father that convinced him to marry her.

Frédéric is grateful to his wife for making this departure from France possible. He thinks of all those who have been left behind: his father jailed, tried, and stubbornly refusing to call the Queen the "Capet Woman" when questioned; Arthur Dillon on the battlefield fighting for France, his fate under the Revolution uncertain.

Why had they all been so blind? Why had he not realized how dangerous the spreading lack of discipline in the army would be? Why had he not foreseen the possibility of civil war? Why had he not grasped how dangerous his friends were, a group of young, idealistic liberal aristocrats at the Palais Royal: the Lameth brothers, and the Vicomte de Noailles? Why had they not realized that they had done so much damage to their own authority, throwing away the keys to the kingdom? He recalls the clandestine literature they passed on to one another and enjoyed surreptitiously. How they all had laughed at the King's maladroitness and the Queen's lack of tact. Why had they believed themselves secure, while playing with public opinion, rumor, and scandal-mongering? Why were they not aware how dangerous the King's cousin was, the scheming Philippe d'Orleans, with his gold? And what part had Philippe played in the Revolution? Had he really started the Réveillon riot? The storming of the Bastille? That he hated the Queen and that his secretary and friends would have liked to see him king, was all too clear.

As the boat continues lurching through the night, he reflects on what he had not foreseen at the time: what Lucy has really meant to him. When so many have perished, she has saved him, so far.

# PART FOUR
# Courtship

# I

FEBRUARY, 1787

She was hiding behind the curtain, waiting for him, though it was hard to hide in that house. Someone was always watching over you. She was rarely left alone and never allowed to venture out into the street unaccompanied. She was obliged to take the carriage or her litter, or if she walked, was followed by her maid. Even when she slept, her governess was in the adjacent room, the door ajar, the sound of her stertorous breathing audible in the night.

Besides, it was hard to hide in the sort of clothes she had to wear, the wide paniers swaying on either side of her waist, the high hair, and the high heels, which made her feel as if she were perpetually reaching up to the top shelf of a bookcase.

She leaned back against the wall, slipped a foot out of her shoe, flexed her toes, and mouthed the name: "Frédéric, Séraphin de Gouvernet, de la Tour du Pin." She was waiting to see him for the first time, hoping to watch him from the violet shadows, behind the dusty velvet curtain, to see him without being seen.

She said his name softly, let the syllables linger sensuously on her tongue, and her breath misted the pane of the long window, and blurred the outlines of the buildings on the street. Snow fell gently, the gray undecided flakes falling from a lowering sky. The light was dim on the Rue du Bac this day in February, 1787. Lucy was still sixteen.

She watched the street. A carriage rolled past with escutcheons

emblazoned on the sides, drawn by thoroughbred horses that stepped
daintily in the city filth; a footman hung onto the back, calling
out something obscene to the beggar woman who sat shivering,
half-naked in the mud; a roaming pack of dogs barked; a thin boy
passed, begging. The girls from the convent down the street tripped
on in double file in their gray capes; carts, a peddler offering to
sharpen knives, a glazier with a rumbling barrow passed: the usual
rank effluvia of early afternoon. Lucy disliked this street: the Rue
du Bac. She would have liked to live like Mme. de Lauzun on the
Rue de Bourbon, which gave onto the river.

*Once, I saw a thief being chased down this street. He ran very slowly,
like someone in my dream when the White Lady is dragging me along, and
I cannot advance. Once, I glimpsed the executioner carrying out a torture
from the window as my footmen carried me past in my litter.*

But Lucy was not thinking of torture or thieves, she was savoring the aristocratic syllables of the name: a Count Gouvernet who
was also a Count de la Tour du Pin and would be a Marquis de la
Tour du Pin one day.

Her grandmother was against this marriage, had already refused
the Count, and had proposed other candidates. She declared he
could only bring trouble: being too old—eleven years older than
Lucy—too small, too ugly, too wild with his and his friends' revolutionary ideas, and too much in debt.

Lucy cared little for these objections, knowing that most people
around her were living lies, politely, gracefully, but still lies. She
knew only too well how her great-great-uncle, an archbishop, a
prelate of the Church, violated religious principles daily. He was
interested in only his own bodily pleasures and the distractions
of the hunt. Her father, who had met Frédéric on the battlefield,
found him valiant, and approved of the match. She trusted him
more than anyone else, in spite of his long absence.

Marriages, she solemnly believed at sixteen and still believes, were written in heaven. It was not entirely in her control. She was ready to fall in love.

Also, though she had never seen him, she had seen his property near Bordeaux one day by chance, the lovely country around his chateau, Le Bouilh. Stepping down from her carriage when she had crossed the Dordogne River, she stood in the flickering sunshine on the bank and watched the light glitter on the flowing water, and looked around her. When she asked her servant to whom all this property belonged, and to whom the river crossing was paid, he had said, "The Count de La Tour du Pin." *I thought how I could own all of this land. The passage across this river could belong to me.*

She wanted this man, and when she wanted something, she had already learned how to fight for it, how to keep her own counsel, how to maneuver in secret, how to plot and plan. "An intriguer," her grandmother had called her, lifting her hand to the cameo at her neck, the one Lucy's mother once wore.

"And if that is what I have become, it is you who have made me so," she had dared to reply, crossing her arms. Now that Lucy was older, her grandmother could no longer threaten her so easily with the convent. She was afraid of what Lucy might say about her to the rest of the world. She had already made her break with many of her mother's friends, making it look as though Lucy had chosen to do so.

So now she watched at the window, making up the scene. She saw the dashing open carriage, brought forth even in inclement weather, come to an abrupt halt before the gate. She already liked the spirited gray horse, which whinnied and pawed the ground with impatience. She liked the way the Count jumped down and bounded up the steps of the house two at a time, purposefully. She liked his dark-gray frock coat lifting behind him, *like a bird on the wing. I thought of the larks in the forest at Hautefontaine, where we had gone in the early spring when Mother was alive. I remembered lying on my back and looking up at the branches stirring up the sky and escaping my body. After Mother's death, Grandmother rarely returned to the house I loved.*

The heavy furniture in this one was spinning around her. The pale light flickered. The snow whirled.

It was true this man was not tall and perhaps others might find him ugly, and who knew if he had as many debts as they said? He was not the sort she was usually attracted to, a slight man, but she liked his military bearing, his agile body, his nose that seemed not quite straight. She pictured him in a collar and hat, which indicated his rank, the kind worn only by a colonel, which contrasted with his smooth-looking skin. She was drawn to his determination to be with her shown in the quick movements of his hands and feet as he flew lightly up her steps. How hopefully, how eagerly he came to her! She liked what she imagined were wide-spaced, soft, melancholy eyes. She wondered what it would be like to kiss his lips.

He would protect her. He would carry her off far from this house, from these relatives she hated. She was in love with love, one she had invented for herself.

She continued to spy on him through the open door as a servant opened it, and he entered the hall of the house. He went into the salon. She heard his light, short steps. His body was not large, but it was impatient, and she imagined it was trembling. She noticed the way he bowed his head respectfully over her grandmother's hand and murmured words she could not catch, but imagined to be courteous and refined. She liked the cultivated sound of his voice, the slight catch in the voice.

The bells of Saint Sulpice tolled as he left the house. He had stayed for only a quarter of an hour, not a good sign. But the bells chimed clear and pure and joyous. They announced good tidings. The sky was light and tender. A wave of joy escaped her heart, flowed fast through her veins. The snow fell gently, but as she watched Frédéric Séraphin go as quickly as he had arrived, everything became distinct, the bare branches glistened as though ornamented with silver garlands, the tips of the iron railing sparkled like the diamonds and rubies she had seen on the young Queen's dress at Versailles.

## II

### March, 1787

Lucy could not move. She sat paralyzed before her mirror, staring in terror at her face and hair: the powder, the pomatum, and the rouge. She was summoned by her governess, Miss B., who stood in the doorway with a hand on her waist and cocked her head to one side, blinking her birdlike eyes and saying, "Come along, Lucy, she is waiting to see you." When she smiled, her eyebrows rose suggestively and her round eyes seemed very blue, as they did when she read aloud from her sentimental novels.

Lucy doesn't remember the names of the novels, but she could not stop herself from listening carefully when Miss B. had been inspired by them to whisper rude things in her ear. Miss B. had pointed out the swell in the tight breeches of a lackey and explained what brought about such a phenomenon. "See how he blooms like a flower in contact with the sun," she had said.

She had told Lucy about the young King, Louis XVI, such a big fellow, after all, and quite strong, yet who had something wrong with his essential organ, and did not know how to use it as he should in the night with his Queen to make a son and heir, until his brother-in-law, the Emperor Joseph, had come all the way from Austria and convinced him to let them take the small snip in the tight foreskin or perhaps simply explained what he must do to his wife in the bed.

"He can get through the door but then just lounges like a laggard in the antechamber," she had explained, making the obscene gesture of drooping one finger lackadaisically inside the ring of thumb and forefinger and letting her pink tongue loll at the same time. She had told Lucy that many of the Bourbon men had problems of this kind. "They are eaters but not fornicators," was how she had put it.

She had even told her what certain people said about the Queen and the Countess Jules de Polignac or even the Princess de Lamballe, with her silvery voice, whom they called the Sappho of the Trianon, and what she did with the Queen in her rustic escapades from Versailles. Lucy was appalled and yet fascinated.

Now Miss B. said, "The Princess is waiting. Your grandmother wants you to come quickly," leering a little as she spoke.

"I cannot," Lucy said, trying to rise from the chair before her dressing table. Her knees buckled under the weight of her clothes and her fear. She knew why she was being summoned. The Princess d'Hénin wanted to inspect her.

Lucy was not afraid of pain. She had borne her grandmother's beatings and her disdain in stubborn silence. But the thought that this stranger, Etiennette, known for her sharp tongue, wit, and beauty, would look her over as if she were for sale, made her tremble. She would be examined from head to toe, like a horse. She would have to stand, while the Princess stared at her mass of blond hair piled a foot high, covered first with pommade to make the powder stick and then powdered so that, if she moved her head too fast, it risked falling onto her shoulders and onto her silk dress, with the heavy, whalebone hoops, which extended on either side of her small waist. The Princess would inspect her skin for its whiteness, its clarity, its contrast with the rouged cheeks.

Miss B. caressed her cheek. "You look lovely, darling. Such a lovely complexion—peaches and cream," she murmured, without looking at her.

*Sometimes Miss B. would slip into my bed at night while I was sleeping and touch my breasts. She slipped her hand gently between my thighs. Her fingers played between my lips, my teeth, to show me what would happen when I was married, what I must allow my husband to do to me in the dark.*

*"Would you like your little lesson tonight? Shall we practice?" she asked and giggled. She trussed up her skirts a little. She put her hands between her pink thighs. She swung her round hips suggestively. "Take a few sips of white wine to warm you before you sleep, dear heart," she said. She laughed her high-pitched laugh that did not seem to come from her plump, beating throat. I would pull down my lips at the sides, lift my chin, sigh. Though I had read in my "Philotée" that we were not permitted to derive any pleasure from our bodies except in marriage, I said nothing. In the dark, I allowed this amoral English girl, who was not so much older than I, who could almost have been the real older sister I never had, to climb in beside me. I moved into her warm, soft arms for the only comfort I was allowed. I forgot my faithful Marguerite, banished and humiliated in the basement kitchen. I liked the blond Miss B. far too much. She did me much harm.*

Now Miss B. told her to stand tall to show off her advantages, and her fingers ran down the décolleté of Lucy's blue dress to her fine waist.

She considered she was not a great beauty like her mother. Her gray eyes were not large and the smallpox she had suffered at four had almost killed her, taking most of her eyelashes. Her nose was straight, what was called Grecian in Miss B.'s novels, but Lucy found it too long and not sufficiently fine. She did not consider that her high forehead added to her beauty, but her fresh mouth, her avid lips, good teeth, and extraordinary forest of blond hair, now piled up absurdly high and decorated with fake poppies, were acceptable perhaps. Above all, she had her youth: her smooth skin, which, despite all the rouge, seemed almost translucent, as though the light were trapped within all the camouflage. She shrugged her shoulders slightly and turned her face away from the mirror.

She wished her mother were here to accompany her now, to hold her hand at this moment. She thought of her grandmother's terrible words: "You never had much to do with your mother, did you?"

"Come on now, why so sad? Let's have a smile. Let's show off our lovely teeth," Miss B. said encouragingly. Lucy attempted a smile, tried to show off her teeth, like a horse, she thought again, but her lips were trembling. She would much rather have been on a horse, galloping far from here through the forest at Hautefontaine.

Paris was in deep winter. Outside the rain fell softly, more like mist than rain, muffling the mire, trickling down the gutters with all the slops into the street. She could hear the wind cracking the branches, snatches of a song. The sad month of March. Not a propitious moment in the year for a new beginning, surely.

Miss B. helped her arrange the heavy hoops beneath her skirt, adjusted a lock of ash-blond hair, dabbed a little more perfume behind the wrists.

She had other assets. She could dance the gavotte and the minuet with grace; she could play the harpsichord and sing; she could read Latin, Italian, and English; she had watched experiments in chemistry at the chemist shop in Hautefontaine; above all she was in excellent health. She took Miss B.'s hand.

Lucy heard whispered words, the rustle of silk. She heard the chink of porcelain. She smelled the sweet, cloying smell of heavy perfume. It was Frédéric's aunt, the Princess d'Hénin, the one called "Jewel" because of her beauty and her sharp wit, the one who lived separately from her husband, the Prince. It was she who put down her cup of chocolate and looked up at Lucy from under her bonnet, appraisingly.

She had come to look her over, to decide if she would do, because

Frédéric's mother, who would have made this visit, had been shut up in a convent, as Lucy's grandmother might have done to her, for what they had told Lucy was scandalous behavior. She was only allowed out rarely to visit her elderly father. What could the woman have done?

The elegant aunt, the Princess, many years younger than her cloistered sister, looked Lucy up and down from the pointed toes of her shoes to the red poppies entwined like trapped birds in her mass of hair. Her knees were reflections of knees in water. Her eyes filled with tears.

The aunt wore an adorable little bonnet with a bow, which covered her luxuriant, dark hair, a frill around the face, and an elegant dark dress. She had been married at fifteen to the Prince, the younger brother of the Prince de Chimay. He was debauched and had deserted her for the famous actress, Mlle. Raucourt, or perhaps it was Mlle. Arnould or both—Lucy did not remember. But the aunt did not look sad. Not at all. She looked as if she were enjoying herself, life, this afternoon's visit in the month of March. Lucy caught her eye, and it was as though a flash of clear summer light had come into the gray winter room.

She was a woman in her late thirties, and though her lovely face was marked by the scourge of smallpox, her large eyes were full of humor, generosity, and intelligence. Her teeth glistened white as she smiled. The Princess rose and embraced her. She cried out with all the exuberance of a passionate nature, "What a slim waist! What glorious skin! What beautiful hair! But she is charming, charming!"

And Lucy wanted to kiss her, to dance her around the room.

"What a pleasure it will be to introduce you to all of Paris. What a lucky man my nephew is!" the aunt said.

## III

*B*Y THE TIME Frédéric sees Lucy for the first time, the King of France has become King Popinjay. There is discrepancy around him, confusion of tongues. Which voice to listen to, which decision to take? France's wars, the Seven Years' War and the American War, have brought nothing but debt. Finance ministers come and go to no avail.

### MARCH, 1787

Frédéric waited impatiently for the articles of marriage to be signed, to see his bride for the first time. He looked around the crowded room, shifting uncomfortably on his ornate, gilt chair. He had not felt welcome the first time he had come into this house, and even now he did not feel entirely so, despite the presence of his own father, his aunt, and even his grandfather, M. de Monconseil, eighty years old, in his black mourning clothes, who had come to assist at the signing, as well as Lucy's relatives, her English aunt, her grandmother, and her great-great-uncle, the Archbishop.

They had already had him wait for what seemed an interminable time in this stuffy room, muffled with dark tapestries with their dim embroidered figures of horses, huntsmen, hounds with dripping jaws, bordered with lilies and blood-red pears; and crowded with all the gilded furniture, the clocks ticking away on the marble mantelpiece, and, before the fireplace, an immense mahogany desk almost entirely covered in papers, an ink stand, and sand to dry the ink. An enormous fire blazed behind an ornate fire screen. It was too hot in the room with all these people. Frédéric loosened the high white collar around his neck and fingered the lace on his chest. He would have liked a glass of wine or at least some water. Why were they taking so long?

The pallid winter light pierced a chink in the velvet draperies and fell on the grandmother, Lucy Cary, who had hardly deigned to address a word to him on their first meeting, and now sat straight and stiff in her high-backed, old-fashioned chair beside the Archbishop and surveyed these goings-on with what looked like disdain. She lifted her sharp chin, pursed her painted red lips, and occasionally glanced up majestically at the ceiling as though the *putti* who aimed their darts at one another might have the answer to her questions.

Frédéric knew she did not approve of him. She had wanted someone else. He jumped violently when she interrupted the notaries to add some clause in her favor to the contract. What would happen if this mercurial woman were to decide to disinherit her granddaughter? Could she do such a thing? What would have been the point of all his efforts to obtain this girl, then?

For Frédéric had rushed around frantically to obtain the necessary formal letter from his father at Le Bouilh. He had feared that if he did not act fast he might lose this girl; her capricious grandmother might change her mind. He had dashed out in inclement weather in his open cabriolet to meet the awful grandmother. Now he wondered if this had been wise.

Lucy, it was true, as her only heir was expected to inherit her grandmother's considerable fortune that had been Lucy's mother's. There had been some scandal over the grandmother's acquisition of her daughter's fortune, her properties: Hautefontaine, with its forests and farms worth 50,000 livres, another house near Paris, La Folie

Joyeuse, with its ravishing park, surrounded by high walls, alleys closed behind iron gates, and fine furniture and paintings, or so he had been told, and this vast somber house on the Rue du Bac, with its luxurious appointments collected by the Archbishop, who was also here today in all his violet robes and buckled shoes, sitting heavily by the grandmother's side and nodding off from time to time while the notaries droned on. He, too, was reputed to be immensely rich but also extremely extravagant. Was it possible he, too, was in debt? Frédéric knew how easily money slipped through fingers at the gaming tables at court, how easily one remembered one's few moments of gain and forgot the losses that were inevitably more frequent.

He knew that Arthur Dillon, brave and generous as he was, possessed nothing besides his Irish regiment and a considerable collection of debts. It was the grandmother who was, somehow, in control.

Now Frédéric felt an unaccountable sense of foreboding. What was he doing here? He was tempted to rise and run down the shallow marble steps. He would have liked, at least, to see the girl, before everything was settled.

He had not expected to see his bride, of course, until the signing had been accomplished, as it always was, by the parents of the bride, or her family, and the groom's presided over by the notaries. But the pompous notaries, in their black robes and their curled and powdered wigs, were taking an inordinately long time, crowded around the desk with all the other relatives, probably enjoying this moment to hobnob with the nobility, or anyway, glad to earn what Frédéric imagined must be their considerable fee.

They had already read aloud Frédéric's title many times: "High and Powerful Lord and Future Husband," which made him grin slightly and raise his eyebrows at his young aunt, who sat at the other end of the table and was capable of appreciating the joke.

He wondered just how high and powerful this future husband

would be, and whether this marriage would bring joy into his life. Would he find this Irish bride to his liking? She had not a drop of French blood in her veins. Might he end up like Lucy's father, being shipped off to fight somewhere conveniently distant to leave the brilliant bride free to dally as she wished with all and sundry at the Court? He had heard the gossip about Dillon and Lucy's mother. Dillon had been given his regiment at twenty-two in order to remove him from his young wife's side and leave it free for the powerful Prince de Guéménée and perhaps others as well.

He wished Lucy's young father were here today to reassure him, to lay his hand lightly on his arm, instead of the disapproving grandmother with her violent red lips. Suddenly, he remembered Dillon fighting a duel. Who was it? The Vicomte de Noailles? A policeman? The man was always fighting duels. He was a brave man, Dillon, but speedy to take offense: *soupe au lait*. The Irish had earned their reputation for violence, no doubt. Might the daughter not be similarly inclined, fighting verbal duels with everyone including her Lord and Master? Yet Frédéric had loved the father and apparently the feeling was mutual.

He had also heard about the relationship between Lucy's grandmother and the Archbishop. Who had told him that? Talleyrand, who knows the family well and admires the Archbishop for his intelligence and culture if not for his morals, most probably. Frédéric stared at them now: Lucy Cary sitting restlessly, tapping her fan against the arm of her chair in her purple taffeta dress, which clashed garishly with the red lips, the Archbishop at her side. He leaned forward and said something in a low voice Frédéric could not catch, and she glanced back at him. Surely it was not possible that they had been lovers for years? But perhaps it was true. Talleyrand made it his business to know everything about everyone.

And what would this young woman be like, brought up in such

a household, with the father always absent, the mother probably promiscuous, and the grandmother involved with the great-great-uncle, a prince of the Church? What would be the result of all this consanguine promiscuity?

Frédéric thought of his own mother, who had not been allowed to come here this day. What had she looked like at the moment of her own signing? Had she worn flowers in her dark, smooth hair? What had she felt? But her presence today would only have been an embarrassment. He had endowed her with all sorts of wondrous qualities.

Looking at the distinctly disagreeable expression on the grandmother's face, he wondered why she was so set against him. Did it have something to do with his connection with Philippe d'Orleans, and the liberal aristocrats around him? The Dillons, he knew, disapproved of Philippe's egalitarian ideas. But surely, certain reforms were necessary, and Philippe d'Orleans seemed an enlightened aristocrat capable of carrying them out. Frédéric had loved, as a young man, the freedom to mingle with the throng at the Palais Royal, at the enclosed gardens and galleries that Philippe had generously opened to the public.

Was it because of the scandal surrounding his mother, his age, or even his appearance? He would always have liked to be taller and broader, and his hair was, indeed, thinning beneath his wig, despite the unguents rubbed into his scalp. He arched his back and held his head high.

And where was the girl, after all? Had she already escaped? Finally, the notaries finished their work, rose, bowed, and left the room. The grandmother now rose slowly, too, and led the girl he was to marry into the room. All eyes were on her and particularly his, of course, as she came into the doorway.

She stood for a moment, looking terrified, glancing around

the crowded room as though it were a jungle inhabited by savages about to consume her. She did not look directly at him, but lowered her glance to the carpet. She advanced slowly across the room, more dragged by her grandmother than walking, it seemed. She was wearing a simple dress in the style that was becoming fashionable since the American War, laced up behind and tied with a shiny blue silk ribbon beneath her breasts, which were half-bared. She looked, everyone around him murmured, "like a portrait." He wondered what sort of portrait they had in mind for her. He didn't think of her as a portrait at all, but as a breathing, suffering creature. He could see she was trembling. Her cheeks were flushed. He had the impression that he could hear the thrum of her heart through her white muslin dress. He, too, felt a physical shock of sympathy at the sight of her, as though his own heart resonated with the thunder of hers. He was so moved by her obvious embarrassment and her painful shyness that tears came into his eyes.

And he could not imagine any painter, even the most skilled, capturing the thick, fair hair that gleamed in the daylight, parted in the middle, pale blond on one side and palely shadowed on the other, or her clear skin, the gray-blue gaze, the determined mouth, the slim waist, and the way she walked, that tentative, trembling gait. He thought of something wild, caught in a net in a forest. He remembered his father telling him that the way to judge the beauty of a woman was from the way she walked.

She continued to look down at the carpet as she came toward him. It seemed that everything around her—the dark tapestries, the gold armchairs, the monstrous desk, his relatives, the uncle, even the terrible grandmother—were part of her and had thus acquired something distinctive. Even the warm air around her was suddenly different: good, sweet, drinkable.

He would have liked his bride-to-be to lift her gaze, so that he could at least convey with his eyes what he was feeling, to put her at ease, but perhaps it was as well that she stared at the parquet.

Though he stood very straight as she came into the room, he realized she was considerably taller than he, particularly in her heels and with her thick hair piled up on her head. He continued to stare at her, as she sat down in silence between his aunt and her English aunt, Lady Jerningham.

His father smiled graciously at her and murmured how happy he was to welcome her into their family. Even his grandfather bent over her hand and murmured an old-fashioned compliment.

He remembered the story of how, as a young page, his grandfather had lit the way for the King, Louis XIV, who was leaving Mme. de Maintenon's bedchamber. Holding the two flaming candelabra aloft with one hand, he had singed the King's wig. As he told the story, this valiant military man's face paled and he trembled all over at the memory, though this had happened seventy years earlier.

Whatever happened to the current King, Frédéric determined, he would remain at this girl's side. He had only known her a moment, but he had already decided he would love her. He watched her now, as she rose and went with more ease through the room. She moved with a certain consequence, as though her existence had acquired a new weight. She was not smiling. Her eyes were alert, her expression serious, self-conscious, and yet wonderfully serene and calmly receptive. He bowed over her hand, and the words came to him with speed and intensity, because he knew it completely: "I know we will be very happy together." He laughed a little, almost as though she were already in his arms. She closed her clear eyes, as though she had understood, and wanted to keep it safe. She put two fingers to her lips in a secret gesture.

# PART FIVE
## Royalty Compromised

On that memorable afternoon, the Princess d'Hénin and the Archbishop accompanied Lucy up the Queen's marble staircase. The Queen had asked to see "la petite Dillon." She wanted to see her now that she had heard from Princess d'Hénin that she was to be married to the Count de Gouvernet, Frédéric Séraphin de la Tour du Pin.

"Bring her to me," she said, speaking of the daughter of her dear, deceased friend whom, of course, she had forgotten within a day. The Princess and the Archbishop walked on either side of Lucy along the narrow corridor that gave onto the room of the Queen's guard. Lucy shook, wobbling on her high heels. Her hair had been pulled upward and arranged with plumes, curled at the back and smothered in white powder. Her burning cheeks, too, had been dusted with powder, and a small black patch was fixed near her mouth like a fly. She kept touching it with the tip of her finger to make sure it was still there. She felt her tight stays suffocating her.

As they walked through the apartments of Versailles, the Princess continued to murmur to her, as her mother had done years before, and to the same effect, "Now don't forget. It's very important to make a good impression. You must be extremely amiable. Don't be cold or distant. She won't like that." The Princess looked at Lucy, touched her burning cheek, and lowered her voice slightly, adding, "My dear child, above all keep away from the windows, from the light. The Queen does not like young women with such glowing skin."

The Archbishop held her arm firmly and propelled her along. There was no turning back. It was a great honor, after all. She would now be able to say, "When I was at Court..." She knew people would give everything for this honor, but at that moment she would have liked to turn back and run down all the stairs that so many courtiers had longed to climb.

They crossed the landing of the Fleury staircase, went through a small antechamber and into the larger one of the Great Dining Hall. The Archbishop grinned in accord with the Princess's remarks. He pressed Lucy against him a little. "Ah!" he sighed, "you cannot imagine how lovely all you young people look to me—even the ugly ones look beautiful, clean, dewy," staring at Lucy who recalled his sermon in the closet.

Now she could not flee. She was dragged forward as in her dream, trapped between them, the one in his violet robes with his blue silk sash, his silk violet stockings, his shoes with the golden buckles, his three-cornered hat in one hand, and the other, who continued to admonish and advise. Lucy was afraid all this scaffolding—the foot-high hair, the wide whalebone paniers, and the narrow heels—would surely give way, and she, too, would crumble before the Queen.

The Queen's serving-women came forward to greet them. Madame Campan, the Queen's reader, and the Countess de la Fayette ushered them into the Queen's presence in her private rooms with obsequious smiles and compliments. Lucy saw everything distinctly, outlined as clearly as in a painting: the Aubusson carpet, with its pink and gold swirls, the chandelier, the fringes, tassels, and plumes, the harp, and the many chiming clocks. All was white and gold here: white wainscotting covered over with gold, mirrors, ribbons, delicate friezes. There were lacquered cabinets, small tables with bowed legs, a little writing table surmounted by a figurine of a lady playing arias on a clavichord, and above the doors the panelling was painted with rustic scenes of sunsets and animals. *All my life I remembered these things.*

The Queen, in a light gray gauzy dress, sat very upright on a sofa and smiled at her. "Come nearer, dearest child. Let me see your face," she said. She lifted a lorgnette to her shortsighted blue eyes. She and her King had at least this in common, their terrible shortsightedness. Lucy moved forward with great difficulty, each step a stab of the knife.

The Queen looked very different from the young woman Lucy had first seen, six years before, at the joyous birth of the first Dauphin. She remembers her clear skin glowing with all the reflected adoration of the crowd. Now there was a fullness beneath her chin, a weight to her bosom. She looked more heavily made up, her face seemed almost red, and her wide-spaced blue eyes glittered with a harsh distant light. Above all, she looked bored, and with her protruding Hapsburg lip, she seemed to pout slightly. Was she waiting to be amused?

Lucy knew the gossip: she was accused of being an Austrian, a foreigner, an old enemy of France. Lucy had seen her presence greeted in her royal box with hostile silence, scorn, and even hissing. People called her Madame Deficit and blamed her for interfering in affairs of state, of increasing the burden of the debt. Others spoke of the notorious diamond necklace scandal. Her name had been tarnished by the Countess de la Motte's insinuations and Cardinal Rohan's testimony in his public trial. The seductive Countess Jules de Polignac had taken the place of the Princess de Guémenée, adding to the Polignacs' already long list of appointments, their wealth, and their nefarious dominance over the Queen.

But for Lucy the Queen was the one to whom she would always owe allegiance. She saw her sitting upright on the sofa in her royal room, reflected in her many mirrors, Marie Antoinette with her ash-blond hair, which was thinner now since the birth of her children and decorated with concealing feathers, her aquiline nose and her small mouth, seen a hundred times, fragmented, splintered. With her fine eyebrows raised slightly inquiringly, smiling benevolently, she would have liked to please. Lucy imagined she was waiting to be amused by someone like her mother, someone capable of softly blending her considerable intelligence with tact and understanding.

The Queen leaned forward and embraced her. She murmured graciously, "La petite Dillon," and Lucy managed to kiss her hand. She could smell her sweet odor of jasmine.

The Queen gave a half-sob and murmured, "Ah, my dear, there is not a day, not a moment, that I do not miss your darling mother!" Lucy drew back with a surge of anger that made her rigid, speechless. She could feel the blood rush to her head. She was certain the Queen, bent on her own pursuit of pleasure, had not missed her mother for one single moment. Others had taken her mother's place immediately, indeed before her death. The Queen's tears had dried fast. Apart from her children, Lucy feared, looking into her shallow blue gaze, the Queen was not capable of sustaining an interest in anyone or anything for long.

The curtains were open in the Queen's apartments. Sunlight played on the parquet, but it seemed dark to Lucy. She could hardly make out the lovely pattern of the silk on the walls, the branches laden with flowers and fruits and birds, the English engravings.

Marie Antoinette stared at her and sighed. She said she did not resemble her poor mother, at all. The Queen turned away from her to greet the Princess d'Hénin and the Archbishop warmly. How healthy and hearty he always looked! What a pleasure he was to see. How reassuring he must appear to the Queen.

The Queen smiled up at him, the popular Archbishop of Narbonne, with his florid face and his sparkling Irish eyes. Her expression, which had seemed haughty, disdainful, was suddenly tempered by sweetness. The young page's words about how the Queen's face expressed too much of what she felt were confirmed. She murmured something gracious to him in a dulcet tone. He bowed low, conveying his respect. Lucy, in her portable prison, drew back stiffly, seeking the shadow. There was nowhere here to hide: all glitter and gold.

The Queen motioned for her to sit beside her. "So I hear you are to be married to the Count Frédéric Séraphin. What excellent news. Your aunt knows I have long been in favor. And is the Count to your liking?" Lucy was unable to reply to her questions, and the Queen was already onto another subject.

"No doubt he is lucky. Your mother, may her soul rest in peace, told me how clever you are. Do you sing as well as she? No? Will you sing for me someday, as she did?" The Queen tapped Lucy's knuckles with her fan impatiently. She was waiting for some modest but amusing response, a compliment on her own voice, her own musical accomplishments, perhaps, but Lucy could not reply.

Tears welled at the thought of her mother, forgotten, displaced, betrayed. She was blinded by her tears of anger, by the Queen's quick, slip-sliding gaze, by her famous flashing diamonds. Tears rolled down her cheeks, but the Queen did not seem to notice. She continued to ask Lucy about her education, her accomplishments. Her conversation hopped about from one question to the next disconcertingly like a frog.

Lucy's head spun. She heard nothing, could see nothing now, not even the Queen's diamonds, which Lucy's mother had told her came from Bohmer and Bassenge, or the Queen's dress, made by

Rose Bertin, who had made Lucy's doll and whose premises were on the Rue Saint Honoré.

The Queen yawned. Lucy feared she must find her a silly, stubborn child with horribly flushed cheeks. The Queen pouted, and the royal lip protruded further. Would she rather have been at the races? Playing tric-trac? Had she expected Lucy to be brilliant and amusing and gay like her mother, or at least sweet and gentle? Did she seem cold and indifferent and not particularly pretty?

*To whom indeed, these days, could the Queen speak? Whom could she trust? Was she thinking of the Countess de La Motte, the diamond necklace Countess, who had been flogged publicly and branded with the V for voleuse? Why was it people felt compelled to write about her, always denouncing her, the Austrian? Why did people want to read such filth?*

The Queen turned her head away. She spoke to the witty Princess and to the Archbishop, who loved pleasure as much as she did. The Queen looked around her room with lassitude and said she thought it was time to change the decor. She was tired of this silk on the walls, of the butterfly caught in its gold medallion, of all these fans and clocks.

"She's very shy, Majesty," the Princess explained, looking at Lucy reproachfully, her eyes saying, "Make an effort, for goodness' sake! What's the matter with you!"

"She's overcome by your loveliness, Majesty," the Archbishop explained, not unkindly, smiling his courtier's smile.

The Queen patted his hand and yawned. "Now tell me about the improvements you have been making on your house. And what are you planting? I hear your garden is beautiful! Beautiful!"

The Archbishop nodded and smiled. "I have my eye on a lovely new painting, a Correggio: *Jupiter and Antiope*. Ah, the light and colors, the sensuality of the nudes!" he said and looked into the Queen's blue eyes.

But the Queen seemed not particularly interested in Correggio's paintings of nudes. Perhaps she didn't know who this Correggio was. Nor did she seem as lubricious as the pamphleteers would have made her out to be. She stifled a yawn. Lucy, in any case, was forgotten, and the reason for her visit also.

Later, as they went down the many stairs, like many courtiers, she thought of all the things she should have said. She thought of all the courageous women before her who had fought for royalty, for France. Visions of the Crusades, images of Jeanne d'Arc leading the troops into battle, of courtly love flashed through her mind. Her awkwardness and anger had made a bad impression. Why had she not shown some proof of her courage? Instead, she had wept at the thought of her mother's betrayal, her early demise! Why had she not told the Queen that whatever awful things the people said about her, whatever dangers she might have to undergo, she and Frédéric would not be afraid to stand by her?

PART SIX

Flying from the Frigate

# I

## MARCH, 1794

Despite the shot of cannon fired by the French man-o'-war, intended to hurry the *Diana* along, he keeps her sail trimmed. He watches with satisfaction as the French ship draws slowly away. It signals that it is making its way northeast to Brest, and that he is to follow. But dark is falling, and as soon as it is thick enough, the captain, feeling rather brave, sets a course in directly the opposite direction.

The wind is high and with all her sails now spread, he takes her off to the west, toward Boston. All is quiet below, his passengers apparently sleeping peacefully, as they travel fast through the night with the wind following, easing the sloop along at six knots. He wonders what Geyer, the ship's owner, will have to say about this new delay, what his poor Sally, waiting and watching patiently, will think.

With the fog continuing and the seas rough on the following day, he finds it impossible to take a bearing. All around them is silence and thick fog and the uninterrupted rhythmic heave of the sloop. The whole earth seems made of water. They might be almost anywhere. In any case he no longer has any idea where he is. For a moment the sky clears and a sick little sun emerges. He attempts to take a bearing, to steer southwest, but in vain. A white gale buries them for days. At moments his mind plays tricks on him: he thinks he sees a vast French man-o'-war approaching, but it dissolves into a bank of clouds.

Days merge into weeks. He is no longer afraid of the Algerian pirates but now of being lost at sea. According to old Harper, they must be approaching the coast of Newfoundland. Harper proclaims he feels a nearness, but his only indication of this is the lighter color of the water. Strong westerly winds drive him back.

Food is becoming increasingly short, and what they have of increasingly poor quality, and he is now obliged to ration water. At this rate they will run out, and he can see that the French couple and their children are growing thinner, the baby quiet at night. He feels it necessary to keep a certain amount of water in reserve for himself.

He is beginning to feel there is nothing he can accomplish, not even bring this wretched 150 tonner safely to its home port. He remembers the day—he had just turned twenty-three, when Geyer had signed him on as captain. It was one of the happiest of his life. The ship, despite its small size, all the dust and grime, had seemed a palace to him then, a kingdom.

He wakes one morning at dawn in the gray severe light from his cabin window. One of his sailors is rapping on his door and shouting that he has sighted a ship through the fog. He is up the companion ladder and on deck in an instant. The ship is coming, as far as he can gather, from Europe. He hails her, and asks permission to come aboard. The day is calm, and he has one of his sailors row him over.

Once on board, he asks the English captain, a thin, morose man with a gray face, all bone and weathered skin, if he can give him a bearing. The man gives him a melancholy grin, jerks his head back contemptuously, and claps him on the shoulder. He asks him nastily what he is doing as captain.

The captain feels himself turn puce—he has not outgrown the ability to blush—and draws himself up and tells him that this is his first charge and that he was obliged to leave his projected course because of his French passengers. In the fog and weather he has become confused, and as he says these words, he wonders if, indeed, his action has been wise.

But the English captain tells him help is at hand. He informs him that they are only fifty leagues from the Azores. Then Captain Pease tells the Englishman of their plight, the lack of provisions on board, the lamentable condition of his passengers, the French-woman and her small children.

The Englishman looks at him for a moment, a glimmer of pity in his eye. He sighs and sends off one of his sailors who returns with a small sack of potatoes and two small earthenware jars of butter, which he is good enough to give them for the Frenchwoman and the little ones.

Back on the *Diana*, the captain knocks on his passengers' door and produces this bounty proudly, keeping back one small jar of butter and a few potatoes for himself.

"Butter!" the Frenchwoman cries, as though it were diamonds, and claps her small hands and lifts them together in a gesture of prayer. She rushes off immediately, with a swish of her dark dress, and the baby on her hip, followed by her little boy, who patters behind her up the stairs to the galley to have the cook boil water for the potatoes.

On her return to the cabin she stands in the doorway, pale-faced, in her dark dress, with her baby and the little boy leaning against her leg, as she leans against the jamb. She brings a whiff of fresh air with her into the cabin, where her husband lies mired in his bunk. She questions the captain about their whereabouts.

When the captain informs them of their proximity to the Azores, the Frenchman's expression changes like the wind on water. A glance passes between the couple. The man makes an effort and struggles to sit up, still stricken with the seasickness but visibly excited by this news of land. Translating the fast flood of her husband's French words, the woman tells the captain that her husband wishes him to have the goodness to leave them there. Then they can easily make their way to England, where so many of their friends have emigrated. Her husband would like to join them.

The captain listens to her lovely voice and stares at her, still in her ugly, stained dress. He looks at her husband with his partly powdered hair, his wrinkled silk shirt and breeches, his gray face. These people want to leave him and his ship! They expect him to change course in order to take them where they wish to go, in order to join their grand friends! How can they expect such a thing! Despite his dreams, where this woman swims naked into his arms, he realizes quite clearly that she has hardly noticed *him*. He is not part of her story, after all.

He draws himself up, his face hot again. He averts his gaze from hers. He apologizes but says stiffly that he is obliged to refuse this request. He is sorry to disappoint them. The captain goes on with some determination now. His obligation is to his ship's owner. Their arrival in Boston has already been delayed in an attempt to keep his passengers safe. He has done what he could. He is sorry, but this would take him off course. What are they thinking? he would like to add.

The man, who seems to understand more than he can express, rises from his cot, staggers toward the chest, where he props himself up, and speaks with animation, and with expressive gesticulations as his wife translates. His face, or what he has seen of it, which has seemed rather ugly to the captain until now, seems suddenly almost attractive, though what he has to say is not. The man dares to grumble about what he calls the lamentable conditions on the ship, the shortage of provisions, the dreadful quality of the food, the uncleanness, the sickening odors, the danger to his health and to that of his family. He has put up with all of this with patience, but it is enough now.

The Frenchwoman stands in the doorway to the cabin with the madras kerchief tied over her head, with her whimpering, pale child in her arms. As she speaks, the captain's dog, Black, stares up adoringly at her with her dark eyes. The captain cannot help listening with pleasure to the lilt of her lovely voice, nor can he take his gaze from the light in her skin, her proud stance, her slightly lifted chin. Despite her disordered attire, her tangled tresses, her stained dress, she has an air of authority which he finds difficult to resist.

"You must take us there," she says simply.

The captain listens politely, while she goes on at some length, but what he thinks is that these people are accustomed to being obeyed. He is nothing to them. Despite their exquisite manners, their elegance, and their fine display of courage, they are aristocrats, arrogant people, used to giving commands, and taking it for granted that people will follow them. For a moment he thinks of Sally, the girl who is waiting for him in Newfoundland, the one who wants to marry him.

The Frenchwoman pauses, and the man looks at him expectantly, sitting up on the sea chest, his slim legs crossed at the ankle, his stockings wrinkled, obviously expecting him to assent. The captain lifts his cap and scratches his head, making a show of considering, but he tells them that he needs to bring his ship to Boston as quickly as possible.

He doesn't say that what he wants most now is to go home, to get rid of the pack of them, to receive his pay for the dangers he has confronted on their behalf. He wants to rest in his own snug house with its bay windows that look toward the sea. He wants to smoke a long pipe, sitting out on the veranda and watching the evening sky.

He wants to sleep through an entire night without being disturbed by worries of wind or cries. He wants to do nothing. He wants to be rid of his dreams of the falling sailor, who swims perpetually to catch up with this ship, his dreams of this Frenchwoman in her perpetual dark dress. He longs to bring this endless first voyage to a successful end.

He decides he will marry his Sally, if he ever arrives home. He is aware now, with the Frenchwoman before him, of just how much he misses the comfort and company of women, in his bedroom under the eaves, in the nights when the rain beats hard against the bay windows. He imagines Sally standing in the half-dark at the top of the stairs and lifting up the hem of her skirt to trip down to him as he comes in the door, throwing her freckled arms round his neck, though she has never done such a thing, not being a demonstrative girl. He sees himself walking hand in hand with her in his back garden in the mist, descending the hill, going through the blue hydrangeas and the wild pink roses to the sea. He imagines the two of them wandering to the beach in the first light, Black frolicking ahead.

## II

Lucy shakes her head, as the captain leaves their cabin. "Nothing to be done, there. A good man, but stubborn," she says. She looks down at Séraphine, who has been whimpering during the discussion, but now sleeps in her arms, a trickle of saliva on her chin. Her face looks thin and pinched beneath its crumpled lace bonnet. She looks old before her time, her little fingers and hands almost as transparent as rice paper.

"Poor child," she murmurs. How will she survive the months ahead? Humbert is playing with his wooden rocking horse with the cabin boy, who seems engrossed with him in their game on the cabin floor. Lucy has promised him a real pony when they get to America. The cabin boy calls Humbert his "boy" and has become his constant companion. Despite his youth—she guesses he is not much more than twelve—and Humbert's limited English, he attempts with great kindness and tact to cheer him up in his moments of despondency or homesickness.

Frédéric says, "I cannot support another minute in this cabin. I am going up for a breath of air." Lucy tells Humbert and the cabin boy to follow him. They must go to cook. The potatoes will be ready with the butter. They should all eat. She will come in a moment. Now she needs a few moments on her own. She longs for food but even more for privacy. She has hardly been alone for more than a few minutes since they boarded the ship.

She sits on the edge of the berth and looks at her sleeping child. She places her hand on the rounded head with its fuzz of fair hair, the closed eyes, the waxy, thin cheeks—this child born at the height of the Terror, a child of the Revolution. Flesh of her flesh, she lies there, squirming slightly, her hands twitching, her little legs lying open in the shape of a heart. She makes her baby noises, purses her lips, sucking in her sleep, sucking on the idea of a breast, an imaginary nipple. This child is forever needy, forever ravenous, with a hunger she cannot sate. Séraphine sucks and sucks, biting at her bleeding flesh, consuming her, in vain. Daily she is growing thinner, paler. Daily Lucy is growing weaker.

Lucy remembers her younger brother, who died not much older than Séraphine is now.

*How easily he slipped from my life. One day he was running after me on sturdy little legs, playing in the laurel bushes at Hautefontaine, calling my name—sometimes I still think I can hear him calling me, "Lucy! Lucy!"— and the next day he was gone. I remember his face when I went to lean over him. Grandmother told me to kiss him for the last time in his white coffin. I could not touch his flesh with my lips. I kissed my two fingers and touched them to his cold cheek.*

She will take advantage of the baby's sleep to do something she has been wanting to do for a long while. She takes out the rosewood necessaire with her toilette articles, and the folded cloths she keeps there for the times of the month when they might be necessary, though she has not needed them during this voyage. The only liquid which has escaped her body is sweat and a thin trickle of watery milk, oozing from her nipples, which has kept her baby alive so far. It is all she can produce.

The thought of another month on this ship makes her want to run up the ladder and plunge off the side of the boat into the sea, like the sailor who fell through the air from the mast. She imagines the long, slow fall through the twilit air and the plunge down, down, into the deep.

She takes off her kerchief and allows her knotted locks to fall about her face. She tries to run her fingers through them. She shakes her head from side to side, and her long, thick hair blinds her, whipping across her face. She struggles in vain to pull a comb through her tangled tresses, but they are matted like the tight, intricate weave of a fine blond carpet.

She remembers a moment during her stay in Spa where she went with her mother before she died, when she was eleven. She was dancing the gavotte in her taffeta dress. She was slipping easily across the smooth parquet floor in green silk slippers, turning, her skirts lifting around her legs, her arms floating from her sides.

*Surrounded by a crowd of people who murmured compliments on my grace, my hair, I was a flower, a precious Dutch tulip, opening in the sun of their admiration. They all whispered, "Extraordinary! What extraordinary hair that child has!"*

She thinks of what her ancestors had to suffer, stowing away in wooden crates to cross the sea from Ireland to accompany their rightful Catholic king. Now she is the Wild Goose, the foolish goose, lost at sea. What is the matter with her? How can she weep over matted hair? What vanity!

She looks into her necessaire. She hunts and finds what she needs. She picks up the scissors and holds them in her hands, looking at them for a moment, glinting invitingly in a thin ray of light. She holds up a thick lock with one hand and with the other takes a snip at it. She hears the satisfying crunch of the scissors on the hair and goes on hacking at her locks, cutting without mercy, with an intense and growing rage, a need to punish herself, until nothing is left but a fine stubble bristling up on her head like a porcupine.

She picks up her mirror and admires her handiwork, a haircut *à la Titus*, she thinks with grim satisfaction. She looks like a hungry boy. Her eyes look enormous, underlined with ashen shadows, her cheeks sunken and pallid. She gets up and goes fast up the stairs and stands in the wind on the deck, holding the thick mass of hair she has cut off in her hands. She goes over to the side of the ship, throws the useless locks overboard, and watches them disappear into a swirl of sea. She feels light, free, unencumbered by her tresses, her useless vanity, her illusions.

She remembers her ridiculous appearance at the ball all in blue chiffon, with the two bluebirds perched in the turret of her hair that had caused such a stir. "The unruly Irish!" Indeed. How absurd she had been! How could she have given so much importance to such trivialities! *Vanitas vanitatum!*

The captain sees her standing there, shorn like a lamb. He stares at her with his mouth open in horror. "Oh, Madam, what have you done! Your beautiful hair!" he shouts at her, appalled.

Frédéric's reaction is even worse. When he sees his wife, and despite the presence of the captain, he holds his head in both his hands as though confronted by an awful apparition. His face crinkles like a child's. He weeps like Odysseus. "How could you!" he shouts, turning his head away from her as though he cannot bear to see this dreadful sight, as though she has destroyed some cherished dream. He staggers from her to the side of the ship, as though she has wounded him. He seems to take this as an act of rebellion, a direct insult to his already wounded masculinity. For the first time on board ship, he raises his voice in anger. He shouts something about a crime, as though she has willfully killed someone, destroyed something precious that belonged to *him*. He has borne his seasickness, the bad food, and the dangers of this voyage with admirable fortitude, but this has undone him.

She pays no attention to his or the captain's comments, but simply says something about her hair having become so tangled it was impossible to comb it free.

"And what would Leonard say if he were to see you now?" Frédéric exclaims with a bitter laugh, referring to her famous French hairdresser.

Lucy shrugs and says, "Much ado about nothing."

Suddenly she remembers how hungry she is. She thinks of the potatoes and her craving for food. She goes to the cook to see what he has kept for her to eat. He is bent over in the galley. He whistles as he tends to his pots and pans, the eternally bubbling beans, his fair hair in his eyes. "Come and eat," he says, lifting up a bowl. He adds some salt. He offers her the rest of the potatoes, which he has kept for her in a wooden bowl. She sits. *In a daze, breathing deeply, I forgot Frédéric, Humbert, my lost locks, even my baby girl.*

Boyd watches her as she grabs the bowl from him, grasps it in both her hands, and hurriedly stuffs the remains of the potatoes and the butter into her mouth like an animal with her bare hands, as though afraid someone might take them from her. She swipes her finger around the inside of the bowl to get every bit of butter and sucks on her finger. Never has anything tasted so good. Her mouth aches with the pleasure of it. She smacks her lips.

*Not enough food to go around. Too many people, and not enough food. A little boy not much older than Humbert, shoeless and shivering in rags, he lifted up an empty bowl to me as I went by in my litter, carried by my footmen in my taffeta dress on the Rue du Bac. "I am hungry! I am hungry!" he cried out. His thin, high-pitched voice followed me down the street. When I asked Grandmother to give him alms, she said, "There are too many of them. There is just not enough to go around."*

When she has eaten, she speaks to the cook. The new provisions the captain has secured will vanish fast; the shortage of food and water has caused her milk to dry up almost completely. She crosses her wrists and puts her hands to her breasts. She is terrified her baby will die of hunger if this voyage continues much longer.

The cook glances at her hands, her breasts, and then looks into her eyes and whispers that she need not worry about the water rationing, he will make sure she gets all she needs, even if she is the only one to drink. He will hide water for her, and whatever else he can find, he whispers, and adds with fervor, "Whatever happens." He will make sure her baby does not starve.

She smiles at the boy who, despite the grime on his face, looks suddenly handsome to her. She puts her head back and closes her eyes for a moment with abandon. She sits wearily, close beside him, leaning against his shoulder.

Then he does something unexpected. He protectively wraps his arm around her shoulder. She is shocked at how good it feels, a rare moment when reality outstrips her dreams. She feels his warmth, the strength of his young body beside her, and an unexpected wave of desire buoys up in her. He seems now her only ally on this ship. She lifts her hands to her head, lets her fingers explore, feel the bones of her head. She scratches at her scalp through her short-cropped hair. She's certain she feels lice eating at her flesh. How close they all are to death. A terrible hopelessness comes over her then, she does not know how: from the loss of her hair, the unexpected food she has eaten too fast, this interminable voyage.

She thinks with bitter sadness of the frivolity of her past life. All the faces, human and animal, all the faces she has ever loved and have loved her back, come to her, shot through with flashes of light. She sees a glimmer of Marguerite's wide cheeks beneath her white cap in the dark of the closet and hears her whisper softly as she unlocks the door, "Courage, child." Miss B. smiles seductively at her, sways her hips, and vanishes. Her great-great-uncle lifts his beringed hand in the air, his ecclesiastical rings glittering; the Princess d'Hénin's blue cats stalk softly through the grass. Lucy's mother's shadow looms on the wall.

"Maman," she whispers to the sea air, "help me!"

*Mother's face was flushed and feverish, her hair damp around her fore-head. She lay on her bed and murmured, "I am going to Naples with Henri de Guéménée."*

She appears to Lucy as she was that night at the Queen's ball in her pink dress, dipping and bowing her head, fluttering her fan, half-covering her mouth, whispering to the Prince de Guéménée, to the Duke de Lauzun, to the Duke de Liancourt. Lucy looks up into the sky and whispers again, "Help me, Maman, please," but all she can see now is the leaden sea and a white gull that rises higher and higher in the sky, a speck, vanishing.

The truth comes to Lucy that her mother, brilliant, beautiful, and generous as she was, and whether she had been the lover of all those men as some said or not, had not cared enough to help her. The appalling thought comes to her: she knows what the mysterious expression on her mother's face was when she saw her: it was surprise. Her mother had simply forgotten her existence, too busy with hopes and dreams of her own.

And where is Frédéric? He has stumbled back down the steps to the cabin, as though mortally wounded. He is once again lying still on his back. It is not he who will save her, but rather she who must carry him.

## PART SEVEN
*Preliminaries*

# I

*T*HE NEW MINISTER of finance, Calonne, persuades Louis XVI to call a Council of Notables to Versailles to consider measures necessary to rescue French public finance from bankruptcy. Despite the many ministers hired and fired, the King fails to choke the deficit, which instead threatens to swallow him whole. Meanwhile the people express their opinions and plot revenge against their oppressors, write pamphlets, hold meetings, and debate the fate of all the aristocrats, even the Divine Right of Kings.

## MARCH, 1787

*I date this moment as the beginning of the revolution, yet I have always thought of this time as one of the most exciting of my life. I was always waiting for something to happen. There seemed to be a link between what was happening to me, and what was going on around me in the country, all the stir at Versailles.*

On February 22, Lucy's great-great-uncle had been called to Versailles with the other notables by the King's minister, to solve the deficit. France's recent wars had left the country with a huge debt. Nobility and clergy being exempt from direct taxation, the burden fell on those least able to pay.

But Lucy was not thinking about taxes or deficits that spring. She was living through her eyes, her skin, her heart.

They left Paris at one thirty in order to be with her great-great-uncle at Versailles for dinner by three. She set off, her grandmother sitting opposite her, Miss B. at her side, in her uncle's carriage.

Lucy had always been happiest when she could escape the Hotel Dillon and go on some official voyage with her great-great-uncle, when he assisted at the yearly session of the States in Montpellier in the Languedoc. Away from home she felt more alive, stimulated. If she could just keep moving, with all the bustle that a voyage entailed, she believed she would be happy. She liked the variety, the opportunity to learn new things, the pace of events. Her mind seemed more active, awake, absorbing new sights around her.

The routine of Lucy's days was transformed by these long daily carriage rides in her great-great-uncle's magnificently sprung coach with its six swift horses. The elaborate process of dressing and undressing, the rides in the park, the visits back and forth, had become suspenseful, had acquired a new intensity with Frédéric Séraphin in her life.

What a delight to put on her clothes with a pleasant quickening of the heart, to hurry down the steps, and climb into the carriage! It was the part of the day she loved best. She leaned forward, looked out the window from her corner in the camouflage of the shadows, with the thick traveling rug covering her knees. In the shifting light, and with sounds of the horses' hooves and the carriage wheels muffling their voices, Miss B. turned toward her to question her in detail, asking about the Count, Frédéric Séraphin. "So, tell me, will he be at dinner today?" she asked in her breathless way.

"Perhaps," Lucy said and shrugged her shoulders as though she did not care, though she was almost sure he would. Frédéric had written to her in his tiny, wild handwriting, which she had difficulty deciphering, saying he would do his utmost to be there today, that all his thoughts turned constantly to her. She was delighted

with her conquest, this intelligent aristocrat from a powerful family who had fallen tenderly in love with her at first sight.

"And will you get a chance to be alone with him?" Miss B.
asked, raising her eyebrows suggestively. Lucy glanced at her grandmother, who dozed or seemed to doze, sitting opposite them.

"Perhaps, with your help," Lucy whispered, opening her eyes
wide, warningly. But Miss B. continued to question, and Lucy, though
she hardly knew him at all, made him up for the eager Miss B.

"He has such a wonderful voice!" she breathed, moving her
hands. "If I had to give it a color, I'd say it was green: a light-
green voice. And he has read so much: history, literature, and phi-
losophy! He has a wonderful memory and quotes long passages
of Horace, Virgil, and Tacitus." She praised his sense of humor:
"And he makes me laugh! He is always in a good mood. Never
cross with me like you know . . ." she whispered, widening her eyes
at her grandmother. She told Miss B. how he made anything she
said sound interesting or amusing. "He's always saying, 'I've never
heard anyone say anything like that before.'"

"Ah! He knows the art of conversation," Miss B. said, rue in
her voice. Lucy looked at her with sympathy and squeezed her
hand. There would be no count, perhaps no husband at all for
Miss B. who had no dowry, Lucy believed, despite her pink-and-
white complexion, her dewy eyes, her warm, eager breath. *Nul-
lum sine dote fiat conjugum.* Miss B. would have to continue to live
vicariously, through the imagined life of others. She would have
to make do with the little light that shone through the life of her
employers.

Miss B.'s ringlets and her plump breasts bounced up and down
with the movement of the carriage. Her round eyes flashed with
interest. She squeezed Lucy's hand in her damp, dimpled one, and
her knee with enthusiasm, and stroked her cheek. Lucy was happy

to talk about the Count to someone who would listen, which her grandmother would not, while she traveled to see him.

Lucy still cringed under her grandmother's constant criticism of Frédéric Séraphin. "Quite frankly, I don't see what you see in him," her grandmother had said to her, disparagingly. "Rather a small man, don't you think? And the hair is beginning to thin, isn't it?" Or she said, "A man with more memory than sense, I deem."

Lucy said nothing in response to her grandmother's criticism, afraid she might change her mind. Her grandmother seemed to have accepted Frédéric out of indifference to Lucy's future, her mind on more important matters. "What the devil, if that's what you and that father of yours want, so be it," she had said, in the tone of one who says, "Now you have made your bed, lie in it."

As they went onward, and as Lucy rambled on about the Count to Miss B., as though her own words had convinced her, she saw him as increasingly admirable. Also, she saw the world transformed, the contrasts exacerbated: the tree trunks dark, the sky blue, the spring light brighter, sparkling. She loved the delicacy of the colors, the changing light. The creamy puffs of cloud drifted lighter and quicker, and the forest, as they entered it, seemed denser and more dappled, the trees wetter and dripping and more exciting. When she saw a troop of deer running, leaping high across her path, she felt her heart, too, leaping.

As they went through the main gates at Versailles, and she drew nearer to her meeting with her betrothed, she felt as she had as a child: as though she had entered a Kingdom of Beauty. As the coach rumbled over the cobblestones, she listened to all the joyous sounds: the shouting of guards, the ringing of bells, the barking of dogs, music on all sides. Her hearing seemed more acute. She heard the sounds of water and reeds and the voices of the people—the lace

makers, the spinners, the ironers, even Miss B.'s high-pitched English voice—in a different way.

She forgot the fetid odors, the exhalations from the swampy,
spring earth, the disorder and the dust from the myriad unfinished
building projects, the uncertainty of the political situation, the rising price of bread. She ignored the swarming of rats and fleas and
lice and saw instead the shade of the chestnut trees in the long alleys
as deeper, more velvety. As they entered the gardens she contemplated le Nôtre's masterpiece, the thicket of trees, the limpid water
trickling over stones, the coolness of the air.

She saw a bronze statue beckoning, a cherub's arm reaching
out just to her, inviting her on. She caught sight of a stone goblet
piled high with fruit against the trees, and Diana aiming her bow
at the sky. Lucy delighted in this running stream of her life and
abandoned herself to it with a kind of rapture without thought of
the future. She felt wholly human, and also, in a strange way, like a
creature of the wild.

When they congregated before dinner in the gallery, Lucy listened to the sound of the servants' footsteps, the chink of silver and glass. The whole world seemed festive. She looked around to see if Frédéric Séraphin had left his regiment to join them as he had promised her. Instead, she saw her great-great-uncle's friend, the Prince de Talleyrand, dressed here exquisitely for the Court in his ecclesiastical attire as the Bishop of Autun. Lucy had known him since she was a young child, and he was kind enough to come over to compliment her on her complexion. Calonne, too, the controller general of finance, stood smiling at Talleyrand's side, looking rosy and suave in lace cuffs and a silk suit. Lucy could smell his odor of lavender water as he bowed over her hand.

Serious matters were discussed but without undue solemnity. If anyone could make light work of serious business, Lucy suspected Talleyrand could, though this day he looked somewhat worried and whispered to Lucy something about the hasty preparations for this event. Looking for Frédéric in the crowd, she was distracted. She leaned forward to look along the endless table in the lovely blue-and-gold room.

Lucy's grandmother sat beside the Archbishop of Narbonne, near the center of the table. She watched over him, as usual, jealously. Beside him sat a short, obese man, whose swollen lower limbs dangled uselessly from his chair. He looked as though he would be unable even to walk, ride, or take any sort of exercise. Despite his plump cheeks, his ruddy color, his pear shape, there was something delicate, careful about him, Lucy thought, as she watched his fine hands picking rapidly at his food.

Alexander de Lameth, the youngest of the three Lameth brothers and Frédéric's old friend, was also present, sitting opposite Lucy at dinner that day.

"Who is the obese man?" Lucy asked Alexander.

He leaned across and said, "The King's brother, Monsieur, otherwise known as His Heaviness, the Count of Provence," and grinned at Lucy. According to Miss B., Monsieur, who was married to the plain, sallow Josephine, not present this day, was suffering from the same difficulty in bed as the King. Monsieur's remarks, as far as Lucy could overhear them, seemed somewhat scathing about the entire endeavor.

"Equality is a very good thing in a republic, but in France we are used to having a member of the clergy preside over any assembly," said Loménie de Brienne, the Archbishop of Toulouse, a man with disfiguring eczema on his face. He, too, seemed not to agree with Calonne's plan for a land tax.

"He's a friend of my great-great-uncle's. I have met him at Hautefontaine," Lucy told Alexander de Lameth.

"Entirely the Queen's man—ambitious, and some say agnostic. In any case, a frivolous man, who spends his time stirring up the clergy," Alexander told Lucy. Lally Tolendal, the Princess d'Hénin's lover, was also present at the table. He sat very upright, holding high his great head, with his small nose and immense cheeks. Lucy knew he wanted to be a writer and had tried his hand at the art and even had her read some of his not very good verses.

Lucy surveyed the nobility at the table, noted the proud heads rising from the cages of clothes on the pliant column of the necks, turning from side to side. The little curls escaped from wigs. The red, red lips smiled and slipped slightly sideways, equivocally. The foreheads were accentuated with pale powder. White hands fluttered quickly, here to adjust a beauty patch to a cheek, or there to tie a bow to a bodice. Frédéric's face was not among them.

Then Lucy saw him enter the room. He came fast through the throng in his formal dress: his lace collar and cuffs, the embroidered waistcoat, his sword at his side. Then he stood quite still for a moment, his weight on one foot, his hand on his hip. There was something about his stance, his sudden stillness, the way he held his head, his steady gaze, that entranced Lucy. He seemed all of one piece. She imagined him naked, saw him like a smooth statue she'd seen drawn in a book: Michelangelo's David. *I did not know it then but this stillness would be something that would continue to delight me in our lovemaking all his life.* Now she would have liked to take him into her arms. Because of his position in society, his ancient family, perhaps, his military training, or his education, he had a certain assurance in the way he entered a room, the way he stood still, turned his head, looked around him, and, when he saw her, put his hand to his sword. It was a kind of beauty arising from self-confidence, class confidence, male confidence that had never been put into question. His self-possession gave her the impression he was listening to something a little beyond this place. She herself was not capable of such stillness, she felt. Her husband-to-be was not placed next to her, but he was where she could see him.

They began with the Almoner blessing the table. The endless meal with its innumerable courses had suddenly become interesting. Lucy was aware of Frédéric's movements: his hand on the table, his sword, which was de rigueur at the Court. He leaned forward slightly to glance at her. He smiled at something she had said, nodded his head. He said something respectful to her grandmother, or her great-great-uncle who sat not far from him.

Her grandmother made sure that the Archbishop was served

the choicest of morsels. At one point she told the servant behind him to bring another dish, not finding the one he was served good enough for him. The food continued to be brought forth on trolleys in great covered silver tureens.

Monsieur, His Heaviness, as though this were to be his last meal, attacked his food with vigor. He devoured course after course: rice soup served with fattened pullet, meat dishes, and fish dishes, wild fowl and skate livers, hare's tongues, mutton sausages, rabbit's head, celery soufflé, ram's testes, followed by innumerable desserts: jellies, *blancmanges*, custards. His waistcoat and doublet unbuttoned and stained with food, Monsieur sweated with the effort of consuming so much and drinking so much wine. He drank red wine, white wine, claret. The bottles kept coming.

Lucy, sitting at the long table where she could see Frédéric, had no appetite at all. No wonder Monsieur was not able to accomplish anything in the bedroom. No wonder these notables were not able to decide on anything! How *could* a man do anything after eating so much food? His eyelids drooped, and he seemed almost to swoon. She was afraid he might fall from his chair to the marble floor and shatter like Humpty Dumpty. Yet this man was the one who supposedly presided over the Bureau of Notables, where Lucy's uncle assisted, and was expected to return to his efforts to solve the problems of taxation after the dinner.

The word "deficit" hummed around her head like a hungry mosquito. Lucy hardly heard the conversations that buzzed so tiresomely around her. How boring it was and absurd.

*At seventeen, politics bored me. Like those around me, I had no real understanding of the importance of the debt and how dangerous the situation had become. Certainly, I was aware of the abuses, the frivolities of the nobility, the need to regenerate the monarchy, but how this was to be accomplished was not certain to me then or now. Despite my disinterest in the matter, it became increasingly clear to me that this assembly had been called forth by Calonne without preparing for it sufficiently, believing quite erroneously he could use it as a rubber stamp for his land tax.*

Lucy glanced at Frédéric, and he raised his eyebrows at her with understanding. He, too, found all of this ridiculous. He understood her without her even saying a word.

Everyone at the table, it seemed, had an opinion on what should be done, but really it appeared to Lucy that what everyone wanted to prove was that he was more intelligent, better informed than anyone else, that he or she alone knew the truth and had the right to voice it.

There were those who said the deficit had no importance. The thing to do was simply spend more and more, to give the impression that there was money in reserve, an endless supply, to restore confidence in France. It all depended on appearances, and anyway, France *was* a rich country, surely, industry expanding, goods and passengers on the move at a faster and faster rate. Many abuses had been done away with—torture, for example, abolished.

Alexander, who wore his hair powdered and tied back at the nape of his neck, said, "But that is what Calonne has done—and look at the mess we are in! France should learn from the English. The English system is superior in every way. Parliamentary government is—"

"And what exactly do you mean by the English system?" Lucy ventured to ask, turning toward him. Everyone answered at once, but, really, it seemed to Lucy that no one really knew.

Alexander said something about the separation of powers, the system of checks and balances, but what was that?

Lucy noticed how Talleyrand cleverly listened but said little.

Someone else spoke of America, of France's alliance with the American rebels. Had they not proclaimed no taxation without representation? Why was this not applicable to France?

"The ancient French nobility—not those who have bought their places—has paid with its blood and not money," someone said scornfully and put his hand to his sword.

Frédéric seemed to Lucy to know more than anyone else. He spoke of the banker, Necker, with some admiration. He asked Alexander, "Have you read Necker's book, the *Compte Rendu au Roi?*" Indeed, Lucy thought, looking at him admiringly, how much he had read. No one else seemed to have read Necker's book. And why had Frédéric not been chosen as one of the notables who were assembled here, she wondered, when he had read so much and spoke so well? Was he lacking something?

It seemed the most qualified people were often not chosen for the positions they merited, she thought, thinking of her father's lot, too. People were chosen because they were liked by those in power. Her father, certainly, had never received the honors he deserved. Instead it was his commander, the cowardly but charming Count d'Estaing, who had been heaped unjustly with the awards her father should have received. The Count d'Estaing had succeeded by charming the Queen, something neither Lucy nor Frédéric had done.

Someone dared to suggest that Necker's book was really something of a fraud, a pretense that all was well in the best of worlds, when everyone knew it was not. "My God, he even wrote about his domestic bliss!"

Lally Tolendal suggested there should be two houses: an upper one made up of the nobility and a lower one to represent the people, as in England.

Frédéric leaned across the table and said in a low voice to Alexander, "According to Necker, everything depends on public confidence and credit."

Alexander added, "Old industries have to be eliminated and new ones claimed. The past has to make way for the future."

Others whispered about Calonne, the new controller general of finance, who had not remained for the dinner. It was he who had replaced Necker and whom the Queen had never liked despite his deference to her. Calonne had told the Queen he would do anything possible for her, and if it was not possible he would do it anyway. Alexander hinted that Figaro's line from the popular Beaumarchais play probably referred to him: "What was required was a man who knew figures; what they got was a dancer!" The Queen, herself, with her indiscretions, his brother Charles suggested, was portrayed in the Countess Almaviva.

Lucy was amazed at the contrast between the King's power, the courtiers conniving and scheming servility, and the extraordinary freedom of language expressing liberal ideas.

She knew the country was increasingly in debt since Necker's departure, though no one seemed able to agree exactly on the sum. According to Frédéric it was reputed that more than 1,250 million livres had been borrowed since 1776. An appalling monthly sum must be paid to service this debt. The expenses of the Seven Years' War and the American War had never been paid. The nobles and clergy were used to taxing others—the toll, tribute, and corvée—but not to being taxed themselves.

The Archbishop, in his purple robes, spoke with brilliance of the importance of regional governments and the advantage of provincial assemblies while eating *blancmange* beside Monsieur. He said, "But remember poor Monsieur de Silhouette, and what happened to him!" and smiled. M. de Silhouette, who had once been controller general of finance, proposed unpopular taxes and was fired after four months, leaving behind only his name, which had come to designate a passing shadow.

The Archbishop, Lucy knew, though he had proclaimed the need for a reduction of the privileges of the nobility, did not seem to include himself among those affected. He was the one who had told the King, when questioned about his constant hunting and asked if he felt he was setting his parish priests a good example, "Sire, it would, indeed, be a grave error for my parish priests to hunt, but in my case, it is simply the satisfaction of a desire developed by my ancestors." What could Louis XVI, who also loved to hunt as his ancestors had done, say to that?

The conversation came back to Necker as it seemed continually to do. His name, like the word deficit, buzzed around Lucy's head. And here, too, no one could agree. Some said he was a dreadfully pretentious Swiss person, full of himself, ambitious, ignorant, and incompetent, and his wife not worth mentioning. Others considered him a genius, a prophet, a savior. Where did the truth lie?

Lucy heard snatches of the conversation of another archbishop, Loménie de Brienne. He seemed to be busy stirring up the clergymen who sat beside him. *The force of intrigue and the force of public opinion were growing dangerous, but no one, including myself, was aware of this.* Among other things mentioned in these discussions, there was talk of resorting to a meeting of the States General, which had not been called for years. This was when the old Duke d'Ormesson mumbled, "You will repent it."

# III

*I*N THE GARDENS at Versailles many people mingle, including the fishwives (the *poissardes*). They throng not only the gardens but the antechambers of the castle, and even express their opinion of the royals to their face. There is an amazing lack of security, for the sanctity of royalty is supposed to provide its own security.

To her delight and surprise, Frédéric rose suddenly, came quickly toward her, and drew near her chair. He leaned down and whispered fast, "Join me in the garden if you can; I cannot listen to another word," and left the room. Lucy glanced along the table at her grandmother, who was holding forth with authority to Monsieur. Lucy rose and left, whispering to Miss B., who was waiting in an antechamber, "We're going into the gardens," and escaped down the many stairs and into the dusty sunlight. There Miss B. was happy to pretend to lose Lucy in the crowd.

Lucy and Frédéric slipped away and walked in the noise and confusion of the great throng of people who were admitted so freely to the gardens and Palace of Versailles. Laughing, they hurried among Princes of the Realm, cooks, and scullery maids. Beggars in rags accosted them and mingled with Mistresses of the Robes. Many of the people were not even decently dressed, but wore torn and soiled clothing, and most, certainly, scratched at lice or even mice in their elaborate hair, and were not able to hide their odors despite much perfume spilled upon their flesh.

"How do all these people manage to get in here?" Lucy asked.

"How to keep them out? There are so many of them, and they keep pouring through the gates," Frédéric said.

A man with a wide-brimmed gray hat lowered over his forehead, his narrow face in shadow, sidled up to Frédéric and pulled something out from the folds of his cape, smiling the sycophant's smile. "Good God, man, have you no shame!" Frédéric exclaimed furiously, his face red, but the man did not move away.

"Out of our way!" Lucy cried, incensed, putting up her hand to protect Frédéric from the sight of an engraving of two women amorously entwined, with the Queen's name evident beneath.

A shadow moved from behind a bush, and a young woman in a bright green dress rushed forward and appeared to swoon at Frédéric's feet, just as they walked by. He crouched down beside her to revive her with a small vial of some kind.

"Some schemer, watching and waiting for her chance in the bushes," Lucy said impatiently, stepping over the woman and pulling Frédéric up by the hand. The woman's eyes fluttered open, and she sat up and let out a dramatic sigh and put her hand to her half-visible breasts.

"Do you think she'll be all right?" Frédéric said, looking over his shoulder.

"Perfectly all right," Lucy replied and continued on along the path through the trees, though her blood ran cold for a brief moment, as she wondered how Frédéric could be taken in by such a creature. How much sense did he possess?

As she walked on his arm, the uncertain sunlight coming in aslant through the leaves of the chestnut trees, butterflies fluttering over the flowers, Lucy caught Frédéric studying her with an expression of close concentration on his slightly careworn face. She thought he looked like someone who was trying to recall a name, a place. She did not know if he found her pretty, but she did know that he liked to gaze at her, like a thirsty person taking a long drink.

He talked to her of his concerns with the officers in the regiment who did not behave as they should, the lack of discipline among them. "If the officers are not prepared to set an example, why should the men obey?" he said.

*Though in company Frédéric could be taciturn, his spirit seemed to flourish in a more intimate setting. The sincerity of his conversation became more engaging when we were alone. Then he gave me the gift of his absolute attention. Together we began to be at ease. We found pleasure in childlike games, silly jokes, and the innumerable private details which captured our hearts.*

*I liked the fact that he was not taller than I. I liked this slightness, his soft, fast words, his enthusiasms, his ability to listen, his generous actions, though I already suspected some of them might not be wise. He seemed easily persuaded, easily swayed, but I liked the fact that he was not always certain of what he believed, that he seemed able to see two sides to a question. I was drawn, too, despite myself, to his pale skin, the pale eyes, the strong shoulders, but above all to his interest in me.*

They walked down to the water's edge, and she suggested they sit down among the people in one of the cafés along the north traverse of the Grand Canal to shelter in a sudden shower. She watched her Count wave his hands with eloquent enthusiasm; listened to his light, easy laugh.

He talked of books. He was rereading Gibbon's *Decline and Fall*, going over certain passages with some difficulty—he read English quite well, though he spoke it badly, he told her—but great admiration. "You must read it," he said to Lucy, who wished he would go on to tell her about his secret life.

He said, "How difficult it is to say anything that is true about the past—well, perhaps even more difficult about the present. You think you know, but then you read a line somewhere, and everything shifts slightly, and you have to begin all over again."

He knew long passages in Latin and Greek, yet he was interested in what she had to say and questioned her about her interests and her early life.

She told him about her early interest in physics and astronomy and how once at dinner, when she was only thirteen, she had dared to bring forth the name that none of the other learned men could remember. She had said in a low voice, "It was Galileo, of course!" and her neighbor, hearing her say the name, said, "Mademoiselle Dillon says it was Galileo, of course!"

Frédéric laughed. "You put them all to shame," he said with admiration.

In his admiring presence, she felt suddenly freed of her shyness, from the terrible constraint her grandmother imposed with her constant criticism, from the fear that she might find fault, and might at any moment decide to turn on Lucy to banish her from her home. She loved him all the more for what she took as his insouciance, which was so different from her own and therefore seemed exotic.

He had the courtier's ability to find the right word, to bow over a hand, to guide with a light gesture, to take pleasure in the sensuality of life. How conscious they were of the movements of one another's bodies, of the steamy air between them on this uncertain day of showers and bright light.

When a gondolier appeared before them, Lucy, who loved the water, suggested they take a ride with him. Frédéric rose and looked up into the uncertain sky. "It might rain," he said but took her hand. A courtier about to get into the boat gave it up when he saw the young couple, and they stepped in. They sat side by side in the back, and Frédéric gave the gondolier a coin and asked him to sing them a song. He smiled and sang in his native Italian, and Lucy listened to his voice and the oar dipping into the water, and the birds calling. She shut her eyes and leaned her head back to catch the sun and conjured up Venice, as she had seen it in paintings.

*I imagined that we would wander like this in this lovely place for the rest of our lives, with our children, our grandchildren. Later we would think of this moment with longing.*

Together they forgot the dreary conversations nearby. At this moment, she did not think of the poor, hear them moan; nor did she think of the vice in the Church, and of the deplorable behavior of the clergy, nor of the folly of the nobles, and Calonne's plans to raise revenue through the salt tax, internal tariffs, the selling of the Church's lands.

Instead, she leaned back on Frédéric's arm. She spoke of her mother, of how lovely she was, "an angel of sweetness and beauty." Frédéric looked at her and replied, "I can well imagine she was," and took her hand in his. Lucy looked into his eyes and liked what she saw there, moved by his longing. She liked his need for her, the light of hope in his blue gaze.

"Since Mother has died, there has not been a day Grandmother has not tormented me in some way," she said. She added with some determination, "She may not know it, but I won't ever let her get the better of me." Frédéric put his arm around her slender waist and gathered her to him and said laughingly, "She will not torment you any longer, my dearest. Your lord and master will be here to protect you," and Lucy shut her eyes and felt his body against hers and remembered the practicing she had done with Miss B., Miss B. with the soft, soft skin. "I'm sure he will," Lucy said. He was a man who had promised her his love, though she had found that promises often held their own lies—her mother who had promised so often to protect her from her grandmother, but had not dared to or had not cared. She decided this would be different, this man would love her and protect her. She would no longer be a pawn in someone else's game. She would move the pieces.

She asked Frédéric why his mother had been shut up in her convent, disgraced. He told her he did not know but that he, too, with his beloved older sister, had grown up in a house with his own grandmother and grandfather. He had missed his mother terribly, he told her. It had changed him, so that he felt that part of him was still back there shut up in the room where she had left him. Lucy put her hand in his and felt she would have liked to spare him all the sorrows in the world.

He spoke of the difficult times in the West Indies, as a soldier, of his commander, the Count d'Estaing—not a brave man, he said, looking grave. "We were lolling down there in the heat, in the steamy air, waiting for something to happen. There is a lot of waiting time in war. The Count had difficulty making up his mind, causing much squabbling and fatal indecision among his commanders."

Frédéric told her how he had been able to rescue her father on the battlefield in Martinique. He had been riding across the field, at the end of a battle, the sun still beating down overhead. He could smell that awful smell of rot and human sweat, but more than anything else of the earth itself, the mud and mire of war. The smell had stayed with him, always, as though it had entered his blood. Flies and ants were already at their work in the heat. All around him, he said, he could hear the cries of men for water, someone calling for his mother. He saw a bloody head rolling, and a man whose jaw had been shot away, who staggered toward his horse and fell. And then, quite miraculously, coming through the glare of light, he had seen her father in the scarlet jacket of his Irish regiment. He knew him at once by his height. He had been wounded in the left leg, his horse shot out from under him. He had somehow dragged himself across the field, the mud, the swampy terrain, through a welter of bloody limbs, innards, the innocent boots and black hats.

Frédéric had jumped down from his horse, gone toward him to hold him up. He had said, "Can I be of service to you, sir?" and her father had replied, "Bring me water and take me to my regiment," and fainted away in his arms. He had lifted him up and lain him across his horse and carried him to safety.

"How lucky that you were there! He has often been lucky in his life," Lucy said.

"He is a brave man," Frédéric said. "But I don't want to make you old by telling you such sad things," he added, looking down at her and smiling.

"Oh, I'm already old, because I've seen too many sad things," Lucy said. But all the sad things had been wiped away from her mind since she had known him, she declared. "All my past, the good and the bad, has disappeared, and in its place is this," and she put her hand to his heart and looked into his eyes, unable to say the word, and he leaned against her and put his hands around her waist and felt her tremble.

He said, "Love." She was drawn to him by the dark smell on him, behind his ears, at the nape of his neck, something from her childhood, the smell of the piece of ribbon she had kept of her father's, a smell of flowers and sweat mixed with darker ones, the smell of earth and death. She kissed him gravely and gave him her hand as they stepped out of the boat.

# PART EIGHT
## *M*arriage

# I

## MAY 20, 1787

The night before her wedding, Lucy lay in her bed in the apartment that had been especially prepared. She was at La Folie-Joyeuse, her grandmother's house at Montfermeil, five leagues from Paris, which had once belonged to her mother. All her wedding presents were clustered around her. The trousseau that her grandmother had given her was worth 45,000 livres. Composed of linens, lace, and dresses of muslin, it lay in the vast heavy armoires that lined the room. *I remembered the prices of these things all my life and would write them down when I no longer possessed any of them.*

For once, she was entirely alone in her room with all her lovely new things. Miss B. was banished. No practicing tonight. She lay awake in the half dark with the windows open and the night smells of honeysuckle and jasmine rising from the garden. Moonlight streamed through the windows and glittered on the wardrobes' glass doors.

The wind rustled in the leaves like a long satisfied sigh. The basket Frédéric had given her, a cornucopia of good things, lay open on the dresser, its contents spilling from its sides: jewels and silk ribbons shone in the moonlight. There were flowers, feathers, gloves, materials, several hats and bonnets, mantelets in black or white muslin.

The Princess d'Hénin had given her the charming tea table with a silver-gilt tea service: teapot, sugar bowl, creamer, and all the porcelain from Sèvres, which was displayed on the table under the window.

Her husband's uncle had given her a traveling case that had its place in her country carriage, his grandfather, M. de Monconseil, a beautiful pair of diamond earrings. A *jardinière* filled with rare plants was by the bed and, what she liked the best, a little bookcase filled with books, among them a collection of English and Italian poets in seventy volumes, all her favorites: Ariosto, Pope, Milton, Chaucer, Bocaccio, Dryden, Donne, Dante, and, of course, Shakespeare. Pretty English engravings decorated the rest of the room, all gifts from her future husband. What a generous man he was! What loving and thoughtful gifts!

She was extremely grateful for this last gift and for the fact that Frédéric had chosen it with such care. She had found someone she could trust entirely, who had the same values she had, values of sincerity and fidelity. She had found not so much a kindred spirit— she was not certain that they saw the world in the same way—as a generous heart.

She turned on her pillow sleeplessly, savoring these last moments of solitude and thinking back on the days of her single life, which was coming to an end. She had no qualms on this last night, surrounded by her newly acquired wealth and by memories of a past she was eager to forget. Her only fear was that her grandmother, at the last moment, might yet stage some terrible scene to stop this wedding. Even that possibility seemed very faint, with Lucy's great-great-uncle on her side and presiding at the ceremony.

On the day of the wedding everyone met in the salon at noon. The guests followed the bride as she walked across the court. She held the hand of her young English cousin, her father's sister's child, a Jerningham, only twelve years old. Lucy wore a dress of white crepe, decorated with Brussels lace, and a bonnet, veils not yet being in style. A posy of white orange blossoms was sewn to the side of her dress and into her bonnet. Her grandmother followed on Frédéric's arm.

Frédéric's mother was allowed out of the convent to be present at the ceremony. Dressed in gray taffeta, her thin fingers laden with rings, she seemed cold and withdrawn. She said hardly a word, just leaning forward slightly to allow her cool cheek to be kissed, smelling of lavender water. Lucy could see she had once been beautiful, her blank eyes large, her skin still smooth and very pale, her hair glossy, dark, and thick. Frédéric bowed over her hand stiffly, but Lucy could see the tears in his eyes.

At the altar, the Archbishop of Narbonne stood resplendent in his violet vestments beside the Archbishop of Paris, M. de Juigne. The Montfermeil curate said a low mass, and Lucy's great-great-uncle gave his blessing to the bride and the groom and made a pretty speech. His voice was deeply vibrant, and despite what she knew about the man's morals, his love of luxury and the chase, his sermon in the closet, his eloquent words touched Lucy's heart. Alfred de Lambeth, seven years old, and Lucy's cousin, Jerningham, carried the canopy.

At four, a dinner was held. Lucy wore a turban trimmed with tall white plumes. They all stood around talking and feeling somewhat bored. Then she and Frédéric made the rounds of all the tables in the courtyard, where the family's retainers, in their colorful blue livery, the peasants and workers, dined. Many of them had known her since she was born, and they showed her their affection openly. They rose to their feet as she came near and lifted up their glasses to drink to her health and fortune. She had often interceded for them in their numerous disputes with her grandmother. They wished her and her husband good fortune, and their good wishes touched her much more than the compliments she had received indoors.

Marguerite, too, was permitted that day to emerge from the kitchens briefly to hold Lucy in her arms.

It was the following day that the Princess d'Hénin informed Lucy that the Queen wished her to be presented at Court that very week, and that she must come to Paris to study with the ballet master in order to prepare for the ordeal. She was not left to linger beside her new husband at Montfermeil. Would she disgrace herself anew with the Queen, as she had done before? Had not poor Germaine de Staël, Necker's daughter, torn the elaborate train to her priceless dress while making her curtsy?

"You have never torn a skirt in your life, I would wager," Frédéric told her, laughing.

## II

The ballet master, M. Huart, powdered, tubby, and skirted to resemble the Queen, sat on his mock throne and gazed beyond and behind Lucy, as though he could not see her but was watching someone else, her double, or perhaps the ghosts of all the young women he had prepared for presentation.

"Now, once again, please," he said. She dipped down before him and made as if to kiss the hem of his skirt, but he stopped her.

"No! No! More liquid, more supple. You are too stiff, too starched. You want to forget yourself a little. You are trying too hard. Think of yourself as a reed in the wind. You want to have an almost boneless movement, to express your complete devotion, your allegiance to the Queen with your whole body. Let me show you, my dear," he remonstrated, and now Lucy, in her morning dress, was obliged to play the Queen and sit on the stool/throne and watch, as M. Huart took up the role of the young Comtesse de la Tour du Pin with *embonpoint*. Solemnly and slowly but with incontestable dignity and an almost miraculous grace, he pulled his glove from his fat fingers and bent down with some difficulty and yet with great gravity, as if to kiss the hem of his sovereign's robe. Lucy, sitting on the skirted stool/throne and pretending to be the Queen, looked across the room at Miss B., who sat watching her. Her mischievous eyes widened with merriment and her little teeth protruded from her short upper lip. They were both overcome by the desire to giggle.

"Once again, *please*, this is of the utmost importance, after all," M. Huart said with pained dignity and a glance of deep distress at

Miss B. He lumbered forward to take up the throne again. "After all, this is the *most* important moment in a girl's life, is it not?"

The following Sunday, after mass, the real thing was to take place. Frédéric, who had been given only a month's leave by the Minister of War, the Count de Ségur, after his marriage, had been called back to his regiment, at Saint Omer, in the north of France near Calais. Lucy was not certain when she would see him again. He would probably not be able to return to see her until August and had been told he would not be allowed to show his face in Paris even then. There were rumors of France entering the conflict in Holland, in which case leave might be deferred for months.

Lucy was accompanied by Frédéric's aunt, the Princess d'Hénin. Lucy wore a corset made expressly for this moment, laced up behind, but not so tightly that one could not see the fine lawn chemise, which showed her pale skin. Her white shoulders and neck were naked except for seven or eight rows of large diamonds, which the Queen had been good enough to lend her. Diamonds were threaded through the strings that laced up her dress in front. Diamonds were in the mass of her hair. Diamonds and pearls and silver were embroidered in the skirt of her white dress.

Thanks to M. Huart's excellent training, Lucy approached the Queen, made her three curtsies, and took off her glove without mishap. The Queen smiled at her and leaned forward slightly and murmured kindly, "I see marriage agrees with you, my dear. You are radiant today." As she went through the room, Lucy felt her own radiance. She seemed to be floating as the Queen had once done in the *Salle des Spectacles* on the arm of the young guardsman.

She was aware that all eyes were on her, and that not all of them were benevolent. She heard whispers. Her grandmother and even her mother, she realized to her surprise, had made enemies at Court.

She overheard the Princess de Lamballe say in her silvery voice, "The daughter is not as pretty as the mother. Let us hope she will be more accommodating." Lucy gave the Princess one of her grandmother's piercing glances. She could hardly see her. The Princess, once the Queen's favorite, now displaced by the Countess Jules de Polignac, was a blur of whiteness: blue-white eyes, blond hair powdered white, white dress, pearls, which glimmered against her pale skin: *white on white. It was said that she was so sensitive that even the sight of the painting of a lobster made her faint. Poor Princess! She was to suffer the ultimate indignity.*

Now Lucy made a deep curtsy and received the King's abrupt and awkward greeting. He squinted at Lucy with his pale, near-sighted blue eyes. He did not recognize anyone more than three steps away. Like Monsieur, his younger brother, the King was terribly stout, his stomach protruding in his lace waistcoat. He waddled away from Lucy awkwardly, with no dignity of presence at all. Despite his magnificent clothes, covered with diamonds, Lucy thought the King, with his high shoulders, looked more like a peasant behind a plow. Perhaps he would have been happier that way.

Lucy pitied him. She had been told that he had not desired to be king. It was his older brother, the Dauphin, who was intelligent, charming, and imperious, who had wanted to be and should have been king had he not died too soon.

*How extraordinary to think that in 1757, only two years before Frédéric was born, Damiens, who was accused of attempting to kill Louis XVI's grandfather, Louis XV, was condemned to the amende honourable on the Place de Grève: his flesh torn from his breasts, arms, thighs, and calves with red-hot pincers; his right hand, holding the knife with which he was said to have committed the attempted regicide, burned with sulphur; and on the places where the flesh was torn away, molten lead, burning resin, wax, and sulphur were poured, and then his body was drawn and quartered, a process that was very long because the horses employed were not accustomed to this work and instead of four, six were used and when that was not enough, they cut off the wretch's thighs, in order to sever the sinews and hack at the joints. Damiens, who was well-known in his life as a swearer, was asked if he had anything to say. "Pardon, my God! Pardon, Lord," he repeated over and over again. Such had been the excessive power of the kings of France.*

*Yet now, the year of my presentation at court, France had a king who could not make up his mind and spent his time counting various things: the number of deer killed in the hunt, principally: so many dead animals. With his eyelids drooping, his lips downturned, he staggered like a sleepwalker through his days. What was he thinking: about his locks, his hunting, or the many finance ministers who came and went so confusingly? Turgot, Necker, Calonne, Loménie de Brienne? Was he really as dull as some said or was he just a bumbler, a fumbler, incapable of taking a decision? Was he really a good and kind and perhaps even an intelligent man put in an impossible position? Was he in a deep depression? Or besotted with alcohol and too much food?*

Lucy was greeted by the King's two younger brothers, the fat and the slim one. The Count of Artois, the slim one, was all charm. He was popular with the young ladies of the Court, affable, with a free and easy air.

By a great good fortune Philippe d'Orleans was absent that day so Lucy was spared shaking the hand of a man she already considered with much suspicion. *With his moon-face and dull glassy eyes, his elegant clothes, his love of pleasure, Philippe d'Orleans was a world-weary man of spoiled blood and sumptuous sordidness. He was stirring up the people against the King and Queen, though I was to see him often and even to assist at dinner at the Palais-Royal.*

From that day on, though Lucy was not yet a lady-in-waiting, the Queen had decided she would be one of the privileged few who had the honor of assisting her every Sunday in her bedchamber and at mass.

## III

$\mathcal{A}$LL IS INTRIGUE at the Court of Versailles. There are factions, cliques, cabals in an effort to gain the Queen's favor or to acquire influence with the King.

Envy is the emotion most frequently encountered. The gentlemen of the Court vie for the honor of holding the candle last for the King before he retires. This gives them a precious additional moment when a request can be placed, a favor granted.

### JULY, 1787

When she received an invitation from the Duke of Dorset, with the blunt order, "Ladies will wear white," Lucy said to her aunt, "This sort of thing annoys me. I don't like being told what to do and certainly not what to wear."

"It is what is requested, and it would be bad manners to disobey," her aunt said. Then, looking at her with a sidelong glance, she added, "But knowing you, I suppose you will do as you please."

Frédéric was with his regiment, so that Lucy went with her aunt as chaperone to the ball. Frédéric's absences, though Lucy missed him and felt lonely at times, also gave her a certain freedom to do as she wished. They allowed her, too, to imagine him as she desired, to preserve her idea of him in her mind.

She arrived late at the party, when the ladies were assembled in their white dresses, white gloves, white fans, and white shoes.

As she entered the crowded ballroom, sallying forth into this sea of white, there was a shocked silence. The guests stared at her. A murmur swept through the room like the wind on water.

She was wearing bright blue crepe, decorated with blue ribbons, blue gloves, and a blue fan, which fluttered in her hand. Perched in the turret of her mass of blond hair, Leonard, the famous hairdresser, had artfully placed two artificial bluebirds.

Despite her urge to do so, she did not smile, but looked around the room cooly, as if to say, *and what will you do about this?*

Her host, the English ambassador, the Duke of Dorset, a tall man with pale eyes and a distinguished manner, came forward to greet her. As he bent low over her blue-gloved hand, he murmured, though not sufficiently softly not to be overheard, "Ah, the unruly Irish!" There was a little ripple of applause in the room, whether for his words or her attire.

That evening Lucy became known as *Bluebird*.

Every Sunday at noon she congregated with forty other chosen women in the salon that led into the Queen's bedchamber. Except for the elderly ones who were allowed to sit down, they all stood, pressed one against another, because of the wide hoops under their skirts. Unthinkingly, they followed the rigid etiquette. The usher called out: "The service!" and the four ladies-in-waiting whose turn it was to assist the Queen, entered, followed by the rest. The shivering Queen had to stand and wait, while her garments were passed from one hand to the next until they finally came to her and she was able to cover herself against the cold.

At twelve forty-five the usher called out, "The King," and in he came, inclining his head right and left, speaking with the women he knew. He stumbled, half-blind, fumbling with his hat and his sword, seeming distracted.

At quarter past one everyone prepared for mass, the captain of the guard going on ahead, with the King and the Queen following. Behind them came the ladies according to rank, attempting to walk as near as possible to the crowd of courtiers, who murmured compliments to them. Lucy, who was popular, managed to find a place on the edges and to pick up many compliments as though she were Ruth, gleaning behind Boaz.

How she loved to be praised! To hear someone remark on her beautiful hair, her fine complexion, her graceful walk, made her cheeks flush, the world spin around her. She had spent so much of her youth alone, almost forgotten in her room on the Rue du Bac. She was like someone who has never drunk wine taking her first heady sip, or like someone who has once, long before, sipped on something delicious and then forgotten about it, only to find it again.

She walked skillfully, doing the famous Versailles shuffle, not lifting her feet, but skating forward as though she were on ice, slipping along on the well-polished parquet so as not to trample on the train of the lady before her. On she went between the mirrors and below the ceilings with their fine paintings. When they came to Hercules's salon, she threw her skirt to one side and rushed down the aisles of the chapel, in order to be as close as possible to the King and Queen and the princesses. A word from the Queen or the King was of great value.

Sometimes the Queen spoke to her and laughingly scolded her for the brightness of her clothes, the poppies she liked to entwine in her hair. In a loud voice, she complimented her from across the salon on her luminous skin, making Lucy blush. The Queen could be tactlessly cruel, offending the elderly women of the Court through this attitude.

Lucy watched it all and listened to the conversations around her. She would remember all of it vividly and would later write down

SHEILA KOHLER

her version of what had happened. When her life had brought her very far from that place and seemed to her like the drawings of scenes from someone else's album, she would take great pleasure in bringing it all back to life, making it live again as she wished others to see it.

*I remember the odor of pomatum that was applied to hold the powder I wore in my hair. I remember the sound of the slippers skating across the parquet, the brilliant light coming in the windows caught in the glass facets of the chandeliers. I remember the whispered compliments and how they flattered my young and starved vanity.*

Unlike many of the ladies at the Court, she did not flirt with the men, treating them instead as if they were her brothers. Frédéric had been made colonel of his regiment at Saint Omer and was obliged to stay there, leaving her free to make him up in her mind.

# IV

## 1787

Lucy wrote Frédéric long daily letters which he preserved until the end of his life. He replied less frequently, and in his wild handwriting, so that she sometimes complained she was unable to decipher his message. He had little time to write to her. He was busy striving to reform his regiment. He had plans for improving the entire army. He would promote men through a series of examinations, testing the ability to understand military matters rather than to curry favor with the Queen or the King. He wrote that the French army, like the Roman, was losing its ability to instill the necessary discipline and strength to fight. Like many noblemen of his age, he had been impressed as a boy with the virtues of the Roman Republic. He wanted to expel from the army an ethos of privilege and replace it with a neo-Roman ideal of patriotic sacrifice, physical courage, and, above all, strict observance of discipline.

He wrote,

*"I received your letter this morning, my dear heart, with great joy. My thoughts are with you constantly, though I am much occupied here and often distressed by the business at hand. The spirit of the regiment is not what I might have wished it to be. It is all, I am afraid, the fault of the preceding colonel, M. d'Ussun, who was married to one of the Queen's Ladies of the Robe, and an indolent fellow himself. He received his position through connections. He allowed the officers to do exactly as they pleased and failed to curb the excesses of privilege or their disorderly conduct. They do nothing*

*but boast of having twenty-eight Knights of Malta among their numbers, carouse through the night, and refuse to present themselves for duty. I cannot get them to appear for exercises at dawn. If they cannot set an example for the men to follow, who will? An army cannot succeed like this, it seems to me.*

When Frédéric was able to leave his regiment finally in August, he joined his wife and his aunt on the Rue de Verneuil. To his great joy, Lucy had written to say she was expecting a child and could thus not travel with her grandmother and her great-great-uncle to Montpellier. She had left the Hotel Dillon to go and stay with the Princess d'Hénin on the Rue de Verneuil. He was glad she was safely with his aunt, who would not torment her as he knew her grandmother continued to do.

In the ground floor apartment, which looked onto a small back garden, Frédéric rose from his bed and went down the corridor into her room, finding his way in the light of a pale and hesitant moon. He parted the curtains and leaned over her bed. She slept more soundly than he did, her breath even and so quiet, that for a moment he was afraid she was not breathing. She did not hear the loud rumbling of the carriage wheels on the cobblestones, the horses' hooves, or the violent cries. A thin shift exposed her shoulders and breasts. Youth, but not innocence, he thought, even in sleep. She was a woman who knew what she wanted. Even her mass of hair seemed to curl around her face with determination.

He leaned over her and breathed her in. She felt his presence and sat up, and he lay down beside her. She took off her shift, and they stared at her altered body in the moonlight. She lay back and turned on her side, reached an arm above his head, and smiled at him. He kept very still, listening to his heart, the pound and pump of it. He gazed at her. She opened his hand and set it on her heavy breast. "Ripe melons," he whispered, looking at the darkened nipples, feeling the weight of the breast in his hand.

She stroked his body, reaching down and down along his legs to his toes and then all the way up to his ears, cupping them in her hands, smoothing the crown of his head, his thinning hair, as though she would have liked to gather all of him to her, to keep him snug within her. He imagined this child, a little Tour du Pin, an heir.

He lay still beside Lucy, luxuriating in the warmth of the summer night, her caresses, the swelling of his heart, the hope of a child. He lay with his hands behind his head, as if indifferent, imagining his child's head resting in his lap. Somehow he knew not to touch Lucy but to wait for her to move first, though all his nerves, his thoughts, his hopes reached out to her from every part of his body like beating wings.

She rose up over him, straddled his legs. He heard her laugh with the pleasure and freedom of it, felt the lap of humid air on his skin. She licked his face, then kissed his lips with such abandon and heat, sighing and tonguing and biting his mouth. He thought he would never know her completely. She would always remain strange to him, this Irishwoman, so unlike his image of his distant mother. He buried his head between her swollen breasts, rooting in her flesh, for her essence. He felt the swing and hum of them, as he turned her beneath him and entered her body, diving down into the wet heat of her, as the night sounds swam through his mind.

She was awake early, and they went out riding at first light. As he rode at her side, following the sun, he forgot the trouble in the army. He watched her galloping, *en Amazone*, with technical precision, head high, hands light and firm and eager on the reins, as they had been on his body in the night, going on beside him, all silvery slim in her gray English riding dress, a blue veil over her face. He watched the gold light and shade flicker fast on her form, as they went through the pines. He marveled at his joy in her.

Though it was fashionable at Court to complain about everything—his friends who were capable of losing huge sums on the gaming table complained at having to give a small sum for the Queen's charity—he felt fortunate to be with Lucy at the Court, so joyous at his side. She told him she was truly happy for the first time. With him she felt anything was now possible.

## V

ENGLAND, FRANCE'S ANCIENT enemy, is loved, hated, and admired. Cultured men and women admire the English Constitution, the English national character, English clothes. The aristocracy even adopts an English accent. English words pepper the French language. A jockey is a *jokei*; a riding coat a *redingote*. English racers are trained for French races. Lucy is admired because she looks English.

### AUTUMN, 1787

Lucy sat beside the Princess d'Hénin in her open carriage. Her pregnancy was not yet visible. Dressed up in her English shoes with the buckles, her blue English bonnet with its ruffle around her face, she accompanied Frédéric's aunt to the races at Longchamp. A stream of carriages, gilded and colorful as moving flower beds, advanced together through the Bois de Boulogne, rolling steadily in the warm late-fall air, under a blue sky. The leaves of the chestnut trees hung down like ripe fruit.

Lucy felt well despite her pregnancy, or because of it, and the hope she carried within her. Her skin had never been more glowing, she had thought, when she sat before her mirror and had her maid prepare her to go out. She did not suffer from morning sickness and continued to ride horseback and to accompany the Princess on daily outings.

She and her aunt also went to the theater. Everywhere she went, her aunt accompanied her this first year of her marriage, for it was not customary for a young woman to go out alone then.

Her aunt did not allow her to mope at home, waiting for Frédéric's return. Besides, Lucy was seventeen, and how could she resist? She had a fierce longing for pleasure, now that she had left her grandmother's dark house and critical presence.

*As I had during childhood, I preferred to combat any inclination to melancholy with action and more action. We were always going somewhere. We continued to laugh and dance, obliviously, on the edge of the precipice.*

With her aunt, who knew everyone and was welcomed everywhere, Lucy felt free to go about as she wished. They visited the three women who were considered the smartest in society, women who had a considerable influence as they received or did not receive: the Princess de Poix, whose husband was so small he was called the Little Pea; the Duchess de Biron, and the Maréchale de Luxembourg. These were the ones whom everyone sought out: intelligent women, impeccably dressed, outspoken, well-educated, and brilliantly accomplished.

Lucy made a point of going to see her mother's old friends, the people who had quarreled with her grandmother. She returned to the house of the Rochechoart family, where all three generations appeared to live in complete harmony. There she joined in the musical evenings. She sang the contralto roles with great pleasure and to much applause.

She visited Mme. de Montesson, who loved Frédéric like a son. Lucy, unlike the unfortunate Queen, understood what Laclos says in *Les Liaisons Dangereuses*: "Old women must not be angered, for they make young women's reputations." The Queen, she was beginning to understand, was not good at choosing her friends.

Lucy was half in love with her witty, elegant aunt, eighteen years older than she, who sat beside her this autumn day, in her bonnet with its bow on the crown and the ruffle around her neck. Her aunt had so generously welcomed her into her home, encouraging her to be a modern woman with a mind of her own.

As they went through the Bois, they saw a carriage approaching, identical to theirs, the double: the proud white horses, the harnesses, the livery of the footmen, even the escutcheon on the side of the coach with the family's arms. Lucy had the somewhat disagreeable impression of seeing herself in a mirror, except that she was not present in the mirror-image. Nor was her aunt. The occupant of the carriage was a flamboyant red-haired woman, splendidly attired in a low-cut bright-green dress and a silk hat that rose like a tower above her head, finished off with plumes and ribbons waving above her. Her parasol bloomed like a giant green flower.

Lucy grasped the Princess's gloved hand and watched her turn slightly pale beneath her rouge. She twitched her shoulders beneath her dark silk wrap. Her eyes turned darker in the bright sunlight. Lucy asked, "Who on earth is she?"

"Sophie Arnould. Actress at the Comédie Francaise," the Princess replied, gazing into the deeper distance, as though she could see no one at all.

Lucy hissed, scandalized, "What gall! How dare she use your livery."

The Princess shrugged. "My only complaint is that the girl is ruining my husband. She's horribly extravagant," and she laughed and turned toward Lucy. She looked at Lucy's face and said, "You will find that morality is worn lightly at the Court." She reminded Lucy what the Duc de Richelieu had said when he found his wife in bed with a lover: "Just think what an embarrassment, if anyone but myself had discovered you!"

Her aunt looked at her and said, "My marriage was arranged

for me when I was very young, and I have never allowed it to stop me from enjoying my life." She spoke of herself as though she were telling an anecdote about someone else.

"Haven't you ever wondered what it would be like to make love to a man simply because he pleases you?" she asked with a wicked little grin.

Lucy scowled and said that, indeed, her husband did please her. She wished he were here. The Princess gave her a tap on her cheek with her gloved hand and said, "Really, darling, and all the time?"

Lucy questioned her aunt about the absence of her husband, the separate lives they led, but her aunt shrugged and replied, speaking of her husband's activities, "I'm delighted the man has found an occupation, my dear. An unemployed man is so dull." She assured Lucy that she had found several substitutes for him. She said, "You will see with time that monogamy can be rather dull." As long as certain formalities were fulfilled, the Princess suggested, anything was possible. She added, "You seem to think of Frédéric as a lover, not a husband. Rather dangerous in my opinion, my dear. Better to preserve a certain distance."

# VI

## LATE AUTUMN, 1787

The Princess d'Hénin was a great admirer of the theories and books of the controller general of finance, the Swiss banker Jacques Necker. When she was invited to Mme. Necker's salon, she insisted Lucy attend with her. "The woman is very powerful. Everyone wants an invitation. We must go together, and you must meet her," she told Lucy. "As Malebranche saw all things in God, so M. Necker sees all in Madame Necker." Lucy laughed. Apparently the severe Swiss woman had been loved by many famous men including Gibbon, whom Frédéric struggled with in English and so admired.

There was a mixed group of people within these halls: philosophers, poor poets, finance ministers, writers of note, and the aristocracy all mingled in a way that Lucy had never seen before. She caught a glimpse of the notorious Laclos, a man in his late forties, tall and angular with cold blue eyes. It was he who had become the secretary to Philippe d'Orleans and was very useful to him with his schemes, her aunt told her in a low voice.

"Now that book will tell you about life," she said, speaking of the *Liaisons Dangereuses*, which had been an instant best seller.

"Would you like to meet him?" she asked Lucy.

Lucy looked him over but thought his haughty appearance and pallid countenance discouraged any kind of intimacy. With his sharp nose and glittering gaze, she thought he looked rather like a rat. "Félicité de Genlis said she would relinquish her position if he became secretary," Lucy said, speaking of Philippe d'Orleans's mistress, the governess of his children and a writer in her own right.

"I doubt that troubled him much," her aunt said, moving on.

They made their way through the throng of people. The Princess pointed out a group who stood around Turgot, the former controller general of finance. "They are known as the Economists, very brilliant, though they don't seem to have found a solution to the national debt," she told Lucy. They spoke to various people, including the Duke de Lauzun, who said Lucy resembled her lovely mother, but when he saw another woman approaching, he muttered, "Oh God! Here comes Suzanne. Be prepared for a long speech. When God made that woman, he stiffened her with starch in and out," and turned from them and disappeared.

They were accosted by a tall, thin, tightly corseted woman, overdressed in a red silk pelisse. She was trussed up, Lucy thought, like a packet of tobacco. Mme. Necker held forth at great length in a pedantic tone. Perhaps it was her deafness which led her to do this, but she seemed too poised and too precise. She became increasingly irritating as she went on about *her* health, *her* fear of imminent death, *her* darling daughter, Germaine de Staël, and the poor in the hospital *she* had established for them. Lucy wondered what her grandmother would have made of her. Here was someone who had not learned the art of drawing others out.

"Each with his own bed and great cleanliness in his care, and all watched over by the Sisters of Charity," she told Lucy and the Princess. She talked of the necessity of filling each hour of the day with a useful occupation. She drew herself up and said somewhat sanctimoniously that she herself, of course, rose at four in the morning. She said, "God gave me twenty-four hours to spend each day and each one of them must be regulated. I have only one aim and that is to please everyone as much as possible."

"A difficult aim to fulfill," the Princess d'Hénin replied with a little smile, but the Swiss woman was not endowed with humor or the gift of irony.

She even confessed her fear of death, or rather of being buried alive. In a low voice she whispered her plans: she would make sure her death was confirmed by all sorts of tests, and her body embalmed in alcohol, so that her husband's and her daughter's could eventually join hers in the mausoleum she was preparing for their death.

"And that reassures you?" the Princess asked, raising her fine eyebrows, glancing at Lucy.

Lucy suppressed her desire to laugh. She did not laugh when Mme. Necker said this extreme fear had come to her at the time of childbirth. She confessed that if she had known what that process involved, she would never have embarked upon it. "Nothing would have dragged me to the altar. How do women do this again and again, risking their lives? Once was more than enough for me," she said to the childless Princess.

Lucy, feeling her baby kick, turned away from this clever woman from Geneva, who had married the wealthy controller general of finance when she was twenty-seven without a penny to her name. With relief Lucy talked to Suzanne's dark-haired, plain daughter, Germaine de Staël, whom Frédéric had mentioned as a friend.

*At twenty-one Germaine was a lively woman. She wore a beige dress showing off her décolleté and plump, rounded arms. She had a warm physical presence, and was not at all the narrow female scholar I had expected. Unlike her mother, she was unpretentious, and anxious to please, and obviously intelligent.*

She stared at Lucy with her wide-spaced dark eyes, which seemed not quite to match, her thick lips slightly open. She said, "I would gladly give you half the wit I'm credited with for half your beauty."

"But beauty, I'm afraid, fades fast, while wit may be preserved, and indeed, improved with age," Lucy replied.

"You seem to possess both," Germaine said and looked directly at her. She had about her a certain dreamy voluptuousness, which contrasted with her quick words. Lucy liked looking into her eyes and felt warmed by her gaze.

As for the famous Necker himself, Lucy caught only a glimpse of him. To her surprise, she saw him sucking his thumb, as he walked in one door and then out another.

But it was at the theater that Lucy met someone quite by chance, who would be even more important in her life. Almost every evening Lucy and her aunt went to the theater, after reading the reviews in the *Journal de Paris*. Lucy enjoyed dressing up and being seen in the Queen's box. She and her aunt were among the few privileged people allowed to use the Queen's box at the Opéra, at the Comédie Francaise, and at the Comédie Italienne.

The boxes were like elegant lounges, well-heated and provided with everything necessary to arrange one's hair or clothes. There was even a table where she could write, and books were provided, and an antechamber for the servants.

They saw Beaumarchais's *Le Mariage de Figaro*; Voltaire's *Irene*; where the Princess d'Hénin told Lucy how she had heard the old man, a sage among sages, celebrated before his death.

In an interval, a young girl entered their box and stood shyly in the shadows in a green dress. She came forward to greet Lucy and moved with the grace of Diana, the huntress. She seemed only fourteen or fifteen, but tall for her age, dark-skinned, dark-haired, and very slim. She spoke with a slight Spanish accent, and her voice was deep. She was Thérésia Cabarus, the daughter, the Princess told her, of Cabarus, a Spanish merchant.

*All the days of my life I would remember Thérésia's lovely face, the blue-black hair, the smile that exposed perfectly regular white teeth, the dusting of dark hair on her upper lip. At the time, of course, I did not know that the beautiful young girl would become Mme. de Fontenoy and later Tallien's lover, and would save my life.*

## VII

It was at the theater, too, one misty evening in the winter of 1788, that Lucy was taken ill. She had been at Versailles, running to arrive at the service on time, and she had slipped and fallen, when her panier caught on the side of a door. Now she had to leave the Queen's box with stomach cramps. She leaned on Frédéric's arm as she felt the warm blood trickling down her leg as it had for the first time that morning as a girl, alone, in her room on the Rue du Bac. Frédéric helped her to climb into their waiting carriage. She bent over in the dark and held his hand, as she felt the promise of this new life seeping from her, staining her dress crimson. She thought of how disappointed her father-in-law would be, this heir to the ancient name no longer a promise. She lay flat on her back, losing blood, hoping to save the baby. She told Frédéric to go to Saint Sulpice and light a candle but in vain.

When they arrived back from Montpellier, a few days after she had lost the baby, she was still weak from the loss of blood, and too melancholy to want to confront her grandmother and uncle. She turned her face to the blue, silk-covered wall. She wanted them to leave her alone. The only creatures she wanted near her were Frédéric, and the two Siamese cats that lay on the end of her bed on the white counterpane, looking almost blue.

She glanced around the small room and thought of Hautefontaine, and the hunts she had gone on with her mother in the summer and autumn. She saw its vast walled garden, where she had been free to roam, the privilege of the silence in the early morning when she woke in her bed. In her mind she wandered through the empty, secret rooms where she had never ventured as a child, peering into the angles and nooks in the garden she had never explored.

Here was a white azalea in the *jardinière*, the petals translucent in the pale morning light. Her baby lost, lying in her aunt's room, she felt hollow, hardly a person, a shadow of herself, a ghost. She heard the muffled voices of her husband, her uncle, and the Princess, outside her door. She heard her grandmother say, "I insist," in a loud angry voice.

Lucy propped herself up on one arm, reached for the glass of sugared water on the nightstand, and drank it down. She hoped Frédéric would stand firm and convince her grandmother to depart. He was often too gracious, too polite, incapable of being rude when he needed to be. "People will not take you seriously if you are always so polite," she had told him.

Now she heard the Princess say warningly, "I assure you, she's really too ill to see anyone. The doctor has ordered—" but her grandmother had already burst into the room in her bonnet, her black taffeta skirts rustling, the cold morning air entering with her. She stared down at Lucy with her dark gaze, which had once, perhaps, been luminous but was now only stinging. She seemed untouched by humanity.

She ordered Lucy to rise and come home immediately. "I suppose this is some kind of trick just to avoid me," she said, coming nearer. "You look well enough to me—rosy-cheeked as usual. You're not the first to miscarry, after all. An ordinary event." Lucy felt her cheeks flush with anger.

She was followed by Lucy's uncle, the Archbishop, who seemed to fill the small room and not know what to do with his large hands, his feet, his hat in this sickroom. He cleared his throat, and said, "Lucy Cary, dear, please—"

Her grandmother sniffed and said, "Nonsense, my granddaughter has always been strong. Never been sick a day in her life, apart from the smallpox and even that took nothing but her eyelashes."

"You are no longer in charge here," Frédéric said at last. Lucy Cary turned her back on him. She ignored this Count she had never liked or trusted, this Count of no account. She moved around the room, picking up a silver-backed hairbrush, a pin, a mirror. She made a gesture, and the two Siamese cats jumped off the bed with a plaintive, childlike cry.

Lucy Cary said to her granddaughter, "You have no need of your grandmother anymore, I suppose. Is that it?"

The Archbishop said, "Please, the girl is suffering, the child—"

Her grandmother turned fiercely, and said, "Rubbish, Richard. Tell my granddaughter to come home now. Enough of this nonsense. Not good to loll about here, feeling sorry for oneself."

Lucy said nothing, but reached up and took her uncle's hand, looking up at him beseechingly. A mistake, obviously.

Her grandmother smoothed down her bodice, adjusted her powdered wig, like an animal fastidiously shaking off any trace of contact, interrupting any current of feeling between Lucy and her uncle.

"I know you've been gadding about. I've heard of your successes, your showing off. Bluebird, is it?" She laughed nastily, working herself up into a rage. "Undoubtedly you're paying for some imprudence at Versailles."

Lucy sat up slightly and said, "I have tried to see some of Maman's old friends. People have been very kind. The Queen…"

"Hah! The Queen! And you've been seeing the Rochechouarts. I can imagine what must have been said about me."

The Princess, who had entered the room with a bunch of freesias in her hand, interrupted softly, "Perhaps *this* conversation could be put off for a more propitious moment, Madame?"

"She certainly seems very comfortably installed here," Lucy Cary responded, striding about the small room impatiently, surveying the fire, the English engravings on the walls, the English books on the windowsill, the plants in the *jardinière*, the French doors opening onto the bleak little winter garden.

"We have done what we can for her, in your absence," the Princess replied.

"Yes, well, she and that husband of hers might just as well remain where they are, then—permanently," Lucy's grandmother said, and plucked a stray thread from her sleeve and threw it emphatically into the fire. Obviously she saw no need to indulge an incompliant world.

"What do you mean?" Lucy's aunt asked.

Lucy looked up at her grandmother and asked, despite herself, hearing the sound of pleading creeping into her voice, which came to her with echoes of her mother's, "You don't want us home, Grandmother, when I am well?"

# VIII

℘EVEN MONTHS HAVE passed since Lucy was banished from the Rue du Bac. A time of excess. Fashions have gone wild: ladies wear their hair piled so high they must kneel to get into their carriages; gentlemen, priceless embroidered waistcoats with hunting scenes and gold buttons, any one of which is worth more than Marguerite will earn in several lifetimes. The King's cousin, Philippe d'Orleans, is exiled to Villers-Cotterets, but when the Parlement refuses to pass any bill unless he is pardoned, he is allowed to return to Raincy.

## OCTOBER, 1788

Marguerite rose at dawn in her mansard. It was a cold autumn morning, and there was no fireplace in her room. As she peered out the narrow window at the gray sky she could see it was starting to rain lightly. She pulled on black stockings and a black dress over the heavy cotton petticoat, which she had not taken off in bed. She donned her gray jacket and a scarf. She slipped a piece of dry bread into her pocket, drank a little water directly from the pitcher, and took up her umbrella and the small valise she had prepared the night before with the white clothes she had knitted. She went quietly and quickly down the back steps, which smelled of urine, slipped out a side door, and stepped into the narrow, malodorous street.

She hurried over the irregular stones, greeting the white-haired prelate with his scarlet sash about his waist on his way to early mass and the apothecary, who already stood on the corner of the street outside his shop. Servants opened doors, buckets of soapy water were spilled, and the floors were scrubbed, the night soil removed.

She went on, turning down narrow streets, the houses tightly packed one next to the other. She went past bars, where workmen already stood drinking a glass of red wine, through the market-place, where women displayed fish, fruit, and raw meat scented with herbs. She walked across squares, holding her umbrella over her head, coming now to another market where clusters of poor women and men with cadaverous faces eked out an existence in squalid filth. The stench of sulphur rose in the early morning air. There was little here that even a dog would consume: potato peelings, eggshells, rotting fish bones. In the gray light she could see these market women huddled beside rows of low hovels, hiding in the protection of anything that might provide shelter. She thought of all those secret hearts beating in the dim light of dawn, and said a short prayer for their souls: *Lord help them and keep them from temptation.*

She had been back to her village that summer to take her wages to her elderly parents, as she did twice a year, and had been saddened by their plight. They had always been poor, but in July there had been a terrible hailstorm that had ruined the crops. There was blight, followed by drought. The grass was burned. Flecks of yellow-brown mottled the leaves. Bread had become dearer. Trade was stagnant. Hunger roamed abroad.

Her father had lifted his blind eyes up to the sky and said, "Consider the lilies of the field, how they grow; they toil not, neither do they spin: And yet I say unto you, That even Solomon in all his glory was not arrayed like one of these."

She turned her eyes away from a young man lying in the gutter, his hat fallen from his head. Dead drunk, if not something worse, she thought. Someone called out something to a policeman, and the crowd huddled around, all of which she ignored, hurrying on, the edge of her black skirt dragging in the mud.

Then she caught sight of the cart carrying vegetables and her cousin, his back square and broad against the early morning light. He had promised her a lift to Passy, if she could join him early enough on the Rue Sainte Antoine. One of the servants had told Marguerite that Lucy had moved into her aunt's house in Passy, not far from Paris. Marguerite had not seen her darling child since her banishment from the Rue du Bac. She had heard she was pregnant again, though she had been obliged to continue to go to Versailles to attend the Queen for the first three months, but not to mass, for fear she might slip on the smooth parquet.

Marguerite had repeatedly asked Lucy's grandmother if she might have permission to join her for the birth.

"It is not necessary. She has her own people there," she had said haughtily.

Finally, Marguerite, having heard that her cousin was going not far from Passy, had persuaded him to drop her off. Lucy would need her at the moment of the birth.

Now she called out to him, panting a little with the effort of her long, hurried walk through the streets, and he turned in his gray hat and smock, pulling on the reins of his fat dray horse. He smiled, waved a hand, and helped her up onto the cart beside him.

He asked her what was going on in the Archbishop's house. She shook her head and clucked her tongue disapprovingly. There was no religion there. People had gone crazy, in her humble opinion.

Now the drizzle ceased, and the sun shone. Blond stubble of wheat spread around them, and weeping willows trailed their bare branches along the banks of the river. She wondered if the Count would be able to leave his regiment, to join Lucy here for the birth.

All through the hot nights of that summer, sleep had failed Marguerite. She thought of the child, and of her Lucy. Once, she had dreamed that Lucy had given birth to a small furry animal with a narrow black snout. It lay horribly still between her legs. Despite her dream, Marguerite would rise at dawn and embroider the Count's initials on the white baby clothes.

Her cousin dropped her off near the house where Lucy was staying. Looking up at the French windows in the misty late November day, as she walked up the driveway with her wicker valise, Marguerite saw someone striding rapidly up and down with a book in her hands. Then the front door was flung open. "Marguerite!" Lucy called out joyfully, as though she had been waiting for her arrival. Despite her girth, she ran lightly down the steps to greet her.

"She didn't want me to, but I came anyway," Marguerite said.

## IX

𝒯HE ESTATES GENERAL has been called forth by the King for the first time since 1614. "What would Louis XIV have said," the old Duke de Richelieu says.

The national deputies are to meet and the election of deputies to begin. After the failure of the Council of Notables, the Three Estates—the Aristocracy, the Clergy, and the Third Estate comprised of professional men and middle-class intelligentsia—are summoned to solve the question of the deficit. All of France is to be consulted or at least voice their complaints, their wishes, and elect their delegates.

### WINTER, 1789

Water gushed down her legs as her hairdresser piled up her hair. She sent him away and walked up and down in her room, and along the long corridor with its windows on the bare winter garden. She skated along like the women at Versailles in her slippers. "I feel better when I'm moving," she told the doctor who had been summoned and would have her sit down or lie on the bed. Marguerite walked at her side, holding her arm and fanning her face. "Don't you talk," she told her, squeezing her arm. Finally, she convinced Lucy to lie down, to let her rub her aching back. A messenger had been sent to tell Frédéric that the labor had begun.

There was a fire blazing in the fireplace, and Lucy saw the

hibiscus on the windowsill close their petals on the night. Light came and went. There were many people crowded in the room, the doctors, *accoucheurs*, and women around the bed. The curtains whispered the way they did when she was a child, and she thought she caught sight of someone standing in the folds. Something with the laurel crown glimmered white or off white in the corner of the room. This old friend did not surprise her. She remembered her from long ago, when she had the smallpox.

*I will not cry out.* At moments of respite she reached out to clutch Marguerite's familiar rough fingers. She remembered them brushing her hair, helping her to dress, sewing on a button, stroking her forehead, and she smiled at her old nurse, who had taught her what she knows about love.

Then the pain resumed in aching crescendos, and Lucy twisted back and forth on the bed, closing her eyes, concentrating. When she felt she could bear no more, she lost consciousness and slipped away. A great peacefulness descended on her. Much time passed. She was with the White Lady in the field of soft, deep snow.

The dead stillness of the room woke her. Surely there should be more noise, bustle. Something was wrong. There were people near her bed, their faces bending over her as in a dream, strange faces, grimacing. She looked up hopefully into the familiar broad face, the ruddy cheeks. Marguerite was standing over her with the baby in her arms. Lucy reached out. Marguerite said nothing, but wept softly and shook her head.

*Someone else was there. I saw her clearly standing over me. I could smell her rank animal smell. I had always thought she was taller, more commanding, and polite—an aristocrat, after all. Now I realized that she was short, stocky, and even had a slight paunch. An ordinary presence, a commoner, of course, in her dusty white dress, her untidy kerchief, her rumpled clothes—Death.*

Lucy reached up for her baby. She said, "Please." Lucy held her, blue as the bluebirds Lucy had worn so gaily in her hair. She put her hand on the brow, felt the soft skin still warm from her own body, and touched the perfect blue hands and feet, and it seemed to her that the child opened her eyes for a moment and stared at her with her mother's surprised blue gaze.

*The baby had strangled on the cord.*

"The Lord bless her and keep her; the Lord make his face to shine on her, and be gracious unto her; the Lord lift up his countenance upon her and give her peace..." Marguerite said, and gently dislodged the baby from Lucy's arms. Then Lucy slipped away again for a while, wandered across the white field where the air was cool, a breeze blowing.

She believed Frédéric was at her side now. He had joined her in her dream, and they were both running together across the soft, deep snow. An icy wind was whipping her long hair about her face. She could feel her bare feet treading in the snow that gave way, so that she could not advance, and she was terribly cold. She was sinking down through the cold earth. Frédéric's arms were colder than her own, and he was not able to warm her.

She woke shaking with fever and regret. Marguerite was trying to bring down her fever with cool cloths on her forehead. She had succumbed to the puerperal fever.

She saw clearly the dumpy, fair woman in the dusty white dress, Death, who reached her arms out to her. She felt a great lassitude, an aching in her bones. The useless milk oozed painfully from her swollen breasts like pus, the blood seeped between her legs, her breath tasted sour. She was rotting away.

Vaguely she was aware of the women around her: Marguerite and the Princess and even the devoted Miss B., who had somehow reappeared unaccountably reading to her in French most tiresomely from *Paul and Virginie*, with tears in her blue eyes. What was this ridiculous story of a girl who drowns because she will not remove her clothes? Lucy had allowed the midwife to examine her. Better her life than some sort of absurd modesty.

They brought her chicken broth and spooned it into her mouth. They changed the flowers in the vases; she smelled the odor of the stale water being thrown out the window; hands were holding her gently; they rolled her over to change her damp, greasy sheets. She sat in a chair while they turned her mattress. Someone read to her now from the *Gazette*. She knew the gentle, cultured voice, a light green voice. He was reading something about a royal edict. She became aware that Frédéric was at her side, sitting in a low chair by her bed, reading to her. She reached her hand out to him.

"My darling dear, my daisy flower," he said in his terrible English accent, and then continued to read from his paper. He said he was touched at the thought of these many humble men voicing their opinions, electing their parish priests who at least would know how to write down their grievances.

"May the people find a solution to France's ills," Frédéric said and sighed. He hoped to be elected as a delegate in the Isère. He believed this crisis would be beneficial to France. Like Lucy, he felt strongly that certain reforms were necessary, though he continued to believe in the Divine Right of Kings. Was Necker, the Swiss, wise to unleash the French masses? Though this scheme might work very well in Switzerland, where the cantons sent forth their obedient and respectful citizens who gladly elected whomever they were asked to elect, might it fail in France?

Lying in bed, she heard the sounds around her altered, and the room looked different. The curtains, when the maid drew them back, looked thinner, less blue. The sky seemed white. She felt a great weariness.

She remembered lying in bed sick, as a child, and reading *Cleveland* for the first time. How it had delighted her. She had been drawn in immediately by the story of Cromwell's mistress and, how she had been, before that, the mistress of Charles I—what an extraordinary life. The beheading of a King. How could it have occurred? *Perhaps among the English, who seemed able to change their kings too easily, I thought, but not in France.*

# PART NINE

## Revolution

*A*N EXCEPTIONALLY COLD winter, the worst since 1709. Philippe d'Orleans sells the entire contents of his magnificent art gallery at the Palais Royal and distributes money among the poor.

The Queen, annoyed by the people's response to her public appearances, rarely shows herself in Paris anymore. She gives up her royal boxes. The King, expected to bring the privileged into line and to protect the people against the corrupt agencies of administration, continues to hunt in the forests around Versailles. Camille Desmoulins publishes in his pamphlets: "Patriotism spreads day by day, with the devouring rapidity of a great conflagration."

While Lucy recovers slowly in her aunt's house in Passy, the rest of the aristocracy continues to enjoy its amusements. The nobles apparently think of nothing else. The Duke d'Orleans races his horses against those of the Duke d'Artois. Royalty sees nothing and foresees nothing. Intrigue, lies, false dreams, imbecilities whirl like pollen in the spring breezes.

SPRING, 1789

It was coming back from the races at Vincennes in her aunt's carriage, one afternoon, that Lucy had her first encounter with what she came to think of as that fickle and changeable phenomenon: the mob. Four or five hundred people, a coalition of malcontents, were blocking their route in the Rue Saint Antoine. The street was choked with timber, tumult, and the press of men, busily attacking Réveillon's wallpaper warehouse, despite the intervention of the Swiss guards.

She saw someone in the livery of the Duke d'Orleans exciting the mob, with an inflammatory speech that ended with "Long live our father! Long live our King d'Orleans!" She was convinced these people had been bought with Orleans's gold, stirred up, and inflamed by agitators: Philippe d'Orleans's people. She believed this was yet another example of the King's cousin's nefarious doings, stirring up the people against the respectable artisan in order to create confusion.

Some whispered that it was the useless aristocracy's fault, and others blamed France's traditional enemy: England. Whoever was responsible, the poor, decent man, Réveillon, was ruined and had to take shelter in the Bastille. Four or five hundred people had been killed and insurrection had served its apprenticeship.

## II

*I*N May, the delegates arrive en masse at Versailles. They scurry around looking for lodgings. In the Princess d'Hénin's apartment, whose terrace overlooks the Rue de la Surintendence, Lucy and Frédéric Séraphin wish, as many do, that the opening of the Estates General will bring a solution to France's woes. They all hope that the coming together of the three states, Clergy, Nobility, and the Third Estate, the Commoners, will undertake the necessary reforms to regenerate France.

Do they know that walking among the Commons at the opening of the Estates General is a tall and rather corpulent and genial-looking man, the respectable practitioner, the professor of anatomy at the University of Paris, Dr. Guillotine?

### MAY, 1789

That day in May, Lucy, like everyone else who could find a window, or a corner of vantage of any kind, watched the procession that opened the Estates General. Only Frédéric had refused to come and watch, annoyed at not being elected to the assembly when so many of his friends had been, and notably the Viscount de Noailles, the brother of the Prince de Poix.

*Frédéric's vanity, like Marie Antoinette's, was hurt.*

Lucy stood with other women of the nobility, including Madame de Montmorin, and Germaine de Staël, in her brown silk dress, her rounded arms bare, her dark curly hair dressed extravagantly with gray plumes. Frédéric had often spoken of Germaine de Staël and her life to Lucy. She had confessed to him how easily she abandoned herself to any man who found her worthy of his passion. Germaine de Staël, though she had married the Swedish ambassador, still lived with her parents, the Neckers. She was, Lucy knew, also particularly friendly with Frédéric's friend, Alexander de Lameth, who leaned over the parapet beside her and watched the procession.

Lucy did not entirely approve of Alexander. She wondered if his judgment was sound and his revolutionary ideas wise under the circumstances. She was afraid of what might be the result of this nobleman's generous but rash ideas.

Now the plump Germaine stood between Lucy and Alexander de Lameth, and the feathers in her hair shook as she spoke with youthful enthusiasm at this sight, for the first time in France, of these representatives of the people. There was music in the air, as the doors of the Church of Saint Louis opened, and the procession proceeded to Notre Dame.

Lucy watched the six hundred members of the Commons march forth in plain black coats and white cravats. They had refused to wear the uniform the King had suggested for them and had adopted this costume. The grave faces of these dignified lawyers, magistrates, and solicitors showed pride. They stepped forth firmly, hopefully, between the French and Swiss guards who lined the way.

Madame de Montmorin pointed out Gabriel de Mirabeau in their midst. "Good God, look at Mirabeau! What's the man doing marching with the Commons!"

"He was determined to be elected, one way or another, I presume," Alexander de Lameth said.

"As ugly as he is evil," Madame de Montmorin said.

"An excellent orator and rather like Samson, with all that hair, don't you think?" Germaine remarked.

"And like Samson, I suspect, about to pull down the house," Madame de Montmorin said.

*Indeed poor Madame de Montmorin's house was about to be pulled down: she was to die on the scaffold as were her two sons; her husband, like the Princess de Lamballe, would die in the September massacres and her younger daughter would die before thirty, crushed by so much death around her.*

Lucy looked down at the Marquis de Mirabeau with his huge head of dark, thick hair, his pockmarked face, and his height.

"It was the Commons who elected him as no one else would," Germaine explained.

What role would this man play in this gathering? Lucy wondered. A reputation as an eloquent orator, his grievances nursed in long months in prison. One of his mad Riquetti ancestors had chained two mountains together to fulfill a vow, it was said. Would he wish to unchain the fettered of France? My God, how he held up his leonine head proudly beneath his slouch hat, stepping out among them.

"They say his grandfather lay under the Bridge at Casano, body slashed twenty-seven times, while Prince Eugene's cavalry galloped back and forth over him," Germaine said.

"Died there?" Lucy asked.

"Not at all, the grandfather lived to recover and marry and reproduce. A dreadful man with women, his grandson, Mirabeau—poor wife." Then she turned her head toward Lucy and asked her suddenly, "What would you do if you discovered *your* husband were unfaithful to you?"

Lucy laughed and said she didn't believe such a thing were possible. "Frédéric adores me; he tells me everything," she said looking directly at Germaine.

SHEILA KOHLER

"Everything?" Germaine asked.

"He hates me to be away from him for even a night." Indeed, she could not imagine her husband not loving her. She trusted him, would trust him with her life.

"Of course, of course, but *if* it happened—and surely it is always *possible*, what would you do?" Germaine insisted, looking at Lucy and not the parading people before them.

Alexander de Lameth leaned out further to sneer a little at Lucy, or so it seemed to her, waiting for her response.

Lucy gazed at him. "I'd let him know how foolish I thought him, and then I'd go on with my life," Lucy said, watching the nobles now parading resplendent in their gold-worked cloaks of velvet, white-plumed and laced, and with swords glinting at their sides. Lucy recognized many, of course: even her father was there, as a delegate from Martinique. When he saw her, he waved his hat and bowed; she saw the young Marquis de Lafayette pale-faced, imagined his pointed head beneath the three-cornered hat; d'Estaing, her father's and her husband's commander; another Lameth brother, the one married to her sister-in-law; Liancourt, who had once courted her mother with such assiduity; Lally Tolen-dal, with his big head, her aunt's lover; even her father-in-law, who had been elected, though his son had not. She noticed how Philippe d'Orleans stepped ahead of his order, attempting to mingle with the Commons, and was asked to walk with his own.

Germaine said, "And if Frédéric were unfaithful to you with one of your dear friends?"

Lucy shrugged and said again such a thing was really not possible.

*Why did she ask such ridiculous questions? It was a strange habit. It must have been the novelist in her. She was always making up stories, interesting stories, perhaps, though not very likely ones in this case.*

Lucy trusted Frédéric and, certainly, she trusted her dear friends, she said. She leaned against the balcony and watched as the Clergy followed, the prelates in purple and white robes, with mitres, and the priests in their black surplices.

Last of all came the King and Queen. While the appearance of Philippe d'Orleans was greeted with *vivats*, that of the Queen brought forth dead-silence or, worse still, murmurs of "Long live the Duke of Orleans!" Lucy watched as Marie Antoinette stumbled, seemed about to fall. Lucy put her hand to her mouth, appalled, but the Queen regained her footing, lifted her head with dignity, looked around proudly at the silent crowd. Why, Lucy wondered, was the Queen increasingly the target of such scorn? It was becoming a battle of wills between the Queen and her people.

"She looks so sad, poor woman," Germaine de Staël commented.

"How could she not be sad?" Lucy replied with sympathy. The six-year-old Dauphin, who was no longer able to walk, had been brought from Meudon for this ceremony that he watched wrapped in a warm cloak from the veranda of the royal stables. His emaciated body, deformed by rickets and all covered over with sores, lay on cushions so that he, too, could see the splendid procession, a sight that brought tears to his parents' eyes as they passed him.

Lucy thought of the ball that had celebrated his birth, *of the Young Queen, the proud mother, of all that hope of happiness,* who had once seemed hardly to touch the ground, to surge forth through water. *The little boy was to die only a month later.* She thought of her own dead baby, born after so many hours of agony and followed by such sickness. How blue she had been! She wondered at all this death pursuing her.

But Germaine, for some reason, continued with her questions with insistence. "But what would you do?" she wanted to know, "if you found your dear Frédéric in flagrante with an old friend?"

"I would be sad, obviously, at such a betrayal, but I would go on loving him, I suppose. How could I not love him? How could I not love them both?" Lucy said, and looked into Germaine's intelligent brown eyes.

"What a romantic you are!" Germaine exclaimed and tossed her feathers in her hair.

"Not at all. You are the romantic, making up such a story. I'm a practical woman. I would do what was best for me, best for them in the end," Lucy demurred, meeting Germaine's gaze. Then she stared down at the procession. "Will these different groups ever be able to agree on anything?" Lucy wondered aloud, and "How are they going to vote, by head or by estate? That, it seems to me, is the question."

How, with their different needs and desires, would they decide anything in common?

And what about Frédéric? What was he thinking?

He refused even to assist at the opening ceremony of the Estates General. "Too painful," he told Lucy.

"Well, I shall go and see and hear what they all have to say," she said.

"You go ahead. I doubt you will be enlightened," he said.

So she was there in the immense and splendid hall, known as the hall of the Lesser Pleasures that until now had been used for storing scenery, but had been hung with velvet and tassels and decorated with faux columns for this occasion.

Lucy sat uncomfortably with the rest of the nobility, nothing but the knees of the person behind her to support her rigid back watching the King, who made his way with his usual lack of presence, waddling forward blindly, screwing up his face in order to see something without his glasses, wearing a blue costume richly ornamented with jewels. His short speech was delivered with resolution, but he said very little, speaking only of the burden of debt of the American war and the possibility of reforming the taxes but not saying how this was to be done. The Queen in white satin and a diamond aigrette in her hair was full of dignity or pride, depending on the point of view of the onlooker. She listened to the King, but appeared to be troubled, fanning herself continuously with a large fan and looking at the members of the Third Estate, the Commoners, as though she were searching for someone.

There was a low, sibilant murmur as Mirabeau entered and sat down in the benches reserved for the Commoners. The people behind him moved back and those in front of him forward, until the room became so crowded with deputies that the open spaces around the Marquis had to be filled.

Lucy found Necker's speech unspeakably boring and as spiritless as the King's. He went on interminably, with nothing but figures, figures, figures, attempting, as far as she could gather, to demonstrate that the deficit did not exist. If this was the case, Lucy thought, why had it been necessary to convene these deputies of the nation in the first place? Listening to these speeches, the impression she had was that there was no one in charge. Above all she felt, sitting bolt upright in all her finery, that her back would break. She emerged, stunned, into the sunlight after three hours of agony.

## III

$\mathcal{O}$N JUNE 17TH the Third Estate declares itself a National Assembly and its intention of providing France with a Constitution, and on June 20th the National Assembly swears never to separate until the Constitution is established in the Tennis Court Oath. The National Assembly decrees the cancellation and re-authorization of taxes and seizes sovereign power.

### JULY, 1789

On the first of June Frédéric had to go back to his regiment that was now in Valenciennes. Lucy and her aunt went to stay with friends who lived in Berny, not far from Versailles. Lucy was still recovering from the stillbirth and puerperal fever she had succumbed to, which had left her weak and listless. Miss B. had insisted on remaining with her.

Though Lucy dined daily at Versailles with Mme. de Poix, whose husband was captain of the guards, she heard only of the troubles of a few Parisian bakers who were accused of adulterating the flour by mixing it with foreign substances to make it seem more plentiful.

On July 11th Lucy dined with her aunt. While they were eating, her aunt's lover, Lally Tolendal, came into the room to announce the news that Necker had not been seen since that morning. He had left for Holland, it was said.

"What will happen now?" Lucy asked, worried.

"Nothing, I'm sure," Lally who was now an influential member of the Assembly, said.

On July 14th Lucy rode out blithely in her carriage in the mid-afternoon, with only Miss B. and a servant, going through the cool woods of Verrieres.

"The road seems unusually quiet," Lucy remarked. A hot day, and the road, which went from Choisy le Roi to Versailles, did not go through any town, but it seemed to Lucy there was a surprising stillness in the midsummer air.

"There are never many carriages on this route," Miss B. replied.

When they arrived at the chateau in Berny, Lucy looked around the outer courtyard. "But there is absolutely no one here!" she said and ordered the coachman to go through the open gates. Even the inner courtyard was completely deserted. Only a hen pecked its lonely way across the cobblestones.

Then they heard the sudden slam of a door in the stillness, and the concierge came running down the steps, flapping her apron in the still summer air like a white wing. She was shouting something they could hardly grasp, waving her hands around with alarm. She was telling them about something inconceivable: something that had happened at the Bastille in Paris. It had been seized! The guards! The poor Sire de Launay! What a horror! The woman screamed, almost incomprehensible in her distress. The gates of the city had been closed, and the French guards had revolted with the rest of the people.

Miss B. gibbered, "We shall all be murdered! I know it. We shall all be put to death!"

Lucy ordered her to calm herself and hold her tongue, and the coachman to retrace his steps. She returned to Versailles, and went to find her father-in-law, who was able to give her a more precise account of what had happened.

She learned some of the news from him at that moment and some later in the newspapers: the people, hearing of Necker's dismissal, had paraded his bust through the streets. Foreign regiments, sent to obtain order, had been pelted with stones on the Place Louis XV. Crowds, perhaps as many as 20,000 people, had marched on the Bastille in search of gunpowder. They had attacked its crenelated towers that cast their feudal shadow over the quartier Saint Antoine, and held its mysterious prisoners, kept in dank dungeons, it was believed, because of an arbitrary *lettre de cachet*.

De Launay, the governor of the Bastille, a civilian who was born in the Bastille, Frédéric's father said, had been forced to surrender to the almost nine hundred Parisians who surrounded the Bastille. Despite de Launay's desperate cries for reinforcements he had been sent only a few Swiss. The poor man had attempted to kill himself using the knife on the end of his cane but was stopped. The guards then tried to shield the man from the angry crowds who clamored for his death, before they tore him away. He cried out, as surely Damiens would have wished to do, "My friends, kill me fast!"

But they did not. "They took their time, had their sport," Frédéric's father commented angrily. They spat on him, clubbed him, and kicked him to the ground. They pulled out his hair. *"La canaille!"* Frédéric's father exclaimed. Finally he was bayoneted in the stomach and then fired upon as he lay twitching in the gutter. His head was cut off with difficulty with a small knife, and it was carried on the end of a pike through the streets.

"And, after all of this, what did they find in the Bastille?" Lucy's father-in-law asked her, lifting his hands in the air and shaking his head. Lucy waited for him to go on. She remembered reading some of the accounts of prisoners held in the Bastille, where life was depicted as a living tomb. She recalled, particularly, Linguet's memoir where he described the slow stripping away of his identity and the terrible inability to communicate, all of which had impressed Lucy, as well as a story of escape through a chimney with the help of a hundred-foot ladder, fabricated by the prisoner from his firewood all through the winter, only to be caught and brought back in a horrible leather harness.

"A terrible place," she said.

Her father-in-law raised his eyebrows skeptically. "They didn't even find the Marquis de Sade, who had left a week before and had been living there in luxury, my dear, you should know, with his library, perfumes, and family portraits," Lucy's father-in-law said scornfully.

Apparently the pathetic procession that then wound its way through the streets of Paris consisted of only seven prisoners: a few forgers, two madmen, and the nobleman who had been committed with de Sade by his family for libertinism, carried on the shoulders of the shouting mob, one of the madmen waving wildly, believing he was Julius Caesar, as well as the heads of de Launay and the guards on the tips of pikes. "Such is the justice that was accomplished today," he said bitterly, and turned from her to go back to his desk.

Apparently, Lucy was told later, the King, who had been hunting while all this was going on, had asked the Duke of Liancourt on being woken in the night, "Is it a revolt?"

"No, Sire," the Duke replied. "It is a revolution."

It was just the beginning of the violence of the mob.

Lafayette was forced to take the head of the National Guard, and only a few days later Lucy heard of the hanging of the minister Foulon, "From the lamppost" after which his head was stuck on a pike, his mouth filled with straw, his trunk dragged over cobbles until it was shredded. His son-in-law, Bertier, was confronted with his father-in-law's head before being strung up himself. Blood, Lucy understood, was to be associated with freedom.

## IV

## July 16, 1789

And the great flight, the great desertion at Versailles, had begun. Lucy lingered in the dim, silent corridors, aghast. She was struck by the sudden silence, a silence of death around the Queen. She watched as people gathered up whatever they could carry with them and left precipitately. Those who had once clamored the loudest, those who had fought the hardest for the Queen's attention: Lauzun, Vaudreuil, even the Countess Jules, trampled on one another in their haste to get away.

Lucy saw a young woman with a dazed expression dragged onward by a heavyset older one, and it came to her that more than anyone she had encountered, this older woman with the determined look in her bold dark eyes resembled her grandmother, who had already left for England. Then Lucy realized the older woman was Diane de Polignac, the Countess Jules's sister-in-law in the corridor, dragging along the Queen's favorite, the Countess Jules herself.

Lucy had hardly recognized them in their disarray. The Countess, in a fluted bonnet, was picking her way, carrying a yellow caged bird in one hand. They rushed blindly past Lucy and on down the corridor and clattered down the staircase, followed by a small black slave, who was dropping parasols and boxes as he went.

One or two of the courtiers accosted Lucy and advised her to do likewise. "Flee, before it's too late," an elderly nobleman, who had courted her mother, advised her. But most were muffled up, their faces hidden or in disguise, masked, not for any fancy dress ball but for fear of being lynched by the populace. They hurried wordlessly away.

*Gradually over the next few years more and more of the aristocracy was to abandon the King and Queen: a terrible mistake that made the work of my father-in-law, who was minister of war, increasingly difficult. The King, good as he was weak, was unable to stem this seeping of the lifeblood of France.*

Frédéric with his regiment at Valenciennes, heard of these grave events along with all sorts of wild rumors, alarms of war, massacres. He was told that the regiment was to get rid of anyone who would not adhere to the new hierarchy in which the non-commissioned officers were taking the place of the officers. In order to avoid being part of the troops that assembled at the gates of Paris under the command of the Duke of Broglie, he left his regiment at dusk and secretly rode through the night to Versailles. It was to be only the first of many such night rides. He was above all concerned for Lucy's and for his father's safety. On his arrival at Versailles he went directly to the war ministry.

His father, who was about to be made minister of war, urged him to leave with Lucy. He suggested they go to Forges in Normandy, where Lucy could take the healing waters.

# V

## July 28, 1789

Lucy stood at the window watching the road to see if Frédéric was returning from the spa. The sky was hardly stained pink, but she was already dressed in her green English riding costume, her feathered hat, waiting impatiently for him to join her.

They had found a modest ground floor apartment that opened onto the town square. She had spent her time at the spa, or doing her petit point, while Frédéric read aloud to her from the wide choice of books they had brought with them, including his favorite, *Decline and Fall*, which she helped translate into French.

Now she heard a sudden rushing sound: the stamping of feet, accompanied by cries. A mass of townspeople came running into the square beneath her window. The women wept and tore at their hair, the men raged or implored the heavens for protection, children pawed at their mother's skirts.

In the midst of the crowd a man wearing a green velvet jacket, sitting on a heavy black horse, a saber glinting at his side, called out in a loud voice, "The brigands are coming. They will be here in a few hours; they are pillaging and plundering and setting fire to the barns! Run for your lives, Citizens!" and then clapped his spurs to the sides of his horse, rode off at a gallop, and disappeared as suddenly as he had arrived.

She realized the man must be referring to the Austrians, spreading an absurd rumor to frighten the people and stir them up against the nonexistent foreign invader.

*How fear could be used to control ignorant people as one wished. Who was behind these lies?*

Incensed, she mounted her horse that her English groom, Bertrand, had waiting for her. She trotted through the crowded streets, attempting to reassure the people and calm them down as she went among them. "The Austrians are not coming. This is absurd," she called out. "You are misinformed. There are no brigands. There is no need for alarm. Go back to your homes! Someone is trying to frighten you." But the people, seized by panic, rushed around her, paying no attention, gathering up their children, clutching at their belongings, and shouting out to one another to flee.

Panic had them in its power and manipulated them as it wished. Savagery rose to the surface of the crowd. A young man pushed an elderly woman out of his way, and she fell to the ground. A corpulent dowager thrust a frail dandy against a wall as she bustled by him. People staggered on through the streets with their hastily assembled baggage, running this way and that in confusion, clothes spilling from their valises, chickens clucking and rising with a beating of wings in the air.

As she reached the church in the center of the village, she found the young priest about to sound the alarm. "We must reassure the people, not alarm them!" she upbraided him, and as he seemed about to ignore her words, she caught him up by his collar. "Don't be such a fool!" she exclaimed.

Frédéric found her, holding on to the small, frightened man by his clerical collar to stop him from ringing the tocsin. He, too, spoke to the panicked people, trying to calm them. "There are no foreign armies on French soil," he cried. He promised to ride to the nearest town and get news for them. Lucy set off at a gallop at his side, accompanied by Bertrand, who was convinced that all the people had gone mad. "Milady, what has got into them?"

It took them an hour to reach the nearest town, where they were supposed to find the marauding Austrians. Instead, they were stopped by a large Frenchman who stood in the middle of the road and challenged them: "Who goes there?" he cried, and aimed a rusty blunderbuss at them. "Are the Austrians in Forges?"

"Indeed, they are not," Frédéric responded. "And who is spreading such an absurd rumor?"

The crowd screamed at him, "He's lying. He's lying! He's a spy! Arrest him!"

Just then a prosperous-looking man came rushing up, red in the face. He pointed his finger at Lucy in her green riding costume, on her white horse. He screamed, "Citizens, look at her! It is the Queen, trying to escape! Stop her!"

Someone else shouted, "Take her to the town hall!" The crowd surged wildly around Lucy, shouting, "The Queen! The Queen!" A tall, strong man tried to grab at the reins of her horse to lead her away. The horse whinnied and reared up, pawing the air. She feared that the men and women who pressed around her excitable horse risked being trampled to death. "Get back!" she shouted. "Get away, before you are hurt. I'm not the Queen!"

At that moment a locksmith emerged from his shop on the square and stood with his hands on his hips, laughing at the scene. He shouted out, "She is not the Queen, you fools! This woman is half her age and half her size."

# PART TEN
## Arrival

# MAY 12, 1794

Lucy sits on deck with her baby in her lap. Séraphine, at nine months, is thin and very pale, but sits upright in her lace bonnet with the loose pink ribbons fluttering around her face like streamers in the sea breeze. She stares up dreamily through gray-blue eyes at her young mother's cropped hair. She gazes at the sea, the sky, and the slow mist that floats up from the water. A trickle of saliva glistens in the corner of her mouth like a diamond. Lucy looks at her. *I will remember this. I will hold this image in my heart.*

What does the child think of this strange world of sky and sea and mist? It is all she has known for the last sixty days. For the last ten of them, they have been lost again in thick fog. Though old Harper has maintained he could feel land breezes, he has inspired no confidence.

The sun glimmers through cloud, warming them. As the fog lifts, Lucy's heart, too, is buoyed up. She sees birds flying through the air: gulls and gannets and some kind of big black-and-white bird she does not recognize. A pelican dives down for its prey. For several days now, she has noticed porpoises, pelicans, and some kind of falcon and sometimes even ducks.

The birds seem to live from what they can find on the surface of the water and are so greedy and tame, they can be caught with a net like fish. They resemble pigeons with long, bent beaks. The water looks lighter here, and occasionally boats pass nearby.

"Look," she says to her daughter, pointing out a little gray bird with black legs and a yellow beak, and on the top of its head, scarlet plumage. The bird lifts off the water and ripples in a furl of air. She watches the bird intently, thinks her way into it. She would like to know what a bird actually feels, the beat of its hungry heart. She had once studied the anatomy of birds, their hollow bones. Séraphine claps her pale hands, and Boyd lets out a whoop of delight as he catches a crab in his net.

Then Lucy sees seven or eight boats passing by.

Lucy is content just to sit outside for a moment in the warm sea air with her children. Séraphine laughs when Lucy tickles her tummy, her little bare toes, reciting: "She shall have music wherever she goes."

Humbert plays with Black, who runs back and forth, barking excitedly, and then comes back to lick the little boy's hands and jump up to lick his face.

"Whatever is the matter with Black?" Lucy asks. As the fog lifts completely, and a blue sky appears, Lucy stands up with her baby on her hip. She peers through the white air. "Look!" she calls out to the captain, who is on the bridge. She lifts her arm toward the horizon, certain she sees land. Or is she simply taking her desire for reality?

The captain shakes his head, maintains it may be land of some kind but whatever it is, it is more than sixty leagues away. Almost immediately, a small decked-in pilot boat passes near to them, and the man aboard shouts out loudly, "If you don't change your course you'll founder on the point!" Young Boyd throws him a rope, and he clambers aboard and explains that they are in the entrance to the port of Boston.

"Boston! Boston!" Humbert cries out and takes Black's paws and dances with him around the deck. Séraphine giggles at the sight of her brother and Black dancing.

Lucy tells Humbert to leave the dog alone and run below and

give his father the good news. Frédéric staggers forth, pale and shaky, one hand shading his eyes from the glare, the other in Humbert's who leads him forth proudly as if bringing him up from the realm of the dead.

Together they watch as they leave the high waves breaking on the rocks behind them and follow the pilot ship through a narrow passageway into sea as calm as a lake and quite as beautiful as any Lucy has seen. A slight land breeze rises, and the decor changes as spectacularly and as suddenly as one on a stage.

Lucy stands with her baby girl on her hip, and Frédéric at her side, while Humbert and Black jump around them with cries of jubilation, as they emerge from the narrow creek into the harbor, and the little boy sees what he has not seen for months, and what his four-year-old imagination must surely have forgotten: green fields, flowering trees, grazing cows, and all the beauty of a new and luxurious vegetation. "Here we will be safe. No more men in red bonnets," Lucy promises him, holding him against her body, as the boat draws further into the shelter of the bay.

When the boat is safely anchored, the pilot arrives with a magnificent grilled fish, and the family settles down to what the captain calls a "welcome breakfast." Even Frédéric joins the family at the table on the deck, sitting at his wife's side, still partly stunned, but hungry. At Lucy's urging he sips from the jug of fresh milk, throwing back his head with abandon, the liquid trickling down his chin. Even Séraphine is given a little of the fish, mashed up with milk and butter.

The delicious odor of the enormous fish, which the pilot has just caught and grilled, proves irresistible. Lucy turns from her husband and children, and all of her attention is focused on it. Her body craves food with an animal's need. Her teeth sink into the white bread with thick butter. She feels as if she will never eat enough to satisfy her craving for fresh food. It brings tears of joy flooding into her eyes. She feels her heart overflow with thankfulness.

"Why are you crying, Maman?" Humbert says.

"Not crying, just laughing," Lucy replies.

Very soon they find themselves surrounded by a number of small craft bringing fruit, green vegetables, eggs, and even more astonishing, something they have not heard for months: people speaking French.

The news has spread that the *Diana* has arrived from France. Several Frenchmen ask to come aboard and besiege them with a host of confusing questions. One young man, a locksmith by trade, wants to know what is going on in Metz. Another, a baker who comes from Lille, wants news of that city. Lucy tries to answer their urgent questions about the Terror, the beheadings, the fighting. They seem quite amazed and indeed, quite angry, as though it were the fault of Frédéric and Lucy, who can only give them two-month-old information on Paris and Bordeaux.

She considers these people, tradesmen and shopkeepers, probable revolutionaries, who would have happily seen her family guillotined.

The captain, now that his ship is anchored and brought safely into this harbor, seems restless. He keeps jumping up from the table. Finally, he excuses himself. He promises to look for suitable lodgings for them in the town. He leaves as the sun rises high in the sky. They have no letters of introduction and are thus entirely dependent on his good offices.

Lucy uses the interval to have Boyd heat fresh water, which they now have in abundance. She gathers up the children for the great luxury of washing them and herself and changing their clothes, which she has not been able to do for sixty days. She wishes to make them presentable for their arrival in Boston. She sits Séraphine in the tub, letting her pat the warm water with her little hands, water dripping onto the floor. She sponges Humbert's skinny limbs as he stands stiffly before her, shivering in his white shirt. She wraps them up in sheets, gives Humbert a book to look at, and the baby to watch, and puts a blanket up to create privacy. She washes herself, lifting the sponge with the warm water and letting it roll down luxuriously between her breasts, under her arms, her legs. She splashes her face with abandon. She pulls clean clothes from a trunk to dress them appropriately. She puts their affairs in order, finds a simple white muslin dress in her trunks, sandals, and a wide-brimmed straw hat to camouflage her cropped hair, a blue dress for Séraphine, and clean breeches for Humbert.

She waits impatiently for the young captain to come back.

Frédéric, with land at such close proximity, cannot bear to wait another moment to go ashore. He says he will go ahead and visit the ship's owner, Mr. Geyer, whose address he has sent from the port of La Pauillac to his aunt and friends. He wants to see if there are any letters from Europe for them. From the railing she watches him climb down the ladder with alacrity and wave to her from the shore gaily. All his old energy and enthusiasm have returned, and as she waves back to him, one hand on her hat, she remembers how eagerly he first came to her, running up the steps at the house on the Rue du Bac.

# PART ELEVEN
## Trouble

I

*As in a* game of cards, when you start to lose and keep losing and know you will keep on losing but continue to play, Frédéric feels things slipping away from him fast through the month of August. Though he is not a member, he assists at the National Assembly and hears the windows rattle and sees the curtains billow and the air fog up with the shouts of exaltation as his fellow noblemen vie with one another in an orgy of self-sacrifice, renouncing corvées and tithes, rents and revenues from the salt tax and tolls. All of Rousseau's dreams are being signed into existence by the noblemen, his cousins, close relatives such as the Duke de Noailles. The press is now free; innumerable journals are sprouting like wild, poisonous mushrooms: Mirabeau has his and so do Marat, Desmoulins, and Brissot; the Third Estate is supreme. On August 26th the National Assembly promulgates a founding manifesto to guide its work: the Declaration of the Rights of Man.

AUGUST 28, 1789

That August, Frédéric was asked to carry out the execution of two of the men accused of creating a shortage of food in Paris. The day before, the mob had pulled down the gallows and pillaged the bakeries, and he had deemed it wiser to delay the execution until the next day.

It was a hot summer morning. He rode across the cobblestoned square at dawn, the air glittering dangerously, the smell of rotting refuse, burnt animal horn, and manure rising around him. As usual, D'Estaing, his commanding officer, was not there and had sent no word of his whereabouts. It was obvious that Frédéric would have to carry out the unpopular sentence alone, if at all.

He surveyed the men of the National Guard as they arrived, late as usual, and muttering among themselves ominously, sloppily attired. Decked out in their tricolor cockades, their tricorne hats, they took up their bayonets as ordered, but from their stance and the surly expressions on their faces, it was quite clear that they had no stomach for it. Frédéric was not certain they would follow his command.

But order, Frédéric thought, looking at his men slouching and grumbling before him, must be maintained. Discipline was essential. He would not give in to the rule of the mob. He spoke roughly, his voice sounding too high pitched, too angry in his ears. He told the men that he, himself, would lead them, and that if any man refused to follow his orders, he would be struck off the rolls.

"Bring the prisoners forth," he shouted, a note of hysteria in his voice, and watched as the two men were marched across the square to the sound of the drums. They were dragged to the steps of the gallows. They moved very slowly, it seemed to him, in a shimmer of summer light. Though he has seen violence of all kinds in battle, limbs cut off, heads rolling, horses shot down beneath him, the sight of these two young and struggling bareheaded men, in their shirtsleeves, unnerved him. He had been told they had each confessed to the crime, but how had such a confession been obtained?

They were forced up the steps, their heads put into nooses, as they violently protested their innocence. He could see the look of outraged indignation and surprise on their faces. How could this be happening to them? their wild eyes seemed to be saying. They looked around at the white sky, the glistening summer leaves, at him on his black horse—at life, as though they wished to hold onto it. But there was no possibility of halting the execution at this point.

When he gave the order, the bodies were dropped, and they dangled limply, life departing from them instantly. He felt his own head swim and had to turn away, afraid he might pass out and tumble down to the cobblestones beneath him.

## II

The great opera hall at Versailles was decked out for the banquet for the Flemish regiment, summoned there for the Court's protection. The floor had been raised and there was a splendid gilded screen covering the stage. Music played:

*O Richard mon roi, l'univers t'abandonne.*

The air was filled with the mingling smells of roasting suckling pig, sage stuffing, and fresh-baked bread. Though Paris was suffering from scarcity bordering on famine, here there was abundance.

Lucy and Frédéric's sister, the Marquise de Lameth, sat on either side of Frédéric at the end of one of the long tables. They watched the magnificent scene, as her sister-in-law, in a silver dress, spoke of her concern for her little boy who was very ill. The doctors had been unable to help, the cupping taking what little strength he had left. Lucy held her hand with sympathy and thought of her own pregnancy, her third, which had been progressing well. As usual, when she was pregnant, she felt full of energy and hungry.

Around them various toasts were raised. In a moment of enthusiam, Madame de Maille, a young blond woman of eighteen, handed out white cockades for the officers' hats.

Frédéric whispered to Lucy that people were getting unduly aroused.

Then, a voice announced the arrival of the King and the Queen. Lucy looked at Frédéric. "They are coming here? Now?

How imprudent," he whispered. The Queen made very few official appearances these days. Officers and men now rose from their seats and raised a loyal shout of welcome to the royal couple.

*The Queen walked down the room in white and pale blue with matching feathers in her hair. She wore her most bewitching smile. She was greeted with a sea of cheers, tears, cries of devotion and loyalty. Someone threw his hat in the air. The Queen leaned her head back slightly. Tears glittered in her eyes. She was visibly abandoning herself to the joy of hearing herself applauded once again. For a moment she had regained the illusion of the sun-haloed princess, who swims on through the sea of applause and adulation in the story that ends happily ever after.*

*Though the Queen had no tact and though she had never learned the useful art of winning people to her cause by shrewdness or flattery, she was at all moments capable of great dignity and courage. She carried the little Dauphin, her second son, Louis Charles, proudly and led her daughter, Marie Thérèse, by the hand.*

A Swiss officer asked if he might put the Dauphin on the table. The little boy was led around in his lilac sailor suit, apparently quite unconcerned by all the shouting.

The next day the newspapers were full of the orgy at Versailles and announced that the Queen and the Court were planning to assassinate the people. They had made the soldiers drunk to seduce them and trampled on the tricolor. Patriots beware!

## III

$\mathcal{T}$HE MARKET WOMEN march on Versailles and storm the palace, while the soldiers, including Lafayette sleep, earning himself the nickname, "General Morpheus."

### TUESDAY, OCTOBER 6, 1789

Marguerite's head was buzzing. Her temples throbbed. She had not slept all night for worry. She was desperate to reach Lucy in the Princess d'Hénin's apartment on the Rue de la Surintendence, where she had gone the day before.

Marguerite had watched the women arrive at Versailles in the rain, shapes and colors shifting suddenly, a slow lean of bodies coming on, among them one extraordinary figure on a black horse, sporting a plumed hat and carrying pistols and saber. Drums rolled. Then they were swarming everywhere, going into the Assembly, poor wretches arriving half-dead, carrying sticks, cudgels, and knives, confused and wrongheaded, their eyes glazed with fatigue, some with their skirts over their heads against the rain, all drenched to the skin, cold and hungry, their shoes squelching with mud after walking the twelve miles from the city. They had marched all the way to the palace, their voices hoarse with cold, wet, and anger, shouting "When will we have bread?" and dreadful things about the poor, foolish Queen. Marguerite was not certain that all of them were women, for she had spotted some thick, hairy arms, stubble on the cheeks. She imagined they were most likely hired by the Duke d'Orleans for liquor and money.

Lucy and her sister-in-law had taken refuge with her aunt at the Chateau. A servant had told Marguerite that she was afraid there might be further mischief at the Palace. Something more was about to happen.

She ran down the steps of the War Ministry in her white apron and cap and tried to make her way through the noisy crowd. Protesters, anarchists, and the dregs of the town were all milling around. She was hemmed in. Someone picked up a stone and threw it. There were skirmishes. They were crazed with freedom, with violence for violence's sake. A tall man with a long beard, looking like an artist's model, with a gleaming sword in his hands, was hacking off the head of one of the King's dead bodyguards.

Marguerite felt this was a scheme; someone had deliberately manipulated the legitimate anger of the women with hungry children. It was less likely that women would be fired upon.

She struggled on, stopping at the fountain opposite the Princess's apartment to splash some water on her face and remove her spotless white cap and apron. She was afraid they might make her conspicuous. As she did so, she noticed a familiar figure, a gentleman, boots splashed with mud, a riding crop in his hands. It was the King's cousin, the Duke d'Orleans, she was certain. He looked calm and rather pleased with himself. At the sight of him, the crowd took up the cry, "Long live our King d'Orleans!" He put his finger to his lips in a gesture to quiet them.

This was all his doing, she thought. He had been planning for months, with his secretary, the clever Laclos, to take his cousin's throne for himself.

She climbed the steps to the Princess's apartment. There she found Lucy and her sister-in-law, half-dressed, walking up and down in great agitation, looking out the window.

Then she heard a low rumbling sound, a gentle thunder, gathering volume. She joined Lucy to look out the window for confirmation of the sound of many feet, tramping up the steep road of the Surintendence. Then she saw the mob of ragged men and women coming on armed with axes and sabers, entering through a side gate that was usually kept locked. They heard a shot.

A large group of women, led, Marguerite imagined, by some traitorous insider, must have found the small door that opened on the secret stair leading to the Royal Court just under the part of the building where they were. The shouting, gesticulating women came rushing up the stairs and into their rooms, surrounding them. They were looking for the Queen and, once again, took Lucy for her. Marguerite pressed up against the wall. Then she heard a familiar voice, the Count telling them to follow him. He was pushing through the women, seizing Lucy's hand. He took her and his sister's hands, and in the confusion Marguerite managed to follow, as he led them through a secret passage upstairs into the great gallery, known as the Oeil de Boeuf, where many of the courtiers huddled in great anxiety.

There they learned that the Queen, showing considerable courage, had narrowly escaped death, thanks to a few loyal guards who had warned her of the mob's arrival. Lafayette dramatically kissed her hand on the balcony. Then the mob forced the royal family to abandon Versailles and accompany them to Paris.

Frédéric watched them go, a strange, slow, sad cortege miles long, going through the gates, with a splashing and a stamping, the carriage in the midst of the din, with the King, the King's sister,

the Queen, and the two royal children and the heads of the murdered guards hoisted on pikes before them, the pikemen and the
pikewomen, with loaves stuck on the points of bayonets, women
mounted on cannons with green boughs stuck in gun barrels, and
on carts, hurrahing, uproaring, and chanting.

The King had ordered Frédéric's father to stay behind at Versailles and shut it up, making sure all was safe, and preventing loot-
ing as far as he was able. Frédéric remained with him.

Lucy left her place of safety and came to find him there.
Together, hand in hand, the two of them wandered through the
alleys and the endless, empty rooms, only the sound of their footsteps echoing, where they had once roamed with so much bustle
and confusion, among so many other courtiers and supplicants with
such hope for happiness. Sinister figures slipped silently through
the grounds as dusk fell, waiting, Frédéric was certain, for their
chance to destroy the palace. The only other sound that now came
to them was the clacking shut of doors and shutters that had not
been closed since the time of Louis XIV.

Together they went into the Queen's room and stood side by
side, looking at the ripped bedclothes on the royal bed, the silk
slippers lying there, the stockings still awaiting the royal foot. It
seemed to Frédéric in its sepulchral silence like his mother's room
after they had dragged her from his small beseeching arms. He
turned to Lucy now and held her tightly.

# PART TWELVE
## *Boston*

# I

## May, 1794

Frédéric trips fast along the quay in flickering spring light, his eyes brimming with tears, light-headed from lying on his back and hardly eating for two months. His legs are weak, shaky, not his own. The world dances around him and settles down again, becomes stable for a moment, then dances again.

He smells all the land smells, the city smells, dung and kerosene and smoke, breathing them in like perfume. His nausea passes. He is alive! Lucy has saved him with her mad flight to America in a teacup.

He passes people in the street, ordinary people, going about their business in an ordinary fashion, plain women in neat dove-colored dresses, and men without red bonnets or baggy trousers or tricolor cockades. No one pays him much attention.

He stops to catch his breath. He remembers a blue evening in The Hague where he went as plenipotentiary minister for the King, only a few years before. It was after the King's bungled flight to Varennes in 1791 and his subsequent imprisonment. Frédéric's sister, who was already consumptive, had gone along with them, with her two little boys, as she could not bear to leave him. Lucy, Frédéric, and little Humbert had all lived together with her in a pretty house in the town.

A ball was given in their honor. They had all danced under a sky wild with stars. His refusal to wear the orange ribbon of the

Stadholder's party had caused such a furor, which had amused him at the time. As he danced, he brushed against the Princess of Orange's large, comfortable bosom. She was a solid, fresh-cheeked, cheerful lady, who was wearing an almost identical dress to Lucy's, her hair dressed by Lucy's hairdresser. The women had attempted to copy everything Lucy and his sister did. They mimicked Lucy's smooth gestures, the sound of her voice, the words coming fast and with assurance, the erect way she walked, her remote expression.

How short-lived it all was! His dismissal had come as soon as Dumouriez was made minister of foreign affairs, and his father had called Frédéric to England. It was while he was there that the terrible September Massacres took place in Paris, priests and bishops murdered in the prisons by the mob, and the poor Princess de Lamballe carved up, her heart carried on a pike to be shown to her great friend, the Queen.

Now Frédéric is ushered into the shipowner's splendid paneled office. Mr. Geyer rushes in, wiping his hands with his lawn handkerchief. He welcomes Frédéric warmly, addresses him by his title, uses his *particule* with evident pleasure—though he muddles up his name; "Count Frédéric de Gouvernet, de la Tour du Pine," he says a couple of times, as though Frédéric were a tree—wrapping his tongue around all the syllables like bonbons, savoring the words, which Frédéric has not heard for many months: Count! Not Citizen! Frédéric can hardly hide his grin, as Geyer bows over his hand almost unctuously, as if he were a king.

He makes a point of telling Frédéric that he has no revolutionary sympathies. He speaks slowly, simply, repeating his sentences, making sure Frédéric understands. Like many of the Boston merchants, he took the English side, and he has been shocked and dismayed by the carnage on French soil. "Whatever has happened to reasonable, rational, civilized French society?" he asks, shaking his head with consternation. Frédéric nods, smiles, and half-understands. He omits to tell the man that he himself had fought for American independence, that they might have killed one another in battle.

Geyer, in his English clothes and wearing an English wig, surrounded by his English furniture, repeats, "I am delighted you have arrived safely!" He is apologetic about the most unfortunate delays. He was most concerned about them, about the young, inexperienced captain, so slow in bringing them to their destination.

Frédéric accepts a cup of tea, followed by a glass of excellent port wine. He eats a biscuit free of weevils. He sits in a comfortable English leather armchair in the sun. He stretches his legs out, crosses his boots, hardly listens to the man who is obviously enjoying this conversation. He doesn't know how long it has been since he has felt so good.

Geyer is one of the richest men in Boston, their young and naive captain has told them proudly. Frédéric smiles at the thought and looks around at the elegantly paneled office, the leather armchairs, the bound books. Having money, he is beginning to realize, is a kind of grace in this country. He already senses how important it will be here where it is the only thing that sets people apart.

He seems never to have enough of it, he thinks, his mood darkening. He has always lost it too fast on the gaming tables, with women, with friends who have forgotten to pay him back. He has never known how to hold onto it. He was not brought up to think of it as important; or rather he has been brought up to live as though there would be an endless supply of it, that his name and position would always stand, would serve him better than money ever could.

He is painfully aware that they have very little left. But they do have influential friends, he is reminded when Geyer tells him he has a packet of letters for him.

## II

"What a charming man he is!" Frédéric exclaims, climbing back up the gangplank, waving the pile of letters at Lucy. She stands shimmering before him in her white dress and straw hat, her face shining, ready to disembark.

Humbert says, "We are ready to go, Papa. You should have come sooner." Lucy laughs, saying, "Such an impatient young man."

Seeing her standing there laughing in her straw hat and white dress, he thinks again of his older sister, so lovable, and dead so young. He remembers the etched delicacy of her features, her large artless green eyes, her laugh: an unexpected, contagious one. She had died of consumption in The Hague, leaving two small boys behind. He was not with her, having been summoned to England by his father, but Lucy had refused to leave her. Lucy had stayed on in Holland through the September Massacres, only returning to France with him in order to claim his chateau at Le Bouilh.

He remembers a day during a voyage the three of them had made shortly after he had married Lucy, to see his sister's husband, the Marquis de Lameth, in Lille, where he was stationed with his regiment. They had been riding across the summer wheat fields together, red poppies spotting the edges. They were amused at something—he doesn't remember what, perhaps at nothing at all. How his sister had laughed, her cheeks flushed, her long dark eyelashes wet with laughter. How carefree and careless the three of them had been! How thoughtless riding across some poor peasant's crops!

"Where on earth is our captain? What is he doing?" Lucy asks now.

How charming she looks to him in her flushed impatience, a blue sash tied beneath her breasts, a slanting straw hat shading her lively face. Séraphine balances on her hip and lifts her hands out to him.

They have escaped the tragedy that has taken over their former world. Everything here looks as though a cloud has been lifted from the earth. The sun shimmers on Séraphine's fair head, on her long blue dress. It's on Humbert's fair skin. There are rainbow colors in Séraphine's hair, tiny soft beams of light. Frédéric notices the intense blue of his daughter's eyes and her clear fair skin, and she seems to him, at that moment, intensely beautiful. He reaches out his arms to her, takes her from her mother.

He thinks that from the moment he caught this child in his hands at her birth, he has felt nothing for her but the most spontaneous love. He holds his little girl in his arms in her clean blue dress and smells her skin. She smells of sea and air and scented soap. At the same moment the captain arrives, saying he has found lodgings for the family on Market Square.

# PART THIRTEEN
## *Danger*

# I

*A*FTER THE BOTCHED attempt to escape to Varennes, King Louis has been recaptured, tried for treason, and guillotined. The Queen has been separated from her children and moved from cell to cell in the Conciergerie. She, too, has been brought to trial and cross-examined for many hours and accused of every baseness, even incest with her eight-year-old boy. The Terror is at its height.

Aided by these internal divisions, France's foreign enemies advance on all sides. Northern towns have fallen, Flanders and Alsace are threatened, and Spaniards ravage Roussillon.

Frédéric and Lucy and Humbert have been hiding out, first at Le Bouilh, and now in this house at Canoles near Bordeaux, awaiting the birth of their baby.

## SEPTEMBER 15, 1793

When the labor began, Lucy asked that they open the windows in the big bedroom on the ground floor of the house, so that she would not miss the sounds from the vineyards and the three roads that surrounded the house. From time to time she could hear a horse's hooves. Then she would clutch at Frédéric's hand, until she could hear only crickets pulsing in the night.

Her thoughts jumped about, wild with pain as she was, but fearing more for Frédéric than for herself. If the revolutionaries found him, they would arrest him immediately. His name, his rank, his father's station and recent trial, would mean certain death for him. Still, it seemed impossible that she should be separated from him at the moment of her baby's birth, when her body lay raw and open and vulnerable, separating from the child she had carried these difficult nine months. She needed him more than ever.

A servant had been posted on the road to give Frédéric the time to escape.

M. Brouquens had told them they would be safer in his house at Canoles rather than their chateau, which had been sealed. A man much beloved in Bordeaux by the people though not in favor with the revolutionary government, Brouquens was, however, in charge of the army's food supplies, which gave him a certain status. He was saving money for an emergency. A young doctor from the Sorbonne, Dupouy, had been persuaded to be present despite the danger.

She could only pray for a quick delivery, less for her own sake than for Frédéric's. She was terrified he might be found. She prayed for the pain to increase, knowing that the worst pains harbored the end. They came fast and furiously, burning through her body like bolts of lightning.

Marguerite, too ill with a high fever to attend to her, was in another part of the house. Lucy suspected the young maid, Marie, who was looking after the three-year-old Humbert, of revolutionary sympathies. Not assured of her loyalty, Lucy had nevertheless kept her on, fearing, if fired, she might denounce her mistress.

Dupuoy, knowing she was an aristocrat, remained beside her through this fierce travail, watching her with a terrified look in his violet eyes. Lucy was not certain if he was terrified for himself, for her, or for them both. She lay on her bed near the window, covered only by a light sheet, her thick hair damp around her forehead, her hand clutching Frédéric's.

Dupuoy told her to move to the edge of the bed and bear down as the pains increased, so that now there was only one long unbearable burning in her belly. She bore down with all her strength to push this child out into the world, as fast as she could, lifting herself up on her elbows to watch the crowning of the head.

The baby, obedient to her mother's wishes, made her appearance with such a rush that Dupuoy, waiting with trembling hands, nearly dropped her, slim and slippery as she was. But Frédéric reached out and caught this tadpole swimming its way so precipitately into life and held it in his hands, telling Lucy they had a little girl. Her face bathed in sweat, tears on her cheeks, Lucy reached out her arms to hold her child. "Come to me, darling heart," she said.

Dupuoy, remembering his role, managed to produce his instruments to cut the cord, and to clean away the afterbirth, the blood, and excrement, and place the baby in Lucy's arms.

Lucy looked down at her baby girl, touched the pointed head, the pink fingers and toes, the face still red from this sudden and swift arrival. She had not thought ahead as far as a name. It was not wise in the birthing business, she had found. Her mind had been only on Frédéric Séraphin's safety.

"We'll give her your name since you caught her: Séraphine," she said, lifting the baby up high to Frédéric Séraphin for his blessing.

He held the child in his arms and as there was no priest nearby, said the Latin words easily, words coming to him from his childhood when he had attended mass each morning in hope of bringing his mother back: "May the Lord bless you and keep you. May the Lord make his face to shine upon you."

"You must go, my love," she told Frédéric, who bent down to kiss her forehead and place the baby back in her arms.

"We will live in one another's thoughts," Lucy said.

"I will send you word as soon as I can," he said to Lucy. She wished there were words to express all the love in her heart.

She was determined not to watch him go out the door. She would keep him safe in her mind, just as she had closed her eyes on the darkness as a child, keeping a faint illumination shining inside the dark of the closet.

She could hear his footsteps in the night garden, going through the vineyards to the stables.

*Then he was gone, neither of us knowing if we would ever see one another again.* She lay with her baby girl, the blood seeping fast from her raw body. She was terrified that her strength would leave her, that she might swoon away, contract the puerperal fever as she had done before. She willed herself to stay alive, to stay well for her baby and her sleeping son and for Frédéric.

*Go away, I commanded the dumpy woman in white who lingered at the door. I turned to the young doctor for help. Poor Dupuoy.*

For the doctor had tears of terror in his violet eyes, and his hands were damp and slippery with perspiration. He stood trembling helplessly at her side, muttering his prayers. She told him to hide himself with the maid and Humbert.

Then she decided she must sleep. Her whole body ached from her efforts, but it was imperative that she rest. She wanted to enter a sea of sleep, to sink down into deep blackness, into a dark resting place, unhaunted, safe. While the rain began to fall hard, the odor of damp earth rising in the air, she fell asleep, with Séraphine clutched in her arms, *for at twenty-four one sleeps soundly even at the foot of the guillotine.* All too soon she felt hands shaking her roughly and opened her eyes to see Brouquens's elderly servant leaning over her, panting.

"What is it?" she asked.

"Those cutthroats are here, Madame, at the house, and they have dragged my master along with them to look through his things!" she exclaimed. The servant slipped a little bag containing five hundred gold coins under her pillow, money Brouquens had saved for them.

## II

Frédéric had borrowed a servant's cloak and hat and ridden off into the night. He held on to the baby-smell as though it had entered his flesh. He had kept one good horse with the pretext of visiting his farms through the summer, and he pressed the nervous mare onward at a fast pace, going through the dark. Raindrops fell hard as he rode, running down his back, like ants, soaking through his cloak and his shirt, his hat, his hair, filling his boots, his mouth, his eyes. Mud spattered his legs and boots, and lightning illuminated the dark sky, frightening his excitable horse, so that she reared up and he feared being thrown to the stony ground.

He cursed the foolishness of his fellow countrymen, his own foolishness, his idle days in the salons of Paris, the idle conversations about the English system, the idle projects for aristocratic reforms. He, too, had wanted necessary reforms without realizing what they would bring in their wake.

He knew that even if he were able to reach the royalists, in the Vendée, he would not be welcomed. Anyone who had stayed on in the King's service, once the King had signed the Constitution, was considered to have betrayed the royalist cause. His fellow noblemen had even accused his father of treachery.

His intention was to go to his house at Tesson, near Saintes, which he knew had been requisitioned, hoping the concierge and his wife, good people and faithful to his family, might be willing to help him. He was not certain. He felt like a general who has come back from the battlefield with the stench of defeat on him. Whether the money stowed in his leather saddlebags and the fake passport in the name of Citizen Gouvernet, useful all through the summer during his journeys back and forth from Bordeaux to Canoles, would suffice, he did not know.

As he left Saint-Genis, day was beginning to break, and a peasant called out to him from the doorway of a small stone house inviting him to stop and take shelter. Frédéric was exhausted, cold, and shivering, so weary from the night in the saddle that he feared his legs might crumple if he dismounted. Moreover, he hesitated to accept this invitation, aware of the danger of discovery. He could smell the delicious odor of grilling cheese and he needed to rest his half-dead mare. Almost falling from his horse, his saddle squeaking with rain and sweat, he hitched his horse in the shadows under the eaves of a small shed, right by the farmer's door.

"You yoke your oxen early," he said to the old man, attempting to play the grain merchant and adopting, as best he could, the Bordelais accent.

"It isn't even eight o'clock, but I need to be there early," the man replied.

"You are taking your oxen to the fair at Pons?" Frédéric thought to ask him.

"Going to buy grain," the man explained and ushered him inside where Frédéric found another elderly gray-haired man, with a high forehead and a sober air, already warming himself by the large kitchen fire. Frédéric glanced at him warily but now had little choice but to sit down beside him, sprawling a bit, as much as the rush-covered chair would allow, playing the role of a grain merchant. For a while the halting conversation centered on the safe topic of the high price of grain, and Frédéric was able to warm himself and dry off somewhat, only muttering a few expected phrases.

There were the damp smell of wet wool and the reek of perspiration in the long, low-ceilinged room. Beyond the single window, bluish in the faint light of day, the fields lay motionless beneath the birdsong of early morning, the distant lowing of cattle, a cock crowing. The grilling cheese was not offered, but instead his host offered a beaker of rum which Frédéric accepted, drinking it down fast, his hands trembling. He noticed the other visitor was not drinking, but looking at him from time to time askance, with suspicion.

Then the heavy man rose rather suddenly to his full height. He left the house without a word, his boots scraping on the stone floor, only to return a few minutes later wearing a mayor's sash. Frédéric's heart drummed, his mouth dry. He sat down again beside Frédéric at the side of the fire, the wicker chair creaking beneath his considerable weight. He stared at him with shrewd brown eyes and asked, "I presume you have your passport, Citizen?"

Frédéric, realizing that his grain merchant pose might not have been entirely convincing, only smiled, and duly brought forth the fake passport. He watched the Mayor scrutinize it carefully in the faint light of day, saying at the same time a small silent prayer.

"No visa for the Charente Inférieure, I see. I'm afraid you will have to remain here until later. I'll have to consult the Municipal Council," the Mayor said, turning to look at him more closely. Frédéric stared back at him, seeing not the man's face but his own death.

## III

Already, events were crowding in between them.

Lucy told the young maid to push her bed and Humbert's cot into an alcove. Dupuoy huddled there beside them, trembling and pale, looking as if he feared his last moment had come, muttering prayers in Latin. She told little Humbert to lie still, not to make a sound.

She asked the maid to bring her a hand mirror and a pretty rose-colored scarf. She sat up, combed, and bound up her locks loosely. She sprayed her body with perfume, propped herself up painfully, positioning herself so that her head was bathed in morning light, pillows behind her back, her swollen breasts decorously visible. Though her baby was hardly a day old, and she was exhausted and weak from the labor and blood loss, she could only hope that if all else failed, her powers of seduction might still be sufficient to protect them.

She ordered the maid to put out all the paté, wine, and liqueurs they had for the soldiers and to make herself as amiable as she could.

Half an hour later, she heard the clatter of the sabots on the tiled pathway. To wear boots or shoes would have been considered a lack of patriotism. The loud voices of rough men came from the garden, questioning Brouquens, who was stammering responses as best he could. They were examining the outside of the house, asking about the various rooms, the dependencies. Then she heard the clomp-clomp of the sabots on the parquet floor in the drawing room. The raucous voices could easily be heard through the thin partition.

She tried to hold her baby to her breast, but there was a weakness in her arms, and she was afraid she wouldn't be able to lift her child to her nipple, to quiet her. Her heart was pounding so hard she feared she might faint. For a moment nausea made her close her eyes. But when she reached for the baby it was all right, and the child shook her head back and forth, rooting until she found her nipple, and began to suck, though Lucy had as yet no milk. She kept her gaze fixed on the door, willing it to stay closed, but expecting at each moment to see it burst open and herself discovered there, with the suckling child.

She felt that all of this had happened before: that this terror was something ancient, something she had already felt long ago. It could have been what she felt as a child, hearing her grandmother stomping along the corridor in her heavy leather riding boots to come to the closet and drag her forth and beat her.

Eventually she heard the feared question: "Who is in that bedroom?" One of the men rattled the doorknob. She heard Brouquens say rather gruffly that it was impossible for him to comply with their wishes. He could not tell them what they wished to know, as it was a secret. Lucy wondered what the man had in mind, and if any sort of story could possibly stay these men. When they insisted, he began speaking in the embarrassed tone of someone a little ashamed of what he is saying. Lucy marveled at his inventiveness and audacity.

*He was like a good novelist but with the addition of working fast and in dangerous circumstances and with considerable courage and resourcefulness. The man managed to remain sufficiently close to the truth to be convincing, but distorted it in an original way for our own ends. I wondered at such audacity.*

*I had not thought this respectable, middle-aged businessman capable of such powers of imagination.*

What he told them was that the daughter of a friend had been entrusted to him so that she could bring forth her illegitimate child in great secrecy. The young girl had been here, hiding her shame, and was quite ill and very delicate besides. He was certain they would be capable of understanding, that to intrude on her under these circumstances would be cruel and unnecessary.

For a moment there was silence. Then, to Lucy's complete amazement, these same men who had watched thirty heads fall that morning on the Place Dauphine now must have taken off their sabots, for she heard them tiptoeing quietly about the house in their bare feet, so as not to disturb the young sinner while they searched the other rooms. After two interminable hours of eating and drinking, they left, taking Brouquens with them. Vulgar guffaws could be heard along with crude farewells offered to the young mother in trouble, as the men tramped through the vineyards.

## IV

The old peasant, who had been listening to the interchange between Frédéric and the Mayor before his fireplace with some visible signs of embarrassment, cleared his throat, walked up and down, moved to the door, and looked up at the sky. He said cheerfully, "Weather seems to be clearing. It may be, with a little luck, a fine day."

Helped by his hint, Frédéric rose with what he hoped was an appearance of calm, walked slowly toward the door, and stretched his hand out, as if to confirm this remark and sample the elements. At the same time, in the shadows of the eaves, he managed to unhook his horse, which was tethered there. Continuing to speak of the weather, he vaulted on his horse with one light leap and dug his spurs into the sides of the startled beast, his passport still in the Mayor's hand.

He did not dare ride to Pons now, but decided to seek refuge with a locksmith who had been recommended to him. This man, for a considerable sum, offered him shelter. Frédéric had always hated confined spaces. This one was worse than any ship's cabin. It was a dreadful, dark hole separated by only a thin plank from the shop below, where the forge and the bellows roared all through the day. But what choice did he have?

He was let out only at night by the locksmith and his wife. It was then that he was allowed to go into the kitchen, to eat, read, and write to Lucy.

He had found a young boy who went to Lucy with a "special loaf of bread for the wet nurse," with a letter hidden in it. Lucy wrote back that she had taken advantage of Dupuoy's presence to learn what she could about medicine: about surgery and mid-wifery. In exchange, she taught the young doctor how to knit and embroider and to make clothes. He was more adept with his hands at knitting and sewing than at catching babies!

# V

Her maid was knocking on her door. What did she want at this early hour?

Lucy stood at the window, looking over the flat autumn vineyards into the pale sky, Séraphine at her breast. She could smell the warm earth and her baby's skin. She was up early, awakened by her baby and fear. Sleep failed her often now, with Frédéric gone. There was no one to speak to. What was there to say? She didn't trust Marie, and Marguerite remained distressingly ill. Lying by her baby at night, she tried to read herself to sleep in the light of the candle. She had managed to bring some of her favorite poetry books that Frédéric had given her as her wedding gift. She read Milton: "Avenge O Lord! thy slaughtered saints, whose bones lie scattered..."

Poetry made her conscious that she was still alive, and Frédéric, too, though she had heard nothing recently. The brief rhythmic lines gave her hope. They were like breathing out and in, like life. She read Herrick's poem: "Fair daffodils we weep to see..." But sleep bypassed her. Every sound in the old house, every creak was a presage of disaster. She found herself making odd movements with her mouth. The palest thought carried a deep shadow. The thought that someone might harm her children or that she might be separated from them appalled her. She gazed up at a slice of moon, still visible above the vineyards in the crystalline sky.

"What is it?" she asked Marie.

The maid told her someone was waiting for her. Lucy lifted the curtain on the upstairs window and saw a young man standing before her door in the early morning light. He wore a red night-cap, a tricolor waistcoat, a rough black-shag jacket, black-shag spencer, and sabots, and he sported an enormous mustachio and carried a long, fierce-looking saber, swinging from his shoulder.

"What does he want?" she asked, instantly white, clutching Séraphine closer.

Marie smiled her thin, devious smile and said vaguely, "God is merciful, Madame."

"I thought you said you were an unbeliever?" Lucy said.

"He says his name is Bonie and was sent by Brouquens."

"Tell him I'm not—; I've gone out," Lucy said, hesitating to speak to someone dressed in such attire.

"So early?" the maid asked pertly, hand on a hip.

Lucy nodded. "Go ahead," she said, wishing she could tell the girl to leave, too. But the man waited outside her door until the sun was high, and the maid banged pots and pans loudly in the kitchen. "He insists on speaking to you. He will wait all day if he has to," Marie said.

Brouquens had, indeed, sent him here. "I might be able to help you," he said almost tenderly, as they sat side by side on the sofa in the small salon. Bonie, as the man was called, suggested Lucy might want to move everyone from Canoles to his hotel in the Place Puy-Paulin, which was empty and well-hidden behind a sort of wood shop. He lived there entirely alone, his wife having recently died in childbirth. They would be less conspicuous in the city.

"And you live there without danger?" Lucy asked him, looking into his striking eyes.

He explained that he was in no danger. He belonged, he told

her, leaning forward, his large hazel eyes intensely focused and seemingly alight with curiosity and goodwill, to the Jacobin Club in Bordeaux and was known for his bloodthirsty speeches against aristocrats and for using the informal *tu* to address all and sundry.

"I see," she said, smiling at this description. The man certainly played the part of a revolutionary most convincingly.

There was no doubt that the situation in Bordeaux was growing daily more dangerous, and Brouquens, who remained under house arrest, had already told her that her prolonged stay at Canoles might attract notice, particularly because of her English looks. The English were being rounded up and imprisoned.

"I will come with you," Lucy said.

She found his place as he had described it, well–hidden behind the wood shop in a small side street. It was also dusty, gloomy, and dilapidated. The large empty rooms would house her and her people. She noticed with delight that the salon was blessed with an old and somewhat out-of-tune harpsichord, and that the thick walls might make the playing of music possible, though they did not shut out the sound of the drums announcing the fall of another aristocratic head.

## VI

## OCTOBER, 1793

Lucy was able to get a letter to Frédéric, telling him of her move into town. She told him about the large rooms shaded by the chestnut trees and about Bonie.

She wrote, *He comes and goes in his revolutionary attire looking very fierce. Yet he has such a good face—I do not believe he will betray us despite his large moustache and sideburns and his long sword. Help comes in the most extraordinary disguises, is it not so? From a Jacobin, no less.*

*I pray we may be together soon. Your baby grows fast and is a voracious eater! I so wish you could see us, my dearest heart, me in my new peasant clothes in which I hope to be less conspicuous.*

For Lucy had decided to acquire the local dress. She contemplated herself in the mirror. She had lost all the weight she had gained during her pregnancy, indeed, with the meager rations available she was slimmer than before. Like her mother, she was tall and slender. She was clad in a short skirt, which showed off her ankles and her clogs, a tight waistcoat, and two red kerchiefs, one tied with a knot on the side of her head and another knotted about her neck. She caught a glimmer of her mother's face in the reflection, a wisp of her triumphant smile. Suddenly she remembered her mother saying good-bye one evening before going to a ball, putting her hands to her slim waist, laced into a similar peasant waistcoat, turning on her high heels, so that the short, bright skirt of her peasant dress billowed out around her ankles.

Lucy felt giddy, as though this disguise had turned her into someone else, someone younger, freer, one of the people. She remembered her fantasies as a child when she had imagined she, too, was a peasant.

# VII

"They say that Tallien's lover, the beautiful Thérésia Cabarus, has come to Bordeaux to join him," Marie told Lucy one morning, as she pulled Humbert's shirt over his head. She was raucous and brightly colored and as heedless as a tropical bird. There was an excited glitter about her that worried Lucy.

"Thérésia Cabarus, Madame de Fontenoy, is Tallien's lover?" Lucy asked, aghast, remembering the young girl slipping shyly into her box at the theater in her green dress. Diana, the huntress. "How on earth did she meet a man of that kind?" Lucy had heard that Tallien, an editor-turned-revolutionary, was called the Pluto on earth, the one with the keys of Tartarus. Would Thérésia play Proserpine and soften his heart?

Thérésia had met him in prison, according to Marie, where he had not only saved her life but fallen hopelessly in love with her.

"A romantic story," Lucy said. "What I have heard, which sounds more likely to me, is that the man was a peddler in drugs and the sale of arms."

"Now they say he has grown rich, selling life and death," Marie said and cocked her head and looked at Lucy, rather like an animal, Lucy thought, considering her prey. The girl, with her red curls and saucy tongue, knew too much.

Lucy remembered how graceful and charming Thérésia was

as a girl of fifteen, in what had already begun to seem like another life. Might she be able to help her? Lucy wrote to her:

*"A woman who met Mme. de Fontenoy in Paris and knows she is as good as she is beautiful asks her permission for a moment's audience."*

The immediate response being the one Lucy had desired, she was on her doorstep half an hour later. Despite her sabots and the bright kerchief around her neck, Thérésia recognized her immediately and embraced her with effusion. "Ah, my dear Madame de Gouvernet. How happy I am to see you again!" she exclaimed. "How charming you look in your disguise! *La belle grisette!*"

Thérésia apparently had no need of such a disguise. She was in a bright-dyed Greek costume, her dark tresses snooded with a glittering antique band, her feet naked except for sandals with pink silk ribbons tied around her fine ankles.

Lucy explained her situation, which Thérésia considered to be even more perilous than Lucy did. "It's a miracle you have escaped thus far. You must leave Bordeaux immediately," she urged Lucy.

"How can I leave my husband or abandon my children?" Lucy replied. Thérésia urged Lucy to see her lover, Tallien, and ask his advice. "You will be safe with him, I promise you. He will do anything I wish."

Lucy stared up at the young woman, wondering at her goodness. She had met her only once before, and that briefly and a long time ago. Though she had been in the same convent with her sister-in-law, Lucy could hardly believe the woman would do this for her. She seemed to Lucy at that moment of gratitude more beautiful than any other woman she had ever seen. What she would have liked to ask her was why she sacrificed herself to a man who signed the death warrants of innocent people daily.

The next day a letter arrived, saying, "This evening at ten o'clock."

Lucy walked up and down her room with her baby girl on her breast, Humbert trailing behind her, his hands over his little ears. For young as he was, he understood the meaning of the sound of the drums rolling on the Place Dauphine. Was it wise, after all, to meet with this upstart, who had used the revolution for his own ends and had so many aristocrats put to death? Might he not, despite Thérésia's intercession, destroy her instead? What if Thérésia, like so many before her, had overestimated her powers of persuasion? At twenty, surely, such a thing was quite possible.

# VIII

Just before ten o'clock that evening, Lucy decided she had no choice. She would have to take her chances. She left on foot for Thérésia's house, not far from her own, dressed in her local dress and her sabots. There, to her surprise, she found a large number of well-dressed people gathered in her salon. They were drinking the excellent wine from the area, a Saint Emilion. From which aristocrat's cellars did it come? Lucy could not help wondering, though she took some for courage.

Grim generals of the new Republican Army gathered in enormous horse-collar neck cloths, their hair in one knot, and *citoyennes* in sandals despite the cool evening air. They might have stepped from one of David's paintings, she thought. They all looked somewhat askance at Lucy in her peasant dress, causing her to smile at the irony of the situation.

Thérésia wore a soft white dress with a high waist, her dark hair coiffed smoothly, snooded with pearls around her forehead. She moved among her guests gracefully, sipped the wine, and gave no sign of remembering why she had summoned Lucy there.

There was no sign of Tallien either. Obliged to make polite conversation with these people, Lucy could hardly contain her impatience.

Then she heard the heavy sound of rolling wheels, which shook the cobblestones. The rolling stopped just beneath Thérésia's windows. It was impossible to mistake Tallien's carriage, as his was the only one allowed to pass freely through the streets at that hour.

Lucy drained what was left in her glass of wine quickly. *I imagined it might be the last drop I would drink.*

Thérésia rose and left the room and a few moments later returned. She came up to Lucy, who sat talking distractedly to a young man who kept leaning too close to her from the edge of his red velvet chair. Thérésia bent over her and whispered in her ear, "Tallien is waiting."

If she had announced that her executioner were waiting, Lucy could not have felt differently. She followed Thérésia down a narrow, dimly lit passage, holding her by the hand. At the end of the arched, whitewashed corridor, she saw a door open on a room with candles burning on a mantelpiece above a large fire. She thought of her first interview with her aunt. If only the Princess d'Hénin were here with her now, with her wit and her courage. Thérésia, like Miss B., was obliged to give Lucy a little push forward into the room, into *the den of lions*, Lucy thought. Then she heard the sound of the heavy door shutting firmly behind her.

Lucy did not dare raise her gaze to the monster she had conjured up in her mind but advanced half-blind, knees trembling, to a corner of the fireplace where two candles flickered. She grasped the marble mantel, leaning all her weight against it. Someone, she was vaguely aware, leaned against the opposite corner. A rather high-pitched voice asked her quite gently what it was she wanted of him.

Her voice faltering, she requested permission to go to Le Bouilh and have the seals removed from the chateau where they had been wrongly installed on her father-in-law's property.

The voice interrupted her to say abruptly that this was certainly no concern of his. It added, in an even sterner tone, "So you are the daughter-in-law of this Marquis who had the audacity to insist on speaking of the Capet Woman as the Queen at his trial. And your father is a royalist general, no?"

"Arthur Dillon," Lucy said proudly, lifting her head a little.

"Ah, Arthur Dillon, is that it? Well, all these enemies of the Republic will have to be eliminated!"

As he spoke, Lucy was seized with indignation. She felt her cheeks flush and dared to do what she had not until then: lift her head high and look him directly in the eye.

This enabled her to see what she had not yet seen: a slight young man, not much older than she, twenty-four or twenty-five. He had a pretty, insignificant, girlish face with a rather long nose, which tilted upward with a kind of optimism. Fresh color bloomed in the cheeks, which were surrounded by a mass of reddish curls, which had escaped from beneath his large military hat, itself covered with shiny material and surmounted by a long, waving, and rather absurd tricolor plume. He wore a wide leather belt, and a long, shiny saber like Bonie's hung from his shoulder. He looked, Lucy thought, like someone in a play dressed up as a bandit. He reminded her of the Queen's page, that evening she had first gone to Versailles, with a similar feather in his hat and a wandering hand.

Taking the measure of the man, and recklessly angry, she lifted her chin high and straightened her back. She relinquished her marble support and said, "I have not come here to hear my family insulted nor to hear their death warrant. Since you cannot grant my request, I will not take more of your time," and she inclined her head slightly as if to dismiss him.

These words seemed to have amused him or, anyway, taken him aback, for he allowed himself a half smile. His dark eyes turned bright, and he laughed, turning toward her and saying, "You are very bold to speak to me thus."

When she arrived home she rushed in to take Séraphine from the arms of the maid, who was walking her up and down, trying to still her crying. She gave her her breast and held her in her arms.

"What have I done to you?" she whispered into her baby's soft fair hair, terrified she had made their situation worse.

She received a letter the next day from Thérésia who wrote:

*I don't know what you said to him, but you made an excellent impression. He has promised to see that you are not arrested. I accused him of not doing enough for you and told him I have ordered you to depart immediately for Le Bouilh.*

## IX

*T*HE QUEEN IS carried to her death in a cart drawn by heavy horses. She wears a plain white dress and a widow's pleated bonnet, her white hair hacked short by Sanson's huge scissors, her hands, unlike the King's, bound tightly behind her back. The actor Gramont leads the procession to the scaffold. He stands up in his stirrups and shouts out: "Here she is, the infamous Antoinette. She is *foutue*, my friends!"

An ill woman who might have died in any case not too much later, with blood secretly weeping from her ailing body, she apologizes to her executioner, on whose foot she has accidentally stepped, and is then guillotined to the exultation of the crowd.

OCTOBER, 1793

From Lucy's apartment she could hear the almost continuous sound of the drums rolling as the heads fell on the Place Dauphine. At night, from the gardens adjacent to hers, raucous shouts and coarse epithets filled the air; she could hear the singing of the *Ca ira les aristocrats à la lanterne*: the "Friends of the People" sang to show quite clearly what they intended to do to any aristocrats they could lay their hands on.

*Looking back, I cannot believe how I survived.*

She was aware that their only hope now was to find some way to leave the country. What protection Tallien had been able to afford her would soon amount to nothing, if indeed it did not prove harmful.

Lucy received Frédéric's letters and his news infrequently. Fewer people were willing to hide him and those who did, did so with increasing reluctance, and with constricting conditions, because of the extreme danger to their own lives of such an awkward guest.

One clear evening, after a day of rain, Lucy received a visitor. Marie announced, "Ferrari, the singer," and ushered in a portly middle-aged man. Lucy had seen him before, she was certain, and she knew almost immediately he must be a spy. He wore dark clothes of a rather demodé cut and had a high, broad forehead.

"A great pleasure to see you again," he said in a pleasant voice, bowing over her hand. From the voice she recalled him vaguely from her days at Court or perhaps at the Rochechouarts' house. She was not certain where, but she must have heard him perform somewhere and remembered his fine voice. A tall man with a wide face and ironic brown eyes, he reminded her for some reason of her great-great-uncle, who was, she had heard, safely in England with her grandmother. Despite her intimate knowledge of her uncle's vices, she missed his reassuring presence, his fine mind, his enthusiasm, his love of luxury.

Surveying her dim, silent domain, Ferrari confirmed her suspicions. He was in Bordeaux, he admitted to her in a low voice, as a secret agent for the King's brother, the Count of Provence, the one known as Monsieur, who had also escaped to England. Lucy thought of Monsieur, His Heaviness, and remembered the meal she had watched him devour so voraciously that day at Versailles. She recalled his delicate fingers picking adroitly at his food, and wondered if he were losing weight on English food, and what his role had been in his brother's undoing.

"Dangerous work you do," Lucy said.

"I've made several important acquaintances with the representatives of the people," he said, and laced his fingers across his stomach.

The singer, who remembered her better than she did him, from her days at Court, walked over to the old harpsichord, opened it, and let his fingers linger on the keys, playing an arpeggio. He turned his head, smiled, and told her he remembered how well she sang. He had heard her at the Rochechouarts' house. Would she perhaps like to sing something with him? Would it not distract her?

"And why not?" she said, looking down at Humbert, who had wandered into the room, putting her hand on his shoulder.

Ferrari sat down at the old harpsichord, adjusted the stool, and opened up the music. "Shall we do this one?" Ferrari asked, turning to a page with a duet. They sang together.

"Lovely, lovely," the Italian applauded her, when they had finished. "Wasn't that fine?" he asked Humbert, who nodded with polite enthusiasm. "You sing very well, sir," he said.

"And your mother has a fine voice. You could have been a professional singer if you had wished to, Madame. And you read music very well, too."

She smiled at the Italian's compliments, which she did not believe, but an idea had come to her with his flattering words. She invited him to share the evening meal with her and proposed her plan.

Could she leave France with him, passing herself off as his widowed daughter, with her two children, and her husband as his servant? Could they disguise themselves as singers and go from town to town?

He responded with enthusiasm. "We could give concerts all along the way in Toulouse and Marseilles! But we must practice. And I'll ask M. de Morin to accompany us on the piano. He'd snatch at a chance to get out of France, too."

The next evening M. de Morin arrived, a thin young man with

powdered fair hair, who had a faint blue scar, just a line, above one eyebrow as if a pillow had marked his forehead. He looked ascetic in his tight, creased black clothes, the trousers a little too short. He looked green, obviously half-dead with hunger and fear. He had no identification card and could not go out in the day. He had been one of Bordeaux's Association of Young Men, a group of royalists who were wanted by the revolutionaries.

A glass of good wine went immediately to his head, so that he began to giggle and engaged in play with Humbert, running around the place, hiding and seeking, and then singing little Séraphine to sleep with a lullaby. He was one of six children and missed being with his brothers and sisters.

When they could drag him away from the children, he took up his music at the piano. His hands were small and soft, and his attenuated fingers trembled as he played the harpsichord with feeling and expertise.

The idea of playing a singer intrigued Lucy. Could she pass herself off as a professional singer? Could she sing as well as her mother had once done for the Queen? She remembered the Queen's tactless question: Could she sing better than her mother?

*Nei giorni tuoi felici*, Lucy and Ferrari sang, while M. de Morin played Paisello's duet, his fingers trembling on the out-of-tune harpsichord.

For a while the music had its own magical effect in the dimly lit room, and they forgot where they were or why they were practicing these songs. Then they looked into one another's eyes, and Lucy could divine a small glint of amusement in the Italian's dark, ironic gaze and even a mad glimmer of laughter in de Morin's pale blue one. She was caught up in a sudden, wild burst of laughter and obliged to double over, and the rather pompous, portly Ferrari in his embroidered waistcoat followed suit in a wonderful and sur-prising belly laugh. Morin stopped playing and joined in, giggling a high-pitched, panicky giggle.

*Had I died then, my soul would have gone on singing in Italian, I'm certain,* Nei giorni tuoi felici. *There could have been worse deaths.*

# X

## WINTER, 1793

De Morin was captured and guillotined, as were all the young men in the Bordeaux Association, Ferrari told Lucy sadly. He, himself, would no longer be able to duck into the wood store and mount the slippery shallow wooden steps to Lucy's apartment. He was leaving for England. She would have to come up with some other plan.

Walking alone in the street one winter afternoon, phrases and tunes from the songs they had sung flitting through her mind, she came to a halt. She stood dead-still in her madras scarf and shawl, watching aghast, her back to the wall, hardly able to believe what was before her eyes.

In the pale winter light, a group of scantily clad women and disreputable-looking men went past her through the cobbled street. On their shoulders or aloft in their culpable hands were ancient silver chalices, precious plates of gold, crosses, sacred paintings of saints, and even their sacred remains, plundered from all the altars of the churches in Bordeaux: from the Cathedral, St. Seurin, St. Michael. Prostitutes and drunken criminals strode along gaily with their precious burden, singing and laughing and calling out insults. Behind them followed everything they could not manage to carry, piled high in carts. Before them, swinging her wide hips as she sauntered along, a chosen one of their number, a well-endowed woman, painted and half-naked in a diaphanous Greek-style pink tunic adorned with a crown of laurels, carried the richest of the sacred objects, a heavy silver plate filled with rosaries and silver communion cups, which she balanced on her head like the woman with a bucket in the New Testament, going to the well for water. It was she who had been selected to impersonate the Goddess of Reason.

Lucy followed the procession in shocked silence to see what would happen. When the procession reached the Place de la Comédie, all the precious objects were piled high on an enormous pyre and burned. She returned home in a state of terror and shock at this sacrilege. She was even more horrified when she received a letter that evening from Thérésia telling her that Tallien had suggested that Lucy herself would make a wonderful Goddess of Reason.

## XI

### January 26, 1794

One morning at the end of January, she visited Brouquens's house, where he was still confined under house arrest. He was sitting at his desk, writing a letter. She could hear the squeaking of the nib, moving across the paper. Seeing a newspaper lying open on a table, she leaned over and began reading idly. It was then that she read of the *Diana*, a ship of 150 tons that would leave for Boston in eight days. She was about to leave the room, without a word, when Brouquens looked up from his letter, and asked her where she was going in such a hurry.

"I'm going to America," she said, like someone in a play.

She went directly to see Thérésia, whom she found at home, dressing to go out. Thérésia sat before her mirror, putting on her diamond earrings. She had not, apparently, been obliged to sell her jewelry.

"A brilliant idea. You must go. You don't have a minute to lose," she said. She got up and began to pace back and forth, her hands clasped. She added, "Tallien's position is increasingly threatened. Ysabeau has denounced him. We are both in great danger."

Lucy hurried home. She would have to find someone to bring Frédéric to Bordeaux in time to board. When she entered the apartment, she found Bonie talking to Marie in the kitchen. She asked him to come into the drawing room and shut the door. She explained that there was a possibility of their all leaving France, if Frédéric could get back to her before the boat left for Boston eight days hence. "Eight days," he said. "There is only one man who could undertake such a dangerous trip and get back here in time, and you are looking at him!"

Lucy looked at this young man in his rough frieze jacket, called the *carmagnole* after a revolutionary dance. Could she entrust her dearest being in the world to him? But what alternative did she have? And the man had certainly proven trustworthy so far.

She embraced him and thanked him for his generosity. She told him she would tell him when he should leave to fetch Frédéric. First she needed to obtain the passages on the ship and the permission to leave France.

She went immediately to find an old friend of her father's, a shipowner who was also a broker. As she walked to his house, she wondered if she would be able to take Marguerite with her, but considered that the voyage and the life in America would be too hard for her devoted old nurse who was still not well enough to face the rigors of a sea-crossing in the winter on such a small boat. Surely no one would hurt her if she were to remain in France?

Her father's friend promised to reserve a passage for her and Frédéric, if she could obtain the permission to leave France. He said that would be the difficult part.

The following day, while Lucy was lunching in the garden below her apartment, Marie came out to tell her that guests had arrived. At that moment, Tallien walked in through the French doors with Thérésia leaning on his arm. She smiled at Lucy and put a finger to her lips.

"Forgive me for disturbing you, Madame," he said, all amiably. "I understand that there is some way that I can make amends for my former faults?"

Lucy deigned to smile slightly. Some friendly word should be ventured. She offered them a glass of her good wine and asked them to sit down with her and share her meal. When Tallien was seated beside her, she explained in her polite manner that her financial interests made it imperative that she travel to Martinique. She needed passports for her and her husband and children without delay.

"Ah! Financial interests in Martinique? Important indeed," Tallien said, smiling a little and shaking his tricolor feather at her. He drank his glass of red wine in one gulp and added, "And where, may I ask, is your good husband, Citizen?"

Lucy continued to eat, wiping her lips with her napkin. "You will understand, I'm sure, if I keep that information to myself."

"As you wish," Tallien replied gravely, bowing his head a little toward Thérésia who was wagging a finger at him.

Two hours later Lucy received the precious piece of paper, ordering the Bordeaux municipality to give her the passports she needed.

## XII

She had calculated every minute that the dangerous trip should take. On the third day, toward nine in the evening, she expected that the ferryboat that came daily to Blaye would bring Frédéric to her. Unable to wait for another moment in the room with her children sleeping at her side, she rose, wrapped a shawl around her shoulders, and slipped out of the house and along the dark, dangerous streets, avoiding the revolutionary patrols.

In the moonless night, she went down to wait on the banks of the river for the ferry that was to bring Frédéric. She stood with her shawl about her shoulders and her face, as there were police posted along the river at each of the places where the ferry stopped. There was the dank smell of the riverbank, the sound of water lapping, the chill of the winter night.

Suddenly, through the darkness she saw the lantern of a small boat coming through the silence of the night, and heard voices speaking in English. Recklessly, she called out in that tongue to ask, "Is the tide ebbing?"

The response came loud and clear, taking her breath: "It's been ebbing for an hour!"

She gave up hope for Frédéric's arrival that night, as no ferryboat could land in such shallow water. She returned home hurriedly, entering the room where her children lay sleeping, Humbert lying on his back, her baby curled up on her side, her second finger in her mouth. She sat up watching over them, images of Frédéric passing vividly through her mind. She saw him being stopped and

SHEILA KOHLER

interrogated and recognized; carried in a tumbril to the Conciergerie, going under the archway with the red lantern swinging
above his head, thrown into a dank prison filled with wailing, desperate prisoners, listening to the Seine lapping while rats roamed
around him; she saw him climbing the steps of the guillotine. She
strained her ears for any sound that might be construed as a foot-
step or the opening of a door.

*Alas, never had a house been so still.*

In the morning, after a sleepless night, Marie came sauntering
into the room to help dress Séraphine.

"By the way," she said nonchalantly, as she lifted the child from
her cot, "Bonie is here and asks if you are up and dressed?"

Lucy could hardly control a cry. Making an effort to appear
calm, she left the room to find Bonie.

He reassured her in a low voice that Frédéric was hidden in the
house, that they had arrived the night before but had not wanted
to wake her.

"Dress as if you were going out to do some shopping, to fool
Marie, and I'll meet you in the street, and take you to him," he said.

Frédéric stood immobile before her, gazing at her from the
shadows, as though he could not believe she was there. She rushed
to him and clasped his slight body tightly against her, feeling the
thrum of his heart against hers. She had lived this moment so many
times in her mind. She was without speech. They sat down side by
side on the bed, the springs moaning. She traced his face with the
tips of her fingers: his eyes, his nose, his mouth. She stared at him.
"We have aged many years," he said, looking at her in her local
dress. He was weeping.

"Such joy," Lucy said, but she, too, was weeping. He looked so
dreadfully pale, so thin and exhausted, his eyes so shuttered, blank.
He had left six months before, and someone else had come back.

- 256 -

Reading her thoughts, he explained that they had been walking for three days with very little food and no shelter. At one point he had thought he could go no more. Fortunately, a peasant had passed them and taken them in his trap, impressed by Bonie's revolutionary attire. As there was no ferry at that late hour, the resourceful Bonie had rented a flat-bottomed boat that they had managed to land in the shallow water.

"You arrived in the night. How could you imagine I would be asleep?" she said.

"I remember how soundly you can sleep!" Frédéric laughed in her ear. He was alive, free, and laughing by her side. She was finally able to hold the dearest being in the world in her arms here in this transient room.

*In every lifetime there are a few luminous memories that explode like sparks in the darkness of the mind.* They were not out of danger, of course, but for a moment they were happy, and death that had been so close to them for such a long time did not frighten her at the thought that she could meet it now with her beloved at her side. Her life and his, in the little prison of the dark room, had ripened, grown luminous for the while.

## XIII

### MARCH 3, 1794

With his hat pulled low over his forehead, his face in shadow, Frédéric walked ahead with Bonie, going into the passport office. Lucy followed at some distance, dressed as a shabby lady in a straw hat, carrying Séraphine and holding Humbert by the hand. She entered the crowded passport office with the piece of paper she had acquired from Tallien clutched in her hand. Asked to wait, Lucy was careful to go into one part of the crowded room with the children, avoiding Frédéric, who sat against the stone wall on the other side of the room with Bonie on a low wooden bench. They waited, not daring to look at one another, through the crowds of people gathered there, or to protest the passing hours despite the knowledge that if they did not receive the passports this day it would be too late, the *Diana* being scheduled to depart the next day. Even the children, somehow sensing the danger, remained quiet, Séraphine on Lucy's knees, plugging her mouth with her fingers, and Humbert leaning against Lucy, looking up at her with terrified eyes. From time to time she produced a little bread and butter for Humbert, which she had stored in her pockets for him, and, covering her breast with her shawl as best she could, fed her baby.

Dark began to fall in the long, low room, its beamed ceiling blackened by smoke and grime. The clerk, who was slowly issuing the passports, picking his teeth, talking and laughing, and generally taking his time, called out, "That's all for today."

Lucy watched in amazement as Bonie leapt lithely over the counter in his revolutionary attire, his sword clanging against the wood. He said, "Citizen, if you are tired, let me write in your place." The clerk looked surprised by this apparition, shrugged, and said if he wished to, he could go ahead, but to make it snappy. He wanted to go home.

"It won't take long!" Bonie said cheerfully. He then took up the clerk's place and gestured to Frédéric to come forth. "You next," he said in a rough and commanding voice, playing the revolutionary. Bonie dipped the clerk's quill into the ink pot before him, writing fast, hurriedly making out a collective passport for the Latour family. He handed it over to the clerk for his official signature.

The clerk grasped the precious piece of paper and looked up at Frédéric. "Come closer and take off your hat, so I can see your face, Citizen. I need to make sure you're not some aristocrat trying to escape the guillotine," he said and laughed. There was a terrible moment as Frédéric hesitated to comply. Humbert, who stood at Lucy's side, threw himself against her knees, burying his face in her skirts and covering his eyes in terror.

But Frédéric regained his faculties fast, removed his hat with a flourish, and gave the clerk a grin. "Do I look like one of those!" he dared to say. The clerk gave him a cursory glance and signed the passport.

# PART FOURTEEN
## America! America!

I

MAY, 1794

Lucy shakes hands and says good-bye to the entire crew. The cabin boy weeps as he embraces Humbert, whom he has come to consider his own boy.

Lucy shakes Boyd's hand and notices a tear in his blue eyes, but she, herself, is perhaps saddest of all to leave Black behind. Boyd has assured her the captain would never want to part with his beloved dog, so she does not suggest his accompanying them, and the dog is tied up to prevent him from following.

In the spring sunlight, they leave the small ship where they have been confined for two long months. Lucy, though her muslin dress hangs loosely about her, has found a blue silk sash in her luggage, wound it twice around beneath her breasts, and tied it tightly. She has covered her thin shoulders with a deep blue velvet shawl and found a gay plume for her hat. She steps forth with her children and as she feels American soil beneath her feet her heart lifts with a new buoyancy, but the land seems to give way beneath her, heaving and falling. She can hardly walk and has to hand Séraphine, light as she is, to Frédéric.

"Terra firma," Frédéric says with satisfaction, taking his little girl who throws her arms around her father's neck. Frédéric seems to have regained all his vigor and his good temper from the moment he caught a glimpse of land. Lucy takes her husband's arm and leans against him as he strides beside her with their baby in his arms, and young Humbert skips happily ahead of them, looking around in wonderment, following the captain who leads the way. Is it possible they are really safe now? Will they all survive in this new country? At the thought, Lucy says they should eat.

They repair immediately to a good inn that the captain recommends where they find the wooden table spread with all the good things they have craved for so many days at sea. Here they eat fresh meat and vegetables and fruit—bananas—and drink fresh water.

They go toward the house of the Pierces, where the captain has found them lodgings on Market Square, their baggage being sent on ahead.

Lucy looks around at the light glistening in the tendriled foliage, on the cobblestones. She listens to the bees' joyful buzzing in the spring grass: the miracle of grass. Good God, green grass! She keeps saying the word over and over: *grass*. The magic of saying the word makes her skin prickle with joy. She is drunk with joy. She wants to dance, to shout. She wants to lie down in the grass, feel the solid earth against her back, watch the blow-weed drift; she wants to lift her arms over her head and roll in this small square of city grass as she did as a girl at Hautefontaine, rolling down the bank, before her mother had died.

And with this small square of dusty city grass, the dusty city spring flowers: ordinary pale daffodils and wilted daisies, all the colors of the garden come flooding back into her gray, fog-filled world, the colors of the flowers in her mother's summer garden: the small walled garden outside her window at Hautefontaine: the mauve of the foxglove, the deep blue of the cornflower, the gold of the marigold, the pinks, the scarlet of the poppy, all the flowers that were left to go to seed, to wilt and die, their petals falling to the ground, when her mother died. She sees all her flowers again sprung up anew in her mind in this new, safe place, in all their summer glory. Her dancing head is suddenly full of summer flowers. Their strong fragrance spreads in her mind like a veil. She brings them forth, restores them miraculously, as she has been restored. The *Diana* has come into port. Everything swims around her, and she closes her eyes and leans against a stone wall.

They say good-bye to their young captain at the Pierces's door. They thank him for their safe arrival, and he shakes their hands and rushes off in a great hurry, not stopping to wave.

"Someone waiting for him, I wager," Lucy says to Frédéric, who nods his head.

The three Bostonian women greet them warmly, clustered together, peering at them with curiosity, in the small dark hall of their house. There are potted ferns in a *jardinière*; and narrow stained-glass windows, and an odor of camphor in the air.

The Pierces do not speak a word of French, and seem relieved and delighted to find that Lucy speaks perfect English. They are eager to hear all their news, clearly fascinated by the drama of it all. They can hardly wait to usher them into the parlor and offer them a cup of tea, before they insist on Lucy telling them, with all the gruesome detail she can muster, about the dangers through which she and her family have come that provoke a flood of good-natured sympathy from all three generations equally.

When Lucy takes off her hat in the late afternoon sunlight of the parlor and exposes her short, blunt-cut hair, the three women all fall silent, their faces solemn, tears in their eyes. Lucy can imagine what they must be thinking and she hastens to reassure them, but though she repeats several times that really it is she herself and no one else who is responsible for this massacre, they insist on believing that Lucy's haircut is due to the famous executioner, Sanson, in preparation for the guillotine.

"How terrible!" the youngest Miss Pierce, Sarah, who must be about sixteen, says, clasping her hands to her breast, the thrill of tragedy in her large gray eyes.

"But we have been two long months on board ship! After all, my locks would be quite grown out by now," Lucy reasons to no avail.

In order to cut short their effusions, Lucy asks to see the house and their rooms. Mrs. Pierce, Sarah's mother, a heavy woman of some energy and elegance, who wears a dove-gray dress with a white fichu around her shoulders and a white cap, shows them around the place that gives onto the square. Their rooms, as indeed almost any rooms would at this point, delight Lucy with their light and air, their proportions, their stability: the small drawing room with its fireplace, large windows, and a yellow silk settee; the big bedroom, with one large bed and two cots, up a short flight of stairs, seem the most delightful rooms she has ever seen.

Lucy is happy, too, to let young Sarah, Mrs. Pierce's blond, plump, fresh-cheeked daughter, take over her Séraphine, which she seems extremely eager to do, and little Humbert, who is an outgoing child and remarkably precocious, used as he is to being left with strangers of all kinds, trots off happily with the older Mrs. Pierce, to see the chickens in the back garden.

Alone and safe that evening in the big bedroom with her husband, for the first time in so many months, Lucy removes her sandals, unties her sash, flings herself down, and stretches out across the wide bed on her back, her arms spread-eagled. She is finally free of the halter which has bound her in such close proximity beside her baby girl, rocking sleeplessly through the nights. She is exhausted. She wants above all to lie close beside Frédéric, to taste his lips again, and to sink into the deepest sleep. She looks at him in the flickering light of the fire. He looks thinner and softer.

He moves toward the window to draw the curtains and then rakes the fire.

"Come to me," she says, which he needs little encouragement to do.

What a luxury to have her breasts, her limbs, her body back to herself, to be able to lie flat on a wide, soft bed, to move about freely and above all, to reach out, which she does now to feel Frédéric's body beside her while she listens to the sound of the wheels of carriages on cobblestones, the chirping of the night birds, the wind in the leaves. She breathes in the smell of dust which rises in the air like perfume.

Frédéric runs his fingers through her cropped curls, and she asks him if he has forgiven her. He laughs, amorously, playfully, and for the first time in many months responds to her caresses, buries his head and licks hungrily at her breasts, her nipples. Together they laugh at their good fortune.

Lucy's plan has miraculously succeeded. She has single-handedly rescued them all. She is greedy now for life, for love. She offers up her body to her husband. They fumble awkwardly like new lovers, laugh at one another, not accustomed to the reality of one another's bodies. They have lived for so many months in one another's dreams. And Lucy is greedy for sleep. She wants to sleep forever. She sleeps as if she will never wake again.

But she does wake. Lucy wakes in the middle of the night to the sound of crying. For a moment she thinks it is her baby, Séraphine, that she might have fallen ill, but Séraphine is fast asleep on her stomach, one finger in her mouth, her head to one side in the cot beside their bed. It is not a child crying, but a dog howling and howling in the night. Lucy turns over and tries to go back to sleep. Let the dog continue to howl, she is not going to rise from her bed. But the dog goes on howling. The dog is scratching at the Pierces'

door. Lucy climbs out of bed and looks out of the window and recognizes, in the light of the moon, the captain's dog: Black. How on
earth has she found them? She runs down the stairs immediately to
let in the soaking wet dog and clasps her in her arms. "Where have
you been, Black darling?" she asks her, though it is obvious she
must have been in water for a long time. The dog licks her face, her
hands with her warm, wet tongue.

She learns the next day that she had been kept chained up on
the ship until ten o'clock that night, but the moment she was freed
she jumped into the water and swam more than a mile for the shore.
She had somehow managed to follow their scent and find the house
where they were lodging and scratch on the door.

Lucy dries the dog off and takes her upstairs where she falls
asleep, exhausted, beside their bed. Lucy climbs back into bed and
stretches out again beside Frédéric, eager to sleep. But Frédéric is
awake now. He lies on his back, his arms folded behind his head,
staring up at the low ceiling. He wants to tell her more about the
letters that he has received.

Now he shares his good news with Lucy. He has letters from
England, from his aunt and also from a friend of his aunt's, Angelica Church, whose family lives in Albany. This American Angelica
interests Frédéric a great deal from her letters: she sounds clever,
and generous.

"And who, pray, is this Angelica Church?" Lucy inquires,
suspicious.

"Betsy Hamilton's sister, apparently, one of five girls, and
according to gossip, also Hamilton's mistress." She has heard of
their plight from the Princess d'Hénin and offers them her help.
They are invited to her family's home in Albany, the home of Mar-
garita van Rensselaer, another daughter of General Schuyler's. Lucy
asks who this general is.

"The second most senior general to Washington in rank and seniority during the American Revolution," Frédéric explains.

Angelica Church's family is anxious to receive them in Albany, the Princess d'Hénin maintains. General Schuyler, Frédéric explains to Lucy, is famous for his role during the American Revolution and for his wealth. He is a lumber and fur trapper baron. Lucy murmurs a response sleepily. They will discuss it all in the morning. She has no desire to move on anywhere. Now she must sleep. She takes his hand and places it on her breast. She feels she will never get enough sleep, never get enough of her husband's loving.

"Perhaps we should go on to Albany, en route to Canada," he suggests.

Frédéric does not wish to stay long in Boston, he says, where he cannot speak the language. Besides, the Princess speaks very highly of this Angelica Church's family. General Schuyler will be able to introduce them to all of Albany and from there they can go further north to Canada.

Lucy says she will follow Frédéric wherever he wishes to go, and certainly, she trusts his aunt's judgment, though she would much prefer to remain where she is. Now she cannot move; she must sleep.

## II

Geyer, the ship's owner, has a farm near Boston and proposes they go and live there.

Lucy likes Boston and the kind Pierces, who are so helpful with her children and have provided her with a comfortable and safe abode on Market Square. She loves watching her children eat. She pours milk and sprinkles sugar over porridge and ladles it into their mouths, each spoonful a source of satisfaction, a small joy. She sees them filling out visibly, regaining their strength, their little limbs lengthening. Humbert is rapidly learning English from young Sarah. Little Séraphine has even taken her first few steps, tottering precociously around in this garden of the New World, in her new brown American lace-up boots. She wants to follow her brother everywhere. They all go walking with the devoted Black, whom their captain has relinquished after this proof of his dog's affection for this adopted family.

Mrs. Pierce takes them around the city, proudly showing them the sights: the column that has been erected on the top of the hill where the people had gathered, she tells them, to pass the first resolutions against the unjust taxes the British government had imposed; they see the part of the harbor where the tea had been tipped into the water in an act of rebellion, and the fine lawn where the first armed troops had gathered at Bunker Hill.

Lucy is full of enthusiasm for this country where the people have managed to make a revolution without descending into chaos and arbitrary violence. What is it, she asks Frédéric, that has prevented tyrants from taking root here on this soil as they have done in France? Are there no American Dantons, no Robespierres, nor Ysabeaus?

Frédéric sighs and says, "Perhaps what there is here is less history, and thus less vice and folly to extirpate. Give them time, and they will probably behave like everyone else."

But Lucy is more optimistic. "Perhaps others will learn from our mistakes. Surely mankind can improve." For all seems so new and shiny and safe to her here. She walks with a firmer footing now.

Also, Lucy receives visits from several people in Boston. People are apparently curious and anxious to meet these aristocrats who have miraculously escaped the guillotine, the dangers of the crossing in winter, intelligent, liberal aristocrats, after all, with good manners who are careful not to put on airs. Lucy tells her story, or parts of her story, to rapt audiences, again and again.

*I realized telling my story, altering it slightly, that there was something theatrical about all of this suffering. I saw the dramatic possibilities. How many plays and poems and novels will use these extraordinary events and render them in different ways? There was a pleasure in recounting these scenes. I was able to bring these people to life again, to bring them into the present. I reinvented them, so that at times I wondered if I had not made some of this up, myself, created it. What had really happened? I was already beginning to forget, the story replacing the facts. Had the concierge come down the steps, that day? Had she really flapped her apron at us like a white wing? Had Miss B. really gibbered? Had the women all come flocking into our room at Versailles taking me for the Queen? Had the Queen gone to her death in her white bonnet, hands tied tightly behind her back? Was the blood really seeping from her body, as they said, a bloody rag stuffed into a crack in the wall? And what had happened to the royal children? Were they still alive?*

None of these visits pleases Lucy more than one from a man named Bonamy, a tall, slender man with weather-beaten skin who comes from Santo Domingo where he has known her father well. Bonamy visits her one warm morning in June, bringing the past with him. They sit out together in the small garden, and she questions him about his life and her father's. Bonamy has been declared an immigrant, and so can go back neither to France nor Santo Domingo. He is without a home.

He speaks of her father with much admiration, tells her of his passion for his regiment, his revindication for his Irish men to march the first against the English, of his battles against the English on American soil where he had accompanied the Count d'Estaing. He speaks of her father's bravery in Savannah where he had accompanied him at the ill-fated siege.

"What really happened there?" Lucy asks, remembering only vague accounts.

There was no unity among the French commanders, and much prejudice against the black troops from Santo Domingo. Chaos ensued at times, one officer shouting "Forward" while the drums beat a retreat.

"D'Estaing was more a soldier than a seaman," Bonamy says.

"Not much of either," Lucy retorts, and Bonamy concurs.

Haughty and arrogant, d'Estaing refused to accept the advice of his officers. At times they had all felt, Bonamy maintains, that an evil star hung behind the fog in the heavy morning air. Her father's regiment had been split up, much to their dismay and over his strong protests.

The retreat was murderous. D'Estaing, himself, was wounded. "Their assault was as furious as I've ever seen, and the ditch was choked full of French dead," Bonamy told Lucy bitterly. The whole campaign was ill-advised and monstrously ill-managed, according to him. Her father had had to take over and do his best to save the wounded and dying men on the ships where no provision had been made for such a calamity.

Lucy speaks bitterly of this Count whom the Queen heaped with honors he did not deserve in her mind. "He underestimated my father. And as Frédéric's superior, made himself scarce at each moment of danger. He was always just a little too late."

Bonamy says that her father had proposed a retreat through Charleston, but d'Estaing would not listen.

"A man of little value," Lucy says scornfully. "It was Father who should have had his place."

Lucy is hungry for any small detail of her father's life. There is so much about him that she ignores. Like many children of her time, she has hardly spent more than a few weeks under the same roof with him.

"I'm worried about him. What will happen to him now?" Lucy tells Bonamy as they sit side by side in the safety of American shade, all the horror of the daily violence in Bordeaux coming back, the sound of the drums in her ears.

Bonamy says, "Your father believes that it is sufficient to live without reproach and without fear. I don't know that he has looked for honors in his life."

He rises to take his leave, bends gravely over Lucy's hand, promises to come back to see her again.

Lucy says, "Indeed, I hope you will."

But Frédéric, who speaks so little English, wishes to go further north, toward Canada, and Lucy is in this, as in all matters when he has a mind to insist, ruled by his wishes, though she judges them clearly enough. He is delighted to find friends of his aunt in America. He decides to accept the invitation of the Schuyler and Rensselaer families.

But before they leave Boston, Lucy goes through all the things they have brought with them and sells anything she doesn't feel they will need for the life of a farmer. She is determined to live simply, to dress as the other women do, to give up all the luxuries of her life.

*I had been spoiled, admired, and fêted. I had led an idle life. Looking back on my past, I reproached myself for all my futile vanity. I determined from now on to devote myself to my duty. Without being aware of it, God had perhaps already enlightened me.*

Like her locks, she gets rid of all the fine materials, laces, and porcelain that they have left and that they can sell, as though this stripping will protect her and her family from further violence. Luxury and ease are associated in her mind now with death. Besides, they will need the money to acquire a farm, and they will not need such items in the life that she plans for them.

# III

Frédéric wakes very early and rises. He cannot sleep. He looks at his sleeping wife and wonders at her ability to forget the past. Despite his joy at his family's safety, part of him still desires to be back in his country. His yearning for France comes over him at odd and inappropriate moments and in undistinguished places, standing shaving in the morning, looking into his mirror, for example. His very identity, after all, is caught up with his past. He worries about the fate of his country, about their friends and family, those left behind, those who have not chosen or been able to leave, the absent ones.

He leaves Lucy sleeping with her baby at her side, Humbert in his cot, and takes Black with him. He goes silently down the steps and out through the door and into the quiet streets of early morning Boston, the dark dog following him closely like a persistent memory. He buys the newspapers as he has done every day since his arrival, anxious to read the news from France that is reported here as soon as it arrives in the Union.

He comes back to the house and sits down at the dining room table in the pleasant, bright room with its yellow walls and yellow silk, pelmetted curtains. The youngest Pierce woman, sixteen-year-old Sarah, who has fallen in love with his children, brings him a cup of hot, sweet coffee, before taking Humbert, who is now awake, off for a walk in the garden. He watches her go out the door with his child holding onto her hand, going into the sunlight and down the steps.

Frédéric, though his spoken English is limited, is able to read the language without much difficulty, and what interests him above all: the list of names that he scrutinizes daily, fearing to find the familiar ones of friends or family among the many victims of the guillotine. He has already heard of the deaths of several of his friends and enemies, including his aunt's wayward husband, the Prince d'Hénin, though she had almost never lived with him and he suspects will hardly mourn him.

Today, he reads of the death of his commander, the Count d'Estaing. He has never admired the man who had received many honors he had coveted including election to the States General. Before losing his head he had declared, or so the newspaper reports, "Send my head to the English, they'll give you money for it." For a moment Frédéric feels a certain satisfaction and then is immediately saddened. With the Count d'Estaing goes a whole part of his own life. Perhaps, he thinks, one is almost as saddened by the death of an enemy as by that of a friend.

Frédéric reads of the deaths of some of his old friends from his wild days in Philippe d'Orléans's circle: the gallant Duke de Lauzun, one of Lucy's mother's admirers, who had also fought for American independence, had always proclaimed liberal sentiments, and even fought in the revolutionary French army.

Frédéric wonders about the writer who described his world so well: Chloderlos de Laclos. What has happened to him? Will he keep his head on his shoulders or lose it like Philippe d'Orléans himself? Frédéric thinks of the irony of this death, of this "Citoyen Egalité," the title conferred on him by the Commune of Paris. How had the man dared to vote for the death of his cousin, the King? And in the end, none of this had saved him from suspicion.

He peruses the rest of the long list of names, not all of them familiar to him, and comes to one he has feared to find each day:

Arthur Dillon. The name of Lucy's father is among the list of guillotined.

Frédéric sits quite still, the paper in his hands, but cannot reconcile his image of the young man, his white skin slightly freckled, galloping forward on his horse, his eyes filled with expectation, his body coiled like a spring with strength, with the idea that this head has been severed from its trunk with a blade, and lifted up to the crowds to jeer at, and the rest of his young body thrown onto a cart like garbage.

Because of the slight difference in age, Frédéric has always thought of Arthur not so much as a father-in-law but as a friend to emulate. Indeed, he could never break the habit of addressing him with the familiar second-person singular. Frédéric thinks of himself almost as an echo of his father-in-law: their lives have taken such similar paths up to now; he has followed in his footsteps in the army; they have won and lost in the same gambling games; they have drunk together. Lucy's grandmother had taken advantage of him as she had done with Frédéric, he knows. He had saved his life. This time he was not there to save him. Above all he knows Lucy loves him passionately, despite or perhaps because of the little opportunity she has had to be with him.

He knows he was brought up with Lucy's mother like a brother and married her at eighteen, that he had owned nothing in the world besides his regiment. In an attempt to save the King he had been imprisoned in the Luxembourg Palace and condemned to death. He must have been guillotined while they were at sea on board the *Diana*—on the 13th of April, Frédéric reads, and stares at the yellow walls around him but sees instead Arthur Dillon, hands bound behind his back, carried in a tumbril down the street, mounting the steps to the scaffold at dawn.

Later Frédéric will hear this story. Among those who were in the tumbril with him was a woman, Camille Desmoulin's wife, Lucille, who at the last moment, when the executioner had placed his hand on her shoulder and told her to go ahead, turned to Arthur and murmured, "I beg you, sir, go before me," to which he had replied with courtesy, "There is nothing I can refuse a lady." He mounted the steps and cried out in a loud voice, "Long live the King!"

Frédéric goes slowly and quietly up the stairs with the newspaper in his hand and stands by Lucy's bed. He looks down at her with the early morning light on her face, her fair cropped hair bristling around her head in disarray, like a nimbus, her cheeks flushed, their little girl beside her. She sleeps with a slight smile on her face—his brave and brilliant and lovely wife. How happy she looks. He brushes away the tears that he feels on his cheeks. How can he remind her of the terrible violence they have hoped to flee? How can he be the bearer of such tidings? How can he hurt the one who is dearer to him than life?

IV

He sends their baggage ahead to Albany. Lucy wants to cross the one hundred miles on land by mail coach in order to see more of it. She is excited to see this wild country. It takes them fifteen days to go from Boston to Albany by the post road. They go along a narrow road through thick, dark forest, the carriage jolted terribly by tree trunks that have not been completely removed. Lucy is full of admiration for this unspoiled scenery. Frédéric listens to her exclamations of delight at the sights and sounds of this savage place: the trees entwined with creeper, the dense underbrush, the plethora of wildflowers, the intense quiet of the forest, broken only by the cry of a bird or the wild flapping of wings.

When they stop to water the horses, they let the children and the dog run, and she puts her hand on Frédéric's arm and says, "Listen to the silence." He takes her hand and puts his arm around her shoulder and wants to weep.

They stop at inns on the way, and Frédéric is appalled when they are asked to sleep in a bed with strangers, the women separated from the men! To sleep in a bed beside strangers seems the height of incivility. To demand clean sheets also seems to be considered quite an unreasonable caprice.

"What is this savage place we have come to?" he asks Lucy, but she laughs at his expression and says it is better than sleeping in the Temple where the royal children are still imprisoned. How can he complain? Indeed, what can he say?

On the night they stop at an inn in Northampton, Frédéric

decides he can delay no longer. He is afraid Lucy might read of her father's death herself in some paper. He waits then until after they have dined and the children are asleep, and sits down beside Lucy and holds her hands in his and tells her. He embraces her but is aware she is not conscious of his vicinity: his substance is neutralized by her grief. In his arms her body already feels lighter, slighter, as though part of her has been lifted from him by sorrow.

V

*So much gone: Hautefontaine, the house on the Rue du Bac, Marguerite,*
*lying ill in France, and now this violent premature death, but I will not give*
*in to despair.*

Lucy holds onto Séraphine tightly, lays her hand on her forehead,
feels her pulse, her warmth, the damp of her hair, the beating of her
heart. She breathes in the odor of her hair, her skin, of her life.

*I've got her.*

Lucy lies awake with her child on one side of her and, almost
inconceivably, a strange woman who snores loudly, her mouth wide
open, on her back, on the other. She thinks of Miss B. and remembers the lullably of her stertorous breathing and wonders where she
is, if she has survived all of this, and perhaps even prospered during
these times of change. Lucy cannot but smile at a vision of Miss B.
in a Greek-style dress, her blond curls threaded with pearls, going
through the Bois de Boulogne in a carriage, or walking along the
Fauboug Saint Honoré on the arm of a large dandy, some promi-
nent revolutionary. Lucy hopes all this violence has been profitable
to someone, that if she has lost so much, someone else has gained.
There has been a change of hands at least. Lucy remembers how
Miss B. held her in her arms at the moment of her mother's death.
Now she can only hold her sleeping child in her arms.

Again, Lucy can hear the rain running across the roof. She
wishes she had had more time to ask her father about himself,
about his inner life. Would he have told her? She thinks he might.
She knows only a few general things about him, after all: the sort

- 281 -

of vague and laudatory things her mother would tell her when she
questioned her. Perhaps her mother had never known him well,
either. All she had said was how brave he was, how gallant, how
brilliant. And what does all that really mean? Lucy wonders now.
She knows he, like his brothers, like her husband in his youth, was
a gambler, and that her great-great-uncle was obliged to pay his
debts, which gave her grandmother a considerable hold over him.
She knows he fought several duels, that he was fearless in battle. A
brave man, undoubtedly, or reckless, or rebellious, or all of that.
But none of that tells her much about him.

She remembers the last time she saw him, in March of the pre-
vious year, when they had been obliged to leave Paris for Le Bouilh
in order to hide from the growing Terror. She had embraced him
then without having any idea it would be for the last time. How
could she have imagined the death of such a young and vigorous
man? She remembers his youthful appearance that was due to his
height, perhaps, or his handsome face, his fine, insouciant bearing.
She thinks of his originality of mind and his evenness of temper
that had made him such a fine companion.

She knows he has shown great courage in his defense of the
King. When he learned of the attack on the Tuileries and the over-
throw of the monarchy, he had addressed an order of the day to his
troops in which he renewed his own oath of loyalty to the King.
The result of this declaration was his removal from his command
and his return to Paris. In vain had Lucy begged him not to go,
and she reproaches herself now for not compelling him to return to
The Hague with her. She knows of her father's appeals to Dumouriez who made such empty promises, and she believes his inter-
views with the judges of Louis XVI had one purpose only: to save
the life of the King. On the morning of the King's trial her father
had continued to believe that the vote would be for his imprison-

ment and not his death, which was quite unthinkable to him. How could they have voted for the death of a king? It is unthinkable to her, too, that anyone could have voted for the violent death of her own father. She thinks of his last moments. What must he have felt at the moment of the parting of his soul from his body? What terror as they tied him down to the wooden plank? Would he have felt the blade severing his neck? It is that last moment that haunts her, that she finds unbearable to contemplate.

She has only a handful of memories, shadowy moments from her childhood, comings and goings in great halls and great parks. She remembers watching from the window as he went through the gates on horseback in the early morning mist at Hautefontaine with her mother at his side, going to Brest where he boarded his ship with his brothers for America. Is this all that will remain for her of the man who brought her into the world, to whom she owes her life? Yet, somehow, she feels his love for her has pervaded her life. Her father loved her. Of this she is certain.

From this moment on, Lucy sees the savage beauty of the forests, the wild vines, the rhododendrons, the roses and the lianas that wind their way from tree to tree through the web of her sorrow. The narrow road that separates Massachusetts from New York, the forest in every stage of growth, seems gray to her, all the colors drained away.

# VI

## June, 1794

It is in the evening, after fifteen days of traveling by coach, with the children and Black, that they come to Albany. Looking for the van Rensselaers' house, they arrive in a long street at the end of which lies a large rose-colored mansion, bookended between tall Dutch chimneys, a distinctive balustrade wrapped around white-trimmed dormer windows, surrounded by a pretty garden with flowering trees and white flowers that glimmer in the gloaming. There is a fragrance of jasmine and honeysuckle and some other wild herb Lucy cannot identify.

Lucy calls out of the window of the carriage to ask a young boy in the street whose house this is. He lifts his hands in the air with surprise. "But it's the Patroon's house, of course!" he replies.

"And who might the Patroon be?" Lucy asks. The boy exclaims, "You don't know who the Patroon is? Who are you then?" and runs off in fear and a sort of horror to have spoken with someone who did not know something of this sort.

At that moment, a slim, tall man in a gray waistcoat and flowing powdered hair comes into the garden and opens the door to the carriage. He introduces himself as General Schuyler, and hands Lucy down from the carriage, himself. He has, perhaps, heard the news of Lucy's father's death, or chooses by chance and goodness of heart the very words that would move her more than any others would have done at this moment of sadness in her life.

He opens his arms to her and embraces her. "Now I will have a sixth daughter," he says in perfect French, including her in his family of five girls.

He explains, when Lucy compliments him on his use of the French language, that his tutor as a boy had been a Huguenot minister.

Inside the simple, elegant mansion, they are made welcome by his wife Caterina, whom he calls Kitty. She is a woman in her sixties, tall and upright in a gray dress with a rose at her bosom. She has a long, determined-looking jaw. She must have been determined, Lucy thinks, knowing she has borne the general fifteen children, only eight of whom have survived.

Kitty takes them upstairs to the large guest bedroom that opens off the hallway and tells them that the Marquis de Lafayette has slept here, as well as the Vicomte de Noailles and Lucy's mother's old beau, the Duke de Lauzun. Lucy smiles and says, "We will be in good company," though she knows the Duke has been guillotined like so many of her mother's friends. The ghosts of these men will hover over them, surely.

Frédéric mentions Angelica Schuyler, but Lucy understands quickly that this eldest daughter, her aunt's friend, is not considered without reproach. She has run off and married a man in her youth of whom the Schuylers did not approve, apparently. Another of the daughters, Mrs. van Rensselaer herself, the one who has married a cousin, the Patroon, receives them as kindly as her father has done when they go downstairs for refreshments in the dining room.

Mr. van Rensselaer, her husband, Lucy gathers, is considerably younger than she. Mrs. van Rensselaer asks immediately to be called Peggy. The two families, of Dutch origin, Lucy understands, are inextricably and confusingly intertwined. She is not quite sure of the relationships between these people, but understands that, as in her own Irish Jacobite family, cousins have married cousins, and they have remained almost entirely among their own Dutch kind in this American town.

They have established themselves here and embellished this house with the taste and the solid comforts of the Netherlands. Lucy looks around the dining room with all the shining plate and fine blue-and-white china. While the family eats, the Schuylers immediately show interest in their welfare. They question Lucy and Frédéric about their projects and enter with enthusiasm into their plan. They will help them find a farm, they promise.

The general's daughter, Peggy, sister to Angelica Church, is a woman of thirty-odd years. When they rise from the table she goes to a daybed and reclines beside the fire, despite the warmth of the June evening. Pale and fragile-looking, with large dark eyes and delicately etched features, she wears a deep blue velvet dress, her dark hair smoothly coiffed behind her head. She holds onto Lucy's hand and then insists on holding the baby girl who squirms around in her arms, eager to escape and explore the house, after being cooped up in a carriage for so many days. Peggy tells them she is delighted to have the family in this house, and calls forth some of her people to take the children into the upstairs nursery where her own children are waiting for them. Her people will bathe and put them to bed, she tells Lucy. Black is sent off into the kitchens to eat. Peggy speaks as good French as her father does. Despite her delicate health that has kept her indoors and confined her to her couch, Lucy is surprised and delighted by her conversation that shows superior intelligence and good judgment. She hadn't expected a provincial American woman to be so well-informed about the causes of the French Revolution, the vices of the aristocracy, and the folly of the bourgeoisie.

# VII

Lucy finds Peggy, the next day, in her garden, a white shawl over her shoulders, a basket over her arm, cutting pink roses. A warm day and the sun is already overhead. Lucy sits outside under an oak tree with Séraphine on her lap, talking to her new American friend. The baby in her pink bonnet chews an ivory and silver teething ring, drooling and gurgling happily, her cheeks a hectic red. Humbert is playing with Peggy's little boys in the nursery.

Peggy admires the baby. "She's beautiful. A rose—pink roses in her cheeks!" she says, gesturing to the basket with the roses by her side.

Lucy smiles and says the roses come from the teething, which keeps her up at night, alas.

Lucy asks Peggy about Albany. She wants to know everything about this place, and Peggy, though she tires easily, is happy to inform her. She speaks of the dog days of the Revolution, how ill-equipped and poor Washington's armies were at times. "There were so many moments when we despaired of victory. You cannot imagine," she says. "Without the French we would have been lost. And there was much violence here, too, you know. We feared for our lives."

Once their house had been surrounded by enemy soldiers, she tells Lucy. That day—her youngest sister was still a small baby, about the same age as Séraphine, Peggy says—her father was sitting in his front hall, with the doors open on account of the heat of the summer's day, when he was told that someone wished to see him at the rear gate. Immediately fearing trouble, all the doors and windows were barred and the whole family rushed upstairs, just as the band of Tories came crowding into the hall of the house. They had apparently planned to carry off General Schuyler to Canada. Upstairs the family was busy barricading themselves in one of the bedrooms, putting everything they could find against the door, fearing for their lives, when Peggy's mother gave a little cry. She remembered something: they had forgotten the baby, the youngest girl, who had been put to sleep by a nurse in the basement because of the cool air.

Peggy, without thinking, she says, immediately rushed down the stairs and thrust herself unthinkingly through the throng of soldiers. She swept up the sleeping baby from her cradle in the basement and carried her into the hall. As she ran through the hall, one of the cutthroats threw a tomahawk that narrowly missed her, tearing her gray taffeta gown and making a gash in the wood of the staircase, still visible today. Still, she managed to carry the baby, going past the men and up the stairs. Her father then scared the band of marauders away by calling to imaginary armed men.

"What courage!" Lucy exclaims.

Peggy smiles back and says, "One doesn't think, you know, when one does something of that kind. Besides, it's nothing compared to what you have been through." But Lucy shrugs and says she simply did what was necessary under the circumstances. They have been lucky, too.

"But there were those who remained behind, those who never dared or managed to leave France. And you did," Peggy says, looking at her with curiosity and admiration. Lucy nods and thinks of her father. She says those who remained were perhaps the bravest. *I will not cry. I will not cry now.*

Lucy warms to Peggy's unreserved behavior. She tells Lucy

she is incapable of disguise, and that she shares her trust in private integrity.

Lucy asks Peggy to tell her about the history of this town.

Two years before their arrival, Albany had been almost entirely burned to the ground by a slave rebellion, slavery not yet being abolished in the state of New York except for the children to be born after 1794, she informs Lucy, and then only when they had reached their twentieth year and after the slave had reimbursed his master by his work for the "education" that he had received. One of the slaves, who objected to these prerequisites, had decided to avenge himself by burning down the city, which was almost entirely made of wood. A twelve-year-old slave, who was caught lighting a fire with the straw in her master's stable, was made to confess and gave the names of her conspirators. The slave whose name she gave and six of his accomplices were hanged.

Lucy thinks of Candide in Voltaire's book, and how he comes upon a slave who has no hand and no leg, the hand having been taken from him when a finger was caught in the sugar mill and the leg having been removed when he wished to escape.

From the ashes of this burned city and thanks to the Schuyler and the Rensselaer families, apparently, a new town with brick houses has emerged.

## VIII

Lucy sits at the window and reads some of the letters they have received from Europe, while Séraphine sleeps in her arms, her head on her shoulder. Among them is a letter from Talleyrand himself, who asks where and when he can find them. "Let me know where you are. I will come and see you," he writes. He has been exiled from England where he has stayed at Juniper Hall with the Princess d'Hénin. Now he finds himself in America.

Lucy thinks of him, coming into the salon at the Palais Royal, standing by a table by the fireplace in his exquisite clothes, and then lounging indolently on a sofa, his face unchanging and impenetrable, saying little but lighting up the conversation with a mordant phrase, his small green eyes sparkling.

What was it he said when she had asked his advice about Frédéric? Something like, "Indeed, he would be perfect for you," spoken in his deep, low voice, with his usual inscrutable and slightly malicious smile.

She wonders at Talleyrand's role in her life. Has she been mistaken about him? Despite his reputation for opportunism, she cannot but think of him as benevolent and generous.

When Peggy hears, at luncheon, that Talleyrand is in Philadelphia, she says she is anxious to meet this interesting man. She has heard so many conflicting things about him from her sister, Angelica, and from her brother-in-law, Alexander Hamilton.

"What do you think of him?" she asks Lucy in her direct way.

She wants to know about his role during the French Revolution. What does the man believe? He is, or was, an archbishop and a nobleman, is he not?

Peggy has a way of looking at Lucy across the mahogany table, with her dark inquiring eyes, not exactly trustfully but with belief. She appears to appeal to her judgment, putting simple questions with genuine interest, as if wishing truly to discover the way the world turns.

Lucy tells her that Talleyrand, like her great-great-uncle, the Archbishop of Narbonne, had probably not chosen the priesthood out of piety, but rather for worldly reasons. His family had decided he must enter the priesthood because of one of those accidents so common in childhood. His wet-nurse had dropped him down the stairs or something of that sort. In any case, he was lame and therefore unfit for the military, which, as the firstborn of a noble family, would have been his destiny.

During the Revolution he had made sure he was elected to the Estates General, one of the representatives of the clergy of Autun. He is, above all, an ambitious man, able to charm anyone he wishes. What wit and what intelligence, she exclaims. "After an hour's conversation with him you will forget any reservations you might have had about him." He had obtained the vote of the Clergy of Autun this way, though they also had solid reasons for choosing him as their representative.

Lucy believes Talleyrand was in favor of regular sessions of the Estates General and of the codification of the law as well as education for women. No taxation should be imposed without the consent of the people, was one of Talleyrand's ideas, as well as freedom of the press and free trade. Lucy says, "He is one of those people who, despite his own vices, has an eye and an ear for virtue."

"Really!" Peggy exclaims. She finds it hard to believe that an archbishop belonging to the oldest French nobility would have such ideas. She wants to know, too, in more detail about Lucy's own life in France before the Revolution. She seems to know a great deal about France. She wants to hear the Princess d'Hénin's news, and all about the unfortunate French Queen and King.

# IX

## July, 1794

Frédéric goes out riding daily, looking at different farms for sale in the area. He passes by the inn, on the route to Canada, where the stage stops and where the lands for sale are advertised, pinned up on the door, and then he rides to the ones that seem interesting to him.

One evening on his return to Albany, tired out and hot after a day of fruitless searching, his muscles sore from being in the saddle for so long, he reads his own father's name this time, in the list of the guillotined. This group followed only days after Lucy's father, though the news has only come to them now.

As Louis XVI's last minister of war, he had been left behind at Versailles to make sure the place was shut up and safe, when the King was taken to Paris. He had responded when Fouquier-Tinville had questioned him, stubbornly refusing to call the Queen "the Capet Woman" and continuing to refer to her as Her Majesty or "the Queen." When asked about his son's whereabouts, he had not thought to lie but had simply informed his questioner of his hideout at Le Bouilh.

Frédéric goes up the stairs to the bedroom to give Lucy the news. He stops at the door and stares at her as she sits on the silk-covered sofa, reading La Fontaine's Fables to their children in her gray peignoir, her skin in the light of the lamp rosy, her once-again heavy hair pinned up behind her head. Lucy is in mid-sentence and does not stop. Séraphine sits on her lap, with her head propped against her mother's breast, her finger in her mouth. She studies her father's face, her expression placid. He lifts his arms toward her, and she slithers from her mother's knees and comes to him quietly and embraces his legs. He lifts her up, and she puts her arms around his neck, as though she senses his distress.

Lucy looks up at his face and says, "What is it?"

Frédéric cannot speak. The idea of a public pact, a version of civic order ordained by God, has been cruelly shattered. The social structure that existed, for better or for worse, has been swept away. Should his father have consented to serve the King once he had been forced to sign the Constitution? Frédéric catches a glimmer of a face in the round mirror on the wall above the sofa, a man's face. For a moment he is not sure whom he sees, or what this man believes anymore. He is suddenly struck with a sort of horror not so much at this death but at the continuation of his own life and the impossibility of answering the questions of how to do this. Bravery, honor, and courage—what do these words mean, now? And what is he to put in their place? He feels stripped of his clothing, as though he stood there naked before his wife and children. He says, "Now we are both orphans, or almost orphans."

"Oh, Frédéric," she says, and rises and comes to him. She holds him, takes Séraphine from his arms and puts her down. He places the newspaper into her hands and sits down between the children who watch him, fear in their eyes. Only his mother is alive, safely shut up in her convent.

"What an irony to think Mother is the only one who has survived the Terror," he says, and turns his head away to hide his eyes, moves away from the children. Frédéric sits down on the bed, listening to the sigh of the mattress. He holds his head between his hands, feels his lips tremble and a tear trickle into his mouth. He wipes his lips. His body shakes, and he weeps. He remembers his father's definite, efficient gestures. He can see him at the dining table taking up a glass, setting it down with a little snap. He talked, too, with speed, the words coming without any waste, any extraneous explanations. Not a tall man, but a man of considerable presence and vigor and intelligence.

Frédéric watches the little boy climb back up onto his mother's lap and put his arms around her neck. He thinks how hard his mother's confinement had seemed to him as a boy. He had never understood entirely why his father had banished her to a convent. It was something that had always angered him. But his father had thus inadvertently saved her life. He thinks of his days with his grandmother. The last time he was with his mother was at their wedding. Why has his father's death made him long for his mother again?

Lucy embraces her husband and weeps with him. Then she rises and says, "I must put the children to bed. I will have to make mourning weeds for us all. I must ask Peggy if she has some black material I can use."

Frédéric nods but would prefer her to stay beside him for a moment longer and comfort him. Lucy is almost never still, he realizes, watching her gather up the children. She is always rushing off. She is, in this country, as always, an eminently practical woman.

She leaves him little time to mourn. He watches in grudging silence, half-stunned, as she sets about making full mourning clothes for the entire family immediately. He marvels at her skill, her industry, her boundless energy. He watches her needle fly. She is an excellent seamstress and works quickly and well. Also, she is anxious for them to have a place of their own and encourages Frédéric in his endeavor to find them a farm.

"We cannot stay here indefinitely," she remonstrates, as he lies on the bed with his hands over his eyes, his head aching, in the guest room that has been so generously provided for them.

He, himself, has little energy or desire to do anything. What is the point? The heat increases as the summer advances, a humid stifling heat that reminds him of his time in Martinique under the Count d'Estaing, when they lay at anchor for days in the harbor while the French nobles bickered over what was the best way to attack. Now those French nobles are no more. But he is still here. He sprawls on his bed in the van Rensselaers' large guest room, as he did on board ship, motionless, in his shirtsleeves, sweating, sick at heart, with the shutters drawn on the brilliant summer light, or he walks alone in the garden staring at the light in the summer leaves. Black, who has accompanied them this far, wanders behind him, like a secret shadow, a stain.

*Exceltat in adversis*, his family's motto. Have they really excelled in adversity? Here he is accepting hospitality from kind people without much hope of repaying them. He has become a beggar, worse than a beggar, for he is far too proud to beg. He wonders where it is that *he* has gone wrong? He has tried to live his life with the kind of energy and courage and diligence his grandfather had always displayed. He has attempted to follow his high principles, to put into practice the tenets he had instilled in him from an early age, those of loyalty and fidelity and truthfulness. He has followed Lucy into the New World. Should he rather have stayed behind with his father and died with him? Why should he have been the one to survive? Was this flight nothing but cowardice?

Though the Schuylers and the van Rensselaers show great kindness to his family in this moment of bereavement, Lucy exhorts Frédéric onward. They must attempt to continue with their lives despite these tragic events. They cannot take advantage any longer of this hospitality.

How can he become what she wishes, a man of the earth, a farmer, a tiller of the soil? He is not good with his hands, has never had to use them except with a sword, a pen, on the reins of a horse, or against the soft skin of a woman. Is Lucy really aware of what farming involves in these climes, the daily drudgery, the extremes of the climate: stifling in the summer and freezing in the winter, the hostile indigenous population? Why had they not gone to England, where his friends have taken refuge and where Lucy's family, surely, would have helped them?

He watches with exasperated admiration as Lucy prepares herself for the life of a farmer. She insists on rising in the morning before daybreak, getting him up out of his soft bed, and sending him back out into the stifling summer air to find a farm. She is anxious to have the whole family settled before the winter and in their own place, unbeholden to anyone.

## X

At first, Frédéric's disposition is too melancholy to find this task anything but tedious and unpleasant, but riding out one morning through Watervleit, five miles north of Albany, his interest in the countryside overcomes his dejection when a view of the Hudson River Valley gives him a sudden lift of heart. Here he comes to a farm of two hundred acres. The one-storied house, of brick and wood, is of a type he has seen in Switzerland. It seems almost new, and the dependencies in good order. It stands on the side of a hill, looking over the valley toward the blue hills, which shimmer in the summer light.

The proprietors show him around the house, which is raised five feet above the ground, with a cellar and dairy. The rooms are small but cozy and filled with light. There is one room he imagines he could make into a study and line with books, wallpaper on the walls. As he walks about the house, the doors being opened for him, he does not speak, afraid if he appears too enthusiastic the proprietors might change their minds.

When he walks about the property and sees the large apple orchard, a good-sized vegetable garden, several milk cows and two mares that he is told will bear, and is given the price of the land as two dollars an acre, he almost lets out a gasp. The farm pays Patroon Rensselaer a rent of fifteen bushels of corn a year.

The situation is pleasant, a fertile spot, well-wooded, and rich in pasture. Would he be able to farm this land successfully? He knows nothing about farming, after all.

He brings Lucy to see it the very next day, leaving the children with Peggy. She, too, finds the situation and area pleasant.

"This would be fine for us, just fine!" she says, standing outside the house in the sunlight and looking across the valley in her straw hat, her face shining with perspiration and enthusiasm.

Frédéric follows her around the house looking at the few rooms, which now seem in a state of some disrepair. They go into the kitchen and a beam of summer sunlight slants through a hole in the roof, dust particles caught in the light. There is an unpleasant musty smell in the pantry.

"Something smells dreadful in here," Frédéric says.

"Perhaps some trapped animal," Lucy says, opening up cupboards, hunting. They walk through the rest of the house where a film of dust lies on all the surfaces.

They stand in the dining room, and Frédéric holds his breath, in the still heat. He listens to the silence in the house.

He thinks of his grand, unfinished chateau near Bordeaux, of his father's ambitious plans to build something on the scale of Versailles. Will they ever be able to return there and reclaim their heritage, their lost lives, their position in society? He wants his children and his children's children to live in their proper place. It is as simple as that. Why should they be obliged to live here, almost like beasts? Why should they have to linger on in this country where everything and everyone, it seems to him, is for sale?

He says, "Lucy, is this wise? Do you think we can really do this on our own? What if one of us were to fall ill? We are, after all, not used to physical labor."

Lucy replies, "We are young and strong and intelligent. Why would we not be able to farm this land? Others do it all the time."

She strides around the place, telling him how it might be made more comfortable, suggesting several improvements. They could plaster the walls, fix the roof, and clean out the dairy.

She is a woman who lives in the present without regrets. She doesn't even seem to think unduly about her father. He has never heard her say she regrets anything. One would think she actually preferred this harsh life in America to the sweetness of her former existence in France. Certainly she does not seem to miss France. A capable woman, a good woman, but not a soft woman.

"*Sois douce,*" he would like to say at that moment. He would like to put his head on her shoulder and ask for comfort. He would like to say, let's go home, this is too difficult for me.

Lucy says, "And a pigsty. We will need a decent pigsty, definitely."

That evening, they confer with their friends on the price of the farm, which the Schuylers deem reasonable.

"Let us make a bid," Lucy says.

When their money arrives from Holland, they are able to buy the farm. Frédéric sends letters to his aunt, his friends, informing them of their new home.

In the months that follow he feels mainly fear, as though he has embarked unprepared upon some vast and risk-filled situation. They make arrangements to obtain the necessary equipment for the farm, which costs more money than he had thought, but something other than these arrangements fills him with foreboding. He realizes he is afraid he will die here in these poor, cramped rooms, that he will never return to France.

## XI

AUGUST, 1794

They engage a strong, broad-shouldered local woman, Betsey, to help Lucy with the children so that she can work in the dairy. She has read up about this work and tells Frédéric she is convinced they can make it pay. She believes she can handle it almost on her own.

The farm comes with the two mares of almost exactly the same size and color, but very different temperament, one as quiet as a lamb, who follows Lucy around like a dog, the other a devil that no one can master, until she is put to work between two cart horses. Lucy loves to ride this wild mare who responds to the slightest touch of her heels against her flanks, a sleek black horse who snorts with impatience and gallops until flecked with lather between her haunches and on her neck. If Lucy is happy in her work in the dairy and in the fields of wheat and corn, she is even happier in the open country. The further she rides the happier she becomes and the more plans for her farm come to her mind. She would like to plant hedges, dig a pond, and fence in a paddock for the cows.

As soon as the proprietors move out, they begin the improvements Lucy has suggested, covering the walls with plaster into which a little pink color has been added. Frédéric does his best to help. A French carpenter from Albany is called in to make an elegant small wooden pigsty that is deemed "noble" by their envious neighbors. Lucy makes sure her dairy is neatly paved with red brick and laid out with a proper descent, so that no water lodges in the pavement. She keeps it well washed and all the utensils perfectly clean.

She fences a paddock for the cows to keep them out of her vegetable garden, where they have already eaten all the summer lettuce. She learns to milk them herself, sitting on a small stool, talking to each of them as she greases the udders, making sure she strips them completely.

They acquire all the necessary equipment: milk pans, butter churns, and cheese tubs and barrels in which to ship the cheeses. She keeps eight cows. The majority are Devon, reddish cows with twisted horns, bred to calve at the end of March or early April, with one cow at the end of September, so that the family will have milk all year.

Working in her dairy at first light, her back aching as she bends over, she thinks of the Queen, who loved to play the simple country girl, Babet or Pierrette, and the Queen's sister-in-law, Elisabeth, who had herself painted in a dairymaid's cap. Poor, playacting, foolish women.

*The four essential components in the dairy are: milk, the curdling agent, the curd, and finally the cheese. As the whey rises to the surface it can be skimmed off with a ladle. The butter-making takes place mainly in the spring and early fall, and the cheese in the summer.*

Lucy rises before dawn and dresses in the dark. On her farm she dons a new disguise. She will dress like the other farmers so as not to stand out. It is safer to be one of the crowd, she has learned in Bordeaux. She will not make herself remarkable. She wears a blue-and-white striped skirt of wool, a little bodice of dark calico, and a colored handkerchief around her neck. The exterior of the under-dress is a garment lined and quilted, extending from the waist to the feet. The shoes are high-heeled, made of tanned calfskin or cloth.

She wears her fair, heavy hair parted, and piled up, held in place by a comb. The effect is pleasing to Frédéric, he tells her. He finds her at twenty-five even prettier than he did when he first saw her at sixteen, he says wistfully. He watches with amusement and laughs at the transformation when she drops her peasant disguise to visit the Schuylers or the van Rensselaers. She decks herself out anew in the few silk French dresses she has kept, and a superb hat she has made herself.

She has taken to farming immediately, as though she had been born and bred for this hard occupation.

"You must have some peasant blood somewhere," he says.

*He said of me what would be said of Napoléon, a few years hence: "Anyone who could teach that man a little idleness would benefit the universe." Frédéric would have liked a little more idleness in his wife.*

"How can we?" she says simply, when he reaches for her in the night. It would be impossible to be pregnant now. She has her hands full as it is.

Goodness, courage, and industry, Frédéric thinks, can be used as a weapon. How he longs for the softness of the air, the tenderness of the light in the Ile de France, the silkiness of his wife's skin.

## XII

It is on her farm that Talleyrand finds her, one warm, clear morning in late September. He has ridden up from Philadelphia, where he has taken refuge after being exiled from England. He has no intention of lingering on in the colonies, but for now he bides his time. He rides up the hill, sweating on this unusually warm fall day, noting the splendor in the leaves, the foliage—he has never seen so many colors—and the smell of the pigsty. As he goes on toward the small farmhouse, which he supposes to be hers, he is appalled to see a lithe young woman in peasant garb lifting up a hatchet in the air. The little girl at her side stares up at her mother as he halts his horse.

"My God!" Talleyrand murmurs, recognizing her as she lifts up a hatchet with a haughty snarl. She is engaged in preparing to cut a lamb bone from its carcass. Talleyrand, who has last seen her at Court in her presentation dress, curtsying before the Queen, calls out in French, "It would be impossible to cut a leg of lamb with more majesty."

Lucy turns and laughs, still holding her hatchet in one hand, coming toward him. He descends from his horse and limps toward her to embrace her and young Séraphine. He has thought to bring a doll for the little girl, as he did once for Lucy. He has bought it in England and produces it now from his pocket, like a rabbit from a conjurer's hat: a porcelain doll completely dressed in a chemise and silk stockings that makes the child smile up at him and clap her hands.

Lucy, too, greets him warmly. "How lovely of you to have thought of Séraphine and to have remembered the one you bought for me. You had it made for me by Rose Bertin, when I was about her age."

She is obviously glad to see a familiar face here. She looks remarkably well, her cheeks flushed from effort, her eyes luminous. A woman with a pioneer spirit, he marvels. She seems quite contented in this savage place, he thinks, looking around him at the burrs and weeds, the rows of corn, the hawthorne thickets, and smelling the odors of manure and smoke from the fire. He has known her since she was a child, and though he suspects she does not entirely approve of him, he has always admired her beauty, her intelligence, and her virtue. Now he also admires her courage and energy.

She says proudly, "Let me show you my farm," as though she has acquired a grand domain. He would much prefer to go inside, out of the heat, have a glass of wine with Frédéric, and rest his leg. He mumbles something about being rather thirsty.

Lucy doesn't seem to hear, so he is obliged to limp after her, careful to avoid the mud and mire, afraid of getting his boots wet and catching a chill. She insists on showing him everything, holding her little girl, who seems to be a good walker, by the hand. He is obliged to admire it all: the apple orchard, the fields of wheat, the corn, the pigsty, and even her cows, which she calls to in their pasture by name, as though they were her children, her friends, or perhaps, he thinks, her enemies. Indeed, she has humorously given them royal English names: Elizabeth, called Lizzie, and Mary, called Meg, Anne, Katherine, and Jane.

Talleyrand is not particularly eager to get too close to these cows, which rather terrify him with their dangerous-looking horns.

As a boy he once had a rather shameful incident with a bull, which chased him across a field. He had had to climb up a tree and be rescued by his nursemaid. He hangs back, as Lucy calls her favorites to come and meet him. "Come meet the Archbishop of Autun, my girls, my beauties," she says, leaning over the fence and turning her head to grin at him. He watches the big stupid beasts trot up, one in front of the other obediently. Their tails switch at flies, their skins shudder. They make a sort of mazy motion with their mouths. He backs up, lifts his lawn handkerchief to his nose, and, when Lucy prompts him, gingerly stretches out a hand to touch a shiny fat cow's reddish flank with the tips of his gloved fingers. Séraphine looks up and laughs at him. "Maman, the Archbishop doesn't like cows," she says quite clearly, clutching her doll to her breast. The precocious child must not be two years old, but apparently already speaks in sentences.

He, too, recalls Marie Antoinette playing the country girl, but this is no game. This woman takes her work seriously. She is telling him with pride how much money she plans to make from her dairy, her butter, which is already in some demand. She shows him the results, daintily prepared and stamped with her crest in the cool of the dairy. She wants to show him around it, asks if he would like to try his hand at milking. He lifts both of his pigskin-gloved hands in the air, appalled. "There I draw the line," he says.

He has always liked Frédéric, whose intelligent conversation, aristocratic ease, and playful erudition he enjoys. Lucy insists he return the next day to join them for the roast lamb she is preparing.

## XIII

As Talleyrand had foreseen, the roast lamb is crispy on the outside and not overdone, the way he was obliged to eat it in England. The freshly baked bread would rival any French baker's. He compliments Lucy on her cooking, but she laughs and says she knows he is a fine flatterer. She has simply followed the instructions in her cookbook. She turns the conversation toward the wider world, to more serious subjects, and questions him on news of France. He notices how closely she listens to his answers, so that her further questions display genuine interest.

The conversation flows with the excellent wine, which the couple have brought from France. With what assurance this young woman carries herself. Talleyrand is struck by her easy warmth, her calm grace, her mixture of sympathy and curiosity. Where does her self-assurance come from? He remembers her miserable childhood, the early death of her mother, her grandmother's cruelty and neglect. He remembers her painful shyness as a girl and realizes that beneath all of that she must have been made of sterner stuff.

Despite these qualities, despite her beauty, her exceptional complexion, the lovely light in her fair hair, she is not the sort of woman he would want for a mistress. Oh, my God, no! Not that he is against intelligent women, or women who think for themselves, on the contrary. But he has a passion for play. He cannot quite see Lucy entering into the play he would envisage for her. Pity.

He thinks of the succession of women in his life. He remembers the first one, a young actress he met in the shadows of the portico of a Gothic church. He saw her hesitate to venture out into the rain, lifting up a bright kerchief to protect her blond head. He had seized the opportunity to offer to share his umbrella. His life has been made up of a series of such opportunities, seized at exactly the right moment. He learned the art of timing at a young age.

He wonders about Madame de Flahaut from whom he has heard nothing recently. He thinks of the grand dinners she gave in her apartment in the Palace of the Louvre, which she had inherited from her mother, one of the many mistresses of Louis XV. He remembers the flickering light of the candles in the silver candelabra, the fine china, the white linen tablecloth. How she played with both him and the American, Governor Morris, deliberately making them jealous and yet at the same time able to like one another. There was a woman whose wiles he understood. How charming he had found her at those moments of, well yes, perverse pleasure.

Lucy, undoubtedly, would have disapproved of such behavior. Nothing perverse about Lucy Dillon. He wonders what it would be like to make love to such a matter-of-fact woman, and considers it might be unnerving. He is not sure he would quite be up to the task. He wonders if Frédéric is. Talleyrand thinks of a certain dark-skinned lady he has just met in Philadelphia. He has enjoyed shocking the burgers of Philadelphia walking through the streets with her on his arm. He thinks of the blue garter against her slim black leg, which pleases him inordinately. His mind drifts for a moment from the dinner conversation to an erotic reverie, his body growing warm and swollen like a lustful youth.

Then he looks at Frédéric, who sits in the middle of the table but does not seem to be suffering. Frédéric stares across the table through the charming bouquet of pink and yellow wildflowers and autumn leaves, which Lucy has arranged with so much taste. He gazes with adoration at his young wife. How he admires her! Lucy is amusing with intimate details of her beloved cows. Madame de Flahaut would have had trouble with cows.

He wonders why Lucy chose a man like Frédéric. He remembers suggesting this marriage to both of them, playing Puck rather mischievously. She had responded with enthusiasm, and the man also, apparently. They had him to thank for this good marriage. He has heard that it was at least partially her decision to marry him. She could have married anyone she wished, he would wager. Yet he is not sure that they are well suited; they seem very different from one another. As much as he likes and esteems Frédéric, he is afraid that, unlike his wife, he is not a person of much enterprise. It is from the mouth that Talleyrand can see that he lacks ambition and worldly wisdom. No, not an ambitious man, or one capable of adapting to different situations, different codes of honor, as Talleyrand knows himself to be. Yet a good man, loyal, and undoubtedly useful as a friend. Talleyrand is certain Frédéric will be useful to him at some point in his life, and he intends to cultivate them both. He is well aware of how useful women can be.

## XIV

After dinner they return to Albany to the home of the generous General Schuyler, his host. Talleyrand had been eager to meet this wealthy and well-educated American, having heard about him from his son-in-law, Alexander Hamilton.

They find Philip Schuyler waiting for them, striding up and down on the terrace in the late afternoon light, his powdered hair brushed back from his face, brandishing his newspaper in the air triumphantly.

"Great news!" he exclaims, as they come up the steps. "Robespierre himself, after Danton, has fallen victim to his own infernal machine and has thus brought about the end of the Terror. He was guillotined on the 24th of July, after apparently shooting himself in the jaw, in a failed effort to kill himself and cheat the blade."

This news is greeted with great joy, though it has come too late for so many. Their black clothes are the visible signs of their losses. Talleyrand, however, is particularly pleased, as he believes his sister-in-law, mother of three young children, has been spared the guillotine. But reading the newspaper later that evening, he discovers her name in the list of the executed. She has been in one of the last tumbrils of victims executed on the last day, the 9th Thermidor. Despite his grief, he cannot help thinking that perhaps now he will be able to return to France. He longs to be back and to take up the pieces of his broken career. He is already planning how he might use this change of circumstances to his advantage.

How deeply separate we are from our fellow human beings, he thinks. That evening, he writes an amusing letter to Germaine de Staël, telling her that Lucy and Frédéric actually sleep in the same bed! What is the world coming to in this savage place?

XV

Between October 25 and November 1, winter comes suddenly to the region. Lucy has never experienced a winter like this. The sky is covered by a mass of cloud so thick, night seems to fall when it is still day. Canoes and ferries are hauled out of the water or turned over keel upward. The snow falls so thickly it is impossible to see anyone at ten paces. Paths along the side of the Hudson are marked out with pine branches. She learns to dress herself and her children for this weather. From the natives in the area, the Onondagas, a tribe of the Mohawks, she buys moccasins made from buffalo skins and embroidered with dyed bark or porcupine quills.

Now they go for rides in the snow in their sledge, which is rather like a shallow box that holds the whole family. At the back is the main bench, mounted over a cupboard for packages. She sits there beside Frédéric with her children close beside them on either side, buffalo skins and sheepskins over their knees and feet, their breaths condensing heavily in the frost.

She likes speed, the cold air on her face, and the freedom of the vast spaces of the American night. She remembers her great-great-uncle's carriage with the six swift horses driving them back and forth to Versailles in the spring, and she holds Frédéric's hand. *I was so glad we were both safe in this new country. I felt he loved me, cared for me tenderly, though he found the farming life hard.*

As they work together in the kitchen making apple quince, Betsey tells Lucy that a young Negro, Minck, wishes to leave his master and the property on which he was born, because of the severity not only of his master but also of his own father, who belongs to the same master and who beats him.

"He wishes us to buy him from his master?" Lucy asks. "I am entirely against slavery," she says. "I have not come to this country of freedom to acquire slaves."

Betsey adds, "I've told Minck about you and what a generous mistress you are. He'd be much better off with you. You would be doing him a favor, and he would be grateful and work hard."

Lucy asks, "But would he be allowed to leave his master?"

Betsy nods, saying the letter has been written, giving permission for Minck to leave and find another master. "He would be happy to sell him."

When Lucy asks Frédéric, he says he would be glad for the help of a young man on the farm and agrees to acquire him. They climb into their red-and-yellow sledge drawn by the two black mares, whom they call Devil and Angel. They leave the children with Betsey and drive through the stinging snow and sleet to the farm where Minck is to be found. All the farms around here are owned by the same Dutch family, the Lansings.

After taking several wrong turns, Frédéric and Lucy arrive. A formidable-looking lady in a black dress, who reminds Lucy of her grandmother, opens the door for them. But this woman speaks with a heavy Dutch accent and wears a clean white cap that Marguerite would admire. It is the lady of the house, Mrs. Lansing, who stands stolidly in the void of her coldly soaped and well-waxed circular hallway. The large round silver platters gleam on the table behind her. The hall table gleams. A bowl of dried flowers stands on a table in a corner.

Appraising them with shrewd eyes, without further ado she asks them, in her halting English, "Do you have the money?" and ushers them into the parlor with its large fireplace covered with a tapestried fire screen and shining brass implements. The winter light comes in aslant through a low window. Lucy thinks of a Vermeer painting, *The Interruption of the Music Lesson*, which she has seen in Holland.

Frédéric counts out the money Lucy has been clutching in a leather pouch under her cloak. They have received it as a bequest from Lady Dillon, one of Lucy's English relatives, so that they will wear appropriate mourning on her demise. Lucy watches the counting of the coin on the gleaming table, listens to the chink, and wonders what Lady Dillon would say if she knew to what purpose her money was being put.

At that moment, a tall man, dressed in a good cloak of homespun gray, enters the room without a word and with a severe expression.

"My husband," Mrs. Lansing informs them. He then duly counts the money again and locks it up in a strong, well-polished box.

Mr. Lansing then calls forth Minck. He comes in shyly and stands against the wall, head bent, turning his hat around by the brim, glancing up hopefully at Lucy and Frédéric.

*I saw his shyness and remembered walking into the room on the day I was engaged to Frédéric. I, too, had wished to leave the house where I was held in what I had felt as bondage.*

What must this young man be feeling at such a moment, she wonders. She would like to be able to think her way under his dark skin. She would like to say something reassuring to him.

Mr. Lansing beckons to him to come forward. He reaches out, takes one of Minck's hands, and places it in Frédéric's. "This is your new master," he says. Minck grasps Frédéric's hand and looks up at him with large dark eyes. They stand for a moment holding hands like a couple before the altar, as Lucy and Frédéric once did with such joy...

Lucy, who feels her face burn, wishes to leave, but Mrs. Lansing, now that she has her money, is suddenly hospitable. She insists they stay, and wine and cake are served. Minck is sent to prepare for his departure. When Lansing hears that Frédéric has represented the French King as a plenipotentiary minister in Holland, he would have them stay still longer, waxing suddenly loquacious, offering to bring out his best Madeira.

They find Minck already installed in the sledge in his best clothes, which he tells them he has paid for with his own money.

"Where are all your things?" Lucy asks. He shows them his few possessions, which might have fitted into the hat that he has already put in the locker of the sledge. He seems already to have made himself at home. Then he turns to them, touching his cap like any well-trained coachman, and lifts up the reins. Angel and Devil set off at a gallop.

# XVI

Lucy works beside Minck, milking her favorite cow. She sees a shadow in the entrance to the dairy and hears a cough. She looks up. A tall, dark-skinned man stands before her with his hat in his hands.

Minck makes a noise which might be a cry of either delight or sorrow.

"It is my father," Minck says, rising, and knocking over the bucket of milk beneath the cow he is milking. "Oh! Pardon," he says.

"My name is Prime," the father says, bowing his head. "You must buy me. I will help you run your farm properly." He comes forward with a confident air, picks up the milk bucket his son has knocked over, clucking his tongue and shaking his head. He begins milking the cow with an expert hand while Minck stands by, his mouth open. Lucy wonders if this, perhaps, has been the father's aim all along. A clever man.

*Word had spread fast that these French aristocrats, unlike the local Dutch farmers, were benevolent employers.*

She says to him firmly, "I would like to have you work with us on our farm, on one condition. There is to be no trouble with your son. You must promise not to lay a finger on him."

"Like master like slave," he says, and grins.

## XVII

WINTER, 1794

Prime convinces Lucy to buy yet another man to help them.

"Thomas is a good man," he tells Lucy. "He will work hard for you. We need another man on the farm. It will make Master's work easier," he says shrewdly, with a glimmer of complicity in his eyes. She nods her head and grins at him. It is clear they do need more help. Frédéric has not developed a taste for farming. So she is to become a slave owner, here in this country of freedom.

When Thomas has hardly arrived and been established in a room in one of the dependencies, he says he has been separated from his wife, Judith, for fifteen years. If someone will offer to buy her, and she wishes to leave, her master cannot keep her anymore, though in practice such a thing is often almost impossible to arrange. The slave owner has all the power. Lucy needs another woman on the farm, as Betsey has now left to marry, so she agrees to speak to Judith's master.

"He is a bad man. Be careful," Thomas tells her.

"I'm not afraid of some Dutch farmer," she says scornfully.

Nevertheless, for this acquisition she deems it wiser to dress in her fancy French clothes, or what is left of them, and an elaborate plumed and beribboned hat she has made.

Once again Lucy sets out in her sledge, the money under her cape, this time without Frédéric but with Minck driving. She arrives at the small wooden house one winter morning. She is greeted by a certain Wilbeck, a tall, stout man, who is walking down the wooden steps, his face shaded by his hat. She steps out of the sledge as if it is a grand carriage, and offers him her gloved hand, which he hardly touches.

She says, "I believe you work for our friend Mr. van Rensselaer," and smiles her most condescending smile.

"I have that honor," the man says, glancing at her warily.

She tells him that she has come to buy his slave, Judith. She has heard that he wishes to sell her.

"You are ill-informed. I have no such intention, ma'am. Indeed, she is very useful to me," Wilbeck replies, adding that he is in a hurry to leave.

Lucy stands before him, not moving, blocking his path. Some seconds pass. He surveys her with small dark eyes. A muscle twitches at the corner of his mouth.

"I believe that it is unlawful to keep a slave who wishes to be sold," Lucy tells him and smiles again, graciously.

"She has no wish to be sold." His voice has become rancorous and he is obviously annoyed. They stare at one another and in that moment, detest one another. He is about to say something else but stops, clearly deciding not to say what has come to mind.

Lucy says her sources tell her otherwise. Wilbeck glances darkly over her shoulder at Minck, who is sitting in the sledge, holding the reins of the horses and looking straight ahead.

"The girl is quite content with me," Wilbeck says. He adds, "If that settles the matter, I must leave."

"Not at all, sir. Nothing is settled." Lucy smiles at him. "Apparently you have been waiting for someone who wishes to acquire her. As you can see, I am here. Be so good as to call her forth, and tell her she has now found her new mistress," Lucy commands, as though Wilbeck had not spoken.

He studies her carefully and directly, taking in the fancy silver dress, the leghorn hat, the feather, the kid gloves.

"I'm sure Mr. van Rensselaer, our dear friend, will be pleased with your decision," Lucy adds and smiles again at him, going past him with a rustle of her gown, up the steps of his house in her high heels. She puts her gloved hand on his door handle, hoping he has not noticed how it is trembling.

He takes out his key, opens his front door, and calls forth his slave from the interior.

Judith appears in the doorway almost immediately, as though she has been waiting. A tall, thin woman with a worn, gray face, though she must still be quite young, she wears a gray skirt and dirty white apron and cap. She stands with her hands clasped and her head lowered, glancing up at Lucy from the side of her eyes.

"Come on, Thomas is waiting for you," Lucy says.

She counts out the money, takes Judith by the hand, and leads her out to her sledge.

# XVIII

## 1795

Spring comes as suddenly as winter here.

Lucy watches with satisfaction as their apple trees bloom, the delicate white blossoms like thick fallen snow on the branches. The crop promises to be plentiful. They have followed the old Bordeaux custom of hoeing a patch four or five feet square around each tree. They hunt in Albany for a number of Bordeaux casks instead of the new porous wood that is used here to keep the cider. The cellar is prepared with as much care as if it were to store the fine wines of Medoc.

The crops are springing up: the corn and the wheat, well-ended, well-weeded by Minck, Prime, and Thomas. There are no wild poppies on the edges of these fields.

Sometimes in the evenings when her work is finished, she rides her restless black mare, Devil, out onto her land. She loves to ride with the beautiful ladies' saddle that Talleyrand has generously given her, complete with bridle and saddle cloth. She trots out alone into the evening silence of this new land. She feels a deep joy in her physical well-being. *I was alive and well. In this new country we had managed to acquire a farm and to keep everyone alive. With our own hands and the help of our people, we were able to farm the land successfully and even make a profit. There was enough for everyone to eat.*

She revels in this moment of solitude after a long day of hard work. She feels the horse's restless body move beneath her, cantering. Her step is light, and the mare seems hardly to touch the earth.

It seems possible to fly, possible to be both body and spirit in the freedom and silence of this vast space. All this savage beauty belongs to her for as far as the eye can see. She has never felt so free.

She does not often have time to go riding for her pleasure. She rises before daybreak and goes to her cows. Then the milk is set aside and strained and cooled. The fires are lit, and breakfast, which is eaten at eight o'clock, is prepared. She finds herself so preoccupied by her chores that she often forgets to eat. Her own need for food seems slighter, and she hardly notices that she is growing thinner. She does not dislike being so light, which enables her to move quickly about the fields or the dairy, but Frédéric protests. She promises that her appetite will come back when their crop has been harvested in the fall.

During breakfast, she watches the milk for the cheese warm over the fire in a large brass kettle. The milk from the eight cows is enough to make ten or fifteen cheeses, each of about eight inches in diameter and four inches high. About eight cheeses are made a year in this way. After dinner, the cheeses have to be turned and rubbed.

She makes her butter in collusion with these same fat cows. To make butter, the milk is set for twelve hours in summer and twenty-four hours in winter, to let the cream rise. Then the cream is scalded, till bubbles rise and the cream changes its color. After standing for twelve hours more, it is ready to be skimmed and put into a tub or churn for beating or dashing until butter comes. It is then washed in many different waters. She finds the vertical movement of the butter churn fatiguing, and she requires the help of her men to turn the common churn and the barrel churn. Sometimes she flavors the butter with caraway and sometimes she rolls the little cakes in pepper.

*You think when you are very young that you will do something that will last forever. Lasting is what is important. But if you step back and look up at the stars you realize that nothing, nothing will last much longer than a small cake of butter, perfectly made.*

Every morning Prime takes the sledge to the market in Albany, where he sells wood as well as the butter, cheese, and cream. He brings back fresh meat for the family. Like Marguerite, he can neither write nor read, but he keeps his accounts so accurately there is never the slightest error. He brings back a not inconsiderable sum of money from the market.

Lucy likes to earn money with her own hands. She would like to earn more and suggests they acquire more cows and buy additional acres to farm, but Frédéric demurs.

In the summer they are lent a mill for pressing their apples, which is harnessed to an ancient horse. There are two interlocking grooved pieces of wood like ratchets, which are turned by the horse—a present from General Schuyler. The horse is harnessed to a wooden bar. Round and round the ancient horse walks. Humbert proudly sits astride the horse and rides all day while the apples fall into the hopper, convinced his contribution is essential.

Lucy's butter becomes in great demand. People have heard her story and are curious. Besides, the butter does not taste of winter feeding. She cuts it carefully into small pieces, stamps it with her crest, and arranges it daintily in a clean basket on a fine cloth. Her cream is always fresh.

At sunset the cows are milked again, the milk strained, and the day's labor has ended. Lucy likes the hard work and working side by side with her women and men on her farm, milking her cows and making her butter and cream.

At nine in the evening tea is served, the bread spread with the excellent butter and a Stilton cheese Talleyrand has generously left them, together with the beautiful ladies' saddle.

# XIX

Riding along a narrow path on her wild mare in the cool of the thick forest, Lucy is startled to see a tall, broad-shouldered man, stark naked, his dark skin glistening. He walks calmly toward her through shadow and light. He lifts his hand in greeting and approaches without fear or shame. He tells her in good English that his name is John. He asks if he might cut willow branches for her and weave them into baskets. She thanks him, her voice a little strange in her ears, attempting to keep her expression from showing surprise and her gaze from lingering on certain well-made parts of his body or on his tomahawk, which he holds lightly in one hand.

He suddenly reappears, a few weeks later, one summer day, as Lucy rides out alone late in the afternoon. Again he walks along almost naked, but this time he carries six closely woven round baskets, all fitting one into the other, in his arms.

He refuses money but asks only for a jar of buttermilk. He would like to taste the milk from her dairy. He has seen her cows, the butter she makes. She takes him to her dairy, dismounts, and serves him from a wooden bowl, as Boyd had once fed her in a moment of great hunger and despair on the ship. She watches him drink the buttermilk with the same pleasure she still has when she sees her children eating plentifully. *Not enough food to go around*.

The Indian women, too, come to the house and sit motionless beside her door in the evenings. Humbert likes to go among them and talk to them, now that he speaks such good English. He asks them why they wear such funny clothes, and they laugh at him. Sometimes when they get up to go, they take him by the hand and he wanders off with them. Judith calls out to him. "You must not go with the Indians," she tells him. She has told Lucy that the Indians sometimes steal white children. But Humbert doesn't listen.

One of the women is known as the "Old Squaw" because of her advanced age. She is dressed scantily, wearing only a sort of apron of blue cloth and a small shawl thrown over her shoulders fastened by an acacia thorn. She frightens Judith, who insists that she must be a witch, and might put a curse on them. She must be placated at important moments, such as the calving of a cow, the birth of a child.

Lucy has been warned not to give the Indians rum, but she finds some artificial flowers, feathers, and ribbons, which she has kept from her days in France, and which the women accept with great delight. Old Squaw is particularly pleased.

Despite her advanced age, Old Squaw loves to adorn herself and is delighted when she is able to admire her reflection in the mirror, which Judith brings out to her. Old Squaw takes Lucy's gifts with many compliments in her good English. "Mrs. Latour, great lady, from the old country," she murmurs to Lucy. She loves to use the tip of an old feather, a knot of ribbon, or even an old fake flower for this purpose, winding them into her hair as Lucy did once the bluebirds into her own. Lucy remembers the elderly women at the court of Versailles who dressed up their hair with identical vanity.

## XX

In the fall Frédéric receives a tiresome visit from a French nobleman who was an officer in his regiment. The man, who has escaped
the Revolution, wants to become a farmer, too, but knows nothing
about farming, speaks no English, and has neither wife nor children to help him. Nor does he show much industry, but rather
lingers late in his bed and arrives at the breakfast table expecting
to be served his chocolate and brioche. He eats copiously but does
not offer to go out into the fields with Frédéric. He complains of a
headache and lies on the couch through the day, staring wistfully
out the window, or nodding off over the book on farming Lucy
has thrust into his hands.

Finally Lucy suggests he come riding with her one morning to
see the countryside. She studies his portly frame and languid movements and suggests he ride the more docile of her two mares. But
he begins to lag behind, almost immediately, and she can see he
needs a riding crop to spur on Angel. He has not thought to bring
one, and she never carries one, having no need for one on Devil.
She is growing impatient at his slow pace, his inability to make his
horse advance, and his inane conversation, when she hears a slight
rustle in the grass. She catches a glimpse of her friend John, who is
walking through the bush toward them, the spring sun shining on
his broad, bare shoulders.

"Hallo John!" Lucy calls out to him gaily, waving her gloved
hand, glad of the interruption.

The French officer watches with an indescribable expression of horror and surprise as the tall Indian emerges from the bush, coming toward them almost naked, only a blue cloth fixed by a cord between his legs and to his waist, a tomahawk in one hand, his other held out in greeting to Lucy.

"My God! Savages!" he cries in terror, turning his horse in the opposite direction and digging in his heels, managing to take off with considerable speed.

Lucy speaks to John for a moment in English, exchanging pleasantries about her companion's desultory riding style. John glances at the Frenchman cowering on his horse at a considerable distance, hiding behind the trees, and grins at Lucy and says gravely that the man certainly looks as if he is in dire need of a crop.

Before Lucy can explain anything to her horrified companion, John is off and reappears, leaping lightly from the top of a hillock, his tomahawk still in one hand, in the other a stick, stripped of its bark, which he politely offers to the Frenchman.

He grasps it and uses it immediately to good effect on his horse's back.

"And what if you had been alone!" the Frenchman mutters, his face flushed with horror, when Lucy has caught up with him.

"I should have been exactly as unalarmed," Lucy replies with a laugh. She cannot resist adding, "And, you know, if I had needed to defend myself from *you*, John would gladly have thrown his tomahawk at your head."

## XXI

A vegetable cart often passes before Lucy's door. The driver, a respectable-looking man well-dressed in waistcoat and gray home-spun trousers, always stops and offers his wares. He tells Lucy he is a Quaker. He belongs to a reformed branch of Quakers and his settlement, which is not far from their farm, is bounded on one side by the thick forest belonging to the town of Albany and on the other by the Mohawk River. Lucy invites him into her kitchen, where he sits down at her table.

He explains to her that an Englishwoman had made a number of converts to this sect in the states of Massachusetts and Vermont.

Lucy always buys something from him, but he refuses to take the money from her hand. If she finds his price too high, he says, "As you please," and she puts the money she wishes to pay down on the edge of the table.

"You should come and visit our settlement," he says one afternoon.

"I would like that very much," Lucy replies.

It is Prime, who knows the country well, who leads her and Frédéric to their settlement. He rides on ahead of them to show the way. Frédéric and Lucy ride side by side in silence along a vague path, then the path becomes clearer and better kept. They go on for three hours. Lucy begins to suspect Prime must be lost, when they pass the barrier that marks the boundary of the Quaker property. Then the path becomes even better marked, almost a road. They go through pleasant meadows, with horses and cows who have been turned loose to graze, until they come to a clearing where there are a number of buildings: a brick community house, a church, and school.

They are greeted kindly but with considerable reserve by one of the Quaker men. Prime takes their horses to the stable, for there is no inn. Their guide offers them no refreshment after their long ride, nor does he speak to them. The Quaker simply leads them in silence through a neat but charmless vegetable garden where other Quakers are tilling and weeding. They are taken to visit a boys' and a girls' school, the stables, and the dairies, all of which impress Lucy with their cleanliness if not with their charm. Everywhere they go, Lucy is struck by the order, the cleanliness, and the silence. Not one word, not one song disturbs the air. All the women wear the same gray woolen cloth and toil in silence. There are no small children.

Eventually, a bell rings, inviting the community to prayer. Lucy and Frédéric are asked if they would like to join the community and are led to opposite ends of an immense room. Lucy is taken to a chimney corner and allowed to sit down but warned to remain silent, though there is no one with whom she might converse.

While she admires the cleanliness and the high shine of the white pine floor where rows of copper nails appear, wondering what might be their purpose, a bell peals and sixty odd girls and women but no children are ushered into the long, cold room by an ancient woman. They all stand motionless with the toes of their shoes on the lines of nails until the ancient woman gives a sort of cry or groan, when they all change places. This happens several times. The elderly woman then mumbles some words that Lucy does not entirely understand, though some of them seem to be in English. Lucy bows her head and says her own little prayer in French. She asks God to give her strength to continue her work in this new country.

# XXII

## Fall, 1795

Lucy is obliged to ride to Troy to fetch a new milk can for her dairy. Frédéric is working in the fields with the other men, so she leaves the children with Judith. She sees the Indian women sitting immobile by her door and watches Humbert go off with them. She goes into the stable. Her nervous black mare nickers as she crosses the threshold into her stall. She approaches and saddles her, slipping the bit into her mouth. She will make the trip a quicker one though she can be hard to handle, startling easily at the slightest sound or movement in the grass. She sets out alone at a canter, waving to Séraphine, who runs a little way after her on pink legs, calling out "Good-bye," as Lucy goes down the hill and across the fields.

Her business in town takes her longer than she had thought, and when she rides back, night is already falling. She rides her mare fast to the ferry, which is crowded at this evening hour. With several other passengers, she waits for the ferryman to push off, and chats with a young man in a gray cloak who admires her restless horse. The river runs darkly. She looks up at the stars. Just as the ferry is about to leave the bank, a farmer arrives driving before him four large oxen. He calls out to the ferryman and waves to him, telling him to wait for him.

The ferryman tells him to wait for the next trip, the ferry is too crowded, and his oxen will frighten the young lady's skittish horse. But the farmer, a large man himself, insists, arguing vociferously and insistently. At this point the farmer throws him a coin, and the man shrugs his shoulders and stops.

The farmer and his oxen crowd onto the ferry. Lucy's mare bucks and strains at the bit, and she leans forward and strokes her neck and whispers soothingly in her ear, to calm her down. Her first impulse is to get off the ferry, but it is completely dark now, and she is afraid Frédéric and the children will worry if she does not get home soon. She gets down from her horse and holds her by the reins.

In mid river, the four heavy and thirsty oxen, all unyoked, lean over the side of the ferry to drink. It tips dangerously to the side. Water pours in, wetting her boots and soaking the hem of her riding dress. The ferryman shouts to her to let her horse loose and to hold onto him instead, but she continues to hold onto her horse.

One of the passengers, the young man in the dark cloak, has the presence of mind to stick his knife into the rump of one of the oxen who plunges into the river. All the other three follow suit, and the ferry rights itself, though not before everyone is standing in water up to their calves and the farmer is swearing loudly at the young man who has saved them.

Safely home, she has bad dreams. She awakens at dawn, shivering and light-headed, but insists on rising and going about her work. She wraps a wool shawl around her shoulders and goes into her dairy to her cows with Séraphine. "Lizzie, little Lizzie," she sings to her favorite cow, as she leans wearily against her flank. She puts the bucket under the cow's udders, greases her teats. She is convinced her cows know her, understand their names, know what she is feeling, and are quieted by her singing.

At breakfast she drinks bowl after bowl of milk and then evacuates all of it in a furious gush. Judith obliges her to lie down with the shutters closed. She feels she is rocking, as though she were on the ship again, and she dreams of her two mares: an Angel and a Devil, who are both talking to her at once. When she wakes, her face is wet with tears.

She rises the next day and goes about her work, but every evening the fever returns at the same time, and with it the thirst and diarrhea. She refuses to go to bed. The farm needs her. The children need her. She drags herself through the days.

## XXIII

At breakfast one morning, Frédéric watches as Humbert enters the kitchen barefooted, his unbrushed hair falling into his eyes. He slouches by the kitchen table and puts his finger into the jam jar, licks it, and sticks it back in again. Frédéric looks at Lucy as she moves around the kitchen expertly. How thin and pale she has grown. She has something sharp about her face now, something sly that makes him think of a fox, and her neck looks strained. Humbert continues to eat the jam with his finger. Frédéric admonishes him.

Frédéric says to her, "That boy needs to learn some manners." She shrugs her shoulders.

"At his age my grandfather already had me studying my Caesar," Frédéric says.

"What are we to do?" she asks, sitting down opposite him. He can hear the worry in her voice.

"It's high time this boy learned something," Frédéric says. "He is left too much to his own devices all day long: he wanders off with the savages or rides bareback on one of the horses. He is running wild. He needs schooling, someone to teach him his letters, Latin, mathematics, discipline, and neither of us have the time or the strength." He wants his child to have the education that he feels has been his means of survival. His rigorous French education, the best in the world surely, is what has given him the strength to continue and an idea of who he is, despite all the upheavals in his life.

Lucy agrees and says they need someone like Combes.

"Well, there's no one like that around here," Frédéric says.

"Could we ask the minister's wife to give him some lessons?" Lucy asks.

"She lives too far away to come here daily. We would have to send him to stay with her," Frédéric says.

"You wouldn't think of sending him away, would you?" she asks.

"What else can we do? There are no adequate schools for him here. He needs an education more than he needs his mother or his father," Frédéric responds, and thinks of his own mother with her dark smooth hair.

"He won't want to go off," Lucy says. "He is so tall for his age and full of energy and high spirits. I worry about him on the horses. He's likely to get hurt one of these days."

Despite her protests Frédéric decides to leave Humbert with the minister's wife, who is childless and loves children and offers to care for him, to teach him to read and write and devote herself to him. He tries to comfort Humbert by saying he can take Black with him. He feels he must do what is best for him, watching his weeping boy leave in the carriage.

He thinks of his dead father, his mother still cloistered, his aunt in England, and wishes his family and friends were nearer. Without Lucy's health, how will they manage on the farm? Would it not be wiser to return to France, now that the Terror has ended?

## XXIV

Frédéric hands Lucy a letter from Talleyrand, inviting them to New York City as soon as possible. They must stay with Mr. Law, his friend. There are papers that Frédéric needs to sign. Talleyrand has somehow heard of the imminent bankruptcy of the bank where Frédéric has left their money. He has managed to force his way into the banker's office and demand that he relinquish the Count's money before declaring bankruptcy. Thanks to Talleyrand's foresight, Lucy understands, Frédéric has been spared a huge loss.

Frédéric says he doesn't understand. "The bank seemed such a respectable and safe one," he says. "I spoke at length to the banker, a very nice man, and he assured me there was no risk."

Lucy does not like to think what this means, or why he was not able to discover what Talleyrand did. How had he handed over their precious remaining money to an unreliable banker? She cannot help but think of her grandmother's words: "More memory than sense."

She thinks of the contradictions in her husband's character; such an intelligent, learned man, but such an unworldly one, better with abstractions than the reality of everyday life. Why has he so little ability in finance? America, where finance is so important, is perhaps not the best place for him.

They leave Séraphine with Betsey, who comes to stay on the farm with her new husband.

They take a boat down the Hudson River to New York, boarding the ship the night before, as it leaves early in the morning. The journey takes twenty-six hours, though much of that time is spent at anchor.

Though Lucy admires the houses, villages, and the hills along the side of the river, she shivers, first hot then cold, and her head aches. Her fever has returned. Why does she not get well? Sickness makes her impatient. She has so rarely been sick. She feels that an effort of will should overcome all. She insists on going ashore to visit West Point.

When Talleyrand greets her on their arrival at Mr. Law's house he sees immediately that she is ill and insists that she rest.

"Just a little tired after the voyage. I'll be all right tomorrow. I want to come with you to Philadelphia to meet the great Washington," she says enthusiastically, for her husband has told her of the plan.

"Nonsense. There is no possibility of your traveling with us. You are going to stay here until you are better." Talleyrand, unlike Frédéric, dares to talk to her like a father. Frédéric, though he has been with her every day, has not been aware of what Talleyrand has spotted immediately: her increasing weakness. Sometimes she feels Frédéric no longer sees her as she is but as he would wish her to be.

Talleyrand convinces her to let the housekeeper at Mr. Law's house put her to bed and take care of her while he and Frédéric leave for Philadelphia to sign the necessary papers at the bank.

Lucy lets the housekeeper help her undress. The stout woman has a gentle face, though something severe around her mouth. Her hands are red and roughened with work, which gives her nobility. There is a question in her eyes, a quietly enquiring gaze, which has something devout about it. Lucy thinks with longing of Marguerite and her quiet but profound piety. She must be wondering about me, Lucy thinks. She cannot even write to her, as Marguerite has never learned to read. Will she ever see her again?

The housekeeper puts her to bed in the large, quiet bedroom with the red velvet curtains and bedspread. What a luxury, she thinks, as she sinks down into the clean starched sheets. She runs her fingers over the embroidered initials.

It is months since she has slept in such a luxurious room with a wide, comfortable, clean bed, with someone to help her take off her clothes. How strange to lie down in the day like a child forced to take a nap. She struggles to stay awake to listen to the sounds of the house, the carriages in the street, voices. Outside is the City of New York. She would like to go out and explore the busy streets.

Finally, she is obliged to close her eyes, now that there is someone competent to care for her. She surrenders herself to the blissful underworld of dreams. She sleeps, her head bathed in sweat, her legs and arms spread-eagled, as though crucified. She loses herself in a passion of sleep, though aware at moments that someone is watching over her. It seems to her that the housekeeper keeps coming into the room in her navy dress, bringing her a cup of steaming broth.

She dreams of her farm, the hills sloping down to the valley dotted with cows. She sees her children approaching through the long grass. Her little girl's eyes are filled with panic, reaching out her arms beseechingly, her mouth open in a cry for help. She wants something fiercely, and Lucy cannot help her. Increasingly, Lucy's dreams become disordered, and she is obliged to give herself over to her sickness. There is pleasure in just lying in the bed alone, succumbing to the fever, though at moments when she is fully conscious she thinks of her husband, who will have the opportunity of meeting General Washington. She would like to see him, shake his hand, speak to him. She has heard he is very tall: over six foot four and a man of commanding presence.

The sun is shining into the room. "Close the shutters, could you? The light makes my head ache," she says, and closes her eyes.

By the evening she is delirious again. The White Lady is dragging her across a field of snow. The earth tilts and rocks beneath her. She is frightened of falling as the sailor did from the high mast, his arms flailing at the rigging.

After four days the hot and cold fits end, and she wakes to find Frédéric sitting at her side. She reaches out her hand to him.

"You came back," she says.

"Of course, I came back," he says. "I always will."

# XXV

When she has recovered, she joins her husband, Alexander Hamilton, Talleyrand, and Law. They sit outside on the terrace in the warm evening under a sky filled with stars. She says little but listens with pleasure. She immediately likes Hamilton, a man just under forty years old, she judges, who speaks excellent French. She likes his delicate bone structure, his fresh complexion, violet-blue eyes, auburn hair. She finds his face distinctive, his manners gentlemanly, his mind intelligent, well-informed, and full of energy.

They speak of Hamilton's father-in-law, Philip Schuyler.

"He has been so kind and helpful to us," Lucy says, and tells Hamilton how Schuyler greeted her when she first saw him in his daughter's garden.

Hamilton tells them how Schuyler was defeated by Aaron Burr in his race for the U. S. Senate. Hamilton, himself, has recently resigned from the Treasury and resumed his legal practice. "I had little choice if I wished to leave any legacy to my children," he says.

Lucy finds his frank and critical conversation intriguing. She gathers he has his disagreements with Jefferson.

"A utopian visionary with a misguided set of political principles," he says bluntly. He is not much kinder to John Adams, but it is Aaron Burr, obviously, whom he despises. "No principles at all," he declares. Lucy is surprised by all the intrigue and animosity among these men. *I had thought they would be above such bickering in America.*

Hamilton describes the War of Independence with brilliance. He tells them how he led an infantry assault, jumping over a parapet in a desperate bayonet charge against the entrenched British at Yorktown. He speaks of his fiscal program for the new nation. He seems to consider the problems of the world as though they were personal challenges. Lucy likes this enthusiasm, this optimism, and his small fine hands, which he waves around in the twilight. She thinks how different this account is from the insipid one given by Lafayette, alias General Morpheus, whom she considers a decidedly silly man who sought nothing more than his own glory.

One afternoon, Hamilton offers to take them on a tour of the city. He takes them to see King's College in Lower Manhattan, where he attended classes, explaining how his studies were interrupted by the American Revolution. He shows them the tavern run by Samuel Fraunces, which was popular with the revolutionaries. He takes them to the house on Cherry Street where Washington lived.

The weeks go by quickly and Lucy is enjoying her life in New York with this agreeable company, until Law, their amiable host, brings these pleasant days to a sudden end. He warns them one morning that there is yellow fever in the town, that they might be trapped there.

## XXVI

Séraphine runs to her and flings herself against her legs. Lucy lifts her up, and she tips off Lucy's hat and puts her hands into her hair, pulling out the pins. "Don't leave me again," the child orders, beating her fists angrily against Lucy's shoulder. The child smells of wild air and grass. She has been running wild on her pink legs under the trees.

Lucy has been away a whole month and hugs her, full of delight to find her well and happy, to feel her warm, lively body against her own.

She returns to her tasks full of ardor. She resumes the washing and the ironing. They work together in the clean, orderly dairy. She goes to her cows in the early morning, walking across the field through grass wet with dew. Her cows greet her, lifting up their heads, flicking their tails joyfully and lowing gently, as she enters the cool of their stalls. She likes the slightly sour smell in the dairy and lingers at the cows' sides, calling them by name.

A new calf is born, whom she calls Liliac. She stays with the mother in the field through the labor and comforts her and then watches her lick her calf all over and then sees the awkward, trembling, endearing first steps the calf makes by her mother's side. She refuses to let her Negroes take the calf from the mother as they want to do to increase the supply of milk.

The apple crop is harvested and magnificent. Their cider is sold at a high price. Lucy's Negroes work hard by her side. Frédéric, too, works beside them in the fields harvesting, though with less enthusiasm. He finds this work monotonous and likes to slip away into his study to read or to wander off a little way with Séraphine. Lucy watches them go and hopes he will eventually be happy as a farmer.

Indian summer is a time of peace and prosperity. She has fallen in love with this land, the breadth and stretch of it, the blue hills in the distance, the fall leaves in all their variety, the gold of the light, the smooth blue of the sky, the wildness of the dense forests. She likes the variety of the people here—the Indians, the Negroes, her Dutch friends, and particularly Peggy van Rensselaer, whom she visits in Albany whenever she can.

## XXVII

She wakes one morning early to hear her child crying. For a moment she doesn't move, the sky still dark and the cry soft. Then the crying becomes louder. She rises and puts on a gown, and goes into Séraphine's small bedroom with its faint odor of flowers and urine, its pink flowered wallpaper she has put up with her own hands.

"What is it, my love?" she asks, standing barefooted by Séraphine's bed, her loose hair falling in her face. Cramps have rolled her child into a small ball. Her quilt is on the floor, her little fists held tightly against her stomach. She is doubled over with pain, her face as white as her gown. Her throat and bowels disgorge together.

"Oh, child!" Lucy bends over her, feels her damp forehead and cold hands. She lifts her from her bed to clean her.

The child has no fever but lies pale and conscious, her large eyes, her father's, fixed on her mother, in terrible pain. She complains of thirst. Lucy brings her water to drink, but she vomits it up and continues to moan. She asks her mother to take away the pain.

Lucy remembers the child's hunger on the ship, when she sucked so helplessly at her dry dugs. She remembers how fast and furiously she had arrived in the house at Canoles with the night sounds running through the fierce travail.

Séraphine asks Lucy if the little van Rensselaer boy, her playmate, could come and hold her hand, but Lucy has heard the night before from Peggy that he, too, is ill with the same troubling and mysterious stomach pains.

Lucy sends Frédéric to fetch the doctor. From the window she watches him gallop across the fields on Devil. She sends Judith to see that someone milks her cows, whom she hears lowing in the pasture. She sits by the child's side and holds her hand and wishes Marguerite were here to help.

When the doctor arrives, it is already noon, the sun hot and strong. Outside all is quiet on the farm. There are flies buzzing against the windowpanes as he enters the room. His boots are dusty. His bag creaks as he opens it and then snaps it shut. Frédéric stands beside him and watches as he examines the child in silence.

The doctor asks the couple to step out into the corridor. He tells Lucy and Frédéric that there is no cure for this illness, that many children are stricken, and there is no hope. He has come from the Rensselaers' house.

"There must be something we can do!" Frédéric says, but the doctor shakes his head.

Lucy asks if there is not at least something to help with the pain.

She goes back in to sit beside her child and gives her a teaspoonful of laudanum. Séraphine lies still, her big eyes open, looking up at her mother. "Am I going to die, Maman?" she asks.

Lucy looks down at her, this child who has made the long voyage across rough seas with them.

"Hold me tight. I don't want to leave you," the little girl says.

Lucy gathers her up in her arms and carries her over to the window to see the oak tree and across the valley the blue mountains in the distance. Frédéric stands beside them. He says, "See the light in the leaves, my darling," but Séraphine is looking up at her mother's face. She lifts her hand to cling to Lucy's loose hair, as the light of understanding goes from her eyes, and her fingers slip through Lucy's locks.

## XXVIII

They bury the little body under the oak tree in the garden. There is no Catholic priest in the vicinity, and Frédéric will have no other, so he reads the mass for the dead in Latin himself as he once recited the blessing at the child's birth. They stand side by side, the crickets rasping, and the birds crying out as they do at twilight. The air smells dry and dusty. The leaves are all the colors of the rainbow. Frédéric bows his head and prays, remembering the little girl to the Lord and asking his pardon. *Levavi oculos*: "I will lift mine eyes to the hills; from whence cometh my help? My help cometh even from the Lord." *Dominus regit me*: "The Lord is my shepherd."

Then he can read no more. He leaves Lucy and shuts himself up in his room, the small study he has made for himself with its green wallpaper and books. He will see no one, eat nothing.

Waking at dawn in despair, Lucy goes outside and finds herself standing by the child's grave. She kneels in the fallen leaves by the side of the small lozenge of a headstone. The earth is hardly displaced by the little coffin.

She thinks of her days in New York, listening to Hamilton, visiting the city, while her little girl ran alone under these trees. How could she have known her time would be so short with the child? Among the many images that come to her is her own face in the mirror with the housekeeper, helping to pin a blue flower in her yellow hair. Vanity of vanities.

She lifts her hands and presses them together and prays for courage. She thinks of the words that she has read: "Master, go on; and

I will follow thee, / To the last gasp, with truth and loyalty." She thinks of her Jacobite ancestors, following their liege and marching so bravely into battle for a lost cause, dying with valor for a displaced king. Is that life then? Is that all? Her mother, she knows, lost her little boy. Mothers lose their children again and again. As her grandmother put it, "An ordinary event."

She lifts up her face to the sky and feels the first drops of rain fall on her skin. The sky is filled with moving clouds and the wind blows the branches about wildly. Acorns fall to the ground, on her head. All of this is in the semi-dark. A slice of moon is still in the sky. There is a strange light, a sort of mist in the air, or perhaps it is the tears in her eyes. Everything around her is full of energy and life. A storm is coming fast like the travail that had brought forth her child who had arrived so suddenly and so furiously as if wishing to send her father forth safely from Canoles.

She lies down on the grave with her face to the earth, her hair spread loose around her shoulders, her arms spread out, her hands holding the earth: the drama of the position of despair a comfort. Her whole body presses down toward the ground that holds her child. The wind rolls over her. The fields heave and hiss like the sea. The wild rain falls fast, beating against her body. She weeps and begs God for strength to continue to lead a decent life, to do what is right without bitterness at this senseless blow. She murmurs into the earth, into the grave, the words of the prayer her nurse taught her as a child:

"Our father, who art in heaven, hallowed be thy name," she says the familiar prayer. She feels a new softness and sweetness in her voice, muffled by the earth, the sound of the rain and the wind, as though these oft-repeated words could create a small miracle. She abandons herself to the mechanical flow of her words, as she once did to the notes of music, the songs she had sung with joy: "Thy kingdom come. Thy will be done on earth as it is in heaven."

*My head reeled. My face burned. My whole body trembled. I was thrown into a state close to rapture as I watched Christ, his face swimming toward me from the depths of the earth. His face was twisted close to my own as if he was about to cry out to me. "Lucy, come to me!" The light was in my eyes like water. In a daze, breathing deeply, I forgot Frédéric, Humbert, even my lost child. It seemed to me that Christ had covered me over as I lay on the cold earth. I thought only of the Lord who had come to me, half-light, half-illusion, my illusion, my promise of peace, brought forth by me in this strange, wild place.*

She feels a peace descend on her then, and she rises to her feet in the fall beauty. Somewhere in the depths of this savage earth her child's spirit lingers. She leaves her child in a place she now feels is sacred and forgiving. In her wet clothes, her hair in her face, mud in her mouth, she is re-created by her own words. She has brought forth God from this earth to comfort her. When she goes back into the house, her face smudged with earth and tears, her clothes sodden, her shoes ruined, she tells Frédéric they must bring their little boy home.

# XXIX

## WINTER, 1795

Frédéric's days and nights in this place are terrible beyond description. This time seems an eternity of woe, infinite hours of dullness and despair. He lives day by day with Séraphine's death. Images of her inert body lying in Lucy's arms come and go. All happiness has gone from his life. He cannot control the terrible ache on waking every morning and a weariness that stretches through the day. His complete lethargy shocks him. He feels he has lost a living part of himself.

All through the winter he wanders in a dream, isolated from everyone around him, most of all from Lucy, whose touch he cannot bear. Silence lies like a weight on his house. During those first months without Séraphine, it is as if Lucy does not exist for him. She is a vague unwanted shape, moving about constantly on the edges of his vision in her dark peasant garb, going about her work with the cows, riding across the fields or along the snowy paths, Humbert always at her side.

Grief poisons everything. The weather is foul, or so it seems to him, and the rain continues day after day, or a cold mist, and then a thick blanket of snow. He hates the harshness of the winter, which had once seemed exotic and joyous here. He refuses to go into the fields. He lies on the bed, his pillow sodden with tears, sweat, and saliva. His body smells of sweat, and his breath is sour. Sometimes he walks out with Black, the sounds of his footsteps on the ice following him as he moves. The bad weather, his own uncleanness, his dark unshaven face in the mirror is comfort of a sort. A blue sky, a bath, a razor would be a slap in the face, an insult, incongruous. Like everyone faced by the death of a beloved, he thinks: How can the world go on? How can the sun rise and shine, the rain fall? How can Lucy rise at dawn and go about the farm so purposefully? Her false cheer makes him grit his teeth. At such moments he hates her.

At night, he discovers in sleep what the daylight hides: the darkness of every object, and even more, the night shadows that flow over the landscape like water. He does not reach Séraphine even in his dreams. He dreams he is back on the *Diana* and returning to France, but his little girl is no longer in his arms.

One night, he goes into Lucy's room and finds Humbert lying asleep, one hand in her hair. He swoops up the child with one swift, angry movement and carries him into Séraphine's room that has been left untouched since her death. Black follows them there, her tail between her legs as if fearing a kick, though Frédéric has never done such a thing. He stands in the middle of the small room with the sleeping child in his arms and looks around. Nothing has been moved, the small silver-backed brush on the dresser with the child's initials, Talleyrand's doll propped up on a wicker chair, the ivory teething ring, the little dresses in the closet, a bowl of dried white flowers on the table between the windows. He looks down at his boy, his heir. He feels a sudden surge of terrible hate for this living child. How dare he go on living! He wants to drop him or to dash his head against the stone floor. He lays him down in Séraphine's cot where her breathing body once lay, warm and soft.

He goes back into Lucy's bedroom and stands by her bed, looking down at her. How can she sleep so peacefully? He folds his arms, trying to expel this awful hate from his breast. Then he sees she is awake and watching him with her steady gray gaze. He rips off his clothes, as though they are contaminated, lies down beside her, takes her roughly into his arms, drags her to him, though she protests at first, then lies limp, surrendering to his superior strength. He pries her legs apart, enters her body brutally, coming into her in a way he has never done before, without a word, without a preliminary caress, without pleasure. He is just there, thrusting deeper and deeper, drowning in her flesh, going into the depths of the sea of her body, not breathing, swimming with his lungs bursting, gathering up the silt of the seabed, letting it sift through his fingers, looking through waving seaweed and coral and rocks for his child. She is down there somewhere not taking in enough air in the depths of Lucy's body, he knows, if he can just keep on swimming. He must find her and drag her up into the air. Then he sees the tadpole of her little body swimming toward him, as she had swum forth into life with such exuberance that day in Canoles, coming fast into his hands, her silver body slippery and soft with life and love.

# XXX

## Spring, 1796

Letters reach Frédéric telling him that thanks to the joint efforts of their friends, Bonie and Brouquens, the seals will be removed from their chateau, Le Bouilh, but only in the presence of the proprietors. They are given a year's delay to come home. France is victorious through all of Europe, a new government is in place.

He does not hesitate. He rises and goes to the door of the house immediately with the letters in his hands, looking for Lucy. He sees her in the fields. The wind is blowing the branches above her head and her skirts about her legs. From where he stands in the door of the house, the fields are rippling seas of spring color: brilliant yellow, fuschia, ash-blue. Everything is moving, blooming in this place.

Lucy is at work in the pasture, rounding up her cows. He can see Humbert, too, running after them. He is helping her round them up for milking. Bareheaded, barefooted, bare-chested, his fair skin burned dark, stick in hand, shouting and laughing, he could be any French peasant boy. Lucy, too, in her dark peasant garb, her stomach swelling, her cotton blouse half open on her breasts, her straw hat on the back of her head, looks like a peasant.

The wind drops, and there is a moment of complete stillness, the stillness of mid-afternoon. He hears only the hum of the bees. A Dutch landscape painting, perhaps a Hobbema or Cuyp: a young pregnant woman, her boy, and a dark dog with cows in a pasture, a farmhouse in the distance.

"Like a portrait," he remembers them all whispering, when she first walked into the room that day long ago, in her white dress. The truth is, he realizes, he does prefer nature in a painting, as he prefers words in a poem to spoken ones. Lucy, though he loves her so, he sometimes prefers as an image in his mind, an idea, *Bluebird*.

He walks toward her. As she leans forward to grasp a cow's collar, he hears the cowbell ring. Her swollen breasts glisten in the sunlight. "Come on, my girls," she is saying, "come to me." She hasn't yet noticed him, and as he watches her for a moment, a shadow of prescience falls over him. She will not want to leave. She will not want to go back to France.

"Lucy!" he says, but not loud enough for her to hear him.

It is Lucy who has made this farm work. Her butter, her milk, her cheese are a success. She makes money from them, with Prime's excellent help, and from their cider. She runs this farm for both of them, directs her people with a generous and a steady hand. She has the gift of command as she does on a horse, as her father once did with his regiment. They are people who inspire allegiance. She allows these people, who know farming, to guide her without ever completely relinquishing the reins. She is there beside them from sunrise to sunset, working as they do, yet listening to their advice. They would follow her anywhere. She is the one who makes the decisions and takes the responsibility for the mistakes. It is she who has brought forth the fruit from this earth.

Frédéric has failed as a farmer. He has worked in the fields beside his men, but never as well as they do and never with the kind of camaraderie Lucy has established with them. He is not as strong or as good with his hands as they, and truthfully, manual labor bores him. The monotony of the days in the fields. He prefers his books, his plans for reform, abstractions. He prefers to command a regiment, a body of men trained according to military tactics established centuries ago. He is grateful to this new country, which he has fought for, grateful for the asylum it has given his family, but he has always longed to go back to the country of his forefathers, to find himself anew in a place where they speak his language, understand his customs, and share his education. His spoken English has not improved here, though he reads it fluently. He wants to reclaim his inheritance, some part of his past, his home. He wants to take up his military duties, to reorganize the army as he had always intended to do, or at least find his place within the government, the leaders of the country. He senses that strong new leaders are now needed in France to take up the fallen reins of the government. Will he be among them? Talleyrand, he is certain, his old friend, will prosper under any regime. Frédéric will even face the sea voyage to accomplish this aim. He cannot spend his days as an American farmer any longer. He has done his best, but he was born a nobleman, a man of refinement, destined to lead his country, to protect its honor with a sword, not to till some savage place's soil. Here, he feels, birth, position, honor, even education count for nothing or next to nothing. It is money that rules this country, nothing else, and he has never been good with money. He was brought up to believe he would always have it, an endless supply from his patrimony.

"We must go home," he says firmly, as she stands with her hand on Lizzie's flank. She is talking to the cow, not listening to Frédéric: "You are a pretty girl," she says, as though he has not spoken, and pats her rump familiarly, leans against her, rubs her face in her fur. She talks to her animals more than she does to him, these days. She stands in the bright sunlight, the shadow of her straw hat on her flushed, sweating face, looking at him.

"What is it?' she asks him abruptly.

Lucy has the effect of interrupting the flow of his will, so that for a moment he loses his conviction. He glances at her blouse where the swell of her white breasts glistens with perspiration in the light. He draws his hand over the stubble on his chin. He must disgust her in the state he is in. He must bathe, clean himself.

She asks him what he is talking about, and looks at him a little as her grandmother did, as if he has lost his reason. There is a glint of pity, too, in her blue-gray eyes. He takes advantage of that glint to put his hand over hers, to draw closer to her.

He gives her the letters to read. "We must leave as soon as we can sell the farm. A year to reclaim Le Bouilh, or it will pass into other hands."

She doesn't look at the letters, hands them back to him, moves away. She says, "I cannot go back there. I have nothing but memories of horror in that place." Her hand lingers again on Lizzie's back. A cow. She wants to remain with her cows! Her words have brought tears to his eyes. He turns his back on her and tries to regain control of himself but finds he is being held by Lucy, her head leaning against his shoulder, her hands firmly around his waist.

"Surely not, Lucy," Frédéric says as he turns to her, feels her supple, slender form against him. His heart tilts with longing and flutters and thumps against his ribs. He takes her hat from her head and lets it fall back on the ribbon around her neck. He puts his hand to her face, touches her cheek lightly, a gesture of request. "Surely you have good memories as well as bad?" His hand rests against her cheek, and she does not withdraw. Nor does she yield. His voice sounds weak and cajoling to him. In his sorrow he has forgotten the art of wooing.

She says, "Those memories are of no use to me now. I have no interest in memories. I want today and today and today."

He thinks that she has always looked like a foreigner to him, an Englishwoman, an Irishwoman, a wild Irishwoman with her blue-gray eyes, her fair skin, that mass of wheat-colored hair shining in the light. It was what drew him to her at first, this difference. It is part of her charm, yet it makes his possession of her seem tenuous. She has never entirely belonged to him.

Humbert, as though he senses his father's thought, looks up at him and takes his hand. He asks if they will be safe in France now.

"It took less time to kill Robespierre and Danton than it did the King. They have destroyed themselves as well as everyone else," he says bitterly, looking down at his son who looks up at him blankly.

"So many deaths. And who is to say there will not be more. And what about our farm, our land? What about the grave under the oak tree?" Lucy asks.

Frédéric puts both his hands up to his eyes, as though Lucy has struck him. How he would like to take the little bones to France where they belong, to rest beside his ancestors in the cemetery at Le Bouilh. He hates to leave his child behind, so far from home in this savage earth.

"What about the animals? What about our people here? What will become of them?" Lucy asks, following, relentless, and waving her hand toward the hills.

"We cannot just give up our home, our inheritance, our place in society, the chance to take up the life we were born for!" Frédéric says, aware he has not spoken so many words for many months.

"You believe we will be able to do that? Turn back the clock? Would you wish to? And what might still happen there?"

"For Humbert's sake, for our boy, so that he can have a French education, reclaim his inheritance." Frédéric puts his hand on Humbert's fair head, drawing him closer to his side, aware he is using this child he has hardly spoken to for months for his purposes.

Humbert says, "Can we take Black? Can we take Black, please!"

"Of course, I wouldn't dream of leaving him behind," Frédéric says, looking down at him.

Lucy can say nothing to that, surely, or to the thought of Frédéric's unborn child within her. She has told him she is certain the child is another girl, and she has already chosen a name, a hopeful name: Charlotte, the name of her father's sister. Lucy stares across the valley toward the blue hills.

She speaks, her words coming fast, in a passionate plea, talking, it seems, half to Frédéric, half to the sky. "How often I have seen the dawn flood this valley and the sun turn everything bright. There is nothing here to distract me from the light and the sky and the beauty of the land—from God. I want to stay here, Frédéric. To stay where we have lost our baby, but where I have found something else. What awaits us in France? What sort of a home has it been to me?"

"You will not follow your Lord and Master?" Frédéric says with a half-smile she has not seen for a long time, but his heart is beating like a drum. Humbert looks up at Lucy and puts his hand into hers.

Lucy looks at Frédéric. She sighs. "Let us stay here, Frédéric, please," she says, but he hears how her voice wavers. He adds for good measure, sensing he has already won, "Etienette tells me she saw Marguerite in the street. She's awaiting your return." He feels he has the upper hand now. He takes her into his arms, nuzzles her neck, breathes her in.

She says, "I will do what you want, Frédéric. I promised to obey my Lord and Master long ago, but there is one condition I insist you fulfill. You must free our people," she says, "all of them."

## XXXI

"If you leave, what will become of us?" Judith asked Lucy anxiously, when she saw the letters arriving and heard the news. Now Lucy calls all four of her people into the drawing room. They stand before her in a row. Judith, holding her little girl—the two-year-old Maria, born on the farm—is pregnant with a second child, her belly swollen beneath her neat blue skirt like Lucy's own. Judith stands next to her husband, Thomas, and beside them are the father and son who have learned to live and work together, if not in harmony at least in some kind of peace, Prime and Minck. Lucy looks at them in their neat clothes, their heads held high. What will their lives be like when she has gone, even with their freedom?

Lucy makes a little speech. She says, "My dear friends, I have good news for you. We are obliged to return to Europe." She sees the fear in their eyes. She goes on quickly. "I don't want to leave this farm, where I have been so happy with all of you, but I am obliged to follow my husband—you will all understand that—and he wishes to return to France. You have given us both such excellent service. Without all of you, your industry, your honesty and hard work, it would never have been possible for us to farm this place as we have done and prospered. It is right you should be rewarded for this, and we have decided to give you your freedom."

For a moment there is silence in the room and incomprehension on the faces of these people, who look at one another with wonderment. Then, first Judith and then her husband and then Minck and finally his father sink to their knees at her feet and lift their hands. They all speak at once, crying out, "Is it true? Do you mean we are to be free?"

Lucy turns from them and says, "You are as free as I am myself." Then the four of them surround her, weeping with joy, and she weeps with them.

The next day the public ceremony of manumission takes place. All the Negroes of the town congregate to watch. The Justice of the Peace, one of Mr. van Rensselaer's employees, at the last moment makes his displeasure known. "This is not wise; it will set a bad precedent," he says to Frédéric. He maintains Prime is too old, anyway, to be freed. "This slave is clearly older than fifty," he says. But Prime, the wily one, has foreseen this difficulty. He takes out a birth certificate to show he is not yet fifty, the age after which freedom is no longer possible.

The four of them kneel before him, and Frédéric puts his hand on the head of each one in token of his or her liberation, as was done in ancient Rome.

*It occurred to me, as these people walked away slowly and gravely, that it was not I who was going away and leaving them. I did not have it in my power to leave this country I had come to love, but rather it was America that was retreating from me, slowly, like the ebbing tide.*

*This farm, these people, my friends, my animals, and my foes would all remain in my mind through the many remaining days of my life. I would keep a little of them within me, as I boarded the* Hispaniola *for the voyage back to France. I carried with me some faint illumination to remind me through dark days ahead that there was light out there and sound and above all, space, freedom. In my mind, over the years, I would keep the illusion of flying free through the trees in the sunlight, the illusion of being the Queen of my own destiny.*

PART FIFTEEN

# The White Lady

She wakes from a bitter sleep. Her legs are heavy, and the pain is like knives in her feet. Someone familiar stands at the foot of her bed, a white shadow.

"Ah, there you are, my darling!" she says and reaches out her hand, and the shadow comes quickly to her side.

She can hear the soothing sound of running water. What river is she near now? Not the Dordogne. This is not at Le Bouilh. The grand, unfinished chateau, like all the rest of them, was lost long ago.

She remembers waiting for Frédéric's boat from Blaye, that night in the dark, and calling out to the sailors to find out if the tide was ebbing. She remembers the deep darkness, her fear, and the silence in the house.

Secret moments from their life together, moments only she would know about, burst upon her like the first beams of light, which penetrate through the half-closed curtains. She feels the cool stone of the fountain and a hand over hers and hears the fresh sound of water running in the gardens of Versailles. She sees herself opening the loaf of bread with trembling fingers and finding his crumpled letter within with the words of love. She feels him standing beside her in the shade of the little wood in the wild place. He holds her shoulders, as she leans against him.

"Where have you been, this long time?" she asks with some impatience, but the shadow does not reply.

"Have you really come back to me?" she asks, her words a soft moan in her throat.

Faint sunlight flickers on the carpet. Why is there such an ugly red carpet in her room? Why is this room so small, almost like the little boat that carried her to freedom, and indeed, she is rocking as if she were on one. Why is she so tired, so tired? Everything spins again as it did when, as a child, she came back from the hunt with a broken leg.

*I will not cry, I will not cry. I will not cry.*

The figure sits down close beside her, knees touching her side, and takes her hand. "Now, now. Lie still, Lucy," it says, speaking in a strange, muffled voice.

"But I was so afraid they had taken you from me forever."

The figure says nothing but smiles at her, and she notices the long, yellowish teeth. She stares, thinking that the thinning hair does not seem as white as Frédéric's. When she looks carefully, Frédéric's fine features seem diluted in this face. And what has happened to his military bearing? She cannot help noticing that the sharpness of the nose, the energy of the cheekbones, and above all the intelligence of the gaze are all diminished here. What a great gift intelligence is in one's nearest and dearest. One does not notice it until he is gone, and one has to explain everything too slowly.

There is something different about the length of the arms, too. The arms are too long for the body, as in an awkward painting, and the legs look a little bowed to her. This cannot be Frédéric; she has confused her desire with reality.

"How cold it is in here," the figure says fretfully. Is this someone habituated to warmer climes, a traveler from afar, perhaps?

"The pinecones are expensive," she says dryly. She knows this sort of thing, but then she has often been surrounded by impractical people. She has always been aware of the price of things. She has so often had to handle matters of money. She does not blame Frédéric for the loss of their properties, or the poor choice of an attendant for Le Bouilh, but often she has had to manage things on her own.

She remembers her private interview with Napoléon, when Frédéric had been dismissed from his position as Prefect in Brussels. She had rushed to the Trianon the moment she heard the news, traveling overnight, afraid Charlotte's marriage as well as Frédéric's position would be lost. She had been accorded an audience the next day, as Napoléon liked to hobnob with the old nobility. They had walked up and down together arm in arm on the terrace in the white morning sunshine. She was in her silver dress. The Emperor had conceded the esteem in which her husband was held in the town. "Will one at Amiens do as a replacement?" he had asked her apologetically.

Yet she feels splintered now; she is here, in this chilly room, with its odd bits and pieces: the apricot-yellow wallpaper, the armchair with its ugly green damask cover, the rosewood secretary against the wall with the pens and paper she rarely uses, her precious books, and the wobbly table where they would take their meals, the two rush stools, the china eggcup that her maid seems to have forgotten to remove, the white half-stove made of earthenware in the brick alcove where they burn the pinecones. She turns away from the figure toward the window.

The wind lifts the light curtain, and the pale spring light flickers on the carpet. They will all be arriving now, she supposes, those few who are left to her. It must be time.

"Where is Cécile?" she asks. "She is coming, is she not?"

How she misses her beloved grandchild, Charlotte's child, whose father wrenched her from her arms, when Lucy could no longer be of service to his family. She remembers saying good-bye to her, the clinging of the soft arms around her neck. She remembers Cécile's wedding day that recalled her own.

The figure has risen and stretches lazily, saying nothing, retreating slightly, walking without dignity, in creased, stained clothes until it stands half hidden in the shadows of the thin curtains. Lucy lifts her head from the pillow to get a better view.

Being old, feeble, and sick is rather like being a prisoner. People can come whenever they will, interrupting your thoughts. They are not the ones you want. They talk at you as though you had already departed, believing you will be grateful for their company. She wants only Frédéric beside her. Like a cat, she thinks, she would prefer to crawl into a corner of the barn and hide her sorrows, her sufferings. She remembers the time she went to prison in the Fort du Ha with him. He had refused to sign the papers of allegiance to Louis Philippe. "Not the son of Philippe d'Orleans! Not the son of the man who voted for the death of the King!" he had said. So she had followed him into prison and slept in the cell with him. She had swept the floor and made the tea, and really they had done quite well there together, though she recalls the ceaseless voices rising up from the courtyard day and night, the jailers opening doors with a key when they wished.

She had always followed him and applauded his moments of glory. She remembers the invitation he received from Talleyrand to accompany him to the Congress of Vienna. She had tried to comfort him in moments of great distress, but perhaps Frédéric is happier where he is now, with God.

She remembers the Prince de Poix driving up with the news that made Frédéric go mad with grief. He had advised Humbert, telling him it was essential that the hypothetical young *Mousquetaire* fight, not realizing Humbert was describing himself. "Your companion should be all the more zealous in the defense of his honor because he has not yet paid with blood for his rank, as his older and more experienced opponent has," he had said with conviction. The

opponent had begged Humbert not to fight him over an insignificant remark about a uniform. "Why should two good men die?"
he had asked, or so everyone said, but when Humbert, his father's
words ringing in his ears, struck him with his gun across his face,
he took aim. "Poor boy. Poor mother," the older man was reputed
to have said. The bullet went straight through her boy's heart.

Suddenly, she knows who is here with her. She recognizes her,
the White Lady, her most faithful companion. Unlike Frédéric,
she has never left her side. How she has hovered near her, dogged
her heels, watching and waiting through the years. She has been
waiting for this moment, a moment of feebleness, of distraction, of
exhaustion, eager to embrace her.

She has come for her children, one after the other, first her
babies, and then her grown girls: little Séraphine, then Charlotte,
and then Cécile-Elizabeth, then her darling boy, who ran wild on
the farm with her, struck down at twenty-six with a bullet in his
heart. Now, she has only one left, her beloved Aymar, her youngest boy, who is here with her, being brave and imprudent and full
of rash ideals. He must be out now, trying to sell the "Renaissance
boxes" he makes to keep them alive.

She has known three revolutions, two invasions, different
kings, an emperor, rough sea voyages, the sight of strange coasts,
glut and famine, but what she remembers are the odd things: the
joy on the faces of her slaves when Frédéric freed them; the seventy
volumes of poetry she found in her room on her wedding night;
the battery of implements she used to churn the butter and stamp it
with her crest; the taste of the fish she was served in Boston harbor
for her "welcome breakfast"; the shout of the man in the mob who
saved her life; her neighbor's description of her "noble pigsty."

She will she never forget Bonie waving to her wildly, the
first person she saw on the quay on her return from America, or

Marguerite coming to her for the birth of Charlotte, at Le Bouilh, while brigands roamed the countryside.

She would like to escape the White Lady one more time, but she has caught her by the heels. Arthritis has attacked her legs, and the gout has her feet. Her smile and her outstretched hand are so inviting.

She has seen her many times, but never quite this close. She will not go to her just yet. There are still things to be accomplished, surely, and above all things to be learned. She has always felt one could never know enough, that one must go on learning at each moment, up until the end. She remembers reading Tacitus while her hairdresser decked her hair and the Abbé Bertholon's physics lessons, her singing lessons with the Italian, Ferrari, in Bordeaux, while hiding from the mob.

She recalls rising early to go to her cows, the smell of them, the warm udders in her hands. She remembers each of their names: Lizzie and Meg and Jane. Once, she had put her mouth directly to the teat, and sucked as she pulled, and felt the warm milk spurt into her mouth.

The river runs. The odor of spring perfumes the room. Sunlight honeys the parquet floor. She watches the thin curtain lift hopefully in the breeze, and the pain in her legs lightens. It is quite enough to be free of pain: the silence of the organs. Outside lies the town, the red rooftops, the church, the narrow streets, the orange trees, the river. Pisa, she remembers now, of course. She is in Italy because of her boy, Aymar, who was banished from France. She is with her only remaining child. Though she has always loved the countryside, in town she likes to watch the people go by from her window. The White Lady fades. She reaches out, once again, for her pen.

*There are still these moments in the early morning, which come to me from time to time, small miracles, when I feel the pain in my legs diminish and a lightness in my feet. I feel I could rise and almost dance the gavotte as I did as a girl in Belgium with Maman when we went there for a cure. I feel I could outdance, outrun the White Lady. I am filled with a kind of hopefulness, yes, even happiness has possession of my heart, as it has done again and again over my long life. Suddenly, I want to call the maid to bring the mirror. For I need to remind myself of my great age. Surely I cannot be eighty-three?*

*For I feel so young, so young, almost sixteen, waiting at the window for Frédéric.*

AUTHOR'S NOTE

My Lucy Dillon is Henriette, Lucy Dillon's double, a fictional character on whose behalf I have taken many liberties suited to her nature, as I have with the numerous other historical personages given their proper names in this book. I wish to acknowledge the many modern historical studies and biographies, the memoirs and letters of the period, and particularly Lucy's own wonderful memoir.

# ACKNOWLEDGMENTS

I want to thank my dearest daughters: Sasha, Cybele, and Brett Troyan for their advice and continuous support; my husband's family: his parents, Joe and Jean Tucker, and his sisters, Sally and Jane, for their love and encouragement; my friends: Marnie Mueller, Regina McBride, and Ronnie Sharfman for careful reading and judicious comments; and all my colleagues at Bennington, particularly Liam Rector, Martha Cooley, Phillip Lopate, and Alice Mattison.

I am deeply grateful to Joyce Carol Oates, Raymond Smith, Edmund White, Lyndall Gordon, Amy Hempel, and Elizabeth Strout for their continuing generosity; to my excellent editor Rosemary Ahern for much hard work and many perceptive comments, to my publisher, Judith Feher-Gurewich; and my agent of many years and many books, Robin Straus.

I wish to acknowledge the great gift of a year at the Cullman Center at the New York library where much of this book was written.

Finally, as always, I am in debt to my darling husband, Bill, who has read these pages as he has all my pages with so much love and dedication and an eagle's eye.